Let Sleeping Dogs Lie

D0050437

Also by

SUZANN LEDBETTER

HALFWAY TO HALF WAY
ONCE A THIEF
AHEAD OF THE GAME
IN HOT PURSUIT
WEST OF BLISS
NORTH OF CLEVER
SOUTH OF SANITY
EAST OF PECULIAR

Let Sleeping Dogs Lie

SUZANN LEDBETTER

MIRA®

If you purchased this book without a cover you should be aware
that this book is stolen property. It was reported as "unsold and
destroyed" to the publisher, and neither the author nor the
publisher has received any payment for this "stripped book."

Recycling programs
for this product may
not exist in your area.

ISBN-13: 978-0-7783-2636-6
ISBN-10:   0-7783-2636-5

LET SLEEPING DOGS LIE

Copyright © 2009 by Suzann Ledbetter.

All rights reserved. Except for use in any review, the reproduction or
utilization of this work in whole or in part in any form by any electronic,
mechanical or other means, now known or hereafter invented, including
xerography, photocopying and recording, or in any information storage or
retrieval system, is forbidden without the written permission of the publisher,
MIRA Books, 225 Duncan Mill Road, Don Mills, Ontario, Canada M3B 3K9.

This is a work of fiction. Names, characters, places and incidents are
either the product of the author's imagination or are used fictitiously, and
any resemblance to actual persons, living or dead, business establishments,
events or locales is entirely coincidental.

MIRA and the Star Colophon are trademarks used under license and registered
in Australia, New Zealand, Philippines, United States Patent and Trademark
Office and in other countries.

www.MIRABooks.com

Printed in U.S.A.

For the unsung, everyday heroes who often put their own lives on hold to care for a loved one in need.

ACKNOWLEDGMENTS

Once upon a time I was four feet ten inches tall,
like my character, Dina Wexler. I even have vague recollections
of climbing up the kitchen cabinets to plunder Mom's stash
of Brach's milk chocolate stars and brushing my teeth
with my chin hovering a skosh above the basin.

A now-five-seven adult's memories of a time when much of the
world was beyond my reach and everyone was literally looked up
to weren't enough. Huge thanks go to Veda Boyd Jones and
Mary Guccione for insights on the grown-up and short-statureds'
daily frustrations and creative adaptations and the fact that larger
than life has everything to do with heart and nothing to do with
height. I am in their debt and stand forever in their shade.

Thanks also to John Bragdon, consumer assistant at Jacuzzi, Inc.,
in Dallas, Texas, for product information critical to my homicide
scenario. Darrell L. Moore, Greene County (Missouri) Prosecuting
Attorney, keeps the legalities straight and factual, and lets me
pick up the lunch tab once in a while. Pat LoBrutto, dear friend
and opera buff, filled in on the finer points of *Pagliacci* and
sang a few bars of an aria on the phone. Without Jean Edwards,
Comair customer service representative at the Springfield-Branson
(Missouri) Regional Airport, I'd have flubbed my plot-oriented
flight plans six ways of Sunday. The mythical Park City, Missouri,
has several more connections elsewhere than available in fact,
but the beauty of fiction is getting the basics right
and taking it from there.

Lara Hyde and Mary-Margaret Scrimger at MIRA Books were
excellent, devoted editorial glitch finders; any remaining are mine.
A hearty salute also to Robin Rue, Writers House, LLC, for the past
twentysomething books. Thank you, team. You *rock*.

As does Dave Ellingsworth. One day, maybe I'll find the words
to tell him how lucky I am to be his wife, best friend
and forever partner in real life.

1

"Aw, c'mon, Cherise. Be reasonable." Jack McPhee's lips pulled back in a grimace. The heel of the hand not holding the telephone receiver clunked his temple. Too little, as recriminations went, and definitely a couple of words too late.

"Be reasonable" was number nineteen on the list of sixty-two things to never say to a woman. Any woman, whether you were dating her, sleeping with her, married to her, called her Mom or she knew "the usual" was Chivas on the rocks with a twist.

Therefore, it was hardly a surprise when Cherise Taylor's normally dulcet drawl could have etched granite. "So," she said, "it's *un*reasonable for me to be upset about being stood up for dinner. Again."

"No, no, of course it isn't," Jack said, tired of reciting dialogue from a familiar script and the revolving cast of leading ladies. Any second now, she'd say…

"We haven't seen each other since Thursday at lunch."

"When I told you I had an out-of-town job to take care of." An off-the-books, expenses-only one for a friend, Jack might have added, but what was the point?

"Yeah, and I stayed home all weekend, in case you called." A derisive snort, then a plaintive, "You've heard about floors clean enough to eat off of? You could take out somebody's spleen on mine."

Jack tapped a pencil end over end on the desk blotter. He'd flown to Seattle by way of Dallas and Denver, logged twelve hours' sleep in seventy-two and the majority of those after he fell into his own bed last night. "If I'd had a chance to call," he said, "and you weren't home, I'd have tried your cell phone. If you didn't answer, I'd have left a voice mail."

"Oh? Then it's my fault I was bored out of my mind all weekend."

Pretty much, he thought. A bit harsh, maybe, but before he came along, Cherise volunteered on Saturdays at a library teaching English as a second language. Sundays, she'd meet her married sisters for a girls'-day-out brunch, then hit the flea markets, catch a chick flick or zip north to Kansas City to shop at malls identical to those in Park City.

Sniffling now, Cherise went on, "And you don't even remember what day this is, do you?"

The obvious trick question disqualified Monday as the correct answer. Jack's eyes cut to his page-a-day calendar. July 7 was blank, apart from a sticky note to remind him to drop his suit at the cleaners before the bloodstains set.

"Who cares if tonight's our anniversary?" *Sniff-sniffle.* "No big deal."

Jack pulled away the receiver, examining the sound holes as if the pattern would reveal what the hell she was talking about. Anniversaries commemorated wars, major battles, natural and unnatural disasters and wedding ceremonies. None of those applied, yet all of a sudden, the commonality seemed oddly significant.

"For six months, I've put up with your weird hours. With dates canceled at the last minute and knowing your mind's anywhere but on me sometimes when we *are* together. But have I complained? Uh-uh. Not even once."

I wish you had, Jack thought. Repeatedly and often.

On a shelf above the microwave at his apartment was a framed sampler that read: "The lower the expectations, the higher the probability a man will tunnel under them." His ex-wife had cross-stitched it and given it to him for a divorce present. Whether she'd coined the phrase, or copped it from Gloria Steinem, a louse with good intentions should have it tattooed on his forehead.

"I'm sorry, Cherise," he said. "I really am."

A lengthy silence acknowledged the subtext. "Me, too." Cherise's sigh implied a middle-distance stare at the ceiling, select memories scrolling behind her eyes, her head shaking in futility. The image skewed somewhat at her muttered, "Honesty in a relationship, my ass."

Jack scowled. "Hey, now wait a sec. I *have* been honest with you. A hundred percent from the first time we went out."

"Sure you were," she agreed. "But how was I supposed to *know* that?"

His mouth fell open. Bereft of an intelligible response, he raked his fingers through his hair and wondered if a lapsed Episcopalian was eligible for the priesthood.

"First date," she said. "Between the beer course and the pizza, I asked you to describe the perfect woman. I expected the usual answers—Julia Roberts, Angelina Jolie, Salma Hayek. If you'd said your mother, I wouldn't have stuck around for the cinnamon bread."

Jack could do worse than a gal like the one who'd married dear old Dad. And had more times than he cared to count. "For the record, my mom's a wonderful woman, but not exactly my type."

"I gathered that when you said 'The perfect woman for any man doesn't confuse supportive with taking his crap and making excuses for him.'" Cherise laughed. "Ten points for creativity, but you really didn't expect me to believe it, did you?"

Actually, he had. For one, it was the truth. Plain, simple, straightforward. For another...

He didn't have another. Couldn't imagine why he'd need it. "Look, I—"

"*Don't,* okay? Let's leave it at we had fun, it's over, no hard feelings, time to move on." Cherise hesitated a moment, her voice somber, the drawl more pronounced. "I'm gonna miss you, though."

Jack nodded, as if she were seated across the desk, not downtown in a triwalled cubicle with less square footage than a municipal jail cell. "Same here, kid," he said, curbing the impulse to suggest a fresh start.

Barring dual amnesia, there was no such thing as a mulligan in a relationship. Jack's crazy uncle George once owned a beater Oldsmobile that wouldn't shift out of Reverse, but for most people, going backward to go forward was a dumb idea.

Cherise knew that as well as he did. "Let's leave it" was code for "Goodbyes hurt, but we aren't in love and in like isn't enough for the long haul." Still, the handset's glowing redial button dared Jack to ask her forgiveness. To give him a second chance at being the dependable, thoughtful guy she deserved.

Uh-huh. Sure. He docked the phone. And while he was at it, he'd learn Parsi, buy season tickets to the opera and take up water polo.

By noon, Park City Florist would have delivered the half-dozen pink carnations Jack sent to Cherise's cubicle. Figuring she'd understand the quantity, but not the symbolism in their color, he'd asked the clerk to write "I'll never forget you" on the card. Although sincere, his latest failed romance was the last thing on his mind as he cruised by the Midwest Inn's guest entrance.

The three-story, stucco-clad motel was situated on a back-filled knoll facing I-44's prime business interchange. From the air, the building was shaped like a capital M with a swimming pool puddled between its legs. Tourists seldom traveled through southwest Missouri in helicopters, so the snazzy architecture was wasted on pigeons, drive-time traffic reporters and the local hang gliders' club.

The all but deserted rear parking lot angled in concert with the M's ascender points. Jack knew the checkout time was 11:00 a.m., and check-ins were prohibited before 3:00 p.m. The black Lexus sedan and a forest-green minivan parked several discretionary spaces apart credenced the adage about rules being made to be broken. Or at least bent, in exchange for the folded fifty-dollar bills Jack had slipped to the desk clerk. Two President Grants was the agreed-upon bribe for the clerk to call Jack's cell phone with Mr. and Mrs. Smith's room number and precise location.

He pulled in beside the Lexus and lowered his side window. It was risky to forgo tailing his quarry to the motel, but he sensed he'd been spotted at last Friday's rendezvous at a Best Western across town. The rapid metallic ticks emanating from the Lexus's engine confirmed the greedy desk clerk's ETA.

Shifting his aging Taurus into Park, Jack left the engine running and snagged an equipment case from the backseat. While the building's height shaded the asphalt for a few yards behind his car, air-conditioning wasn't optional when midday temperatures flirted with the century mark.

He snapped photos of both vehicles with a still camera, then switched to a digital. Elbows propped on the steering wheel, he aimed the telephoto lens at room 266's plate-glass window and adjusted the zoom.

The miniblinds were closed, as always, with the slats tilted down, rather than up. From Jack's or anyone else's ground-level vantage point, the interior view was akin to lurking at the bottom of a stairway to peek up a lady's skirt.

Motels and hotels provide drapes for a reason, and it wasn't just to give the bedspreads something to match. If married couples hot for a nooner with someone other than a spouse knew how the law defined an expectation of privacy, Jack would have to find another line of work.

Domestics weren't his specialty. Maximum sleaze factor and aggravation—minimum challenge. But it'd been a slow summer and a guy's just gotta do what a guy's gotta do to cover the rent. Whether Cherise believed his excuse for canceling their date tonight or not, Jack hadn't lied about meeting a client for dinner. Hopefully there wouldn't be a scene, until after he'd polished off his steak and steamed veggies. Either way, he'd leave the restaurant with a check in his pocket and craving a long shower.

A couple more shots of the lovebirds' striptease were all Jack needed and all he could stomach. The camera was whining its second electronic high C when the Taurus's passenger door swung open. The young man tilted the whole car as he crammed himself into the seat. "Mr. McPhee," he said, huffing a bit from the exertion. "This is your lucky day."

A fleshy inner tube oozed from under his rock-band T-shirt and spilled over the waistband of his jeans. He smelled like a deep-fried *Esquire* cologne sample. Two days' growth of stubble fanned from a goatee and bristled his chins. A ham-sized knee, then the other, wedged against the glove compartment. The .38 Police Special inside might as well have been in a bank vault in Wisconsin.

Then again, if Moby Dick was a carjacker, he'd need the Jaws of Life to stuff that gut behind the steering wheel. Jack eyed a manila folder clutched in the man's fist. A process server would have shoved a subpoena at him and waddled off. There'd be balloons and a camera crew if the dude was with that magazine outfit's prize patrol. Besides, you had to enter to win.

"Who the hell are you?"

"Brett Dean Blankenship." He offered his hand. Jack didn't take it. Nonplussed, he went on, "Pleasure to meet you, sir, but who *you* are is why I'm here."

A smirk exposed teeth not many years removed from orthodontic appliances. Attention turning to the folder, Blankenship recited, "You'll be forty-one on October 4. Married once, divorced, no kids—" he glanced sideward and *heh-heh*ed "—as far as known. You've got a B.S. in criminal justice, graduated from the Park City Police Academy, then resigned two years later. You bounced around from rent-a-cop to long-haul trucking, dabbled in auto repair, retail sales and telemarketing. For the past fifteen years, you've been a marginally successful private investigator."

Jack took exception to "marginally successful." He'd had many a good year and a fair share of great ones. Self-employment ordained lean ones proportional to sweet ones. It kept you humble and out there hustling. Or it should.

"Not too shabby for a one-man operation." Blankenship handed over three sheets of paper. "But it's safe to say, you ain't setting the world on fire."

The pages' bulleted lines noted Jack's Social Security number, previous and current home and office addresses, savings and checking account balances, registration info on the Taurus and his pickup, average utility bills at his office and apartment… Junior G-man stuff either in public records or easily obtainable if you knew where to look.

What raised Jack's hackles was an account of his activities over the past week. Blankenship had tailed him and Jack hadn't even noticed. Which explained the Lexus driver's sudden hinkiness last Friday.

He balled the sheets and tossed them into the backseat. "Whatever your game is, sport, I'm not playing. Now get outa my car, before you void the warranty on the shock absorbers."

Blankenship blanched, then exhaled, as though a lung had collapsed. "I worked like a dog on that report. I thought you'd be *impressed.*" He stretched a shirtsleeve to mop the sweat trickling down his muttonchops. "The correspondence school instructor said that showing we can run background checks is the best résumé we can have."

God deliver Jack from schmucks with matchbook private-detective-school diplomas. And from the Missouri law mandating a year's apprenticeship with a licensed investigator. That and a written exam weeded out the wanna-be overnight Sam Spades, but presented certain liability issues. Like mentorship being a pain in the butt for a working, marginally successful P.I.

"I live with my mom, so I can work for free," Blankenship wheedled. "Double the manpower, double your billable hours. Maybe triple 'em."

Halve them was more like it. Jack needed Baby Huey under his wing like a duck needs a concrete flak jacket. "Sorry, but like you said, McPhee Investigations is a one-man agency."

"It wasn't when it was Gregory, Aimes & Watkins." Blankenship shrugged. "Okay, so Watkins was dead and Aimes's wheel was throwing spokes before Chuck Gregory took you on. If it hadn't been for him, you wouldn't have a license, much less your name painted on the window."

With uncustomary patience, Jack said, "I was in the right

place at the right time." His inflection relayed *as opposed to you.* "Chuck wanted to retire and he loved showing rookies the ropes. Me, I'd rather hang myself with them."

Desperation edged Blankenship's laugh. "Come on, gimme a thirty-day trial. If it doesn't work out, no hard feelings. At least I'll have a month's experience to add to my résumé."

Jack's eyes rose to room 266's window, then lowered to the dashboard clock. By the time Blankenship extricated himself from the passenger's seat, Mr. and Mrs. Smith could waltz out arm in arm from the building's rear entrance.

He'd also bet McPhee Investigations hadn't topped Blankenship's list of employment prospects. The Park City telephone directory's business pages advertised about two dozen agencies, including a pricey nationally franchised outfit. If the kid had a brain, he'd started there and worked his way down.

"What I will do," Jack said, stashing the camera equipment on the floorboard, "is give you some friendly advice, while I drive you around front to your vehicle."

"It isn't here." Blankenship yanked on the shoulder harness. "I took a cab so I wouldn't blow your surveillance."

Well, well. That hiked Jack's previous estimation a few notches. Not enough to hire him, but maybe the kid had a brighter future than he thought. Wheeling around the motel's east side, he said, "Where to?"

"1010 West Danbury."

Jack gripped the steering wheel tighter—1010 West Danbury was his office address.

"I can't wait to show you what I can do with a computer. The background check on you? Just a warm-up." Blankenship played an air-piano solo. "Finger exercise."

Jack reconsidered a long-held supposition about predestination. To wit, days that started off swell were fated to free-fall into the toilet. Conversely, days beginning with a cosmic swirly would inevitably improve—though the increments ranged from microscopic to worthy of a parade with lots of tubas, bass drums and scantily clad majorettes.

So far, this one was a crapper with an automatic flush.

He didn't need a computer geek. A trusted subcontractor provided information above and beyond Jack's expertise or time constraints. Much as he sort of admired Blankenship's chutzpah, he'd sabotaged his fledgling career from the get-go. Ditto, no doubt, at every other agency in town. Giving him the hows and whys wasn't Jack's purview, but if the kid listened, he might wise up.

"You'd do about anything to score an apprenticeship," he said.

"Yes, sir." Blankenship grinned. "As long as it's legal." The latter inferred illegal activities weren't off the table, depending on the likelihood of police involvement.

"Then make a list of everything you've done to impress me, then do the opposite when you apply somewhere else." Jack braked for a traffic light. "Starting with your wardrobe."

Blankenship looked down, thoroughly bewildered. "I paid a bundle for this shirt at a Sister Hazel concert. It's a collector's item."

"Frame it and hang it on the wall. The grungy jeans and tennis shoes? Garbage." Jack adjusted his tie, a maroon silk with understated silver threads. "You want to be a professional, dress like one. Buy a razor and get a haircut. Want to work at a car wash? You're all set."

"Easy for you to say. Got any idea how much clothes cost when you're my size?"

"So drop a hundred pounds." Jack reassessed the belly garroted by the lap belt. "Make it a hundred and a quarter. Big as you are, one foot pursuit and you're DOA from a massive coronary."

Blankenship's face flushed beet red. "Sure, I'm a little over-weight, but I was born with a really slow metabolism and—"

Jack plucked two sesame seeds from his chin whiskers. "How many Big Macs did you slam for lunch?"

"Three, but—"

"Large fries?"

"Yeah, but—"

"Here's a guess. You chased it down with a diet soda."

A horn honked behind them. Jack accelerated a half block, then joined the queue in the left-turn lane. "This is America, kid. Eat whatever you want, whenever you want, but find a desk job. Investigating's too physical for a guy your size."

He hooked a right off First Street onto West Danbury. "Voice of experience. I stacked on seventy, eighty pounds driving a truck. Losing it was a bitch, but eating half as much, half as often did the trick. To put some distance between you and the fridge, sign up for some college courses—psychology, criminology, basic photography, Finance 101. Computers are fantastic, but not the be-all, end-all."

Another stoplight allowed a sidelong look. Blankenship glared out the windshield, as if picturing Jack's entrails smeared like a dead june bug's.

"You think I'm an asshole," Jack said. "Fair enough. I'll stake tomorrow's lunch money that I'm also the first one who's taken the time to tell you what you're doing wrong. Which is just about everything."

He ignored the tacit "Go fuck yourself" radiating from the passenger's seat. "Don't ambush a prospective employer when he's working. Don't background-check him, either. It screams zero scruples about running anybody and everybody through the mill just because you can."

The seat belt latch clicked open. Blankenship pushed himself through the door with considerably more grace and speed than he'd entered.

Jack called, "Hey, I'm just trying to—" a slam juddered the window glass, then reverberated through the chassis "—help," he finished, watching Blankenship jaywalk around an adjacent delivery truck.

Gee, that went well, he thought. Evidently honesty really wasn't always the best policy. It had, however, shored up the contention that mentoring wasn't one of his specialties.

On the other hand, the kid's eight-block hoof to his car wouldn't hurt him. Maybe allow pause for thought, not to mention counteract his six-thousand-calorie lunch. Or would, if Blankenship didn't salve a wounded ego with a banana split at the diner next door to Jack's office.

The pedestrian crossing light flashed "Hurry up or die." Blankenship materialized in the intersection, seemingly oblivious to the warning and the vehicle cranking a last-minute turn on yellow. The car's tires whinnied on the pavement; its driver saluted Blankenship with an extended middle finger.

The kid didn't notice. Didn't flinch when the car gunned past him, fortunate the side mirror didn't pick his pocket as it roared by. Still walking, closing the distance to the curb, Blankenship's eyes locked on Jack. His head turned, then tipped slightly forward when his neck craned too far for comfort.

His unblinking stare didn't project anger, defiance, disdain or the type of pity bestowed on those who've cast aside a golden opportunity.

Stone-cold hate, Jack said to himself. And a promise to make good on it. He looked away, confused and a little unnerved by its intensity. Keeping his own expression impassive, he glided forward with traffic.

He put a block, then another behind him. And couldn't shake the feeling that Brett Dean Blankenship still had him in the crosshairs.

2

Dina Wexler dropped the box of macaroni and cheese on the counter and shut the cupboard door. She stepped down from the wooden stool, then side-kicked it in front of the refrigerator.

Someday she'd have a kitchen where all the food, especially junk food, lived on her level. For her, using drawers as ladder rungs to reach the cereal and a bowl to put it in was a climbing stage you never outgrew. Not when you'd stopped at four feet ten.

Count your blessings, she reminded herself. Like the man who complained about having no shoes, until he met the man who had no...

The TV in the living room went mute. "Di-*na*," her mother called. "When you get a minute, would you bring me the *TV Guide?* I left it in the bedroom and there's a show on at four o'clock I want to watch. For the life of me, I can't remember what channel it's on."

Dina grabbed the potato chip bag off the top of the fridge. The crackling cellophane mocked her frazzled nerves. She rested her forehead on the freezer door's cool metal face. It was only one-thirty, for God's sake. Lunch was a half hour late, as were her mother's medications that must be taken with meals.

In the hallway, a fabric mountain of laundry banked the utility closet's bifold doors. The yard needed mowing. Both bathrooms were a mess. The kitchen floor hadn't been mopped in recent memory.

Breathe in, Dina thought, breathe out. Make yourself one with the refrigerator. Better yet, *be* the refrigerator and chill the hell out.

The mental image of herself standing on a kid's alphabet step stool getting Zen with a major appliance brought a whisper of a smile. No wonder *Peanuts* had always been her favorite comic strip. Charlie Brown refocused his *chi* with his head against the wall. She bonded with freezer compartments.

"Sweetheart?" her mother called, concern in her voice. "Are you all right?"

"Sure, Mom." Dina sighed and stepped down on the ugly starburst linoleum. "Everything's fine."

A Park City car dealer's commercial now wending from the living room reinforced their unspoken bargain. Harriet Wexler could keep pretending that her daughter was a human Rock of Gibraltar; Dina wouldn't let her mother see it was a prop made of chicken wire and papier-mâché.

She put a saucepan of water on to boil, then spread some diet saltines with sugar-free peanut butter. Laying them on a saucer, she sidled past the early-American dinette set and into the living room.

The vacant midcentury modern duplex had seemed open and airy when Dina toured it with the landlord. The narrow galley kitchen dead-ended at a window painted shut a couple of decades ago, but the dining area's merger with the living room gave an illusion of spaciousness. Off the hallway was a full bath, a small bedroom and the larger master with a private three-quarter bath.

A security deposit and two months' rent had been scraped

together in advance, and then there'd been furniture. Truckloads of Harriet's dog-ugly, alleged heirlooms that Dina and her younger brother wouldn't wish on a homeless shelter. Their mother's insistence that her circa-1978 pine-and-Herculon-plaid home furnishings would go retro any day was attributed to the side effects of digitalis.

Dina pushed back the tide of prescription bottles, moistening swabs, tissues and assorted medical paraphernalia to make room for the saucer on the metal TV tray beside Harriet's glider rocker. On the opposite side, another tray table held a cordless phone, paperbacks, a water glass, a dish of sugarless candy, the current crochet project and the queen's scepter, otherwise known as the remote.

The cushioned ottoman supporting Harriet's feet was surrounded by a paper trash sack, a tripod cane, bags of yarn, her purse, a discarded pillow and a mismatched pair of terrycloth slippers.

"Gosh, Your Majesty," Dina teased. "The throne's getting kinda crowded, isn't it?"

Harriet made a face, then pointed at the crackers. "I thought you bought bread at the store yesterday."

"I did." Dina peered into the plastic drinking glass—half full. "I'm working on lunch, but you need to take your pills."

"I can wait."

Dina knuckled a hip. "So can I." The water began to bubble on the stove. She pondered the tardy renter's insurance premium and what effect a semi-accidental kitchen fire might have on their coverage.

Harriet nibbled a corner off a cracker. Nose wrinkling, she plinked it back on the saucer. "It's stale."

Petulance was as wasted as the coral lipstick she swiped on to disguise her mouth's bluish tinge. "No, it isn't," Dina said. "I just opened a fresh box."

She hadn't, but it wouldn't matter if elves had just carted them over from the magic bakery tree. The issue was that her mother couldn't be trusted to take her meds unsupervised. Harriet's newest shell game was removing the pills from their bottles and stashing them in her bra, the way Dina had palmed brussels sprouts at the dinner table and hidden them in her socks.

Harriet Wexler wasn't senile. A bizarre sense of empowerment derived from outfoxing a caregiver she'd given birth to thirty-two years ago. On some levels, Dina understood and sympathized. On most, the pharmaceutical roulette drove her nuts.

Her mother glowered up at her, snapped a cracker in half, then shoved the whole thing into her mouth. "There," she mumbled around it. "Are you happy now?"

"One more, and I will be." Dina shook the appropriate pills from their amber bottles. The cost of each equaled a month's rent and utilities. "Clean your plate and I'll applaud."

Sips of water, fake choking, a bit of breast-beating and voilà, the medicine went down. "I hope you're proud of yourself, Dina Jeanne. You're nothing but a bully."

Dina recited in unison, "Thank heaven your father isn't alive to see how you treat your poor old sick mother." Leaning over, she kissed a prematurely white head that smelled of waterless shampoo and hairspray. "Daddy's definitely rolling in his grave knowing I'll bring your lunch, test your blood sugar, hook up the nebulizer, change your sheets, tuck you in for a nap, do the laundry, fix a snack, give you a shot, poke down three more pills, walk you twenty-five laps up and down the hall, then start dinner."

As she straightened, her mother's never warm fingers circled her wrist. "Oh, sweetheart, I'm so sorry." Tears glistened in eyes once as blue as a summer sky. "I don't know why I say such awful things to you."

Because now I'm the parent and you're the child and you hate needing the snot-nosed kid you potty-trained to help you to and from the bathroom sometimes.

"It's okay, Mom." Dina swallowed audibly, then cleared her throat to mask it. Aged ears dulled to soap opera dialogue and the radio remain subsonically attuned to the slightest emotional nuance. "Besides—" she forced out a chuckle "—when have I ever listened to a word you say?"

"Humph. If you ever did, you never let on." Harriet plucked at the sheet draping her legs, as though the air conditioner was set at sixty-two instead of eighty-two. "I thought Earl Wexler was the stubbornnest critter that ever walked on two legs. You bested him from the day you were born."

Dina tapped her toe, waiting for the upshot. It came right on cue. "I don't know what I'd have done if Randy hadn't been such a happy, sweet-natured little fella. Hasn't changed a bit, either, in spite of all the disappointment and heartache he's suffered."

"Uh-huh." Dina turned and started for the kitchen. "Life doesn't get any tougher than playing drums for a wanna-be rock band for ten freakin' years."

Her younger brother was everything she wasn't: tall, blond, charming, funny, gifted and as irresponsible as a golden re-triever puppy. Harriet outwardly adored the child who'd needed it more, thinking the daughter who denied being anything like her would be stronger for being pushed away. Earl Wexler had spoiled Dina, loved Randy inwardly and didn't notice which child never laughed at his joke about the hospital switching Randy with his real son.

Politics isn't just local or exclusive to public office. Before children can feed themselves, instinct discerns the balance of power and how to work it. The Wexlers' parental duopoly should have triggered sibling rivalry on a biblical scale. Rather than fight each other, Dina and Randy had joined forces to sandbag the adults.

And the little shit still is, she thought. Except now I'm the adult, I'm flying solo and it sucks. Drummer Boy's sporadic twenty-five or fifty-dollar money orders mailed from towns Dina had to squint to locate in an atlas were *so* not like being here.

The doorbell rang, startling her. The prodigal's return? Dina glanced around, as though a Lifetime channel camera crew might have sneaked in when she wasn't looking. Torn between water spitting on the stove burners and rescue fantasies, Dina threw open the door. "Randy, oh my—"

The two men on the stoop recoiled. The shorter one retreated to the concrete walk. Feeling her face flush scarlet, Dina stammered, "Th-thanks anyway, but we don't need to be saved. We're Jewish. Orthodox."

She used to tell roving God squads they were Catholic, but some well-meaning missionaries took it as a challenge. While Dina's knowledge of Judaism was gleaned from *Seinfeld* reruns, the tack had effectively decimated any hope of conversion.

"Are you Mrs. Wexler?" the taller man inquired. He consulted the clipboard in the crook of his arm. "Mrs. Harriet Wexler?"

Dina eyed the medical-supply-company insignia above his shirt pocket. The doctor-prescribed oxygen machine was scheduled for delivery on Monday, July 11, between 8:00 a.m. and 6:00 p.m. This, however, was Sunday. The tenth. She was absolutely almost certain of it.

Thinking back to the previous evening for confirmation, she realized that *it* had been Sunday, therefore this *was* Monday and a good chunk of it was gone. Small comfort, knowing time warps were the purview of mothers with young children and the housebound by choice.

Behind her, Harriet inquired, "Is that the Avon lady? Get me a bottle of that lotion I like. A big one. That skimpy thing you bought before didn't last a month."

The deliverymen—both named Bob, by their lanyards' photo IDs—gave Dina the tight smiles she'd dubbed "Oh, but for the grace of God go I." They probably had sisters to tend the sick, too.

Dina let them in, then excused herself to ward off a kitchen disaster. Leaving the nearly dry saucepan in the sink to cool, she wiped peanut butter across a few more crackers, poured her mother a glass of milk and grabbed a banana.

A diabetic diet's food exchanges and substitutions weren't that complicated. Meal timing was as crucial as the menu. The object was balancing calories and carbs to maintain blood-sugar levels. Lunch included a vegetable serving, as well, but it'd be a miracle if Harriet ate a bite of anything.

Dina returned to the living room as her mother was saying, "Y'all go on about your business and leave me be. I signed a paper way back saying I don't want a machine breathing for me."

"That's a ventilator, Mom." Dina's elbow evicted the tissue box to make room for the milk and fruit on the tray table. "They brought the oxygen machine Dr. Greenspan ordered to lessen the strain on your heart."

The cardiologist had also scripted a portable tank to trundle along when Harriet left the house. Which she didn't, other than for doctors' appointments and lab tests. Harriet had nodded amiably during Greenspan's treatise on blood oxygenation, simultaneously blocking out parts she chose not to hear.

"But there's nothing wrong with my heart." Her mother stuck out a bony wrist. "Feel that pulse. Strong as an ox, I tell you."

Everything was wrong with her heart, but Dina replied, "And the doctor wants you on oxygen full-time to keep it that way." She waved the men toward the hallway. "So while you finish lunch, Bob and Bob and I will move enough furniture in here to make room for the machine."

"Oh, no you *won't*."

The Bobs halted midstride.

"I'll go to a nursing home before you'll shut me up back there all by my lonesome."

"Mom, please. Don't fight me on—"

"What in Sam Hill am I s'posed to do all day? Time and again, I asked you for a cable gizmo in my room." Harriet grabbed the remote and clasped it to her bosom. "Stick that machine on the roof for all I care. I ain't budgin' from this chair till the undertaker peels me out of it."

Dina scrunched her hair in a wad, battling the urge to scream. To run out the goddamn door. To call the constant bluff and pack her demanding brat of a mother off to whatever nursing home would have her.

She hadn't given the TV a second thought. Why, she couldn't fathom, other than life-sustaining oxygen taking priority over *Golden Girls* reruns. The excuse for a single cable outlet was that Harriet needed rest and wouldn't, with a TV blaring in her room all night. In truth, Dina couldn't afford the extra installation fee or monthly charges.

"Uh, ma'am?" Taller Bob said. "We can—"

"It's not a problem, really." Dina's arm dropped to her side. "Don't worry, Mom. You'll have your TV. Everybody just relax and give me a minute to think."

She crossed to the patio door on the far side of the room and looked back to the dining area. Taking stock and mental measurements, she said, "Okay. What we'll do is shove the couch around over there, then move Mom's bed in here. The oxygen machine can go between it and her chair. Easy access, whether she's lying down or sitting up."

Tall Bob and Other Bob exchanged weary, all-in-a-day's-work looks. Like carpet cleaners, home-health-care equipment employees' job descriptions entailed a lot of heavy lifting.

Wait till they got a load of—literally—Harriet's monster, dark-stained pine cannonball bed. And the matching hutch-top dresser and highboy they'd have to finesse the mattress and box springs past without disturbing a jillion dusty knicknacks and framed photographs.

Harriet whipped back the sheet. Pushing upright, she grabbed her cane and hobbled off down the hall. Dina guessed she wanted to hide the personal, even intimate items that age and illness remanded to plain sight on the nightstand.

Dina continued, "The coffee table, end tables, bookcases—crap in general—we'll dump in Mom's room." To herself, she added, And when Mom isn't looking, I'll sneak Randy's crap out of the second bedroom in there, too.

Thumps in the hall preceded Harriet's reappearance. Clutched in a quaking, blue-veined fist was Earl Wexler's long-barreled revolver. "You boys lay one hand on my things and I'll blow it clean off." Her glare and the gun wobbled to Dina. "That goes for you, too, missy. I'm not an invalid like your daddy was. I'll be damned if you'll make me into one."

Having lost the argument about pawning the gun, Dina had removed the bullets on the sly. The garbage seemed the obvious disposal method, until she pictured city sanitary landfill workers running from a hail of exploding shells. Safer, she decided, to bury them in the backyard.

A subtle head shake informed the Bobs that the revolver wasn't loaded. Evidently aware of the number of people who die every year from "unloaded" guns, both men faded back behind the TV stand.

"Of course you aren't an invalid, Mom." Dina eased toward

her. "Far from it. But if the TV has to stay where it is, it only makes sense to bring *you* to *it*."

"Loll around where everybody that comes to the door can see me." Harriet snorted in disgust. "Why, I'd sooner plunk myself in Penney's front window at the mall."

Dina removed the heavy revolver from her mother's hand before she dropped it and broke a foot. Staring down at it, she remembered her father making the same Penney's window remark to a hospice volunteer. She should have known that for his widow, setting up a bed of any kind in the living room was a death knell. A small, terrifying step away from the hospital type brought in for Earl Wexler's final months.

That time would inevitably come again. A year from now, two, five—the doctors were continually astonished by Harriet's resiliency. When they remarked on it, she always said, "The secret to livin's being too mean to die. God don't want you and the devil's scared of what you'll do if he gets ya."

Dina laid the gun on the dining room table, then faced her mother. "I understand about the bed. I don't have the money to put cable in your room. Dr. Greenspan wanted you on oxygen weeks ago, but you had to get sicker before Medicare would pay for it. Telling me you won't do this and I can't do that isn't getting the machine in here, where you can use it."

She turned to Bob and Bob. "Which these very patient, very kind men will put wherever they think best." She smiled at them, adding, "I'm not passing the buck." A shrug, then, "Okay, I am, but now that I've royally screwed up and pissed off Bonnie Parker in the process, you're in charge."

Harriet grunted. "They should've been in the first place."

"I know." Dina cupped her elbow to guide her back to the throne. "I ought to be horsewhipped for trying too hard to make you happy."

"You're nothing but a bully, Dina Jeanne."

"Uh-huh."

"And you're gonna be sorry when I'm gone. I'm changing my will. Randy gets everything. Lock, stock and barrel."

Dina steadied her for the awkward, off-balance descent into the chair. Her mother's shallow, raspy breathing scared her. A glance over her shoulder at Taller Bob telegraphed, "Hurry. Please."

3

Jack McPhee eyed the redhead striding into Ruby Tuesday's dining area. So did every man at the bar and seated at tables. Their female companions' heads turned, following their gazes, curious why conversations halted in midsentence or lunch dates suddenly forgot how to chew. To a woman, the object of such dumbstruck attention fostered death-ray glares.

Belle deHaven always had that effect on people. A teal silk, hourglass-tailored sheath contributed to it. So did an impeccable pair of mile-long legs, a flawless complexion and green sloe eyes. But it was the inner, indescribable *something* she projected that deeded the room to her.

Jack stood and pulled out the adjacent chair. "You're late, as usual." Belle kissed his cheek, then scrubbed off the evidence with her thumb. "After all these years, you'd be crushed if I was on time."

"The shock might be fatal."

Laughing, she sank into the chair and laid her clutch purse on the table. "Careful, McPhee. I know CPR, and it might be fun getting you in a lip lock again." Belle hoisted the cosmopolitan he'd ordered for her and took a sip. "You were a lousy husband, but a world-class kisser."

"Oh, yeah?" Jack cocked an eyebrow. "Sounds like my replacement could use a couple of pointers."

"Dream on, hon. Carleton is everything I ever wanted. Smart, handsome, respectable—"

"Rich."

Belle shrugged. "That, too, but money really doesn't buy happiness."

You're just now figuring that out? Jack thought.

She drank again and sighed. "Poverty wasn't as romantic as it's cracked up to be, either."

"It's not like we starved. It just took me a while to figure out what I wanted to be when I grew up."

"As if…" Four tapered, manicured fingers grazed his jacket sleeve. A squinted visual inspection elicited a gasp. "Armani? Good God, Jack. Are you robbing banks on the side?"

Hard as he tried, he couldn't tamp the blush creeping up his neck. A former girlfriend who managed an upscale resale shop introduced him to the concept of gently used clothing. Fleeting thoughts of recycling dead men's wardrobes gave him the willies for a while. So did the chance of acquiring Carleton deHaven's castoffs, until Jack realized his ex-wife's hotshot husband was about twice his size.

Across the shoulders and trouser inseams, he allowed. Where it really mattered…well, he had no complaints and damn sure hadn't received any.

"It's been a good year and there's a lot of it left." If you're gonna lie, sport, lie big. "Make that a great year. Business slowed down a little last month, but all in all, I thought I was due a few new threads to celebrate."

"Threads?" Belle chuckled and leaned back as the server settled a plate of Dover sole garnished with squash and broccoli in front of her. Jack had ordered it for her, as well, timing the arrival perfectly.

"You are such a dweeb," she said. "Fortunately, it's one of your charms."

"Thanks." Jack snorted. "I think."

After assuring the server that he wasn't the dweeb to whom she referred and that nothing else was needed, Belle picked up her fork, then frowned at the still empty place between Jack's elbows. "You're not eating?"

"Can't." He glanced at his watch. "Got to meet Gerry Abramson at his office in about fifteen minutes."

She forked in a bite of fish. Her expression inferred it was tasty, but nothing special. "You should've told me when I invited you to lunch."

"If you hadn't been forty-five minutes late, it wouldn't have mattered."

"I'm punctual in my own way." She waved at her drink and plate. "You could have eaten something while you were waiting. Grazed at the salad bar, at least."

Jack shook his head. "Mama raised me better than that." He added, "And I scarfed a stack of flapjacks at the diner, before you called."

Actually, before Gerry Abramson had called. If Belle had called earlier, Jack wouldn't have gone next door for breakfast. The food at Al's 24/7 Eats could torture Jack's gut, even when it didn't feel like a pretzel that slipped under a couch cushion last New Year's Eve.

Jack took a drink of ice water and wished it were Chivas. A slug of liquid relaxation would take the edge off his premeeting jitters. He couldn't care less what type of work the independent insurance agent offered. The domestic Jack expected to collect on Monday night had run sobbing from the restaurant. The heartbroken client stuck him with the dinner check, in lieu of a personal one.

By Wednesday afternoon, the office's quietude had him clicking on the desk phone's handset, hoping the line was dead. It wasn't. In fact, the dial tone had an increasingly mirthful quality, as though Ma Bell were having a few laughs at his expense.

"Jack," said the gorgeous, similarly named redhead dissecting her entrée. "Are you okay?"

He hesitated. When someone asks if you're okay without making eye contact, it's probable that he or she is anything but. Misery not only loves company, but it also graciously cedes the floor to yours, so his or her own appears empathetic.

Except the woman who'd been his wife for eight years and his best friend for twice that was a straight shooter. It had attracted him at the outset. After Belle dumped him for being an immature moron, her brand of honesty was what he'd missed most in subsequent relationships.

Maybe hanging with the country club set was finally wearing off on her. You can't fake going with the flow forever. Eventually the current sucks you in, or you say "Screw this bullshit" and wade to shore.

"This year hasn't been that good, and the suit's secondhand," Jack confessed. "This and a couple of Brooks Brothers set me back a friggin' fortune. Not counting alterations."

"I guessed as much."

Frowning, he reached under his arm, thinking he'd pulled a shrewd move like forgetting to clip off the price tag. Nope, and nothing up his sleeves but shirt cuffs, either. "So how'd you know?"

"Guys who can afford designer clothes don't wear them with Kmart shirts. Or ties. Or twenty-dollar watches." Instead of smug, Belle looked concerned. She pushed away her plate and fingered the stem of the martini glass. "How bad *is* business?"

"Flat." Jack smiled. "And about an hour from an uptick with Abramson's retainer."

"For what? A slip-and-fall? Workman's comp case?"

Both were a P.I.'s bread and butter. Insurers and attorneys hired investigators to expose phony personal-injury claims and employees pocketing compensation pay for job-related accidents. It was astonishing and pretty sad how often paid leaves for, say, a ruptured disc inspired a claimant's urge to reshingle his house.

Jack said, "Abramson mentioned taking a hit from a string of residential burglaries." He stifled an impulse to check the time. Belle, of course, wasn't wearing a watch. "So, how's life treating you?"

Meaning, Carleton better be treating her well, or Jack would cheerfully break him in half. Too cheerfully, he admitted, but protectiveness fueled it, not jealousy.

"Just between us, I'm a teensy bit bored. Nothing a baby wouldn't fix, if my ovaries would cooperate."

Belle signaled the server for the tab, then pointed at her plate, requesting a go box for it. "You have no idea how many times I prayed to my crotch to get with it when my period was a little late. Now I'm hollering up there, 'Swim, boys. *Swim.*'"

Jack was supposed to laugh. He said, "I didn't think you wanted kids." Pride bit off, With me.

"Woman's prerogative. One baby would be okay. Wonderful, actually." Belle drained her glass and blew out a breath. "Carleton isn't the paternal type, but I'll be damned if Abdullah Whatthefuckever will be our sole heir."

"Abdu—oh. The dog."

"How dare you call a champion afghan hound a *dog*. The old biddies at Westminster would have your head. So would the harem he's servicing in Florida." Belle autographed the credit card chit. "That hairball on stilts is higher maintenance than I am."

Jack chuckled. "That's saying somethin', kid."

Motion outside the window caught his eye. Vaguely attuned to Belle's continued slander against man's best friend, Jack leaned over the table, expanding his view of the restaurant's parking lot.

The lunch crowd had pretty well winnowed to vacationers as logy as over-the-road truckers who were seventeen hours into a ten-hour day. Jack's Taurus was baking in the mid-July sun. Belle's café-au-lait Mercedes coupe was parked a half-dozen rows east and farther from the restaurant's entrance.

Here and there, customers prolonged goodbyes, nodding and talking over the roofs of their vehicles. No familiar faces among them—no white-and-Bondo-colored subcompacts in the vicinity.

Still scanning the lot, Jack said, "You haven't noticed anybody, um, hanging around outside your house lately, have you? A strange car cruising by, anything like that?"

When Belle didn't answer, he looked at her. "Hey, no cause for the big eyes. Just curious, that's all."

Belle extracted a pair of sunglasses from her bag and slipped them on. Swiveling in her chair, she said, "I *knew* you were in trouble. What is it this time? Another pissed-off husband swinging single? Somebody pink-slipped after your background check?"

"I'm not in trouble."

She pulled down the shades an inch and peered over the frames.

"I'm not," Jack insisted, then groaned. "There's this mope—twenty-something, big as an upright freezer. He tagged me for a job, I turned him down, gave him some excellent career counseling and sent him on his way."

Belle's stare narrowed, but remained as steady as twin-beam halogens. Her fingers waggled, *Keep going.*

Jack peeled back his suit coat sleeve for a look at his watch. If he didn't haul asphalt in three minutes, he'd be late for the appointment with Gerry Abramson. "The kid thought he'd impress me with my own résumé, financials and an activities report."

"You mean he tailed you?"

Jack scowled at her apparent amusement. "If I hadn't been working a domestic, I'd have spotted his crap-mobile—" he snapped his fingers "—like *that*."

"Uh-huh." A fingernail clicked a riff on the tabletop. "You think he's stalking you."

"Not really." Saying it didn't make it true, but Jack liked the sound of it. "Trust me. He's about as built for covert surveillance as Sasquatch."

Belle pondered a moment. "Then you're afraid he'll use info from the dossier on you to stalk me." It wasn't a question. And there wasn't a molecule of fear in her tone.

"It occurred to me." Jack stood and held the back of her chair to steady it. The scenery below provoked a mental wolf whistle. Belle McPhee deHaven had an unquestionably fine set of legs, but it was the peek at her cleavage that brought back many a fond memory.

She and Jack epitomized a couple who should never have parlayed friendship into matrimony. He was damn lucky he'd escaped the latter without destroying the former.

He walked her out, saying, "Okay, I'll admit, this dude gave me the heebie-jeebies. You know the type. A schlump, except the eye contact's too long and a touch too intense."

"Does this schlump have a name?"

"Brett Dean Blankenship." Taking Belle's keys, he pressed the fob's remote button to unlock the Mercedes's door. "About six-three and four hundred pounds of solid flab. How he packs it into a Chevy Cavalier defies physics."

Belle scanned the parking lot, as if daring Moby Dick to surface. "Thanks for the warning."

"At most, it's a heads-up." He kissed her lightly on the lips. "Sorry I have to run."

"I'm used to it." She flashed a no-insult-intended smile.

Jack couldn't tell through her sunglasses, but bet it didn't reach her eyes. Something was bothering her. He could feel it. "How about meeting me for a drink later? If Abramson's retainer is over a couple of grand, I'll even buy."

"I wish I could." Belle sighed as though she meant it. "Carleton and I are meeting some people for dinner at the club."

Bars kicked off happy hour at four, but Jack gave her a rain check. "If you, uh, want to shoot the breeze some more, you know the numbers."

She nodded and pulled the car door shut.

By the time Jack reached the Taurus, he decided his imagination was working double overtime. An occupational hazard for a semi-underemployed snoop. Belle's admitted boredom wasn't a crisis, even if the rival for your husband's affections was a trophy dog. And he hadn't seen Blankenship as much as sensed him.

He dawdled a moment beside his car to let the blast-furnace heat escape the open door. Belle was right about his being a lousy husband and provider, he thought. But for all the things she'd ripped him for, boredom had never been one of them.

The National Federated Insurers' office was housed in a remodeled Asian restaurant. The mud-brown exterior and pagoda roof reclad in cedar shakes evoked *Jackie Chan Does Sante Fe,* but the parking area was large enough for employees, visitors and a bank's repossessed-vehicles sales lot.

Jack perused a sweet electric-blue speedboat marooned on its trailer. Babe magnet. Babe-in-a-*bikini* magnet. He could be the Captain and she, his Tennille. The fantasy shimmied and vanished, like a cartoon genie into a bottle. Babes young enough to wear bikinis probably wouldn't know the Captain and Tennille from Captain Kangaroo.

On that depressing note, Jack entered the insurance agency's reception area and gave his name to the blonde behind the counter. Without missing a beat of her cell phone conversation, she pointed over her shoulder at Gerry Abramson's private office.

A double row of desks resided where buffet steam tables had fed the all-you-can-eat multitudes until a health department inspector contracted botulism. Three of the agency's four workstations were unoccupied. At the back on the window-wall side, Wes Shapiro waved Jack on.

The office manager wouldn't be picked out of a lineup if a witness had a snapshot of the assailant. Medium build, medium height, medium everything from buzz cut to wingtips. One of those guys who looked the same at his high school graduation as he did at the thirtieth reunion. And not in a good way.

"How's it going, stranger?" Wes stuck out a hand. "I haven't seen you since the snow was flying."

Park City received a total of three inches all last winter, but the slip-and-fall claim Jack investigated turned out to be genuine. When the victim's civil suit against the negligent store owner went to court, Jack would testify for the plaintiff. Gladly testify. Last he'd heard, she was still in a wheelchair.

Wes lowered his voice. "I told the boss to call you two months ago." A thumb pinched an index finger. "The cheap son of a gun has the first dollar this agency ever made."

"Framed and hung on the wall, no less." McPhee Investigations' first dollar was encased in Lucite on Jack's desk. Classy.

"Tell Gerry I'll have the files together in a few," Wes said.

"He'll nag me on the intercom anyway, but the photocopier's a two-speed model. Slow and broken."

Jack continued on, turning into a corridor with gender-specific restrooms on his right. Wes's parting remark was an ode to middle management. Nowhere to go but out imposed a constant straddle between indispensible and justifying your existence.

He and Gerry Abramson shook on their mutual gladness to see each other. For as long as Jack had known him, the independent insurance broker had threatened retirement. Today, a hypertensive complexion and bulldog jaw implied a fatal coronary might punch Gerry's ticket before dinnertime.

Jack asked after Letha, Gerry's wife of forty-seven years. The vivacious grandmother of nine was battling Parkinson's disease.

"She has her good days and bad." Gerry winged his elbows on the arms of a leather desk chair. "The doc's put her on a new course of treatment. It's experimental and costs the moon, but it seems to help."

He shook his head. "Almost a half century in the insurance business, and I'm fighting tooth and toenail with our carrier to cover the meds." A bitter chuckle, then, "And losing."

"Then chumps like me don't have a prayer." Jack rapped on the visitor chair's oak frame. A sole proprietor fears extended illness and a debilitating injury more than the IRS. No work, no income. The flu bug can knock a zero off a month's earnings.

"Time was," Gerry continued, "and not that long ago, when I felt good telling customers not to worry. Fire? Surgery? Hail damage? We've got you covered."

A crooked finger ratcheted down the knot in his tie, as though it were the source of discomfort. "Nowadays, I'm the villain with a briefcase full of loopholes and exclusions." He grimaced, levering the collar button backward through its corresponding hole. "And a lot smaller check than they hung their hopes on."

Jack wondered why Gerry didn't sell out and retire. What kept him coming to this cozy, thick-carpeted office paneled in genuine walnut and adorned with framed certificates of achievement and appreciation? A national newspaper's bar chart recently rated the public's attitude toward various professions. Attorneys historically ranked number one in the most-despised category. The poll's results now placed insurance agents in the lead by several percentage points.

Gerry Abramson had two first loves. Clinging to a semblance of control over an industry he hardly recognized wasn't as painful as watching a bastard named Parkinson steal away his wife and being helpless to stop him.

"How about a soda?" he said, rolling backward in his chair. He opened a minifridge built into the credenza. "Bottled water? Chilled cappucino?" He winked. "Just between us, these juice boxes for the grandkids aren't bad with a shot of vodka stirred in."

Jack declined and was relieved when Gerry snapped the ring tab on a can of diet cola. The man had every reason in the world to spike an orange drink at two o'clock on a hot July afternoon. The Abramson clan photo atop the credenza symbolized eighteen better reasons not to.

"This job you mentioned on the phone," he said. "Since you didn't specify, I'm guessing it's a fraudulent property-loss claim. Probably a high-profile customer."

Gerry glared at the doorway, then jabbed an in-house button on the console phone.

"Here's the copies," Wes said, entering the office at the precise moment his employer's call connected. He cut a look at Jack, as though delivering the punch line of a private joke.

After the handoff to Gerry, Wes pulled over a second visitor's chair. His backside was approaching a landing, but hadn't quite touched down when Gerry cocked his head at the phone. "Three lines are on hold."

Wes nodded. "One for Chase and two for Melanie. They just came back in from their claims adjustments."

"Then take one of Melanie's until she's freed up," Gerry said "And, do me a favor and close the door on your way out."

"Oh. Sure thing." The office manager left the room smiling. Behind him, the door shut with a barely audible snick.

Gerry rolled his eyes. "Wes wants to be an investigator so bad it's almost painful to see."

Thinking of Blankenship, Jack replied, "Doesn't everybody?"

The copied files Gerry parceled out concerned a series of residential burglaries dating back to Memorial Day weekend. "Here's where it gets interesting." He gave Jack a sheaf of police reports. "The same thief or thieves hit last year, starting Memorial Day, then went to ground Labor Day weekend."

He paused to let Jack skim the pages. "Luck of the draw, maybe, but only two of last year's targets were National Federated clients. This year, the so-called Calendar Burglar has already nailed three of my policy holders."

The nickname rang a bell—the tiny baby-shoe kind, not a tolling brass one. By the number of reports, the reverse should have been true. "Why haven't I seen anything in the newspaper about this?"

"The *Park City Herald* focused on it to some extent late last summer. You know, 'Another west-side home burgled while owners on vacation.' Or east side. Or south side. Then the usual PD information officer quotes on home security, warnings about disclosing travel plans to strangers, etc."

Gerry drained the soda can and lobbed it at the trash bin. "Property-theft complaints always jump in the summer and during the holidays. By the time the cops and the newspaper connected these particular dots, the Calendar Burglar vamoosed."

"Feeling the heat," Jack speculated. "Moved on to cooler pastures."

"That was the assumption, except a unit detective followed up in his spare time. Feelers put out to regional PDs netted no thefts that resembled these—the M.O. or an exclusive preference for jewelry."

Gerry allowed that the burglar could have switched specialties, wintered in a warmer clime or been jailed on an unrelated charge. "Whatever caused the lull, he's back. The *Herald* isn't happy about keeping the story low profile, but some influential victims and real estate developers don't want their neighborhoods depicted as crime scenes."

"God forbid." Jack snorted. "They may as well leave out cookies and milk for this dude. A little snack for bad ol' anti-Claus."

"Residential watch groups were alerted in early June. Private security and police patrols in probable target zones have been increased."

"Uh-huh." Jack's finger tapped the prior Sunday's date on the most recent burglary complaint. "Fairly obvious, what a big friggin' bite that's taking out of crime."

"I want him caught, McPhee."

Jack looked up. The tone and content of Gerry's statement weren't particularly open to interpretation. "You want *me* to catch a burglar?"

The insurance broker leaned forward and braced his elbows on the desk. "I hope your schedule's clear enough, or can be cleared to devote full-time to this."

There were some less than lucrative jobs pending on Jack's

calendar. Otherwise, if the schedule had been any clearer, he'd be applying for a shopping-cart jockey's job at the local Sav-A-Lot.

National Federated's retainer would be commensurate with exclusivity, but a scratching sensation behind Jack's sternum hinted that Gerry Abramson was holding something back.

Perhaps an untranscribed chat with a crime-unit investigator who suspected this Calendar Burglar carried an AK-47 in his pillowcase. Most housebreakers aren't armed; county jail or prison-time on a theft rap is measured in single- to double-digit months. Add a weapons charge and it's usually *sayonara* for a long stretch.

But kill somebody with it—say, the P.I. on your case—and it's twenty-five to life. A punishment befitting the crime, Jack thought, except for me still being dead.

"The newspaper may be downplaying the story," he said, "but this victims list must have lit a bonfire under the police chief's butt."

Gerry nodded. "It hasn't slowed, much less stopped these thefts. If the Calendar Burglar isn't arrested before Labor Day weekend, it stands to reason, he'll disappear again."

And bloom like jonquils along a fence row next May. "I understand the reasoning, Gerry. To be honest, just thinking about it has my motor running, and the fee for services could be a beaut."

Jack laid the paperwork on the desk, then sat back and crossed a leg on his knee. "What I don't get is why you think I can make a tinker's damn worth of difference."

"Fresh eyes. Fresh perspective." His gesture relayed "If I'm footing the bill, what's the problem?"

The response was credible, even logical, but a tad too quick. Jack thought back to Wes's earlier remark about advising Gerry to contact McPhee Investigations shortly after the burglaries recommenced. Then the polite bum's rush Wes received when he tried to invite himself to the powwow.

"You think Shapiro's the Calendar Burglar," Jack said. "He covered himself by concentrating on other insurers' clients, then either greed or smarts told him he'd better dip into the home well, or somebody'd get wise."

Gerry's expression slackened. Skin folds lapping his eyelids retracted, as though an instant blepharoplasty had been performed. Chuckles escalated to a belly laugh. "Wait'll I tell Letha. Picturing Wes tiptoeing around like Cary Grant in that old cat burglar movie will be stuck in our heads for who knows how long."

Great. Now that he mentioned it, the image implanted itself in Jack's mind. Sort of like Don Knotts resurrected for a remake. No, not quite that big a departure. Jerry Stiller, maybe. Or What's-his-name—that average Joe born to play average Joes.

"It's as simple as this," Gerry said. "I'm an independent insurance agent. A hub in a wheel with multiple spokes. When loss claims hike, instead of one provider's boot on my neck, it's a centipede." He blew out a breath. "I shouldn't have to tell you, I don't need the stress."

A half hour later, Jack left the building with an armload of files, a retainer check and no idea how he'd earn it.

4

Single-story duplexes are usually long rectangles with mirror-reverse floorplans. By the county assessor's definition, two contiguous residential units separated by a foot-thick rock firewall were patio homes. Very la-di-da, in Dina's opinion, but such was government work. Whether duplex or patio home, the bisected building wasn't rectangular, either, but an L painted a cruddy shade of gray.

The units shared a three-quarter pie-shaped front yard, a sweetgum tree and views of an adjacent redbrick warehouse, but respective tenants seldom saw each other. The jackknifed design had the neighbors facing north at the corner of Rosedale Court and Lambert Avenue; the Wexlers' side pointed due east on Lambert at its intersection with Spring Street.

Visitors directed to the corner of Lambert and Rosedale would idle at the curb, look from one unit to the other and mutter "Eeny, meeny, miney." Occasionally they chose the right "mo." A few hit the gas and drove away in a huff. Those who rang the Wexlers' doorbell in error kept them apprised of the current neighbors' last name.

As Dina cruised up Lambert Avenue at 1:15 a.m., the Rosedale side's windows were dark. Lights blazed from Casa Wexler as if a party was in progress. Where Harriet's energy-conservation policy once consisted of "Flip off that switch when you leave a room. You think I own the electric company?", evidently, she now thought her daughter did.

Dina pulled past the mailbox, shifted the Beetle into Reverse and backed into the driveway. The engine hacked and sputtered. Mechanical bronchitis was typical of vehicles with a couple of hundred thousand miles on their odometers.

Someday she'd have the money to restore it to its original… well, *glory* was a bit highfalutin for an ancient VW. She'd settle for a new milky-cocoa paint job and straightening the Val Kilmer sneer in the rear bumper.

The Beetle was as short in the chassis as she was, but the single garage wasn't deep enough to squeeze between the wall and the car to open the front-end trunk. She shifted into Neutral, yanked on the emergency brake, then slumped in the seat. She was just too pooped to muscle up the garage door, back in the Bug, unload her stuff, then jump for the rope tied to the door's cross brace to pull it down again.

"Someday number two," she said. "I'll have a garage with an electric opener and shutter."

Leaving the Beetle to the elements, she reached into the trunk and wrestled with the magnetic Luigi's Chicago-Style Pizza sign earlier peeled off the driver's-side door. Her hobo bag slung over one shoulder counterbalanced the canvas tote on the other. Quietly, she closed the trunk, then relocked it.

The duplex's front door swung open the moment the key was inserted. Dina groaned in frustration. Sirens and extended commercial breaks often lured her mother from the world that was her chair to survey the larger, outside one. When the TV program resumed, or no disaster was visible beyond the stoop, she'd shut the door and call it good.

Harriet Wexler could not—or would not—get it through her

head that the day was long gone when locked doors and drawn curtains meant you had something to hide.

Inside, an infomercial hawked its wares to an unoccupied glider rocker. The habit of leaving on the TV "for company" impelled silent prayers that her mother hadn't toddled off hours ago to the bathroom and collapsed in a heap on the floor.

Dina left her purse and bag on the table and tiptoed down the hall. Whuffly snores met her midway. In the master bedroom, clear plastic tubing tethered Harriet to the oxygen machine at the end of the bed. Yards of extra hose lassoed the cannonball footpost.

In the light slanting from the open bathroom door, she resembled a child actor made up and bewigged to play her future self. Fingers curled over the bedcovers pulled up to her chin suggested a foil for pixies and their nightly tug-of-war with the blanket.

Dina eyed the machine's distilled-water level, then blew her mother a kiss. "Sweet dreams, Mom."

Naturally, Harriet continued to insist she didn't need oxygen, though her color and energy had improved in the past four days. Dina worried about her tripping over the tubing, but fear of breaking a hip made Harriet extracautious. All in all, the two Bobs' no-fuss, no-muss solution deserved a Nobel peace prize.

In the hall bathroom, Dina ran water in the sink and pretended the mirror above it didn't exist. Off with the black cargo pants, her sour-sweaty top and bra; on went the giant Mizzou T-shirt she'd slept in the night before. Soaping and rinsing her face felt wonderful. A hot shower would be ecstasy, but water tattooing the plastic tub surround sounded like marbles in a cocktail shaker.

Her face buried in a hand towel, she yelped when a voice said, "Where the devil have you been, young lady?"

Dina's head whiplashed toward the door, her pulse spiking a zillion beats a minute. Clutching the towel to her chest, she shrieked, "Jesus *Chr-ist,* Mom. You scared the livin' hell out of me."

By Harriet's expression, she was gratified to know she hadn't lost the ability to strike terror in the heart of her kid from ambush. "That pizza joint closes at eleven on weeknights." She sniffed several times, then puckered her lips. "This is Thursday, you look like you've been dragged through a knothole backward and what I smell ain't pepperoni."

"Oh, yeah?" Dina flinched. Sure, her defense strategies were years out of practice, but they hadn't been *that* lame since fourth grade. What popped out was a snotty, even lamer, "Technically, it's been Friday for almost two hours."

"You said you'd be home before midnight."

"I said I'd *probably* be home *by* midnight." Dina hung the damp towel on the bar behind her, smoothing the wrinkles and leveling the hems. "If you needed me, all you had to do was hit the panic button."

An emergency alert device hanging like a pendant around Harriet's neck was programmed to automatically dial Dina's cell phone. An autodial to 911 would be faster, but a city ordinance prohibited a direct connection to an emergency dispatcher. It was up to Dina to contact emergency services.

"Too many false alarms for a direct call," a city official told Dina. "An average of sixteen a day when the city council passed the ordinance. And *that* was twenty years ago."

A subscription service would relay confirmed panic-button emergencies, but it cost forty dollars a month. Dina couldn't afford it and a cell phone, too.

"I'm sorry, if I—" The doorway was empty. Peering out, Dina glimpsed the tail of a seersucker housecoat rounding the corner into the dining room. When Dina caught up with her mother, she was fumbling with the tote bag's zipper.

"What do you think you're doing?" coincided with the TV announcer's "Only thirty seconds left. Act now, before it's too late…."

"Since you won't tell me what you're up to," Harriet said, "I have to find out my own self."

Paper crackled as she jerked out three white pharmacy sacks, their tops stapled shut. Her righteous scowl deflating, she delved for paydirt at the bottom of the bag.

"What's this?" she inquired, an "Aha!" implicit in her tone. The alleged contraband emerged, cocooned in a plain plastic bag.

"Okay, you got me," Dina said. "You'd think I'd learn it's impossible to put anything over on you for long." She pulled out a chair and sat down hard. "Go ahead. Open it."

Hesitating, her eyes downcast and despair evident, Harriet unwrapped whatever Pandora's box she'd imagined and now wished she'd left alone.

While she stared transfixed at the carton, Dina said, "The pharmacist on the graveyard shift had customers stacked up three deep when I walked in. That's why I was so late. I wanted to ask some questions, or better, get his recommendation, instead of buying just any ol' electronic glucose monitor off the shelf."

Feeling guilty, among other things, for leading on her mother, letting her deliver her own comeuppance, Dina added, "The pharmacist showed me, it really is almost painless. No more finger-sticks to dread three or four times a day."

Harriet ran a knuckle under one eye, then the other. "I shouldn't have—"

"Oh, hush. It's as good a surprise now as it would've been in the morning."

"Yes, and you're the sweetest daughter in the world for buying it, but—" She picked up the empty bag and started fitting the carton back into it. "These things aren't cheap. Why, a fancy gizmo like this—"

"Is top-of-the-line and worth every penny." Dina snatched the receipt from her mother's hand and crumpled it. The shopping bag was taken away and wadded. "You'd buy one for me, if I was being poked and pinched bloody all the time, so end of discussion."

Oops. She grinned, hoping to magically turn the last part, that teensy *finis* which might be interpreted as an order, into a joke. A witty rejoinder. A—

Her mother bent down and kissed her cheek. "Thank you, baby. You shouldn't have spent the money, but it is a trial when my fingers are too sore to work a crochet hook."

She was quick to grouse about everything from foods she craved that were on the restricted list to unwed celebrities who hatched their young like guppies. Aches, pains and physical discomforts were endured in silence.

Bravery was admirable. Except it forced constant vigilance, attentiveness to every subtle twitch, grimace, blemish—any deviation from whatever constituted normal. Had Harriet hovered over Dina and Randy as diligently when they were children, they'd have whistled up the stork and demanded a change of address.

The paper bags contained an anti-inflammatory prescribed for arthritis and two types of ophthalmic drops to control Harriet's glaucoma. One of the latter required refrigeration. As she moved to the kitchen, Dina cocked an eyebrow, angled sideways in the chair, then looked back toward the hall. No oxygen hose trailed along the carpet.

"Something seems to be missing. But jeepers, I can't imagine what it is."

Her mother shrugged and closed the fridge. "So I left my leash on the bed for a minute or two. What's the harm?"

Dina dropped her head into her hands. Maybe it wasn't too late to whistle up that stork.

Jack raised his head from his hands and blew out a breath. It stank of beer, rancid onions from the chili dog and rings he'd gulped for dinner and the five pots of coffee he'd chased them with.

A scrambled egg, dry toast and a glass of milk next door at Al's diner would absorb the acid gnawing craters in Jack's stomach. A glance at his watch, then at the parking lot visible out the office window nixed the idea. Neighborhood bars had poured their customers out on the street over an hour ago, but Thursday-night-into-Friday-morning crowds were different from weekenders.

Rebels without a brain, in Jack's opinion. As if knocking back a sixer the night before the work week ended was a form of social commentary. Clock in Friday with a killer hangover and perfect impression of a toilet bowl's rim carved on your face and that'll by God show the boss who's boss.

"Nice attitude, McPhee," he muttered. "Speaking from experience, I presume?"

He was. His throbbing neck and shoulders brought back memories of regular worship services at the porcelain altar. Hunkering over a desk for hours on end exacted similar punishment with none of the fun of getting there.

Sitting back in his chair, he surveyed the ream of photocopies and newspaper stories separated into categorized stacks. A case beginning with little or nothing to go on was common. One with an old-growth forest in paper form splayed across his desk should solve itself. And might, if he could see the pattern for all the damn trees.

It was there. He was just too bleary-eyed to find it. The usual remedy for mental fatigue was a good night's sleep. A fabulous idea, if he could unplug his overloaded brain and stuff it in his sock drawer. Otherwise, the yammering in his head would be like the New York Stock Exchange after the opening bell.

A legal pad lay on the floor a few yards from his desk. Handwritten notes and jagged scratch-outs covered the fanned yellow sheets. A few minutes ago, the pages rattled merrily when Jack threw the pad in frustration. Tantrums were juvenile and counterproductive. That's why they felt so good.

His bowlegged, knee-bent scuttle to fetch the tablet was peculiar to the elderly, toddlers and those whose spines had conformed to nonergonomic chairs. Jack plopped the pad on the desk, then stretched for the ceiling's acoustic tiles. Crackles and pops sounded like chicken bones in a garbage disposal. He yawned so hard that black specks jittered behind his eyelids.

"Think," he said, still standing, his hands thrust in his trouser pockets. "Gerry Abramson isn't paying you to be dense."

Centered amid the paper rampart he'd dutifully studied was a street map photocopied and pieced together from the Park City phone directory. A colorful four-by-six-foot Chamber of Commerce version was framed on the wall, but the compact tape-job better suited the purpose.

Besides, he'd have to switch on the overhead to see the big one. An island of light shed by the desk lamp was cozy…and less conspicuous to fat, unemployed freaks cruising Danbury Street.

Dotting the miniaturized map were color-coded flags snipped from sticky notes. Each bore the date of the previous year's and current burglaries. A pattern should have emerged. Burglars, particularly pros, as the success rate confirmed, didn't act on impulse or at random.

Eight months of inactivity presumed advance planning for this year's take, hence a corresponding level of preparation the year before. Inherent in both should be a sort of grid effect designed to throw off the cops: hit a couple of north-side homes, then south, then the eastern burbs, etc. The property-crimes unit would chase their tails all over town, unable to anticipate the thief's next move.

In hindsight, that strategy should be obvious. Jack stared at the map. Uh-huh. Sure. He might as well have thrown his ticky-tacky little flags like darts. Blindfolded.

"Gerry's wrong about every victim being out of town when the thefts occurred," he said. "Two hits were in gated communities with manned guard posts. Was it luck, happy accident or genius to hit during a whoop-de-do celebrity golf tournament and the debutante cotillion?"

No answers, including what the debs were coming out *from,* and how three days of brunches, lunches, teas and dinners culminating in a formal ball enabled it.

Talking to himself didn't always rouse any synapses from their stupor, either, but there was something about thinking aloud that worked better than brooding in silence.

His finger tapped each of three widely separated flags. The first marked the Calendar Burglar's alleged debut. The other pair, this year's second and fifth B & Es. "What frosts the cupcake is how he knew to rob *these* folks."

The majority of the robberies occurred in affluent, newer housing developments with names like Grande Vista Estates and Devonshire Downs. These particular three occurred in less target-rich environments: modest homes in older middle-class neighborhoods. The victims' net worth exceeded that of many of the McMansion dwellers, but apparently they subscribed to the antiquated notion that flaunting it was déclassé.

"A lot of Park City natives wouldn't recognize these people's names," Jack said. "They donate a lug of money to charity, but pretty much on the q.t."

Charity was big business—nonprofit status aside. The larger the organization, the larger the administrative staff. Volunteers donated time to causes they deemed worthy, and while that might apply to some on the payroll, logic asserted that for others, it was just a job. And not one that'd earn a down payment on a house in Grande Vista Estates.

Donor anonymity didn't apply to recordkeeping. Federal and state forms must be filed, specifying who gave how much to what and when. A financially strapped employee might shy from out-and-out embezzlement, but initiating a personal collection drive could be irresistible.

Jack tuned out the annoying little bastards in his head questioning how said office worker would know when to strike. He flipped through the police reports for the umpteenth time, scanning one complainant's statement after another.

The remembered reference to charity elicited a gleeful "Bingo!" It was closely followed by a glum "Excellent work, dumbass."

There was Charity all right. Plain as day. Except it was a damn *dog's* name. A poor widdle pooch whose diamond-studded, five-thousand-dollar, sterling-silver-tagged collar got ripped off.

Muttering *f*-worded nouns, verbs, adjectives and not a few common compounds, he threw the reports skyward. Jerked his suit coat off the back of the chair. Switched off the desk lamp. Stomped to the door. Stabbed the key in the lock…then turned, leaving the ring dangling.

Dog. Neither Charity nor charity had tripped an almost imperceptible trigger, much less Jack's temper. And not *dog,* either. *Dogs.*

A report on one of National Federated's insureds noted the homeowner's opinion that not photographing what might be a partial shoe impression on the dog's bed was shoddy police work. Lifting a print off velvet flocked with dog hair was impossible, let alone idiotic. So was arguing with a know-it-all taxpayer.

Jack flipped on the overhead lights. The suit coat was lobbed at a couch clients rarely used and wasn't all that great for naps. Crouched on the floor, he scooped up the mess he'd made and carried it to the desk. Sorting the papers, restacking them neatly, he speed-read each one, looking for another remembered reference to a dog. Maybe a doghouse. A toy. It was there—he was certain of it—imbedded in blocks of cramped cop handwriting he was too weary to decipher.

Provided that pet ownership connected the Calendar Burglar's targets, Jack didn't flatter himself thinking the police missed it. Time was the mitigating factor. Some had slid by before specific thefts pegged a single perpetrator. Determining a link existed and the follow-up ate time off a clock they didn't know was ticking. Then it stopped cold for nine months. When the Calendar Burglar resurfaced, the investigative juice wasn't stagnant, it was freeze-dried.

"They may have already smoked the dog angle, but it's worth a shot. If I can figure out *how* this scumbag operates, the *who* will drop in my lap."

Every burglary victim would receive a call tomorrow to confirm a dog's presence in the home and its whereabouts when the theft occurred. Not from Jack McPhee, of course. Identifying himself as a P.I. guaranteed the person at the other end would hang up or clam up.

Several pretexts suggested themselves on the drive home. A marketing surveyor for a pet-products retailer? Not bad. How about a radio station manager random-dialing for a dog-of-the-week contest? "Decent," Jack allowed, "but start fishing for a specific time frame and the callee might get hinky."

The office's safe line ensured the calls couldn't trace back to him, yet the perfect approach must be slick and instantly for-gettable. He'd think of something. He always did. There'd still be hang-ups and nobody-homes in the mix, but pretexts were as available as the number of otherwise intelligent, cautious people willing to chat up a total stranger on the phone.

"Stranger, my ass." Alone in his car and seemingly the world, aside from a motorcyclist in the opposite lane, Jack tipped back his head and laughed. "McPhee, you're a genius, if you don't say so yourself."

He lowered his voice an octave. "Good morning, Mrs. Victim. This is, uh, John Q. Clerk with the Park City PD. Sorry to bother you, ma'am, but I'm following up on a barking-dog complaint filed on XYZ date at your address…"

5

"Oh, this is so exciting," chirped Ms. Pearl. The confirmed spinster—her word, not Jack's—foisted a pink, doll-sized overnight case on him. "My little girl is going to be a *spy.*"

Actually her loaner Maltese was a four-legged shill. It wasn't Jack's fault that his across-the-breezeway neighbor heard "undercover sting operation" and thought James Bond with fur.

Four hours' sleep had converted last night's genius pretext into a blue-ribbon stupid idea. It would have worked, sure. Then the minute the connection was broken, pissed-off burglary victims would confront the neighbors, demanding to know which one initiated the barking-dog complaint.

And who wanted to waste a day chained to a desk making phone calls? Especially a private investigator who spends more time on the phone than a phone-sex operator.

Jack forced a smile. Not easy with a yappy eight-pound dog in the crook of his arm, two fingers hooked on the handle of its luggage and a leash dervishing at his crotch like a noose in need of exorcism.

The stuffed Maltese toy he'd given his niece for Christmas one year had come with a key in its butt that when wound, played "How Much Is That Doggie in the Window?" Instead of a music box, the real deal squirmed and lunged, as though it had springs where its bones were supposed to be.

"I really appreciate this, Ms. Pearl." Which would be true as soon as Jack dumped her wacko dog at TLC, the city's most expensive boarding kennel. "But remember our, uh, arrangement has to stay between us."

Ms. Pearl's penciled eyebrows lofted, enhancing an already eerie resemblance to Olive Oyl. "It will, Officer McPhee. I won't tell a soul."

He'd never told her he was a cop and hadn't been for many a year. Busting a gangbanger peddling Ecstasy to a middle-schooler in the complex's parking lot was strictly a citizen's arrest. Attempts to correct an assumption that Jack was a plainclothes narc were one of those doth-protest-too-much things. Between his reclusiveness and the weird hours he kept, tenants could just as easily suspect he was a vampire.

Ms. Pearl made oochie-coo noises and crouched down to say goodbye to the Maltese. "I don't know what I'll do without my Sweetie Pie Snug 'Ems. I surely don't." She kissed the dog's button nose. "But I packed your favorite toys and a special treat, so we'll have to be brave girls, won't we? Oh, yes, we will."

Thankfully, Jack's eyes unstuck from their backward roll before he reached the flight of plank stairs leading down to ground level. He loved dogs. His best buds when he was a kid were a brainless Irish setter and a three-legged beagle.

"No offense," he told the wriggling furball playing peekaboo with his tie. "But just because the AKC says you're a dog, you're too short to drink out of the toilet and you couldn't catch a Frisbee with a net."

The parking area behind his building was as empty as it had been full when he'd bailed out of his car around three-thirty. In daylight, the Taurus looked a hundred miles closer to the rear entrance than it had last night. It only seemed farther away with a panting Maltese zigzagging in front of him like a duck in a shooting gallery.

The minisuitcase thumped on the rear floorboard where it would stay until its return to Ms. Pearl—minus the treats. Leave them inside and she'd know the luggage hadn't made the whole trip.

He'd promised to strap down the dog in her safety harness for the ride, too. It wouldn't have joined the suitcase on the floorboard if the white blur now bouncing all over the friggin' car responded to "Sit." Or "Heel." Or "For God's sake, *stay,* you psycho little son of a bitch!"

Bellowing "Hell with it," Jack snagged the leash on the fly and wrapped it around his leg. "Gotcha."

Sweetie Pie Snug 'Ems shot him an "oh, yeah?" glare. Her glittery pink toenails dug into the upholstery. She tugged backward, whipping her pouffy head. When the collar hung up on her ears, she bared her teeth and growled at him.

"Think you're scary, huh?" Jack tilted down the rearview mirror. "Check it out. You look like an attack hamster with a bad perm."

The Maltese stared at her reflection, then blinked her beady eyes. She tucked her feather-duster tail and sat down like the lady Ms. Pearl had raised her to be.

"Good doggy." He loosened the leash a few inches. She hesitated, then sighed and snuggled against his thigh.

He'd told her owner a rumor was circulating about boarding kennels using customer lists for purposes other than mailing Christmas cards. The disclosure was nearer his hunch than he'd cared to admit, yet it hadn't satisfied Ms. Pearl. She'd pushed for specifics. He refused to slander the three, thus far noncomplicit kennels that catered to an upscale clientele: TLC, Ltd., Home Away and Merry Hills.

"You'll just have to trust me on the details," he'd said. To his surprise, she had.

To the Maltese now sniffing at the air conditioner's exhaust, he said, "You're gonna love this gig. In-room movies, an exercise pool, story hour." Jack grunted. "At forty bucks a day, you'd better love it."

The morning rush hour on Denton Expressway was beginning to congeal. The female driver in the car ahead of him was applying mascara and slaloming between the roadway's painted lines. Jack checked his passenger's side mirror, then the rearview. In the inner lane, a Hummer was several cautious yards behind a pickup, as well as Jack's rear bumper. The compact sedan lagging in the Hummer's considerable shadow had a spidery crack in the upper quadrant of its windshield.

Jack's lips curled tight over his teeth. He hugged the dog to his thigh. The speedometer's needle stuck a hash mark past sixty-five, as though it were glued on. Constantly monitoring the mirrors, a half mile clocked past, then three quarters, then…

He punched the accelerator and veered into the gap in front of the Hummer. Tapping the brake pedal, Jack timed the swerve onto Madison Road's off-ramp like a NASCAR contender. The maneuver earned a horn blast from the exiting car he'd cut in front of. Swooping in from nowhere probably scared its driver, but expertise separated careless and reckless from a controlled, slick-as-hell evasion.

Loosening his grip on the Maltese, Jack slowed for the traffic light at the top of the ramp. Below on the expressway, Brett Dean Blankenship's dented Cavalier now tailgated the Hummer like a pesky baby brother. The not-so-ace detective would take the next exit and circle back, for all the good it'd do him.

Jack took a stab at feeling smug. Outwitting the jerk didn't change the fact that four days had elapsed since Blankenship crawled out of his cave and into Jack's car at the motel. Seldom did one ever go by without Jack pissing off somebody, but Blankenship had definitely crossed the line from harassment into stalker territory.

"Lucky for him, you're riding shotgun," he told the dog.

It sneezed and wiped dog snot on his trousers.

"Oh, I hear ya. Moby Dickhead's just begging to get his blubber whipped." Jack signaled for a turn onto Lincoln Avenue. "But a man's got to choose his battles, and Ms. Pearl wouldn't be happy about you seeing me shred that creep like a head of cabbage."

He was still talking tough-guy trash out the side of his mouth and pleased with the effect when he almost drove past Euclid Terrace. Its four double-long blocks surrounded by a crumbling fieldrock wall were a tiny suburb back when lawn tennis and badminton parties were in vogue. By the '70s, the Victorian mansions were shabby white elephants too costly to heat, cool or maintain.

Some chopped up into student apartments were now being restored to their single-family glory, but it was even money which would will out: regentrification or blight.

TLC, Ltd. occupied the former carriage house and stable spared from a suspicious fire that destroyed the main house ten or twelve years ago. Inside the home's granite footprint was a lush, multiflora rose garden with a tiered bronze fountain at its center.

"Looks more like a funeral home than a boarding kennel," Jack said, pulling into the graveled parking area.

It was nearly as quiet as one, too. A Sherwood Forest of evergreens meted the property's lot lines. Disembodied barks and yaps filtered through dense privets enclosing the chain-link runs, but evidently, a customer the dogs couldn't see or smell was nothing to get excited about.

Until the Maltese sounded off. Wriggling against Jack's chest, she yipped and snarled like a streetfighter with a serious anger-management problem.

"Jesus Kee-rist," he yelled, struggling to control the yipping, snapping ball of fur with teeth.

Slamming the car door with his knee, he held the pint-sized Cujo at arm's length. "Listen up, sister."

She licked her bared chops. Her earsplitting barks subsided to motorboat growls.

"I'm operating on four hours' sleep. A three-hundred-pound loony tune's stalking me. If this hunch of mine doesn't pan out or the cops nab the burglar before I do, I'm screwed and so's McPhee Investigations."

If a Maltese could look thoughtful, the one dangling in midair seemed to be taking the situation under advisement.

"So are you with me on this? Or do I take you home and tell Ms. Pearl her spy washed out in the damn parking lot?"

Sweetie Pie blinked, then her head drooped and she heaved a shuddering sigh.

"Good doggy," he said, cradling her under his arm. "And you'd better *stay* good while you're here, too."

Few vestiges remained of the building's original purpose, apart from the redbrick exterior and the interior ceiling's hewed beams and support posts. The plastered walls were painted a soothing willow-green and hung with framed hunt scenes, greyhounds in repose and a huge watercolor chart illustrating more dog breeds than Jack knew existed.

A high counter and a wrought-iron gate divided the reception room from a larger concrete-floored area. Jack supposed the second gate barred a hallway leading to the kennel proper. His apartment should be as clean as this canine hotel—and might be, if it had brass floor drains to hose it out with.

At a rubber-matted, stainless-steel table, a ponytailed twelve-year-old wielded a spiky comb and a blow-dryer. Standing at attention in front of her was a burly Rastafarian with paws. The dreadlocked dog seemed to be in a vertical coma, while she nimbly sidestepped across the row of metal milk crates to offset the height advantage.

A sharp rap drew hers and Jack's attention to a glass partition set in the back wall. A fortyish brunette jabbed a finger at the phone held to her ear, then at Jack.

Nodding, the groomer switched off the blow-dryer, called "Be right with you" over her shoulder, then snapped her fingers. The Rastafarian she was grooming didn't lie down on the table as much as it melted into a prone position.

The girl's soccer-style kick sent a milk crate skirring across the floor. "Sorry I didn't hear you come in," she said, climbing on top of it. "I keep forgetting the door buzzer is broken and that dryer's so loud I can't hear myself think."

"It's okay." Jack made a mental note to get his eyes and perhaps his head examined at the earliest opportunity.

The groomer with the megawatt smile, soft brown eyes bracketed by laugh lines and womanly curves hadn't seen puberty for a couple of decades. Which was terrific, since otherwise, his visual appraisal would be morally reprehensible.

A vague smell of wet dog and flea shampoo was strangely pleasant, exotic even. Most of all, the definitely adult groomer was short. Very short. Short enough for a guy who measured five-ten in leather lace-ups to feel like John Wayne bellying up to the bar in a Deadwood saloon. If Jack had a cowboy hat to doff, he'd have drawled, "Well, hello there, li'l lady."

"Cute dog." She scratched the Maltese's wispy goatee. Not even a suggestion of a wedding band blemished the appropriate ring finger. "What's her name?"

For the life of him, Jack couldn't remember. Then he did, and wished the amnesia were permanent. "Fido." He swallowed a groan. "Yep, good ol' Fido. No middle name or anything. Just... you know...Fido."

"Uh-huh." She chuffed. "Sure."

"No, no, really. It is." Jack stopped himself before swearing to it, but his tone dripped with sincerity—although it was a bit soprano for any kinship to the Duke. A deeper, manlier chuckle preceded, "You've been around dozens of dogs, right? Hundreds, maybe. But I'll bet this is the first, the *only* one you've ever met that was actually named Fido."

On closer inspection, her velvet brown eyes were older, wiser and sadder than a thirty-something woman's should be. It aroused Jack's curiosity and an inner Don Quixote he thought was deader than Cervantes.

"Okay," she said, "no bet. I've never met anybody who named his dog Fido." Her expression implied she still hadn't. "Do you have a reservation?"

"Uh, no." Dogs needed reservations?

"It's a good thing she's small. We're full up on medium and large boarders."

The groomer reached for a clipboard, paged through several sheets, then frowned. "Except if she needs to stay past the weekend..."

"Just overnight." Jack McPhee, private investigator, finally nudged aside Jack McPhee the lovelorn nonromantic. "I'm a sales rep for LeFleur & Francois Jewelers in Chicago." His shrug expressed a redundancy akin to specifying New York in reference to Harry Winston's. "See, uh, our chief designer had an eleventh-hour brainstorm. The sales team's flying in to decide if the piece will be included in the fall line, or held for next spring."

His original cover bio would have been smoother without the impromptu embellishments. Then again, a bumbled inside-the-park homer still counted on the scoreboard.

"So, you travel a lot?" she asked.

"Constantly." A gem—pun intended—of a detail clicked into place. "Normally I lug around a sample case." He sighed. "Thank heaven for small favors, I can leave the case at home for once."

The groomer regarded Fido née Sweetie Pie Snug 'Ems, then her presumed owner. "It's none of my business, but if she hasn't boarded at TLC before, what do you usually do with her when you're out of town?"

An excellent question. Jack scrambled for an answer. "Ah, uh, um, well, Swe—er, Fido—was my mother's dog, then she died. My mother, I mean. I sort of inherited her—the dog—but I do most of my traveling by car, so from now on she can go along and keep me company."

A pause ensued, lengthy enough for Jack to reinflate his lungs and silently ask his perfectly healthy mother's forgiveness. The explanation must not have sounded patently absurd, let alone bullshitic to the groomer, for she expressed condolences, then removed a blank registration form from a drawer.

At her prompting, he supplied his name and an emergency phone number. The given address was a vacant house furnished by the listing Realtor. Its chi-chi neighborhood hadn't yet been scathed by the Calendar Burglar.

"How old is Fido?" the groomer inquired.

"Six" was Jack's wild-hare guess.

"Any food allergies you're aware of?"

A rash with minor welt action would be fair payback for the tie the Maltese was gnawing holes in. Having observed the teeth marks in Ms. Pearl's furniture, throw pillows, shoes and hand-bag, Jack figured the dog's tummy wasn't particularly sensitive.

"Her shots are up-to-date?"

No doubt about that one. Ms. Pearl wasn't the type to deny or delay her little darling's wellness care.

"Veterinarian's name?"

Aw, for crying out loud. The furball wasn't applying for a seat on the next space shuttle. To Jack's enormous relief, the groomer snagged the rabies tag dangling on Sweetie Pie Snug 'Ems's collar and copied the vet's name and office number.

A few minutes later, he walked to his car happily dogless and thoroughly edified in boarding-kennel protocol. Also bereft of TLC's pretty, very short groomer's name and home phone number.

An opportunity to pop those questions hadn't presented itself. Such as her referring to Jack by name, so he could coolly, casually reply, "And yours?"

"Tomorrow, pilgrim." He buckled the seat belt. "First you have to catch the bad guy. Then you get the girl."

Dina cuddled the Maltese. Its button eyes goggled and darted, much like Harriet's when waking in her chair, uncertain whether she'd nodded off or was kidnapped by Martians and returned in the blink of a tractor beam.

"There's nothing to be afraid of, sweetie," Dina murmured.

The dog's head swiveled upward. It looked at her, still a bit perplexed, yet oddly reassured.

She kissed the crown of its silky head, breathing in—

Dina took a second, deeper whiff. Pond's cold cream and Estée Lauder perfume?

"What a cutie patootie." Gwendolyn Ellicot swung open the gate between the hallway and the grooming station. "What's his name?"

"Hers," Dina corrected. "And it's Fido, if you can believe that."

"Not the dog's." The kennel's owner grinned and pointed toward the parking area. "The guy who brought her in." She moved to the counter and picked up Fido's registration form. "By what I saw from my office, he took one look at you and forgot he owned a dog."

Gwendolyn's ruling passions were dogs and fix-ups. Trust her to slap a cutie-patootie label on any man who's ambulatory, old enough to vote and bathes regularly.

There was nothing above average about Jack McPhee. Medium height, medium build. His medium brown hair had an eleven-o'clock part and was blocked in back a half inch above his shirt collar. Even the car rolling down the driveway was midsize and as medium blue as his eyes.

Dina couldn't imagine why a funny feeling, like a hunger pang on spin cycle, had ziggled south of her rib cage when they made eye contact. And now, just thinking about it.

She sloughed it off along with her part-time employer's incurable matchmaking. "Forget it, Auntie Mame. Even if I was interested, which I'm not, Mr. McPhee isn't my type." She patted Fido's pouffy head. "And I'm pretty sure I'm not his type."

Gwendolyn crossed her arms, as if fending off Cupid's evil twin. "Then why was he flirting with you?"

"I wouldn't call it—"

"All right, so that tie of his probably glows in the dark, but the suit was Brooks Brothers. My husband has one exactly like it—or did, until he gave up trying to lose thirty pounds and I took it to a resale shop."

"Will you—"

"Jack McPhee lives on LakeShore Boulevard, Dina." Gwendolyn tapped the registration form, emphasizing each syllable, as one might impress upon a small child a need to clean her room. "Starter homes in that development have four bathrooms."

Not much of an incentive, since Dina couldn't keep two bathrooms clean. She held up the Maltese. "See the collar?"

"Pink. So what? She's female, it matches the leash and—"

"Check out the pedicure."

Gwendolyn blanched a little, then flapped a hand. "You detest painting dogs' toenails, but some groomers think it's cute. And McPhee could have a daughter that thinks it's cute, too."

"Doubtful, unless she's adopted." Dina set Fido on the counter. "Smell her head."

"What? Why?"

"Humor me."

Gwendolyn leaned over, sniffed, recoiled, then sniffed again. "Well, hell."

That's pretty much how Dina felt, too, though she'd never admit it. Mother McPhee's recent demise might explain the lingering aroma of cold cream and perfume, except Fido had been shampooed and trimmed in the past week.

"Life is so unfair," Gwendolyn moaned. "Things were hard enough when all the good ones were either married or dead."

Dina chuckled and handed off the Maltese. "If you wouldn't mind paging Laura to get Miss Fido settled in and give her a snack, I have to finish Claude's comb-out."

The puli-Labrador mix snoozing on the grooming table was one strange-looking fellow. Claude's owners spent a fortune keeping its ropy coat from matting into plaited scales, and it loved being fussed over. Using the table's noose-like restraint on Claude was like tethering a dog-shaped topiary before clipping it. The trick was coaxing Claude down to the floor afterward.

As Dina toed the milk crate back into position, Gwendolyn said, "How's your mom doing with the oxygen therapy?"

"Better." Dina sighed. "When she stays hooked up to the machine, instead of using the portable tank in the living room like a rescue inhaler."

"Then it won't be a problem if Mrs. Allenbaugh is running a little late for her appointment."

Gwendolyn's tone entwined a question with a conclusion.

Dina consulted the antique Seth Thomas above the office window. Mrs. Allenbaugh was always a little late. When, of course, she wasn't a lot early. If the daffy old bat owned a Chihuahua, instead of a standard poodle, the timing wouldn't matter as much.

"How late is late?"

"She promised to be here before noon."

Meaning eleven fifty-nine, but Dina couldn't afford to kiss off her fee and a generous tip. She did some mental clockwork herself. "I'll just have to race across town and give Mom her shot before Mrs. Allenbaugh gets here."

Gwendolyn smiled the smile of a dog caretaker with a six-person staff. She squeezed Dina's shoulder. "Relax, okay? I know Betty Allenbaugh's a pain, but now you have a whole hour between your nine-thirty and ten-thirty to check on Harriet."

Dina nodded and smiled back, as if a diabetic's insulin injections were as mutable as a scatterbrained poodle owner's watch.

6

"McPhee Investigations."

"Great news." Gerry Abramson's telephone voice belied the salutation. "I just heard the Calendar Burglar ripped off another of my insureds last Thursday night."

Jack sat back in the desk chair. Hell of a way to start a Saturday, even though he'd slept away most of the morning. "You're sure it's the same thief?"

"He didn't leave a calling card, but the cops think so. This time, along with the jewelry, he snatched an iPod and a laptop. Both brand-new, still in their boxes for donation to a charity auction."

The police had likely alerted retailers who sold that type of electronics in the event of a no-receipt return. A full-price refund versus a fence's standard dime on the dollar made wonderful economic sense. Stupid wasn't part of this burglar's M.O. to date, but neither was boosting high-tech toys.

Jack copied down the victim's address—a mile from his stakeout last night on LakeShore Boulevard. He reminded himself that Gerry hadn't hired him until Thursday afternoon. It still felt like a "Screw you, McPhee" to have been shuffling police reports and claim forms while the thief made another haul.

A whimper at floor level could be interpreted as "Can we go

now?" The sheltie doing it was Sweetie Pie Snug 'Ems's replacement. Ms. Pearl reneged on her weekend loan, saying she couldn't bear another night in an empty apartment.

The sheltie's owner, Angie Meadows, hadn't been alone at hers, nor happy to be wakened at the crack of eleven by a P.I. needing a favor. The voluptuous server at Jack's second-favorite bar was also a canine loan shark. They'd settled on a hundred dollars to rent a dog shedding enough hair on the carpet and Jack's pants to cost three sheep their livelihoods.

"Your burglary victims," he said into the phone. "You wouldn't happen to know if they have a dog, would you?"

"A dog?" A pause, then, "Now that you mention it, yes. One of those huge, jowly things that slobbers all the time." Another beat's worth of dead air. "Why do you ask?"

"No reason in particular." Jack feigned a chuckle. "Just be glad you pay me by the day, instead of by every weird question I come up with."

"Answers," Gerry shot back. "That's what I'm paying you for."

The click and a dial tone weren't surprising, given the insurance agent's frustration. No doubt Abramson was kicking himself for not bringing in outside help sooner. He hadn't expected results in under seventy-two hours. It didn't stop him from wanting them like yesterday.

So did Jack, though he wouldn't have bet a plug nickel the trap would work on the first try. Common sense just never quite dashed the hope for a little dumb luck. If it did, the only snake eyes rolled in Vegas would be attached to actual snakes.

The sheltie barked. Jack yelped and jolted backward in his chair. Obviously pleased with itself, the dog twirled and bounced on its front paws, like a demented fox subjected to way too many Rogaine treatments. And not nearly enough Ritalin.

Jack's heart gradually defibrillated. "Okay, all right already. One phone call, then we're outa here."

Skeptical it would keep its yap shut, he ripped a page from a legal pad, wadded it and threw it across the room. Forty-three fetches later, Abramson's latest claimant haughtily affirmed the impossibility of a noise complaint the previous Thursday night at her address. As she put it, her English bull mastiff was "off premises."

"I'm sorry, ma'am, but I need specifics to quash this complaint. Was your dog staying with a relative, a friend…?"

"Certainly not. Winston was kenneled, until early this morning."

Jack swallowed to drown any hint of elation. "And the name of the kennel, please?"

"Well, if you must know, it's—" A brief silence segued to murky muffles, as though she'd dunked the receiver in a bucket of oil. Gibberish, then, "He says he's—" A louder summons to "Officer Garble-garble" provided excellent cues for Jack to deep-six the call.

The sheltie gnashed the soggy sheet of paper into molecular confetti, while Jack plundered a desk drawer for the cubic zirconia jewelry he bought for a previous investigation.

Rubbing the fake diamonds on his pants leg restored their sparkly, pimplike luster. A gaudy, similarly encrusted watch replaced his faithful Casio. "Talking the talk isn't enough," he told the dog. "Gotta walk the walk, loud and clear."

The bling aglitter on Jack's pinkies and ring fingers wasn't overlooked by the employee presiding over the counter at Home Away. "Whoa, dude," he said. "Do you have to wear all that for your job? Or do you just, you know, *like* it?"

"The job." Jack lasered the clerks's grubby T-shirt. "Kinda like, you know, all the hair and puppy puke you're wearing for yours."

After the intake information was complete, Jack insisted on a tour of the facility. A potential flaw in his jewelry-salesman spiel had presented itself in about the fourth hour of surveilling the decoy house. Contact with one kennel employee and reliance on an upscale address might not be enough to pique the Calendar Burglar's interest.

Jack followed his slouching tour guide, waving and flashing his bejeweled knuckles like a prom queen at various kennel workers. A fog of dog smell slapped his sinuses the instant he stepped into a wide, concrete-floored exercise area flanked by gated pens. Individually, the aromas might be pleasant. Collectively, not so much.

Breeds of every size and description lunged against the chain-link gates, barking and yipping so loud, the roof should have separated from the ceiling joists. The loaner sheltie spun on its leash like a hairy Baryshnikov, its answering yelps absorbed in the skull-crushing racket.

Jack grabbed the dog, poked the slouchmeister in the back and signaled an about-face. Shoving open the office door, he collided with someone rushing out as he was rushing in.

Their mutual apologies trailed away in unison at "So sorry, I..." Recognition prompted coinciding "What are *you* doing here?" Before either could respond, the tour guide snarled, "It's about fuckin' time you showed up. I told that cocker spaniel's owner two hours, an hour and a half ago."

"Hey, sport," Jack warned. "Watch your mouth."

By her expression, the diminutive groomer he'd almost trampled appreciated the gesture, but could fend off the assholes of the world herself. And had.

Jack said, "I thought you worked at TLC."

"Part-time." She squinted at the sheltie in his arms. "What happened to Fido?"

He died, was Jack's initial thought. Thankfully, it didn't make the verbal leap. "He's fine. Couldn't be better. In fact, he's going with me to a sales meeting in St. Louis." He patted the present loaner. "Butch here belongs to a friend."

The groomer's eyebrow arched.

Whew boy. First Fido, now Butch. *Excellent.* Jack scraped back a bushel of hair at the sheltie's neck. "I swear that's his name. See? It's engraved on his collar."

As was A. D. Meadows and Angie's home phone number. Even barmaids who gave private lap dances on the side use initials for telephone listings, mailbox ID and their dogs' collars.

Jack sensed the foul-mouthed slouchmeister picking up on the groomer's wariness. "A.D. was in a car wreck last night. Poor guy was banged up pretty good and the doc wants him to stay another night in the hospital for observation."

The groomer nodded, as if that seemed reasonable. Then she said, "So you weren't happy with TLC and brought Butch here, instead."

"No, no problems at TLC at all." Jack grinned, as though competing for a most-satisfied-customer award, waiting for a plausible excuse to coalesce. "It's just that…well, Home Away is closer to A.D.'s house, and since he'll have to take a taxi tomorrow from the hospital, it'll be easier for him to swing by here."

Slouchmeister said, "You told me the dog was yours."

"For the next twenty-four hours, he is," Jack replied, truthfully for once.

"Fine, but I need the owner's name for the records." He jabbed an index finger at the groomer. "And you'd best start deskunking that cocker, Dina. If the owner comes back before it's dry, you can forget your part of the service charge."

She bristled, then her lips flattened to a grim line. "Excuse me, Mr. McPhee," she mumbled, and reached for the door to the kennel runs.

Dina, Jack repeated to himself. Well, half a name was better than none. And she'd remembered his. Repressing a smile wasn't easy, but he managed.

When the door closed behind her, he said to Slouchmeister, "I guess she's not what you'd call dependable, huh?"

"Dina's okay, except on short notice." He chuffed at his own lame joke. Stationed again behind the counter, he added, "Like my dad says, if you don't manage the help, the help'll manage to get paid for sloughing off."

Jack assumed the kid inherited his charm from his old man. "Your dad owns Home Away?"

"He took it over when my grandma died." He circled Jack's name on the registration form and noted his temporary custody. "Thank God I only have to work here during the summer."

"College student?"

Nodding, he offered the pencil to amend the ownership line. "Yale. Class of whatthefu—" A gestured "oops," then, "Class of whenever Dad gets sick of paying tuition."

Interesting, Jack thought. And wouldn't it be a coincidence if those Ivy League halls of higher learning emptied right around Memorial Day and refilled Labor Day weekend.

Consideration was given a two-birds-with-one-stone idea. Evidently, Dina the groomer was called in to remedy a dog unfamiliar with a skunk's defense mechanism, not for a full day's work. Waiting around in the parking lot, then buying her a cup of coffee could be edifying in more ways than one.

All in good time, he decided. A casual remark afterward in the wrong ear about her delightful, spur-of-the-moment repartee with Butch's temporary custodian could be a tip-off. Jack using his real name wasn't particularly risky, unless the Calendar Burglar walked his fingers through the phone directory.

"Business before pleasure," he said, with a sigh. "Damn it."

There wasn't enough scotch in Scotland—neat, on the rocks, sucked out a barrel's bung hole with a straw—to blot out the lowlights of the next twenty-four hours.

Not once, but *twice* during Jack's overnight campout in his car, a minuscule Chevy with a cretin at the wheel rolled by the cul-de-sac's entrance. Moby Dickhead had burned the decoy house's address for future reference as effectively as gasoline and a match. Jack stayed put, though, entertaining himself with fantasies of felony assault and battery.

Then just after dawn, while his head was burrowed under the pillow and his mind was deeply involved in an entirely different fantasy and costar, Home Away called to inform him that Butch had jumped a pit bull in the outdoor exercise yard.

The pit bull emerged unscathed, naturally. The idiot sheltie's emergency animal clinic's bill was $422.73. Luckily, Angie Meadows's hobby was hooking, not wind sprints. When he dropped off the bandaged sheltie, she did chase Jack for two blocks, screaming explicit details about the amputations she'd perform if she caught him.

The bar where Angie worked was off-limits for the forseeable future. Finding another second-favorite watering hole wasn't a fraction as worrisome as Gerry Abramson's retainer dissolving in record time.

Provided the Calendar Burglar was identified and stopped, the insurance agent wouldn't freak about Jack's expenses—apart from maybe the veterinary clinic bill for Butch. And if, of course, it was Jack's hunch that led to the thief's apprehension.

And then there was the increasing possibility that he was

loonier than Brett Dean Blankenship. Being wrong about the kennel connection wasn't the issue. He had, however, speculated that the burglar might be a customer, not an employee. TLC's and Home Away's log sheets were both kept in plain view. The thief dropping off his dog just as Jack was dropping off loaners failed to amuse him.

Merry Hills was next and the last on the list. Jack refused to quit two-thirds through the rotation. Come up empty again, and he'd contact kennel owners for a confidential look at their files. As if they'd allow it then, any more than they would have at the outset. Therefore, Jack McPhee, state animal facility inspector—or something equally official sounding—would make unannounced visits.

In the meantime, a new decoy address was a must. A new dog to allegedly reside at that address was crucial. The first grin in recent memory broke across Jack's face. "Belle has a dog."

He sobered immediately. "She also has a husband who thinks you're a bottom-feeder and he's probably at home on a Sunday morning."

Flipping through the Rolodex, Jack called ex-girlfriends, friends, acquaintances and bar buddies he had to describe himself to. Realizing he was visually fitting a dog suit on the one-eared tomcat that roamed the apartment complex, he gave up and dialed his ex-wife's number.

"You want to borrow my dog," Belle repeated. Her tone was normally associated with unsecured loans of large sums of cash.

"Just overnight. You know I wouldn't ask, if I *really* didn't need your help."

"Everybody else you've asked turned you down flat, huh?" She laughed. "Two problems, hon. I'm packing for a flight down to Little Rock to meet Carleton."

Jack pumped a fist. "He's already in Arkansas?"

"He drove down Friday. He's the keynote for another financial seminar. I bowed out of two days of godawful wives' activities, but I'll make an appearance tonight. Then we'll drive on to Hot Springs for a couple of days' R&R."

"If you're leaving town," Jack said, "you need a dog-sitter for what's his name."

"Abdullah, otherwise known as Carleton Jr." She made a gagging noise. "Who's in Florida humping his harem."

"Still?" Jack remembered Belle mentioning the afghan hound's mating marathon last week at lunch. How a dog's life was perceived as a negative, he couldn't imagine.

"I'm sorry, Jack, but I've got to go. I'll call later in the week, okay? Collect on that rain check for a drink you owe me."

"I'll hold you to it, babe. One last thing, though. What kennel do you use for Carleton Jr.?"

"A kennel for an AKC champion stud-muffin?" She chortled. "Abdullah has a nanny, deah boy. She can't speak a word of English, but then, neither can he." A pause, then, "I heard somebody recommend Merry Hills once. It's south of town, off the bypass."

Jack would love to know who that somebody was, but his ex-wife's soon-to-be-empty house solved his location problem.

The Park City phone book had two columns of businesses that rented everything from bulldozers to bridal gowns. For a price, a portable wire dog pen was available, but not a dog to put in it. Local breeders also proved less than cooperative. Jack was reverting to the semiferal-cat-in-a-dog-suit idea when he noticed a small boxed ad at the bottom of the page.

The city animal shelter's desk attendant peered at him through her round, gold-rimmed glasses. "You want to borrow a dog," she said, in precisely the same tone Belle had used on the phone.

"Just overnight." Jack beamed his best "trust me" smile.

"I'll bring it back safe and sound, tomorrow afternoon." The bemusement in her eyes hardened to anger. "If that's a joke, mister, it isn't funny." Her arm swept toward a metal door with a vertical glass window above the handle. "Sixty-eight cats, kittens, dogs and puppies in there need homes. Most were dumped like last week's garbage. Ten percent might be adopted before their time on this Earth ends."

Lips pursed, she shook her head. "If there's anything more cruel than taking one of them out on a field trip," she said, a quaver in her voice, "I can't figure what it'd be."

Jack couldn't, either. The dogs he'd loved as a boy were rejects pushed from a vehicle during the night. He'd known that, yet finding the three-legged beagle in the yard, then later the Irish setter, were like extra Christmases. Both mutts were scrawny and flea-infested, but Jack's loathing for anyone who'd leave a dog to fend for itself or die trying, quickly became fear they'd accidentally wandered from their real homes and their owners would come and take them away.

"I'd give anything to have a dog again," Jack found himself saying. "I kind of envy a couple of friends their dogs, even though one's a Maltese with a Napoleon complex, and the sheltie thinks he's Muhammad Ali."

The attendant's expression softened. "Live in an apartment, do ya? Single. Full-time job."

Taken aback, he said, "So are you psychic, or a really good guesser?"

"After seventeen years, I could spot a dog lover from the far side of the moon. This cockamamie notion about borrowing one comes from wanting a dog for all the right reasons, but you're afraid that by midday tomorrow—before you get attached—you'll have to admit what you think you already know. Your place is too small, the dog will suffer without a yard to play in and it'll drive the neighbors crazy whining the minute you leave for work."

Hearing her vocalize the arguments he'd had with himself and lost—or won, depending—had Jack's hand reaching to scratch the back of his neck. The loaner dogs weren't his bowl of kibble, but K-9 and assistance animals were often apartment dwellers. Rode to work with their owners. Hung out with them all day at the office, keeping them company…

"Except like you said, it'd be cruel to—" Jack looked up, then around. The small room was a warehouse for pet food sacks, buckets of cat litter, baled newspapers, stuffed toys and boxes full of old sheets, blankets and towels.

"Where in the hell did she go?"

The metal door that resembled a drunk tank's swung open. A blast of frantic barks and warm, fetid air accompanied the attendant's reentrance. Beside her, a Wookie attached to a nylon leash lumbered along on all fours.

Its dirt-brown coat was short in some places and cowlicked in others. The tip of a parenthetic tail pointed at its droopy, shoulder-long ears, as though such colossal wind flaps might be overlooked. Overall, genetics seemed to have fused a retriever's legs onto a basset hound's torso. How the dog ran without kicking its front legs from under itself defied all laws of aerodynamics.

Jack backpedaled, palms aloft. "Uh-uh, no way, ma'am. I appreciate what you're trying to do, but—"

"Twenty-four hours." The attendant held out the leash. "If you change your mind by then, bring him back." A wicked smile exposed a gold-capped molar. "The seventy-five-dollar fee is nonrefundable."

"But I—"

"Will that be cash or check?" she inquired. "Sorry, but we don't take credit cards."

* * *

Stripped to his underpants, Jack goosed the dog into the tiled walk-in shower. "Atta boy. Sorry to put you through this, but whatever you rolled in since your last bath, it wasn't roses."

In deference to the dog, water generously described as tepid parted at the back of Jack's head, sluiced into his mouth and up his nose. Puffing and spitting, he dumped a bottle of shampoo on the mutt's head, then smeared it around. The stuff wasn't much for lather, but smelled nice and the label said it wouldn't sting a baby's eyes.

"Feels good, eh, boy? Just don't go getting your hopes up. Nothing personal, but this is strictly a one-night stand and you're spending most of it at Merry Hills."

The dog's muzzle tilted up. A speckled blue eye and a cinnamon-colored one expressed naked adoration. If ever a woman looked at Jack like that, he'd be a goner. A big, seriously ugly, homeless mutt didn't tug any heartstrings. Nope, not a one.

Jack scrubbed the sticky fur on its neck and chest. "I know a con when I see one." He step-pivoted to soap the dog's rump, belly and tail. "Now, Cherise Taylor, my old girlfriend? *She's* a different story. When she gets here, it might be worth your while to give her a 'you are my goddess' look when she picks you up."

A mournful groan reverberated off the ceramic tiles. The mutt's head hung so low, its ears drooped on the floor.

"Cut it out, damn it." Jack unhooked the handheld showerhead for the rinse cycle. "Like I told you, my jewelry-salesman cover is wearing thin and there's no reason not to take full advantage of the deHavens' little trip down south.

"Cherise is taking you to Merry Hills and signing in as Mrs. Carleton deHaven. Belle's never boarded a dog there, so nobody'll know the difference, and I promise, the joint's swankier than anyplace you've ever seen."

Jack shut off the water, saying, "I don't know if they have story hour or not, but I'm talking chopped steak for dinner."

After toweling off both himself and the dog, he threw on a robe and sat tailor fashion on the bathroom floor. He'd never used a blow-dryer in his life, but the clerk at the drugstore offered a few tips.

Careful not to aim the nozzle at the dog's face, it suddenly dawned on him that it needed a name. "We'll leave that to Cherise." Echoes of Sweetie Pie Snug 'Ems and Butch thrummed in Jack's ears. "No, we won't. Being female, she'll stick you with Truffles, or Dijon."

Wookie, his first impression, sounded worse than Truffles. Beast? Appropriate, but a little harsh. Skippy? No. Brownie? No. Cocoa? Fudgesicle?

Jack scowled and muttered, "Shit" under his breath. The dog's ears pricked—a relatively massive undertaking. "Yeah, I'll bet you've heard that one before."

Leaning back, he studied the mutt, like an artist examines a bowl of fruit. God only knew why, but it looked like a Phil. Now that Jack thought about it, even filthy, he'd looked like a Phil.

"Phil McPhee it is." He sighed and shook his head. "Phil. No adoption, no last name required. Just Phil."

His thumb pressed the blow-dryer's toggle switch. "And *just* till tomorrow afternoon."

7

The slow, monotonous drizzle had commenced at dusk. All day, overcast skies suggested a possibility of rain. While some native Ozarkers may have washed and waxed their vehicles to up the chance of precipitation, they didn't skimp on watering their vegetable gardens and porch plants.

Rain shellacked the streets and burbled along the sloped concrete curbing. Pyrotechnic thunderstorms drew watchers to windows and doorways. Tonight's sporadic quivers of cloud lightning and muted rumbles fostered scant, if any supervision.

The gloomy weather, in other words, couldn't be more perfect for a burglary. And less so, for the increasingly narcoleptic private detective parked near the deHavens' highfalutin rock pile.

Slumped in the Taurus's driver's seat, Jack bugged out his eyeballs, rolling them around in isometric tandem. A nest of candy bar wrappers was batted away to grope for the foam drink cup wedged in the holder. Rubbing slushy chunks of crushed ice over his face and neck, he whistled backward, as the runoff trickled down his back and chest, paused ever so briefly at the dam that was his jockey shorts' waistband, then forged onward and irrevocably downward.

He gnawed on the drink straw, yearning for a cigarette. He

couldn't light it if he had one, which is why he'd quit years ago. For a while, smokeless tobacco provided the nicotine buzz without the telltale orange glow. Hating the taste was stimulating in itself, until that dark, unstormy night when he mistook a spit cup for his coffee cup.

The memory alone cleared some of the brain fog. Jack swished a mouthful of diluted soda, as his gaze arced from the driver's side mirror to the rearview, then the passenger's side mirror. His butt and legs were numb. The crotch of his jeans was damp and clingy from the crushed-ice baptisms. He was bored out of his gourd, but at least he hadn't been followed this time.

After Cherise Taylor dropped off Phil at Merry Hills, she'd met Jack at the mall's food court. They'd split a sub sandwich, exchanged keys and vehicles, then traded back at an abandoned farmstead five miles from town.

Great gal, that Cherise. Posing as Belle deHaven at the kennel had been a lark for her. Jack's blip of jealousy at hearing *all about* the fantastic guy Cherise went out with Friday night and Saturday was reflex, not regret. So what if her first date with Mr. Wonderful was a lousy four days after she and Jack broke up on the phone?

"Live and let live." His fingers bobbed for another clump of ice. "I'm happy for—"

He tensed, his eyes riveted on the deHavens' bowed, two-story front window. The drapes, if there were any, hung outside the bronzed metal frame. Belle always had believed the fishbowl effect discouraged intruders.

"Close the blinds and the curtains and a creeper can't tell if you're home or not," she'd agree, then add, "but the neighbors can't see some jerk carting off everything you own, either. Unless he closes them, and if they're always open, that's a tip-off right there."

The opposing schools of thought had equal numbers of fans and detractors—law enforcement and insurers included. Twenty-four-hour convenience stores were constantly warned about plastering advertising posters over exterior windows. Maintaining a clear, well-lit line of sight didn't prevent robberies, but did discourage them.

The deHaven house was dark, inside and out. Jack supposed in her dash to make her afternoon flight, Belle had neglected to switch on any lamps or the exterior lights. Illumination from the solar-powered landscape lights wouldn't attract a self-respecting moth.

Odds were that tiny interior flicker he'd seen was an electronic thermostat cycling on or off. A wink of lightning reflected in a picture or in a mirror. Ninety-nine to one, it was a miserable private detective's imagination begging for an excuse to bail out of his car.

He exited the Taurus, staying to the soggy shadows. His stride was brisk, but as normal as a man could fake whose feet felt as though they'd been encased in concrete. That juke-and-weave-between-the-tree-trunks crap was for spy movies and TV gumshoes. Act like a rational, law-abiding reason exists for walking around in the soup at midnight, and unseen witnesses will assume you're just a schmuck out looking for an escaped cat.

A wide berth was given the motion-detector lights trained down on the three-bay garage doors. The soffit overhanging the solid side wall had no security devices; one lurked under the rear corner, monitoring the gate accessing the backyard.

"Contemporary rustic" was Belle's term for the joint's overall design. Jack figured the thick, six-foot fieldstone wall enclosing the back half of the property met the rustic specs, but it was almost as easy to climb as a ladder.

The moment he dropped to the other side, he crossed the line between a blow-off trespassing charge and the real, indefensible deal. The difference could cost him his license. Fictional P.I.s can afford to play fast and loose with the law. Credentialed investigators don't jaywalk, much less break-and-enter presumably after the fact.

The Realtor who'd listed the other decoy house had obtained permission from its owner for Jack's one-guy sting operation. Here, if worse came to handcuffs, Belle would lie for him. He was almost sure of it.

Jack flattened himself against the house to evade any security camera's electronic eye. Sliding sideward, his windbreaker scraped the irregular stone surface—a noise louder by several decibels to his ears than it actually was. So was the slurp of his crepe-soled oxfords sinking in a shallow gully carved by the downspout's runoff.

Progress halted at a heat-pump unit camouflaged by horseshoed shrubbery. Go around, and a motion detector would nail him. There was almost but not quite enough space to giant-step over the unit's conduits and slither behind it. From Jack's vantage point, the only visible exterior door was the metal-clad utility type that probably led into the garage.

Which begged a question he should have asked himself long before now. If he was pinned to the friggin' wall by the deHavens' security system, how did an intruder slink past it?

Answer—the brief glint of light he'd swear he'd seen inside a minute ago *was* an electronic thermostat control, a wink of reflected lightning, a hallucinatory figment of his imagination.

Those still unsatisfactory conclusions and stubbornness had him twisting off a branch from the heat pump's hedge. Jack retreated to the corner motion detector and waved the stick to breach the monitor's invisible electronic beam.

Nothing. A second box above the utility door scored the same nonresult. He about-faced and proceeded toward a pergola shading the terrace, thinking his suddenly airheaded ex-wife owed him huge for guarding the house she'd forgotten to secure.

In a blinding flash, the patio, yard and the family room inside lit up like a prison compound during an escape attempt.

Jack froze. Dilated pupils reduced the visual field to a fuzzy, round blur. As he whirled to run for the gate, a lower section in the utility door swung upward. Stunned, half-blind, he braced to fend off the dog for whom the pet door was intended. What emerged was a pair of gloved hands, then a stocking-capped head, followed by slender shoulders clad in a dark, long-sleeved shirt.

Jack's wheezy "Hey, you—" was like a starter's pistol at an Olympic hundred-meter dash. The burglar was faster off the blocks, but no match for a flying shoestring tackle. Rolling together on the wet grass, the intruder seemed to have six elbows, knees, an extra set of teeth and no compunction against using them.

Jack's fist hauled back to knock the son of a bitch into next Wednesday. Wrenching away, the burglar's cap fell off. A tangle of long, sweaty hair unfurled like a tent flap.

"Holy—" He squinted at the glowering eye and face behind that hirsute veil. "Dina?"

She kneed him in the groin, tucked, pushed up and took off.

Cursing and cupping his crotch, Jack ape-loped after her.

She was scaling the rock wall when he grabbed her shirttail. Yanking her backward on her butt, he straddled her, detonating fresh, all-inclusive paroxysms of pain.

"Give it up, damn it. I don't wanna hurt you."

Squirming like a ninety-pound wildcat, she panted, "Lemme

go. I didn't take anything—I swear I didn't. Just let me get out of here and I promise, I'll never do it again."

"Gee," Jack grunted. "That's original."

"I *won't.*" With her wrists pinned to the ground, a gloved finger motioned the sign of the cross. "I'm not really a thief—"

"Also original." Jack's head cocked at a siren wailing in the distance. By Dina's expression, she heard it, too.

"Please, Mr. McPhee. Don't turn me in to the police. At least give me a chance to explain."

Explaining his presence to the cops wasn't at the top of Jack's personal hit parade, either. The original plan was to tail the thief home, then tip the police. Nice, neat, unquestionably legal.

The part-time dog groomer and presumed Calendar Burglar he was sitting on could implicate him in the thefts to plea-bargain the charges against her. Or *charge,* if she couldn't be tied to the prior burglaries. Jack's contract with National Federated Insurers should be a nol-pros on an accessory rap. As a rule, he preferred to not mix business with felony arrest warrants.

"C'mon," he said, lurching to his feet, then pulling her up. With her arm clamped in a "don't mess with me" grip, he grabbed the stocking cap, then ran for the side gate.

Struggling to keep up, she cried, "Where are you taking me?"

"My car." He shot the gate latch with a fist, then kicked it shut behind them. "Then as far away from here as we can get."

Floodlights above the garage and entry door blazed like a locomotive's headlamps. He steered Dina into the remaining shadows, the siren they'd heard was louder and closing in fast.

Then it stopped. Silence didn't exactly descend. Not with Jack's pulse hammering in his ears and his undertall captive huffing, "The cops…must've gotten…another call."

"Uh-uh, kid. This is high-roller holler. Siren en route, only."

The one thing he'd done right all night was leave the driver's door unlocked. Jack pushed Dina inside, crammed in behind her and slammed the door. The childproof locks clicked a nanosecond before she jerked the passenger's door handle.

A jittery red halo rose above yonder hill. Jack keyed the ignition, shifted into Reverse and floored it. A hard crank to the right and a sharp left whipped the sedan into an adjacent Tudor's circle driveway. Jamming the car into Park and killing the engine sufficed as brakes without any taillight flash.

"Hit the deck," he said. "And stay there."

To his astonishment, Dina slid off the seat and crouched on the floorboard. Not so surprising was a surly "You said we were getting out of here."

"If we're lucky, we will." Jack curled sideways, his cheek resting on the window ledge and head obscured by the side mirror's housing. "If we're not, the people who live here are, at this very moment, speed-dialing 911."

"But—"

"Look, Ms. whatever your last name is, it's your fault we didn't make it to the car fast enough to drive off into the sunset."

"I was scared to death. I didn't know who'd grabbed me."

"You did before you damn near gelded me."

After a pause that may or may not have contained a stifled chuckle, came a righteous "If you're not a cop and you're definitely not a jewelry salesman, who are you?"

"Private investigator." Jack shrank down as the patrol unit approached the deHavens' address. "Don't make a sound," he whispered. "Boy in blue at eleven o'clock."

A fender-mounted spotlight swept the property from lot line to lot line, then zeroed in on the gate. The cruiser backed up to blockade the driveway. The uniform stepped out of the patrol unit, gandering around as he slipped a nightstick into the loop on his utility belt. Twice, he eyeballed the Taurus parked in the driveway across the street.

It's the housekeeper's car, Jack telegraphed in a convincing, mental tone of voice. Or maybe good ol' Aunt Agnes is visiting from Des Moines.

Another unit arrived from the opposite direction. A consultation ensued, punctuated by gestures and finger-pointing. Armed with Maglites, the officers rang the deHavens' doorbell, checked each garage door, then split up to circle around back.

Cop One disappeared around the far corner of the house. Cop Two slipped through the side gate. Jack started the Taurus, forcing himself not to burn rubber getting the hell outa there.

He waited until a turn onto a curving side street to exhale, switch on the headlights and the windshield wipers. "Ooookay. You can get up now."

Dina took a precautionary peek over the dashboard, then wriggled onto the seat. "That was close."

It still was. Whether the cops heard the engine noise or not, that first responder would notice the Taurus was gone. ASAP wasn't fast enough for Jack to put high-dollar holler behind them.

"You can drop me off anywhere," Dina said as casually as a friend of a friend who'd accepted a lift home from a party.

"My office or the PD." Jack glanced at her. "Take your pick."

"You won't turn me in."

"Care to bet on that?"

"Then why'd you ditch the police?"

"Temporary insanity." God knew, that was true. Jack had never knowingly aided and abetted a criminal in his life. Well, not since he qualified for a P.I. license, anyway. Or during his brief law-enforcement career. And from birth to approximately fourteen years of age.

"I owe you big-time," Dina said, "but I *have* to go home. Tomorrow I'll meet you at your office and explain everything, but my mother's seriously ill, and I can't leave her alone for very long."

She'd never burgle again, she wasn't really a thief and she had a sick mother. All that song needed was Daddy on death row, a lonesome train whistle and a pickup truck.

Jack groaned and shook his head. And he'd probably believe that, too.

8

Jack McPhee had dropped Dina at the street behind the deHaven house where she parked her VW. From there, she hadn't even tried to outrun his headlights etching her rearview mirrors.

Before he unlocked the Taurus's door he'd dictated her name, address, driver's license, tag and phone numbers into a minicassette recorder, then copied them in a notebook. Then again, the impossibility of an escape seldom deterred an attempt.

The thought never entered Dina's mind. The *elsewhere* it had been all the way across town centered on the fact a stranger was about to see her naked. The raw kind, with all her clothes on.

A relief, she admitted, but not in the manner of confessions being good for the soul. McPhee wasn't a priest, and Dina was too pragmatic to believe admitting a sin out loud wiped it and the guilt off the slate, like a divine chalkboard eraser. Especially if you'd committed the same one, over and over again.

He also wasn't a therapist armed with a shovel and a ladder—one to dig for the root of her criminal behavior and the other to help her climb out of the hole. Priests and mental health professionals were godsends for millions, but Dina knew what she'd done was wrong, and why she'd gone ahead and piled on the sins anyway.

Unloading on Jack McPhee had no strings or expectations attached at either end. She'd talk, he'd listen, then he'd take her to jail.

Simple. And yes, a relief, as long as she didn't think beyond that.

McPhee didn't park behind or beside the VW in the duplex's driveway, but at the curb. Supposing the police might impound the Beetle as evidence of something or other, Dina left it outside. The magnetic pizza restaurant signage was peeled off the driver's door, stowed in the trunk, and her purse and tote bag removed from it.

Jack walked up as Dina reclosed the hood. "Did you steal that, too?" he asked, his tone curious rather than condemning.

Realizing he meant the sign, not her ancient getaway clunker, she said, "Since it belongs to Luigi's, I guess I did. I just didn't mean to."

She started for the front stoop. "I used to be a delivery driver—two bucks an hour, plus tips. Except the sleazeball night manager wouldn't give me anything but the college runs, baby-sitter call-ins and dive motels out on the interstate."

"Two bucks an hour," Jack said, "and fifty-cent tips, if the customer felt generous."

"Or too drunk to wait for his change."

The front door was locked, as Dina left it when she sneaked out what seemed like a month ago. She fitted the key and turned the knob, queasy at the thought of her mother having wakened and now lying in wait.

The living room was empty, apart from the Three Stooges assaulting each other on TV. Dina touched a finger to her lips and lowered her voice. "Short story shorter," she said, as though it might distract McPhee from the shabbiness and stale, musty air, "I complained to the manager. He grabbed my boob, offered me a raise if I'd give him one in the storeroom, and I walked out."

"You should have reported him for sexual harassment."

"I threatened to, along with a few other things I'd have enjoyed a lot more." Dina shrugged and laid her bags on the table. "Mostly I wanted a hot shower so much, I forgot about the sign stuck on my car. I intended to take it back when the manager wasn't there and Luigi was, but…"

She motioned at the hallway. "I need to look in on my mother. Don't worry, there's no back way out of here."

McPhee was seated at the table when she returned. He'd removed his windbreaker and folded it over a knee, as though hanging it on a chair back to dry might damage the finish.

After a moment, he said, "Is everything okay?"

Dina hesitated, then slowly shook her head. "You really are a nice guy."

His mouth quirked at a corner. "Somewhat of a minority opinion, but I'd like to think so."

"Well, knock it off." Dina balled her hands in her cargo pants pockets. "Stop acting like you just came in for coffee after a date."

"I could use a cup," he said agreeably. "I could also treat you like public-enemy number one, but if you fit those specs, we'd be at the cop shop."

"Specs?" Dina repeated, thoroughly confused. "What specs?"

"Basic criminal mentality is remorse for getting caught in the act, not for the act itself. You, on the other hand, feel so lousy about it and yourself, I'll bet you had to force yourself inside every house you've robbed."

She had. She'd clutched and run at the last minute more than a few times, too. But how could McPhee possibly know that? And why, coming from him, did it sound so insulting?

Because you're insane was the obvious answer.

"Coffee," she said. "I'll make some."

She fished in the bottom of her hobo bag for one of the stove's burner knobs. To McPhee's askance look, she said, "Mom heated something yesterday and left the burner on, again. I don't know if she spilled a little and doused the flame, or it sputtered out by itself, but the house stank of natural gas when I came home."

"Is she…?"

"Senile" was the implied blank filler. That incomplete question was deemed kinder than outright asking if someone's belfry was missing a few bats.

"Mom's scatterbrained. Always has been. It's funny and endearing when you're young. Pull the same boners when you're old and people who can't spell 'Alzheimer's' think you're the poster girl."

True in general, and a whitish lie where Harriet Wexler was concerned. Her faculties were diminishing. Dina absconding with the stove knobs was a fait accompli that reduced the wear and tear on both their hearts.

From McPhee's chair at the table to the kitchen was an unobstructed nine or ten feet, but he closed the gap. A hip leaned against a base cabinet, one foot crossed over the other.

Self-conscious and resenting it, Dina's face burned as she placed the step stool at the far end of the kitchen. Harriet's decaf was in a canister on the counter. A small can of prohibited, high-octane regular was hoarded on a cupboard shelf behind a barrel of oats. To McPhee's credit, he didn't offer to reach up to get it for her.

"Who's the guy in the photos on the bookshelf?" he asked.

"My brother, Randy, the grunge rocker, punk rocker, white boy rapper, hip-hopper, blues, bluegrass drummer." Dina glanced up while the glass percolator filled under the tap. "Awfully fast search of the ol' premises, McPhee."

"I thought we agreed on 'Jack.'"

"That's when you were a jewelry salesman."

"I'm not sure you ever believed I was a jewelry salesman."

"Yeah, I did." Dina laughed. "A gay, not-quite-out-of-the-closet jewelry salesman." A finger dammed the percolator's stem, while she measured grounds into the basket. "For curiosity's sake, what is Fido's real name and where'd you get her?"

"She belongs to a neighbor," he hedged.

"An older female neighbor, I presume."

"Presume? Oh. The pink collar and leash."

"Nope. The cold cream and perfume. The Maltese smelled like both."

"Huh. Ms. Pearl does, too, now that I think about it."

"And she named her dog…?"

A flinch, then a muttered, "Sweetie Pie Snug 'Ems."

Dina had heard worse, just not lately. "Well, I knew somebody called her 'sweetie' a lot. Her ears perked when I did."

"Pretty sharp, Sherlock. About dogs, anyway. Gay, I'm definitely not. How cold cream and perfume drew that conclusion, I'm not sure."

Neither was Dina. An antidote to instant attraction, probably. She'd married the first guy who'd set butterflies aflutter in her belly—a prelude to emotional evisceration. Fool her twice? Not in this life.

As McPhee inhaled the brewing coffee, his eyelids fluttered in pure bliss. "But if you bought my cover story, why didn't you hit the address I gave for Fido and Butch?"

"Because a Maltese and a sheltie didn't fit the, uh, specs."

He frowned, his gaze ticktocking the length of the kitchen. "Phil did, though," he said, as if thinking aloud. "Well, hell. I was right about the boarding kennels. It never occurred to me the size of the dog mattered."

"Size always matters." Dina added hastily, "If you're female and four-ten, it's an automatic top-of-the-pyramid spot on the cheerleading squad. Great while it lasts, but it sucks pushing around a grocery cart with the handle under your chin forever."

"I'm not exactly NBA material myself, kid."

Dina bristled. "I've been a registered voter for fourteen years, McPhee."

"Jack. And no offense. I call everybody *kid.* I probably called Phil kid when I gave him a shower."

"He's yours?" She grabbed two mugs from the dish drainer. Taking the moral high ground was difficult when hers was a thousand feet below sea level, but she managed. "Then your last name is deHaven, not McPhee. You aren't gay, but you *are* married and you may or may not be a private detective."

She shot him a dirty look. "A dick is what they used to be called, right? Gosh, I can't imagine why."

The ID in his wallet confirmed the Irish surname and his occupation. "Belle deHaven is my ex-wife. Her husband's afghan hound is out of state and they're out of town. The animal shelter let me rent Phil overnight, and a friend registered him in Belle's name at Merry Hills."

"Animal shelters don't rent dogs, McPhee."

"It's 'Jack,' okay?" He hedged, "Phil's out on twenty-four-hour approval. He goes back to the shelter, first thing tomorrow." He glanced at his watch. "Make that today."

Dina stifled an urge to pour his coffee in the sink and bop him with the mug. "Anything to make a buck, huh? Who cares what happens to the poor dog, who I basted in dermatitis cream—no charge—because he was scratching himself raw an hour after you had him dumped at the kennel."

"He was?" At least McPhee appeared contrite. "The baby shampoo I bought was supposed to be gentle enough for—"

"Babies, you idiot, not dogs. Specifically, babies' eyes. Manufacturers amp up the pH to tear level, so it won't sting. Except human skin is about three times thicker than a dog's, which means a high-pH shampoo is about three times too harsh for Phil."

Dina handed him his coffee—grudgingly. "Do tell the shelter manager that he has contact dermatitis, not mange. It won't stay his execution, but they may let him say goodbye to his pals first."

McPhee started as though she'd slapped him. "That's twice tonight you've hit me below the belt."

"If I'd aimed better the first time, we wouldn't be having this conversation."

They glared at each other over the rims of their mugs a while, then he said, "The dog-door modus operandi. That's always been your means of entry?"

Dina nodded. "Some in garage doors, most at the back of the house. Dogs, especially older ones, can't always wait eight hours or longer for bathroom breaks. Leaving them out in the heat, or cold, even with doghouses to crawl into, seems like a crummy way to treat a member of the family."

"Then you scratched up exterior door knobs and deadbolts with a screwdriver or something to make it look like the locks were picked."

She removed a Swiss Army knife from a cargo pocket. "At some house last year—I don't remember which—the front door swung open while I was gouging it."

McPhee chuffed and shook his head. "The surprise is that only one did. People spend serious cash on security systems, then go off and leave the doors unlocked."

"Maybe, but hardly anyone barricades a dog door. They forget it's there, I guess."

"Or think it's too small for a burglar to crawl through."

Seeing no tease or ridicule in his eyes, Dina went on, "Your ex-wife's afghan hound explains why the door I thought was Phil's was so big. If I'd had to squeeze through, I wouldn't have."

"My client gave me copies of the priors' police reports. Those houses must have been scouted in advance. Nobody's that lucky, that consistently." He paused, a hand rising to massage the back of his neck. "Tonight, you chanced it. I figured a one-night trap was a pipe dream, but the rain was too sweet for you to pass up."

She almost did, though. Gooseflesh rippled up Dina's arms, as it had when she'd toed off her wet slippers in the deHavens' pitch-dark mudroom. Creeping through the hotel-sized kitchen, then a breakfast alcove, dining room and on into the living room was like groping through a soundproof Halloween funhouse. The rain-speckled windows seemed to absorb every lumen of exterior light and shed none.

She'd wanted out. Wanted enough swag—just enough—to rescind her deal with God forever. Wanted the courage to push her socked feet into that maw of a hallway taunting her on her left.

Then the penlight she'd gripped, too afraid to switch on, squirted out of her gloved fist. It clattered like a gunshot on the slate floor, winking and rolling lazily away. As she lunged for it, a blinding beam of light outside impaled her. Her heart stopped; her mind shrieked, Get out, get out!

The flimsy slippers on her feet were still damp from the losing race with McPhee. They conjured the yin-yang emotions she'd felt when the judge granted her divorce: failure, the satisfaction that she'd tried her damnedest not to give up, relief that it was over, fear of what the future held.

What she didn't feel were the tears ambling down her face, until McPhee smudged them away with his thumb. "Why, Dina? Why'd you do it? And keep on doing it?"

She sniffed, wiped her nose on her sleeve, but couldn't meet his eyes. "To save my mother's life."

Hearing it, even at a whisper, sounded so ridiculously melodramatic, she expected him to laugh. No response at all freed her to pretend she was talking to herself and crying alone in the kitchen, as she had a hundred times before.

"My dad was a fighter. Cancer should have killed him years before it did, but he wouldn't give up. Neither would his doctors. The bills Dad's insurance, then Medicare, wouldn't pay—experimental treatments, drug therapies, you name it—kept piling up. Then the factory he worked in his entire life announced they'd funded the pension account on paper, but hadn't invested most of the money."

McPhee said, "Then they filed for bankruptcy protection."

"They did. We couldn't. The laws were changed, so medical debts don't count." Dina took a breath, then continued, "After Dad died, Mom sold the house, but after paying off a second and third mortgage, there was barely any equity left. Their savings were long gone, credit cards maxed out thousands above what they could have repaid, if Daddy was still employed.

"Mom had earned 'pin money,' she called it, doing alterations, selling crocheted throws and sweaters, but she never held a full-time job. Couldn't have kept it, if she'd found one, between taking Daddy to doctors, the surgeries, and caring for him at home."

Dina swallowed past the knot in her throat. "Now Mom's heart is failing, she's diabetic, hypertensive—a slew of things medication can't cure, but she'll die without it."

Jack said softly, "And you can't afford to buy it."

"Not since I maxed out my credit cards and the bank turned me down for a loan." A bitter chuckle slipped out. "Medicare covers most of her prescriptions, part of the time. It'd pay for them all, if Mom was sick enough for a nursing home. Real cost-effective, since she'd sooner die, than go to one."

Dina took a sip of lukewarm coffee and set the mug aside. She looked up at McPhee. "Ever hear of the doughnut hole? And I don't mean the deep-fried, sugar-coated kind."

A hesitation, then a nod inferred the *why* he'd asked for was stitching together in his mind. "The euphemism somebody gave the gap in Medicare prescription coverage."

"Cute, huh? Like it's bite-sized and hardly rates mention. What's a measly three-thousand out-of-pocket dollars to bridge the so-called doughnut hole? Medicare *does* cover the first couple of thousand for a few bucks' copay. Once you've spent enough to close that gap, it goes back to covering the expense with the copay, again, till the end of the year."

Jack stared at her for a long moment, his expression grim and dubious. "So for your mother, that gap opens up in late spring and closes in the fall."

A statement, not a question. Dina didn't particularly care for the content or tone. "The middle of April, last year. That's when I applied for the loan. When the bank declined it, I *had* to get the money somehow. Then I scrimped all last winter, saving up for this year's doughnut hole. I almost did, when the cardiologist prescribed two new medications that cost nearly six hundred a month."

Claustrophobia is the fear of small, enclosed spaces. As Dina was distinctly aware, feeling trapped sometimes arises from within. "Mom can't be left alone for more than a few hours. She has dizzy spells. Has to eat at certain times. Takes meds by the clock and in a specific order, but I've worked as much as I could, wherever I could."

"Yeah. Grooming dogs part-time and delivering pizzas."

"Yes! And cashiering at a fireworks stand, a Christmas tree

lot, a Little League concession. In the fall, I pick up walnuts and sell them to a huller, and—"

"Seventy-five grand, kid. That's the appraised value of the stuff you stole last year."

McPhee helped himself to more coffee, as if letting the number and his knowledge of it sink in. "So far this year, you've boosted damn near fifty."

Dina's lips parted. Her head wobbled, jerking from side to side.

He went on, "You had me chokin' up for a while there. Till I remembered the standard ten percent take-home from a fence would fill a doughnut hole as big as a wading pool."

Grade-school addition and multiplication netted a five-figured result—one as ludicrous as it was terrifying. Stealing was stealing, whether her share was $12,500 or less than half that amount.

"I didn't take anywhere *near* that much. I don't care if you believe me or not, it's the truth. I didn't take a dime more than I could earn."

Dina backpedaled, crossing her arms at her chest like a shield. "All right, I did. *Once.* $387.22 more last year, but I didn't keep it. I swear, I put every penny in an envelope and gave to the Salvation Army."

"Oh, puh-leeze." McPhee rolled his eyes. His chuckle branded her a fool and excepted him as a peer. "Next, you'll show me the receipt. No, wait. You would, but you stapled it to your tax return to claim a charitable deduction."

She pushed past him, slopping his coffee on his shirt. Damn shame, it wasn't hot enough to scald. A note to her mother was dashed off on the back of an envelope, then she grabbed her purse.

McPhee stepped in front of her. "Where do you think you're going?"

"The police station. Maybe a *real* detective won't believe me, either, but at least I won't have to listen to any more of your cocky amateur-hour bullshit."

His hand manacled her wrist. "That's three below-the-belts."

"Let go of—"

"You're not bluffing, are you?"

"Ya think?" Dina almost laughed. "Let's review. You have my ID, you know where I live, where I work, and you caught me shinnying out the pet door at your ex-wife's house."

"This is true." McPhee sighed and relaxed his grip. "Everything you've said is true, right down to that donated three hundred and change." A hint of a smile appeared. "Well, up to that 'cocky amateur-hour' remark."

"Before *that,* I told you I don't care if you believe me. I still don't."

"Don't start lying now," he warned. "Okay, I should've realized quicker that anybody with the brains to hang grand theft on a Medicare prescription gap wouldn't drag the Salvation friggin' Army into it." His grin widened. "And it wouldn't surprise me if you do have a receipt."

Dina searched a face that wouldn't send Tom Cruise running for a plastic surgeon. A twice-broken nose always had stories behind it, as would the pale crescent scar beneath his hairline. Worry creases striped his brow, but were fewer and shallower than his laugh lines.

Trust Me wasn't tattooed anywhere. There was scant reason for Dina to do so, other than his reticence to involve the police. Yet.

But why? Was a bounty paid, if his client was notified before the arrest? Was there a possibility the insurance agent could be persuaded not to press charges? Maybe a symbolic trade-off negotiated, like free office cleaning for the rest of Dina's life.

"I deal with cheats, scam artists, swindlers and worse," McPhee said. "In one case I worked, a father smothered his first-then his second-born to make it look like Sudden Infant Death Syndrome to collect the insurance. Convicted pedophiles are known to steal identities to get jobs in amusement parks, schools, day-care centers—anywhere with access to children."

He chucked Dina under the chin. "Constant exposure to the scum of the earth would turn a saint into a cynic. In other words, I wouldn't have made book on catching the Calendar Burglar tonight, but I sure as hell didn't expect to tackle Robin Hood."

"Get your hands off my daughter, mister."

Harriet Wexler stood in the hallway. Her rheumy eyes flitted from Dina to Jack McPhee. "As for you, Dina Jeanne, give him back his money. Every filthy dollar of it."

She raised her cane like an avenging Moses in flannel pajamas. "What you do out on street corners, I can't stop, but I'll sic the law on you, afore you'll bring your merry men *into my house.*"

9

"Mother of God, Mother! You think I'm a *hooker?*"

Jack bit the inside of his lip to keep a straight face.

Dina the dog groomer's sideline as the Calendar Burglar was still a bit of a stretch. Imagining her on the stroll in black cargos, a long-sleeved top, socks and cheap nylon house slippers was hilarious.

"I know you've been sneaking out and back in, late of a night, week after week." Mrs. Wexler snorted in disgust. "Being sick doesn't make me deaf, blind or stupid."

"Well, it doesn't make me a—"

"One day you're crossways about gas going up a nickel a gallon. The next, you bring home gadgets that cost more 'n the moon."

"A glucose monitor isn't—"

"It ain't pizzas you're delivering, girl. Haven't been, for who knows how long."

"And of all the possible explanations a normal person might come up with, you—*my own mother*—decide I'm a whore."

Jack took her first completed sentence as a cue. "No, she hasn't, Dina."

Both women turned on him, open-mouthed and blinking as though he'd arrived by parachute. "I have some good news and some bad news, Mrs. Wexler."

"Who the—?"

"The good news," he went on, "is you know your daughter isn't a prostitute, so that pretty much eliminates me as her john. The bad news is, she's a burglar and I'm Jack McPhee, the private investigator an insurance company hired to catch her."

Mrs. Wexler's withering gaze shifted from him to Dina, then lowered and raised in a head-to-toe examination of her daughter's all-black ensemble. Although several inches taller than Dina, the frail, wild-haired woman seemed to shrink with relief. Her nostrils flared as she inhaled lungfuls of oxygenated air. Slowly, she exhaled a joyous "Thank God."

Jack gave Dina a "See, that wasn't so bad, was it?" smile.

To her mother, Dina repeated, "Thank God? *Thank God?* Like it's okay to be a thief, but not a hooker?"

"Oh, for heaven's sake, Dina Jeanne." Mrs. Wexler shuffled toward the glider rocker in the living room. Coils in the plastic tubing following behind her revolved like a threads on a giant, invisible screw. "Of course it isn't okay."

"I think what your mother means is, there's a difference between selling somebody's jewelry, and selling yourself."

"Don't you put words into my mouth, young man." Mrs. Wexler fell into the chair, as much as sat down in it. One foot, then the other was hiked onto the ottoman. "Even if they're the right ones."

She jerked a tissue from the box and dabbed her brow and neck. Caring for a terminally ill husband and her own failing health must have aged her a decade or two.

Although Jack knew she hadn't believed Dina was earning extra money on her back, waking to an empty house night after night must have terrified her. Death can be a blessing, a tragedy, a peaceful end to a life well lived, but few want to meet theirs all alone.

Dina shared that fear. It didn't matter if she was at a kennel, doing errands, breaking into houses or asleep. Jack had seen the anxiety when she'd hurried down the hall to check on her mother. How Dina endured the constant emotional swings between dread and deliverance, he couldn't fathom.

"I smell coffee," Mrs. Wexler said accusingly. "The real kind, not the brown water that's supposed to pass for it."

Jack said, "I'll bring you a cup."

"Oh, no, you won't. Mom can't have caffiene."

"Pshaw. I drink it all the time, and it hasn't killed me yet." She winked at Jack. "While the cat's away, the old mouse has been known to stir in a spoonful of sugar, too."

"We don't *have* any sugar," Dina shot back. "Knowing you'd cheat, I threw it away months ago and washed out the canister."

Mrs. Wexler started to argue and evidently thought better of it. She minced, "Well, if it isn't too much trouble, may I please have a drink of water?"

When Dina rounded the corner to the kitchen, her mother snatched up a bagful of yarn. From the bottom, she pulled up several restaurant sugar packets. Grinning flirtatiously, she warned, "Don't you tell, McPhee."

"Jack," he said, and held out his hand. "Give 'em here, ma'am, and there'll be nothing to tell."

She hesitated, then dropped them in his palm. "I can get more any time I want."

The eatery's name stamped on the packets had closed two years ago. The old mouse hadn't cheated on her diet and never would. The sugar stash was a rebellion against disease, her daughter, kidnapped stove knobs and a thousand other indignities. Far from the least of which was no one to crow to, other than a stranger who hadn't chirped, "And how are we feeling today, Mrs. Wexler?"

Jack returned a packet to her and slipped the rest in his jeans pocket. "That's enough to get us both in trouble."

Her fingers curled around it. "Thank you, McPhee."

He sighed wearily as he sat down on the couch. What was it with the Wexlers' obsession with his last name? Tacking a "Mr." in front of it, he'd understand. Without it, the semiformality was beginning to sound like a fast-food franchise's new menu item.

"Jack," he said plenty loud enough to hear over a teakettle whistling in the kitchen. "Just plain 'Jack' will do fine, ma'am."

"I thought you said you were a detective."

He nodded, wondering how she'd react to the questions he still needed answers for. And whether Dina would clam up until her mother went back to bed. Or permanently.

"Then you must not be a very good one," Mrs. Wexler said. "Or you haven't been in business long enough to know better."

"Excuse me?" he said, thinking a few key words hadn't registered while his mind was elsewhere.

"A *real* pro never goes by his first name. Near as a body can tell, some don't seem to have one." Apparently annoyed by his persistent bewilderment, she added, "Columbo. Kojak. Mannix. Rockford. Magnum—well, he's an exception, since his buddies call him Thomas, but the show's *Magnum, P.I.,* not *Thomas Magnum, P.I.*"

Rather than point out that TV detectives were as true to life as a talking yellow sponge, Jack thanked her for the advice.

Before the interview concluded, the Wexlers would call him plenty of things besides McPhee.

Dina reentered the room carrying a tray. Water, several tablets and a coffee cup were dispensed to her mother, then the latter to Jack and herself.

"One for all," she said, referring to the whitish skim in his cup, peculiar to instant decaf.

A special circle of Hell should be reserved for its inventor. He swallowed a mouthful, noting that a pinch of arsenic would be virtually undetectable. Hell, a little rat poison stirred in might improve the taste.

Dina set the tray on the floor, then tossed aside a folded bed-sheet at the couch's opposite end. She scooted back into the corner against a bed pillow, her legs tucked under her, as though distancing herself from Jack as much as possible.

"So," she said. "Did the two of you draw straws to see who interrogates me first? Or do you want to do it relay style?"

"Don't be hateful, Dina Jeanne. Let's just have a nice chat, then you and McPhee can help me pack my things." Mrs. Wexler smiled at Jack. "I hope your car is bigger than hers. They won't let me bring much, but that Volkswagen will barely hold one suitcase."

Dina glared at Jack. "What did you say to her while I was in the kitchen?"

"It's my fault you're in trouble," Mrs. Wexler continued. "I do wish you'd been honest with me about the money a long time ago, sweetheart. But as soon as I'm at the nursing home, you won't have to steal things to pay the bills."

To Jack, she said, "Or to make—what do you call it?—uh, *restitution.* Yes, that's the word. She'll pay it, too, then you don't have to take her to jail."

Jack raised a hand to silence Dina. "I'm sorry, Mrs. Wexler, but this situation is more complicated than your daughter bur-glarizing houses to offset your medical expenses. Among other things, there's a serious discrepancy between what she should have been paid for that jewelry and what she swears she received."

"Comes as no surprise to me. Dina's smart, don't get me wrong, but her brother's always had a sharper head for figures.

Why, before Randy started school, he could cipher whether the green beans the store put on sale were any cheaper than the others."

"A financial whiz," Dina muttered, "at begging for money. Even better at getting some out of Mom."

Determined to keep the interview on track, Jack said, "You fenced the merchandise through somebody. I want to know who, how you met, how and where the exchanges went down—everything."

Dina directed a smirk at her mother. "I asked a friend of my mooch of a baby brother which pawnshop would give me the most for my wedding rings."

"You're married?"

"Happily divorced." She went on, "When Randy's friend found out why I needed the money, he took my cell phone number and said a friend of a friend of his might be able to help. A day or two later, a man called, saying he was in the market for upscale jewelry. It took a while to realize he meant hot upscale jewelry. I hung up on him."

"But you couldn't stop thinking about it."

"Not when it seemed like every other kennel customer wore diamond studs as big as marbles. Sapphire tennis bracelets, fancy rings, watches, pendants…" Shame leavened her voice. "And I was canceling Mom's doctor's appointments and telling her they were postponed because I didn't have enough money for the copays."

"You were?" Mrs. Wexler thrust out her chin. "If I'd known that, I wouldn't have taken your guff about my medicine for a second."

"Oh, yeah? Well, putting off checkups is why it scared me to death when I found out you were skipping your meds, or cutting them in half."

"Some of them made me sick, or light-headed, or so sleepy I couldn't keep my eyes open."

"They don't when I'm here to make sure you eat something first, or that you *don't,* if they're supposed to be taken on an empty stomach."

Dina drew up her knees, her arms clamped around them like metal straps. Mrs. Wexler stared at the hallway. She worried the gold wedding band on her finger, mumbling about being a burden.

If tension had a color, it would be chartreuse and the room was pulsing with it. Jack wasn't immune to the effect or the vibe, but should have been. From the moment he recognized the thief's pretty face, he'd felt as if his shoes were on backward.

Seldom was objectivity a conscious effort. Any personal interest in a case was exclusive to the client. Almost without exception, the women Jack had encountered in the course of an investigation were either married, significantly othered or he wouldn't date them if they were stranded on a life raft.

Admit it, he thought. You've felt like your shoes were on backward since the day you met Dina Wexler. She blindsided you, sport. There's no future in it and never was. You didn't know it until an hour ago, but you damn sure do now.

He pushed up from the couch. His coffee cup was deposited on the kitchen counter. A dining room chair was moved into the living room, as though a poetry reading were about to commence.

He pulled a notebook from his back pocket, unclipped the pen from his shirt placket and sat down. "The fence's cell phone number, Ms. Wexler."

Startled by the bad-cop routine, Dina glanced at her mother. Mrs. Wexler sipped daintily from the water glass, content to let her back-talking daughter twist alone in the wind awhile.

Flustered, but loath to show it, Dina splayed her left hand. A seven-digit sequence was recited, then she squinted at her palm. "Wait. I think that last number's a seven, not a one."

Jesus friggin' criminy. The Calendar Burglar the police had chased their tails for two years to apprehend had inked her fence's phone number on her hand.

"Do you have a lousy memory, or does it change pretty often?"

He already knew the answer, and that the fence's revolving contact numbers were linked to untraceable prepaid units, of which he had a sackful. Occasionally, he'd make brief, selective use of a stolen cell phone.

"How do you contact him?" Jack asked.

"From pay phones."

"Never the same one twice, right?"

Dina nodded.

"And he tells you, don't use this contact number next time, use this one."

Another nod.

"You don't know his name, but does he know yours?"

"Just as D.J." Dina frowned. "Unless somebody told him." A pause, then, "I don't think Randy's friend would have, and the man hasn't ever called me Dina or anything."

Odds were the fence knew exactly who she was, where she lived and why she'd resorted to burglary. Multiple receiving-stolen-property charges would bargain down nicely in exchange for particulars on the actual thieves. Even a jailhouse shyster would demand a conspiracy-to-commit charge be taken off the table before the fence flipped on his crew.

"Call him." Jack lobbed his own untraceable, prepaid phone to her. "Say whatever you usually do to arrange a meeting."

Leery, she argued, "He'll know it isn't a pay phone call. He won't answer."

"Try it."

Dina punched in the number and held the unit to her ear.

A quizzical expression, a disconnect, then a second try. She muttered, "Maybe it *is* a one instead of a seven." Her eyes telegraphed an active ring tone. A start, then, "Oh. Sorry. Wrong number."

To Jack, she said, "I don't understand."

He did. A new and legitimate phone number was Dina's pink slip. The fence was feeling heat, or decided she'd become a liability.

"Okay," Jack said, "pretend you've made your haul and a clean getaway. What was the drill from there?"

"I'd call, he'd tell me where we'd meet, he'd look at what I have and pay me."

"No ballpark estimates on the gross? No dickering? Just, 'Here's your ten percent, see ya in the funny papers'?"

The evil eye Dina leveled sufficed as an answer. "For what it's worth, which is probably nothing, I didn't take wedding rings, anniversary rings, anything that looked like an heirloom or was inscribed. Sure, some pieces may have been gifts or had sentimental value, but if I sensed they might, I left them alone."

"Lord in Heaven." Mrs. Wexler moaned and clapped a hand to her face. "You really *are* a thief."

Dina stiffened. Her cheeks flushed, but she didn't respond.

"All I've got to say is, thank God your daddy isn't alive to hear this."

Since "All I've got to say" is usually an intro, not an outro, Mrs. Wexler went on, "Why didn't you tell Randy you needed help making ends meet, instead of this so-called friend of his?"

"I did, Mother. About a hundred times. Including just last week, as a matter of fact."

"I don't believe you." Mrs. Wexler tossed her head. "Randy

is the man of the family now. He'd have come home if you'd asked him to."

Dina looked at Jack. The resentment of a second-favorite child smoldered in her eyes. "Go on, McPhee."

A now familiar flinch tugged his solar plexus. Dina had lived a pressure-cooker existence for years. No time to herself, none for herself. The byproducts of stress and unrelieved exhaustion were a numb conscience and quashed fears of what would happen to her mother if Dina were arrested.

Prison could be construed as a respite. Three hots and a cot, sequestered and protected from the world's problems, responsibilities and hypocrisy. A comparative nirvana, as long as common sense sat down and shut its yap.

Jack slashed underlines beneath his latest note. Every criminal had a sob story. Letting Dina Wexler get to him *was* friggin' amateur hour. He snapped, "Where'd these alleged transactions take place?"

"All over town," she said, taken aback. "It depended on the time of day."

"All over town, *where?*"

"Internet cafés. Library study carrels. Bars with live music. The airport. Once at a moonlight madness sale at the mall." Dina's scarcely audible addendum was, "A Sunday church service. A mortuary during a funeral."

Safety and anonymity in numbers, Jack thought, as long as the crowd's attention is directed elsewhere. Smart dude, this fence. The drug trade had rendered obsolete the traditional rendezvous at a park bench at midnight. Hide in plain sight was safer.

"Never in a car? Yours or his?"

"No." Dina anticipated his next question. "I never saw his car."

Chancy though it would be to walk around with sufficient

cash for the payoff, a metro bus pass could deliver the fence to most of those meeting sites.

"The jewelry itself," Jack said. "How did you know the genuine article from costume?"

A cord worn like a necklace was reeled up from inside Dina's shirt. The black-cased jeweler's loupe at the end resembled a plumb bob. "I logged onto the Internet at the library to convince myself that burglary wasn't just wrong, it was crazy. I'd never be able to tell a cubic zirconia from a diamond, or any fake from the real thing."

She yanked the cord over her head. The magnifier slapped the couch cushion. "Instead, I learned how to use a loupe and what to look for."

"Such as?" Jack's query was half curiosity, half for future reference. Keeping up technologically with the crooks was impossible, but now and then, you'd nab a Luddite.

"Well," Dina began, aware she now had her mother's and Jack's rapt attention. "Zirconias are synthetic, but different than cultured stones that are graded like mined diamonds. Real and cultured may have lasered serial numbers, but nobody does that to fakes.

"Some stones are fracture filled or clarity enhanced, too. That means cracks—flaws—are filled with glass. How, I have no clue." She snickered. "Want to impress a wife or girlfriend without blowing your trust fund? Buy her a fracture-filled headlamp solitaire. Want to rip off somebody? Sell a clarity-enhanced stone for the price of a high-graded one."

Her tone now mimicking a bored socialite, she added, "But do avoid chips, scratches and inclusions—carbon or crystal flaws. They *so* decrease the value. The cut can increase it, but the make—the skill used to cut it? *That's* the fire in the ice."

Mrs. Wexler gasped. "I had no idea you knew all that. You

should apply for work at a jewelry store. It wouldn't be as tiring as grooming dogs, and it's…legal."

The comment was bemused, albeit complimentary, but Dina sneered, "My on-the-job experience is in breaking and entering, Mom. Not in retail sales."

"That loupe," Jack said. "Did you boost it, too?"

"No." Dina didn't say, "You asshole," but Jack heard it. "The, uh, fence gave it to me. Well, he didn't *give* it, he deducted a percentage of the cost from what he paid me."

Crib-noted contact numbers. A jeweler's loupe on the installment plan. The bad-cop schtick didn't prohibit laughing, but Jack was afraid if he did, he'd lose it completely. "Assuming that's a 10X model, how much did he ding you for it?"

"A hundred and fifty dollars," she said.

Double or nothing, the nameless fence had gouged her, but good. By what she'd said earlier, naiveté had also cost her the difference between an experienced thief's percentage and her take.

Fuzzy math might apply to the stolen merchandise's appraised and insured value, as well. Purchase price aside, every appraisal is subjective. If an owner received more than one appraisal, the higher estimate would dictate the insured value for replacement-cost policyholders. Low appraisals could pare down taxable assets for those less worried about theft than an IRS audit.

Therefore, Dina got screwed, the insurance company probably got screwed to an extent and the fence and the burglary victims were smelling American Beauty bouquets.

Typical, Jack thought. Crime does pay. It just doesn't pay dependably or equally. "This library research of yours," he said. "Why didn't you Google up some jewelry Web sites or eBay for price comparisons before you sold the stuff?"

"I thought about it." A silent standoff eventually prompted,

"To go online, I have to use my library card. I was afraid the police could trace the searches back to me."

If only. Jack stifled a grin. The Feds' forensic computer expertise rivaled his own, sad to say. Provided you already knew what to look for and where, it might be found. Otherwise, the Internet was a vast electronic haystack.

"Besides," Dina said, "what if I did find out the fence was cheating me? What was I supposed to do? Threaten to take my business elsewhere?"

Good point, but Jack didn't concede it aloud. "Yeah, well, describe Mr. Loupes 'R' Us for me."

"I never got a good look at his face. He always wore baseball caps and kept his head down a lot." Her teeth sawed across her lower lip, as though mentally formulating an artist's sketch. "Glasses—geeky frames, not wire. Tinted lenses—grayish, maybe—but regular, not pop bottles. Clean shaved. The cap mostly covered his hair, but I'd guess it was brown. About your height and weight."

"Tattoos?"

"Um, uh-uh. Not that I can recall."

"How does he dress? Sloppy? Neat? Soccer dad?"

A frown, then, "Soccer dad, if that means like pretty much anybody over thirty you see at the mall."

"Over thirty? As in forty? Fifty?"

"I don't *know*, okay? My impression is somewhere above grad student and below AARP."

Hence, he hadn't disguised his appearance per se, but anything memorable was unremarkable: baseball cap, glasses, no facial hair, no visible tattoos. The bowed head offset Dina's stature. In addition, both of them wanted the transaction concluded as rapidly as possible.

Jack pictured Dina figuratively if not literally wringing her hands, trying to gulp down whatever internal organ was lodged in her throat. Apart from the burglaries themselves, selling the merchandise was the riskiest part of her crimes. The fence needn't have told her to keep a lookout while he examined the loot.

"His voice, in person and on the phone," Jack said. "Did he speak with a drawl, a lisp—"

"McPhee?" Mrs. Wexler languidly waved the TV's remote control.

Jack had all but forgotten she was in the room. He smiled and said, "Yes, ma'am?"

"Are you taking Dina to jail?"

He checked a nod. The impulsive decision he'd made in Belle's backyard and what he'd learned since advised a consultation with his attorney first, cop house later.

Reverse that order and based on Jack's witness statement, he was reasonably certain Dina's chargeable offenses began at B&E and ended at trespassing. Explain *how* he'd witnessed both before he ran it by a lawyer could get Jack arrested for everything from trespassing to criminal conspiracy to flight to avoid prosecution.

His notes were essentially a confession. By legal definition, they were hearsay, barring her corroborating statement to the police. Dina had either surmised that, or would tick-a-lock after she was in custody, because she wasn't stupid and neither were public defenders.

Absent her self-implication and any concrete evidence— which Jack doubted existed—and the cops might have probable cause for a twenty-four-hour hold on suspicion of burglary. Him, they'd throw in jail for the forseeable future.

The kennel connection was a shoo-in, but circumstantial. A property-crimes unit's second canvass of neighbors surrounding previously burgled homes might result in someone recognizing a photo of Dina's VW. Could that witness swear the vehicle was seen on a specific date, at a specific time or for a specific period of time?

As the world's worst defense attorney would say, an aircraft carrier was easier to torpedo than hindsighted recall.

Even if it wasn't, it was still circumstantial, not direct evidence that Dina Jeanne Wexler was the Calendar Burglar. The trip wire that investigators would inevitably reveal was Dina's income versus expenditures to close the Medicare doughnut hole. Those mysterious, inexplicable windfalls would trigger the prosecutorial avalanche.

And Jack could play bad cop till his skin turned midnight-blue, without the fence, her conviction and a lengthy prison term were nearly guaranteed. Those who steal from the rich and influential don't receive probation. Not if a prosecuting attorney wants to win reelection.

Given Dina's extenuating circumstances, if Jack collared the fence, along with a few of his other suppliers, her testimony might broker a reduced sentence.

"Tomorrow is soon enough to talk to the police, Mrs. Wexler." Jack's gaze flicked to her daughter. "I don't think I have to worry about her being a flight risk."

"Well, then…" Mrs. Wexler's breathless quaver caught his and Dina's attention simultaneously. "Is it okay…if she calls… 911? Think I'm…another…heart attack."

10

"My mom had a rough night last night, Gwendolyn," Dina said into the kitchen wall phone's receiver.

A massive understatement for Harriet's finding out about her double life. When Dina was a kid, she'd known those everyday commandments like "I'm doing this for your own good" and "What you don't know, can't hurt you" were monumental lies. You have to be an adult to rationalize that they're true and actively ignore why the proverbial road to Hell is paved with good intentions.

"Is Harriet all right?" Gwendolyn asked.

"The paramedics checked her over and were pretty sure it was an anxiety attack, not a heart attack. They still wanted to transport her to the E.R., but Mom refused."

McPhee voting with Dina and the EMTs contradicted the precept of majority rule. Harriet insisted she'd been excited about "having company," and should have gone back to bed instead of becoming overtired. Her elevated blood sugar she'd blamed on the decaf coffee she'd barely touched. The real culprit, a stress-induced adrenaline spike, has a corresponding effect on anybody's insulin level. Diabetics are just more sensitive to it.

"Mom's up and around this morning," Dina said, "but she's a little shaky."

"You're afraid to leave her alone," Gwendolyn stated, followed by a pensive sigh. "I would be, too, if it was my mother, but—"

"You have a boarding kennel to run," Dina finished for her. "And I have a grooming appointment scheduled in a half hour."

The line hummed a moment. Gwendolyn couldn't quite mask the edge in her tone when she inquired, "So, how soon *can* you be here?"

From the living room, Harriet called, "*Di*-na. Come here, *quick.*"

Stretching the phone cord to its limit, she leaned around the corner, saying, "I hope before noon…" Her voice trailed away as she saw what her mother was pointing at on the TV. "Oh, dear God."

Dina dropped the receiver on the counter and rushed into the living room. Aiming the remote, Harriet upped the volume on a local station's breaking-news report.

The anchorman doing a stand-up at the end of a residential driveway looked about sixteen and forcibly grim. "A spokesman for the Park City Police Department has confirmed the city's latest homicide victim is Belle deHaven, wife of nationally known investment counselor Carleton deHaven.

"According to unnamed sources close to the investigation, sometime between early afternoon and midnight yesterday, Mrs. deHaven sustained an execution-style gunshot wound to the head. Death was believed to be instantaneous."

The anchor took a breath. "To repeat," he said, "the Park City police have confirmed—"

Dina clapped her hands over her ears. "Turn it down, for God's sake."

The noise level ratcheting down several decibels had no effect on the clamor inside Dina's head. DeHaven. Belle deHaven. The name pounded like a drumbeat. There was no mistaking it or the house with the soaring wall of windows diagonally behind the reporter.

She'd broken into the deHavens' house before midnight last night. Skulked through the eerie, unrelieved darkness as far as the living room, then lost her penlight along with her nerve—for lack of a better term.

A dead woman's house. A *murdered* woman's house. Jack McPhee's ex-wife's house.

That's why he was there. Why he'd hustled Dina from the scene, instead of turning her over to the police. He'd shot Belle deHaven and...

And what? Give or take a few minutes, the first police officer arrived at the deHavens' house around midnight. Jack must have killed his ex-wife some time earlier. He'd then gone back to his car and waited for the Calendar Burglar to spring the trap he'd set that afternoon. What better alibi was there than to pin a murder on a notorious thief?

Dina snorted at the thought. Jack McPhee was a lot of things, not all of them complimentary. But a diabolical, cold-blooded killer? Not.

On the heels of that assurance came a shattering realization. If Jack hadn't been at the deHavens' last night, hadn't practically kidnapped Dina to evade the police, she'd be the prime suspect in the homicide of a woman she'd never even met.

Her knees buckled. Staggering backward, Dina clutched the back of a dining room chair, her eyes shut tight against a swirling ochre-gray haze. What if Jack was at the police station right now, telling them he'd caught her escaping out the dog door? Speculating that Mrs. deHaven must have confronted the Calendar Burglar, aka Dina Wexler. Dina panicked and shot the woman, then ran virtually into Jack's arms.

Stop it. *Stop it.* He knows you didn't have a gun on you. Would have heard the shot if you'd fired one inside the house. Knows you're a thief, yes, and that the deHavens' wasn't the first house you broke into, got scared and left without taking anything. Most of all, he damn well knows you're as steel nerved and vicious as a rabbit.

Dina sucked in a slow, tentative breath through her nose, then another and another deeper one. They ebbed the nausea, but not the sour, burning taste permeating her mouth. She swallowed it back and licked her lips.

Gradually, her vision began to clear. A muffling sensation, like swimming underwater, gave way to the staccato bleats of an unhooked phone receiver, and her mother's disgusted "…this world, this *town* coming to? Fourteenth murder this year, that TV boy said. Like it's a baseball game, for pity's sake, and we're a couple of RBIs from tying up the score."

Harriet threw a wadded tissue at the screen. "Return to regular programming, my foot. First they barge in on my favorite show with the same claptrap they'll have on noon news, then they tack on a string of commercials."

Dina looked from her mother to a national auto-parts franchise advertisement. The relief crashing over her was as dizzying as Jack's imagined police report. She was positive they'd mentioned the deHaven name last night. More than once. Harriet either hadn't heard them or hadn't connected it to the murdered woman's identity.

"Your show will be back on in a minute," Dina said, her voice steadier than she expected. "It's nothing to get upset about."

"Ha! You watch. The clue J. B. Fletcher found that'll nab the killer was in the part they skipped." Harriet's thumb tapped the channel-changer button. "I'll just bide my time with something else till it comes on again on cable at three."

"That'll teach 'em," Dina said, chuckling. Picking up the receiver to call back Gwen Ellicot sobered her immediately.

TLC's owner had been unbelievably tolerant of Dina's frequent and typically last-minute tardiness, let alone no-shows. Mondays were also routinely drop-off days for dogs who reeked from paddling around in the lake all weekend.

Other kennel employees could handle basic shampoos and blow-drys. It was the add-ons, the nonchalant "I know I don't have an appointment, but while he's here, can you trim his nails, scale his teeth, trim his ears, and gosh, the way he's been dragging his bottom, his anal glands might need to be expressed" chores that required a trained groomer.

"Hey," she said when Gwendolyn answered the return call. "I am so sorry I dropped the phone. Mom yelled, and I thought she'd fallen, or—"

"Listen, Dina, don't worry about coming in today." A pause, then, "In fact, well, I wanted to discuss this with you in person, but I've hired a full-time groomer. He wasn't supposed to start till Wednesday, but he's on his way here to cover for you."

Dina was too stunned to speak.

"It's not fair," Gwendolyn went on. "I know it isn't. You're the reason business has picked up. I just can't afford to lose it again because something comes up at home and appointments have to be canceled or rescheduled."

How much business would be lost when the Calendar Burglar's apprehension was splashed across the newspaper's front page? When word spread that a thief had used TLC's, Merry Hills's and Home Away's clientele like a hit list?

It wasn't as if Dina never thought about getting caught. What mental images she'd allowed herself were ridiculously contained and Hollywood scripted: her handcuffed wrists, the prodigal Randy's forced return to take care of and support their mother, her guilty plea before a judge, a prison cell with an X chalked on a wall to mark off her sentence.

"I'm sorry, Gwendolyn," she murmured. "For everything."

The phone receiver she cradled seemed to weigh a hundred pounds.

The turn signal ticked off the seconds Jack waited in traffic at the intersection of Eleventh and Danbury. He couldn't recall ever making the damn light. No once in all the years he'd owned the agency.

Equally immutable was the sallow Methuselah who lived across the street from Jack's office. Rain or shine, summer and winter, the old man sat on his porch smoking cigarettes and flipping the butts into a rusty coffee can. He couldn't see his sneaker laces and wouldn't hear Armageddon, but he waved at passing pedestrians and cars like the hereditary King of Danbury Street.

Jack's gaze swung to the strip mall's parking lot. Scanning for Brett Dean Blankenship's car was becoming habit. Its absence was less notable than its presence—unless the jerk finally got bored or Mommy had cut off his allowance Saturday night and he couldn't afford the gas.

What gave Jack pause was the white Crown Victoria cozied between a Subaru and a Honda Accord. In law-enforcement parlance, "unmarked" referred to an official vehicle without light bars, pinstripes and shield decals. Though stripped of the obvious trappings, flattops radiated an aura. At fifty yards, most people could distinguish a civilian Crown Vic or Chevrolet Caprice from a city motor-pool model.

Crime-unit investigators drove unmarkeds. Specifically, property-crime detectives eager to hear why Jack McPhee and an unknown individual had fled the scene of a residential trouble call last night. The urge was almost overwhelming to abort his left turn onto Eleventh, proceed west on Danbury, then circle around to his attorney's office three hours early for their appointment.

Jack's standard procedure was to notify the cops of a surveillance location in advance. It was a courtesy, sure, but mostly it prevented a stakeout being shot to hell by a uniform responding to a suspicious-vehicle complaint. Dispatch was informed of the prior two traps laid for the Calendar Burglar. He hadn't notified them of Belle's address, for good reason or reasons he couldn't recollect at the moment. After the interview with Dina Wexler, the lapse seemed prescient.

"Up till now." Jack nosed the Taurus into his usual parking spot. "Just play it cool, kid. If that doesn't work, go for dumb. God knows you are or you wouldn't be in this mess to begin with."

Recognizing the investigator exiting the Crown Vic brought a grin to Jack's face. "Corned Beef?" He stuck out a hand. "Man, I haven't seen you in, what, about fifty pounds?"

"Thirty-five. The diet the new wife's put me on has knocked off nearly twenty." Andy McGuire's smile didn't quite reach his eyes. "Nobody's called me Corned Beef in so long, I'd forgotten about it."

The police academy's alphabetical order had McGuire preceding McPhee in everything from seating assignments to drills. Before the first day's training session ended, one of the instructors dubbed them Corned Beef and Cabbage.

McGuire, an African-American, had laughed louder than anyone. At the graduation after-party, the two Micks, as they were also known, contributed a keg of Guinness. Arms draped on each other's shoulders, they'd sung multiple choruses of "Too-A-Loo-Ra-Loo-Ral," because "Danny Boy" was cliché and the lyrics had actual words in them.

"Those were the days." Jack eyed McGuire's tight-fitting summer-weight suit. "So, what plainclothes unit are you with now? Last I heard, you were undercover drug enforcement."

"That was a long time ago, too." McGuire's features hardened, as though their history had gone the way of his uniform and Sam Browne belt. "Homicide. Four years, next month."

The sweat sticking Jack's shirt to his shoulder blades chilled around the edges. He motioned at the office door. "Come on inside. I'll buy you a cup of bad coffee."

"Another time. Right now, I'd appreciate you coming down to the station with me and answering some questions."

"Oh, yeah? In regard to what?"

"Your ex-wife." McGuire studied him a moment. "Don't tell me you weren't aware that somebody shot her yesterday."

"Belle's…?" Jack backed away, stammering, "N-no. Uh-uh. I don't know what the fuck you're trying to pull, but that's bullshit. Total bullshit."

"There's a stack of scene photos on my desk that says otherwise." McGuire asked if Jack was carrying a weapon, then patted him down to confirm he wasn't. "Now get in the car. Please."

Not a word was exchanged as the Crown Vic flowed with the traffic to Fifth, then toward Central Avenue. Jack stared out the passenger's-side glass without seeing the lines of parked cars, storefronts, alleyways or cross streets. Behind his eyes, a tall, willowy redhead pelted him with snowballs, slept on her stomach after they'd made love, glided down the aisle in a white lace gown. She screamed curses with a fist upraised, laughed, cried and jerked her clothes from dresser drawers and crammed them in suitcases. Later, outside the courtroom where the divorce was granted, she kissed him, then promised to always love him and be the friend she should have stayed.

Jack was vaguely aware of walking from the station's parking garage and the elevator ride to the fourth floor. Several quasifamiliar faces looked up from their desks in the homicide unit's bull pen.

McGuire halted at a door with a small, wire-embedded window. He motioned Jack inside a drab, windowless cubicle. "Take a seat, McPhee. I'll be with you in a minute."

Maybe it was hearing the door's automatic lock engage that parted Jack's mental fog. The flickering fluorescent glare of the ceiling lights. It couldn't have been Belle whispering, "Snap out of it, hon. Andy McGuire didn't bring you here to talk about the old days."

Belle was dead. She'd never collect the rain check on that drink Jack owed her. Why he thought of that, why thinking it felt like an elephant crushing his chest, was incomprehensible.

The song that went "I'd trade all my tomorrows for a single yesterday" had it backward. Yesterdays with Belle were his to keep. Tomorrows were luxuries he'd lost forever.

McGuire entered the room and closed the door behind him. He took the chair on the opposite side of a narrow rectangular table. "You're looking a tad green around the gills."

Jack bit back an anatomically impossible remark. He was there to answer questions and extrapolate from them as much information as he could.

The interview started with background information. How he'd met Belle, how long they were married, when they split up and why. Apart from the year of their divorce, Jack couldn't remember the date. *Amicable* understated their relationship since, but sufficed.

"You were the last person she spoke with yesterday," McGuire said. Receiving no reaction, he added, "Why'd you call her?"

"An insurance agency hired me to investigate some residential burglaries. Belle was acquainted with a few of the victims."

Why that satisfied McGuire was clarified by his next state-ment. "Her husband says you've never contacted her on a week-end before."

"Her husband is wrong." Jack nodded at one of the file folders McGuire had carried in. "If any of those are call records and they go back a while, you know I have."

"Not often."

"More than never."

"Maybe Mr. deHaven was mistaken because he wasn't at home when those prior contacts were made."

"Says Mr. deHaven." Jack crossed a leg at the knee. "Is 'contacts' his word or yours? I'm betting his."

"Were you aware Mrs. deHaven planned to meet her husband in Arkansas later in the day?"

"Yes." Gears began to turn in Jack's mind. "What time was her flight?"

McGuire hesitated, then grasped that Jack had affirmed knowledge of her mode of transportation. "Four twenty-six."

The way Belle drove, she'd have left home about three forty-five. Park City Memorial had tightened and complicated security, like every other airport in the country, but passengers soon learned the new, ninety-minute-preboarding rule meant pro-tracted dawdling in the coffee shop. It must surely be a coinci-dence that visitor parking fees now doubled after the first hour, too.

"The .38 Police Special registered to you," McGuire said. "Did you leave it in your other jacket this morning?"

"C'mon, Andy." Jack chuckled. "I'm a P.I., not Dog the Bounty Hunter. I don't pack heat 24/7."

McGuire allowed a half smile. Cops watched Duane "Dog" Chapman's reality show for comic relief. "Then where's the gun? We'll need it for a ballistics test."

"It's locked in the trunk of—" Jack reluctantly corrected himself. "It's in the glove box in my car. The weekend before last, I got bored and drove out to the practice range." Realizing how that sounded, he added, "I do, every couple of months or so."

"You get bored?"

"I target practice. If I ever do need to use it, I'd like to be able…." He cursed himself for running off at the mouth. "You want a ballistics comparison, get a search warrant."

"Oh, really. Well, that may be easier than you think, McPhee."

Two fingerprint-ident cards were removed from a file folder and laid side by side on the table. Placed above them was a photograph of an exterior door frame with a smudge circled in red. "Unless you can explain why your print was lifted off the deHavens' mudroom door."

Jack stared at the idents, then the photo. He didn't remember touching anything, apart from the side fence he'd climbed over and the burglar he'd tackled. And the gate latch, but that was with the heel of his hand.

Except fingerprints don't lie. Thank God, they weren't time-and-date stamped.

As though reading his mind, McGuire said, "The deHavens entertained frequently on the terrace. Barbecues, swim parties, cocktails, after-dinner drinks. Funny thing, though. Mr. deHaven was definite about you never making the guest list."

True, but an allegation wasn't a question. As things stood, it was Carleton deHaven's word against Jack's. The presumption that he and Belle were having an affair was obvious. Also a motive, if she supposedly reneged on leaving Carleton for an encore with Jack, and he'd shot her in a jealous rage.

It fit a wronged husband even neater. Jack said, "I'm surprised my ears haven't burned, much as you and deHaven have tossed around my name."

He looked up at the videocamera recording the interview. "Enough to make you wonder if ol' Carleton's setting me up." His eyes lowered to McGuire. "Where was he when Belle was shot?"

"I'm asking the questions."

"I loved Belle. A part of me always will. If her second husband is all but accusing me of murder, I have a right to know where the hell he was when she was killed."

McGuire gathered the idents and photo and returned them to the file. Another folder slid from the stack and was placed on top. "You don't have a right to jack shit, Jack. But instead of reading it in tomorrow's newspaper, I'll give you a break. DeHaven was in Little Rock, Arkansas. The P.D. there has sworn statements to that effect from a dozen or more people."

They both knew an airtight alibi was as suspicious, if not more so, than no alibi at all. "I guess there hasn't been time to review deHaven's financial records for any unusual cash withdrawals."

"Forget deHaven. Where were *you* yesterday?"

"I slept in. Alone, unfortunately. The call to Belle was one of many related to the job I mentioned earlier. I gave my dog a bath. Went to the mall awhile, met a friend there for a late lunch and chitchatted."

The receipt from the mall food vendor was in Jack's wallet. He didn't volunteer it. Too pat, for one thing. He also wanted photocopies of the original, lest it escape police custody.

"I went back to my apartment—alone. Went out later for a bite, ran into my dog's groomer, followed her to her house. She made coffee, we talked, then her mother fell ill. The mother's a heart patient and an ambulance was called. I stuck around about a half hour after the paramedics left, then drove home."

"I need the names and numbers of everyone you spoke with, by phone or in person."

"Am I being charged?"

"Remains to be seen."

"Then with all due respect, that's confidential." Jack held up a hand. "Why, is also confidential. If you have probable cause to obtain *my* phone records, fine. Otherwise, you're fishin'."

"Does obstructing justice mean anything to you? Withholding evidence relevant to a homicide investigation?"

A citizen might swallow his tonsils. A former cop turned private investigator knew the difference between an interview and an interrogation. McGuire had nearly nothing on Jack. Fingerprints *outside* the deHaven house and no date to go with them. The fatal gunshot was apparently fired from the same caliber weapon as Jack's, along with millions of other .38s, registered and not. Was his phone call to Belle the last she'd answered, much less made? Maybe. Maybe not. Even if it were, it meant zilch.

Yes, his alibi was sketchy. So what? It was Sunday. Normal people don't log their every move. P.I.s don't unless it's billable time.

Jack glanced at the folder moved to the top of the stack. He steeled himself for the big finale. McGuire mentioned it back at the office, after the bombshell he'd dropped to gauge Jack's reaction. A second shock treatment, if it came, he was ready for.

Or so he thought, until enlarged crime-scene prints were dealt out, like a game of gin rummy. Jack willed himself not to look away. To study them clinically. Commit the details to memory.

In the harsh glare of portable stand-lights, the deHavens' master bath resembled a rectangular igloo. The veined marble floors, wainscoting, shower surround and double-vanity counter were in stark contrast to the mahogany cabinetry and trim work.

To the right of the glass-enclosed shower, Belle lay crumpled in a nearly full Jacuzzi. Tendrils of her hair floated beneath her chin, having fallen from a messy upsweep anchored with a clip. Her right leg was crooked over the tub's outer rim, her heel and underside of her calf as bluish-purple as a deep bruise.

The water crested above her breasts, midway to her collarbone, her shoulders slanting downward, molded to the tub's inner curvature. Her head was slightly back, slightly turned, one eyelid hooded. A bullet had obliterated the other.

"Hard for me to look at," McGuire said, "and I wasn't married to her."

The slogan of a long-canceled game show was "It's not what you say, it's what you don't say." Corned Beef McGuire's law-enforcement experience had inured him to horror.

Jack's secret ambition to lead a homicide unit had withered at street-patrol level. He blinked to clear his vision. "No woman deserves to be seen like this. By anyone."

"Then how come you can't take your eyes off 'em?"

Because it's the only chance I'll have, Jack thought. And all I can do for her now is find out who did this.

He raised his head. "The tub. You shut off the jets?"

McGuire didn't respond. It was as good as a no.

"I didn't kill her, Andy." Jack stood. "And this interview's over."

"For now." McGuire moved to the door. "Next time I bring you down here, it'll be in the backseat of the car."

11

After he walked out on McGuire, Jack rode the elevator down a floor to use the washroom. He bent over the lavatory, teeth gritted, splashing water on his face. Both spigots ran liquid ice, as they had when he was a rookie and would have welcomed lukewarm and celebrated hot. Some things never changing wasn't always bad.

Two uniforms strolled in during the frigid baptism. They hardly glanced in Jack's direction, but curtailed their conversation. A civilian, they presumed. One cop checked his clip-on tie in a mirror; neither of them washed their hands before they left.

The washroom's paper-towel dispenser had been replaced with a blower and a roller-towel gizmo. Some joker had inked Caution: Biohazard on the grimy cloth. Yards of wadded toilet paper in the overflowing trash bin said Jack wasn't the first to improvise.

The Visine he squirted in each eye stung like a son of a bitch. A flashback to Belle's fatal wound was resected and shoved in Jack's mental vault.

His gratitude at the elevator car disgorging its occupants on arrival was as fleet as the descent to the second floor. While incoming passengers fanned into the remaining corners, Jack fixed his gaze on the broken indicator panel above the door. The last person to enter the car, an older gent, was left spatially adrift.

At the lobby level, Jack was poised to forgo the antiquated ladies-first drill. As the doors rolled open, his shoe stubbed the uneven brass threshold at the same instant Dina Wexler hoved into view.

Her face went sheet-white; somehow her whisper sounded like a shriek. "I didn't do it, McPhee. I swear to God, I didn't!"

"That's wonderful," he said, and tossed off a rictus smile at the elevator's other passengers. Spinning Dina around, he took her arm and escorted her toward the building's front entrance. Hustling her away from the police was quickly becoming a habit.

"Didn't do what?" he inquired under his breath.

"Kill your ex-wife," she murmured back.

"Good." Jack pushed open the vestibule's wide, bulletproof glass door. "That makes two of us."

His tone must have betrayed him. Dina flinched, then said, "I'm sorry, I— You still cared a lot about her, didn't you?"

"Yeah." Squinting against the sunlight, he steered her to the concrete retaining wall that abutted the steps down to sidewalk level. "So, what are you doing here?"

"I was about to ask you the same thing."

"I beat you to it. Start talking."

She took mild exception to Jack's tone. It wasn't as brusque as Andy McGuire's had been with him, but he was fresh out of friendly repartee.

"Well," she said, "I'm trying to keep from hurting more people than I already have."

"Excuse me?"

"The kennels don't deserve to be punished for what I did, but they will be if the newspaper finds out the Calendar Burglar's been arrested. Everybody in town will know how I chose which houses to break into."

Dina squared her shoulders. "Crime Stoppers tips aren't publicized. I've seen trials on TV where confidential informants hide behind screens and their voices are altered so nobody knows who they are. If I turn myself in and agree to plead guilty, there's no reason the police can't keep the details to themselves."

Jack surveyed her denim skirt, pinstriped blouse, linen blazer and pumps. She was right. Size did matter. In her Monday-go-to-confession clothes, she could be mistaken for the kid on Take Your Child to Work Day.

He couldn't think of anything Dina could wear to allay that living-doll image. Or deflect the verbal head-patting that undoubtedly went with it. Whether she realized it or not, the pet-door M.O. might be a rebellious "Up yours" to the literal larger world.

He scratched an imaginary itch at his earlobe. "That's a nice quid pro quo theory you have there. Allow me to point out a few problems with it."

"Go ahead, but you won't change my mind."

Don't bet on it, kid. "Cops make arrests. That's why you hear, 'The police arrested Donald Duck today on *suspicion* of indecent exposure.' The county prosecutor files the charges."

"Fine." She shrugged. "In fact, that's even better. It'll stay just between me, him and a judge, then."

"No, it won't. Richard '*V* for Victory' Vinyard has to beat a strong same-party contender in next month's primary and a former P.A.'s grandson in the general election. Vinyard's win-loss record in court has snowballed in the wrong direction. He'll call a friggin' press conference. Balloons, hot dogs, ice cream for the kiddies—the works."

Dina's mouth tucked at a corner. Taking it as encouragement, Jack continued, "Once the police are aware of the kennel connection, there's the little matter of Mrs. Carleton deHaven boarding her dog Phil at Merry Hills yesterday."

The color that had returned to Dina's face drained away again. "But I didn't know the woman who brought him in wasn't Mrs. deHaven. Nobody even knows I broke into that house, except you."

"Yep. And you're the only one who can put me there last night." Saying it did unpleasant things to Jack's nervous system. "I asked Cherise Taylor to impersonate Belle, but I didn't tell her why."

Dina stared past him. The tip of her tongue probed a canine tooth. "Okay. Promise not to tell the police about me, and I promise not to tell them about you."

"I already did." At her gasp, Jack added, "Indirectly."

A brief explanation of the interview with McGuire and his highly selective alibi ensued. "As heartless as this may sound, it's a good thing Belle's body was discovered after today's *Herald*'s news cycle. Otherwise somebody at Merry Hills might have recognized her name and already been on the horn to Lieutenant McGuire."

Dina's hand flew up and gripped her forehead. "Channel 8 did a special bulletin this morning. In front of the deHaven house. The reporter identified her as the victim."

"Shit," Jack said, having mentally bleeped the first profanities that came to mind. "I knew I should've picked up that stupid mutt, returned him to the shelter, *then* gone to the office."

On second thought, posing as Carleton deHaven at Merry Hills wouldn't have been exceptionally shrewd, either.

"The kennel is pretty busy on Mondays," Dina said. "All of

them are. If boarding customers don't come by six on Sunday, they have to wait until after two on Monday to pick up their dogs."

Which, Jack recalled, was why he hadn't fetched Phil. As if McGuire wouldn't have waited at the office for him, regardless. He checked his watch. "Maybe Cherise can take off— No, forget that. Accidentally implicating her before the fact is bad enough."

The heat and carbon-monoxide-flavored mugginess closed in and down on him. His heel eviscerated a cigarette butt flicked at a gravel-filled receptacle, then another, girdled with pink lipstick. "For all I know, somebody has already tipped McGuire and Merry Hills is under surveillance."

Dina asked in a low voice, "Could you tell if it was? I mean, would the police watch the kennel from the outside? Or put somebody inside, like he was a new employee?"

Jack chuckled in spite of himself. "I don't think Harriet's the only detective-show junkie at your house." Sobering, he said, "Good God, I should've asked way before now. Your mom is all right, isn't she? No aftereffects from last night?"

"Grouchy. A little woozy halfway through her laps in the hallway, but on her ten scale, I'd say she's about a seven." An upheld finger silenced him. "Cancel the guilt trip, McPhee. Mom had to be told where the money was coming from, eventually. She wouldn't have taken it as well from me.

"You saw how we are. Like a damn button-pushing competition. She's had more practice, but I'm younger and healthier." Dina made a face. "There's something to be proud of. Getting my licks in on a heart patient who needs help in the bathroom."

"Cancel *your* guilt trip, Wexler. It took about ten minutes to figure out that you two are a book-matched pair."

He moved aside for an approaching smoker to douse a cigarillo. Stress had him jonesing to bum a smoke. It always did and probably always would. If Dina hadn't been there, he might have given in.

Settling for a whiff of secondhand smoke, he said, "Which brings up another hitch in your confession theory. Where does Harriet fit into it?"

"I didn't intend to say anything today. I can cover the bills till the end of the month. Long enough for Randy to come home or to make, uh, other arrangements."

Dina glanced down at her outfit. "I'm pretending to be an intersession student. My thesis subject is a hypothetical, law-abiding citizen forced to steal to buy medicine for a chronically ill parent."

Those sad, dark eyes glittered with contempt. "It doesn't make it right, but I'm not the only one who ever has…who *is* doing it, or will, when working, begging and borrowing doesn't stop the merry-go-round. It just goes faster."

No, Jack thought, the situation wasn't unique to her and her mother. Those who take an actual bullet to save someone they love are heroes. Everyone believes they'd make that ultimate sacrifice, too. Jack would for his parents, his sisters, nieces, nephews…and yeah, for Belle, if the bastard who'd shot her had given him the chance.

But take a metaphorical bullet? And keep taking it for the exact same life-or-death reason, and you're a menace to society.

"You'll never pull off the Jane College bit," he said. "Not without a bag over your head. Try it, and any cop with half a brain will read you like *Guns & Ammo.*"

Dina jutted her jaw and plastered on a starlet smile. She hesitated a moment, then slumped. "I look guilty, huh?"

"Worse. You look honest and trying too hard not to look guilty."

"Then I'll practice for a day or two." An eyebrow crimped. "Unless you have a better idea for keeping the kennels out of this."

"Aw, for crissake. That's the least—"

"Since I have an idea for sneaking Phil out of Merry Hills without anybody knowing it."

Visions of a *Great Escape* remake with Dina playing Steve McQueen's role made Jack's head hurt. Then again, her legs were excellent, but too short to reach a motorcycle's pegs. "Let's have it," he said with no enthusiasm whatsoever.

"You give me cash to pay the boarding fee. I'll drop by to see if Phil's dermatitis has improved, then say he needs to be taken outside awhile. That isn't an old wives' tale. Some skin conditions do respond to brief exposure to natural light."

"What if Phil's already outside?"

"Doesn't matter." Her tone suggested the interruption was not appreciated. "I'll let him out the side gate, where you'll be waiting in your car. Back inside, I'll sneak the money into the cash drawer, mark the fee paid and take off."

Jack rested his hands on his hips. "Where *do* you come up with this stuff?" A better question was, how in the hell did she get away with burglary for so long? "If you go outside with Phil, or are outside with Phil, don't you think somebody'll wonder when you go back in *without* Phil?"

"Oh. Hmm. Well, I can wait around in the exercise yard, until the coast is clear. Then I'll…I'll move the dogs around in the pens. Yeah! That'll keep Phil from being missed for a while, and when the fee's marked paid, everyone will think his owner must have picked him up."

"His deceased owner," Jack reminded.

"Okay, but— Look, I trusted you to help me last night. Why can't you just trust me to help you?"

"You didn't trust me. You just didn't want to go to jail."

"I told you everything. I didn't have to. Once I was home, you couldn't have proved I was ever inside your ex-wife's house. Or anyone else's."

She had him there. And knew it. "Let me think about it while you give me a lift to the office to get my car."

They started down the steps, Dina coltish in dress shoes likely boxed in a closet for months, and loath to let them set the pace. "One condition," she said.

Why wasn't he surprised? "Hey, I can take a cab."

"Phil can't go back to the animal shelter."

"He has to." When Jack dragged himself home from the Wexlers, he absolutely had not wished Phil was there, wagging a welcome home. Or stuck a cold, dog-snotty nose in his face this morning and whined to go out. First thing, he'd washed the hair-clotted towels and given the blow-dryer to Ms. Pearl. No bonds to break, no regrets.

"My apartment is small," he said. "Phil is not. Plus, I have a feeling I won't be spending much time there in the immediate future."

"Pets are therapeutic. It's clinically proven they can alleviate stress, depression, hypertension…"

Jack looked at her. "You want him?"

Dina shook her head. "Temporary custody. Fifty bucks a week for his care and feeding, and a promise you'll keep him when I can't anymore."

"Deal," blurted a voice that sounded exactly like Jack's.

Dina saw the car first. She and Jack were in the crosswalk at midblock that led to the visitors' parking lot where she'd left the Beetle. She lagged behind a couple of steps, the tissues wadded in the toes of her shoes as hardened and rough as papier-mâché. Size-four-and-three-quarter pumps didn't exist; fives were nearly impossible to find. Seldom in her life had she worn shoes that weren't a half size too big.

Now skating along more so than walking, she glimpsed a blur streak from the parking lot's exit, turn wide and swerve into the southbound lane. Mouth agape in a silent scream, she slammed into Jack, pushing him forward with all her might.

The burn of skinned knees and the palms of both hands registered before Dina realized she'd fallen. As an added insult, her hobo bag swung up and clouted her in the head.

"Dina!" Jack hoisted her to feet and hugged her tight. "Jesus, darlin', are you okay? Are you hurt?"

Stepping back, he smoothed the hair from her face. He looked her over, as though expecting to see bones sticking out, or arterial bleeding.

"I'm fine." She tottered a little, feeling at once hollow and capable of wrenching up the redbud tree in the parkway and hurling it at…well, *something*.

"Are you sure?" At her wobbly nod, Jack wrapped an arm around her, smushing her against him. It felt pretty wonderful, except she'd really have liked to sit down on the curb a second.

He called across the street, "Hey, kid. Yeah, you. Did you see that car?"

A teenager in what appeared to be chainsawed sweatpants and a T-shirt pointed north. "He cranked a left at the corner. *Haulin'*."

Jack muttered, "No shit, Sherlock," then louder, "Gimme a make, a model."

"You mean like Ford, or sumthin'?" The teen waved dismissively. "I dunno, dude. It was like, you know, like dirty white, I think. Maybe tan."

Behind them, a reedy voice said, "It was a Chevrolet. No doubt about it."

Jack turned, taking Dina with him. The speaker was a well-dressed woman with lilac-tinted hair and the bearing of a retired elementary teacher. "The car was just like my granddaughter's, only hers is blue, and she takes far better care of it."

The woman clucked her tongue at Dina. "That was quite a tumble you took, miss. As crazy as people drive anymore, it's a miracle you weren't killed." She looked at Jack and flipped up her clip-on sunglasses. "In my day, a gentleman walked beside a lady to cross the street, not in front of her."

Dina suppressed a chuckle at his contrite "Yes, ma'am." She ducked from under his protective wing as he reverted to the woman's original comment. "Your granddaughter's car. Do you by chance know the model?"

An apologetic *no* prompted, "What about the driver? Male? Female?"

The woman pursed her lips and looked down the street. "It happened so fast… A man, I'd say, but I really can't be certain."

Jack asked for and received her name and phone, then gave her a business card. "Thanks, Mrs. Norton. If you think of anything else, please let me know."

Dina banked her curiosity until they were out of earshot. "The man in the white Chevy," she stated. "He was trying to run you down, wasn't he?"

Expression stony, refusing to meet her eyes, Jack replied, "What makes you think that?"

"Because he timed it, and he didn't hit his brakes, even going around the corner."

"Mighty observant for a dog groomer." Jack's scowl deepened, as though deciding whether to leave it there or continue. "Assuming it was a Cavalier, the driver's name is Brett Dean Blankenship. I turned him down for a job last week. Saying he doesn't take rejection well is like saying the ocean's wet."

He pulled the Bug's driver's-side door handle, grunted, then reached in the open window and pulled up the lock. "He's stalked me on and off ever since."

"Stalking? Ye gods, McPhee. How about hit-and-run?"

"Missed and ran," he corrected.

Dina stowed her hobo bag on the rear floorboard. She sat down gingerly, the blistering-hot upholstery upstaging her tender, stinging kneecaps. Jack had slid into the passenger's side and was collapsing the windshield's sunscreen, when she turned and said, "But you were in front of me in the crosswalk. Blankenship swung into the other lane, not into the curb."

The folded sunscreen skimmed over her head and flopped on the backseat. "And lucky for me, you throw a pretty mean tackle for a girl."

"You're welcome." Dina depressed the clutch and keyed the ignition. The VW fired up and shuddered in place and coughed exhaust the approximate shade of Mrs. Norton's hair.

Pulling out of the lot, her thoughts flittered like dust motes, a frightening few of them consigned to operating a motor vehicle. "Why did you ask everybody but me about the car and the guy driving it? It was a man, by the way. A big man."

"You were involved. An adrenaline dump sharpens, distorts and narrows perceptions. If you aimed a .22 peashooter at a convenience store clerk, he'd see Godzilla armed with an AK-47 with tiny nicks inside the barrel."

Thinking back, Dina allowed it was true. The car was light colored, but not necessarily white. The driver's silhouette filled the space above the dash and the roof. In the V-dub's passenger's seat, Jack almost fit that description and he wasn't a big man. And an impression of size automatically translated to male.

What Dina couldn't shake was the feeling she, not Jack, was the intended target.

"Left at the next corner," he said, pointing. "Then a right when you get to Danbury."

"Was Blankenship stalking you last night?"

"No."

"You're sure?"

Jack glanced at her, then looked away. "Positive."

Good, Dina thought. Because if he had and the guy was insane enough to try to hurt me, simply because I was with Jack, I'd wonder if he'd…

So did he. She could *feel* it. Equally strong was the sense Jack hadn't lied about last night.

"Left-turn lane," he directed. "See that strip mall? My office is next door to that diner at the end."

Nodding, she downshifted to slow for an oncoming truck and the turn, then wheeled onto the side street.

"Well, I'll be damned."

"What? This is where you meant, isn't it?"

"You made the light." It sounded like an accusation. "Blew right through it, slick as a friggin' whistle."

"It was green," she said. "That means go."

"So I hear. Just pull in beside my car—no, make it a space over, so I can open the door all the way."

Jack unlocked the office for her, where she could, as he said, powder her nose in the bathroom. Her mental picture of a real P.I.'s office wasn't clear, but McPhee might as well have been a tax preparer. A very neat tax preparer, who liked maps, but was too cheap to have them framed.

The sofa was almost as ugly as her mother's. Magazines on a side table were years old. The fake ivy and ferns looked wilted, but the air conditioning was set well under eighty.

A call home wakened Harriet from a chair nap, though she

strenuously denied it. "Where are you? The box thing on the phone said, 'Private number.'"

The corded desk phone was as quaint as the kitchen wall unit at home. Dina had given no thought to the box thing, otherwise known as Harriet's cordless model's caller-ID screen. Odd, that McPhee Investigations—or in digitalese, "MCPH INVSTIGNS"—wasn't programmed into a business phone's menu.

A cordless desk unit Dina hadn't noticed earlier was fed by a separate phone line. A third, detached phone cord inferred he could juggle more conversations than he had ears, as did a multiplug cell-phone charger.

Harriet muttered, "What'd she do, hang up on me?"

"I'm here, Mom. Will you be okay by yourself for a little while longer? An hour, probably less?"

"Well, of course, I will. Stop fussing over—"

"Do I need to pick up anything on my way home? Library books, more juice…"

"Oh, for pity's sake." The line clicked and went dead. Dina interpreted it as a "No, thank you, sweetheart, but it's so thoughtful of you to ask."

The office's half bath smelled of cleanser and Jack's aftershave. The commode's lid was down. The spindled roll of toilet paper dispensed from the front, not the back. A wrapped, spare roll was on the tank.

The sink's chrome fixtures were apparently spot proof, and the liquid soap dispenser, drip proof. A motel-style rack held a box of tissues, stacks of trifolded hand towels and facecloths.

Mr. Clean's wastebasket was empty. Dina took out the plastic liner and flipped over the container on its top. The metal base made a *plinkety-pop* sound under her weight, but the medicine chest's mirror was now visible. And snoopable.

And boring, apart from a box of condoms. Two hermetically

sealed tampons, a razor, shaving cream, deodorant, toothbrush and paste, mouthwash, comb, a travel bottle of shampoo and first-aid items said Jack was equipped for most emergencies and not prone to floss during office hours.

After Dina washed her face and knees, and fingerbrushed her teeth, she found Jack rifling a wide metal storage cabinet. Several of the desk's previously locked drawers were hanging open.

Her "What are you looking for?" was answered with a curt, "Let's go."

With the cabinet, desk, then front door secured, he stalked to the Taurus and opened the trunk. A camera's long lens was replaced with a stubby one. The trunk's lid, inside and out, was photographed. Moving to the front passenger's-side door, Jack clicked off two shots of the window, adjusted the lens and snapped several more.

"Care to let me in on what you're doing?"

Elbow now propped on the seat, he said, "Not from clear over there." When Dina stepped closer, he informed her that his gun was missing.

The lens whirred forward and backward as the glove compartment was photographed inside and out. "The supply cabinet, a desk drawer—I've put it in both a few times. Just not lately. Normally, it's in the trunk."

With a pen, Jack indicated the glove compartment lock's misshapen keyhole. "That, I should have noticed sooner." Of a slit in the passenger window's weather stripping, fine scratches and chips at the top the glass and scuffs on the window ledge, he said, "As for those? Well, I don't ride shotgun in my own damn car."

The Beetle was a one-driver vehicle, too. On occasion, she loaded a bulky or fragile thing in the passenger's seat or floorboard, but usually hoisted them over from the driver's side.

"Your car doesn't have an alarm?" she asked.

"Who pays attention to them, other than getting pissed when they go off? Not real helpful for surveillance, either. A stray cat pussyfoots across the hood and whoop-whoop, I'm the center of attention."

"Can you tell when the gun was stolen?"

Jack shook his head. "No way to determine if the slim-jimmed window is related to the punched glove box. Or the scratched trunk lock, either."

"Common sense says they are."

"Common sense isn't proof." He returned the camera equipment to the trunk. "What I do know is that my .38 was in the glove box a week ago Sunday."

The trunk lid slammed so hard, Dina jumped. "And if McGuire obtains a search warrant, telling him I didn't discover it'd been stolen until an hour after he questioned me about Belle's murder, will make him laugh."

"How many people knew where you usually keep it?"

"It's a pretty easy guess for anyone who knows how I make my living."

Dina did, but hadn't given a gun a thought. Much less, where he'd keep it. "Anyone," she said, "such as that Blankenship guy?"

No answer.

"Okay, then. What are we going to do?"

"We?" He snickered. "Stick with me, kid. I'll get you twenty-five to life on an accessory-to-homicide rap."

"I'm serious."

"You think I'm *not?*"

"Sure you are," she said. "But if I'd never burglarized anyone, the insurance company wouldn't have hired you, you wouldn't have boarded Phil in Mrs. deHaven's name, wouldn't have been at her house last night and couldn't have left your fingerprint on the back door, so it's all my fault you're a suspect in her murder."

She sucked in a deep breath. "That's why it's *we*."

Jack just stood there, slack jawed, as if someone had slim-jimmed his brain and absconded with it. Presently, he said, "I can't decide which one terrifies me the most. When something you say is a couple of quarts low on logic, or when it kind of isn't."

12

Jack was trudging up the steps to his apartment when his cell phone rang. If it's Cherise, again, he thought, extricating the cell from his jeans pocket, it's going to voice mail.

He wasn't being ungrateful or mean. There were just so many times you can reassure someone and so many ways to promise not to involve her, before it became white noise.

Dina's name and number flashed on the ID screen. He'd tweaked her original plot to smuggle Phil out of Merry Hills. It put the onus entirely on her, but she had a legitimate excuse to be at the kennel. Jack didn't.

Now either all was well, or shot to hell. "McPhee," he said, and braced for the latter.

The worst-ever Desi Arnez impersonator replied, "Honey, we're home."

He blew out a breath. "No problems?"

"Oh, I'm good," Dina said. "I am *golden.*"

Jack grinned at the smugness in her voice. He leaned against the exterior wall, grateful the breezeway lived up somewhat to its purpose. "Convince me."

"Would you believe, nobody was in the front office or in the kennels when I went in? Kind of disappointing, actually. I had my lines down cold, but it was cake getting Phil out of his pen and into the reception area."

"How's his dermatitis?"

"Much improved, thanks to me." A pause, then, "I paid the fee, checkmarked the register, then I realized that wasn't enough. Not with Mrs. deHaven's name still there for anyone to see."

Jack's back stuttered down the siding, and he sat down hard on the step. Impending doom tended to have a weakening effect on his knees.

Dina went on, "I licked my finger and tried to smudge the ink. All that did was leave a dirty streak on the paper. I was about to tear out the whole page, when I saw this open can of soda on the counter. I figured if it ate through the gunky stuff on my battery cables, it was worth a shot."

Cola dissolves rust off bumpers, cuts through windshield grime and cleans toilets, too, but Jack kept his "Heloise Hints" fandom to himself. Tough guys don't read her column or "Dear Abby."

"I splashed soda all over the page, like it spilled. Everything it touched smeared a little. In one *particular* spot, a dab here and a rub there pretty much wiped you-know-who off the map. So to speak."

"You *are* golden." Jack shook his head, convinced that whatever guardian angels watched over Dina the Calendar Burglar had smiled on Dina the Phil-napper, as well. "Couldn't have done better myself."

"Ah," she said, "but would you have taken Phil's file out of the wall rack, too?"

Yes, he would have, if given the opportunity, but why burst her happy bubble?

Dina went on to say she'd worked similar sleights of hand on the registration books and files at Home Away and TLC. "Now there's nothing to connect you to any of the kennels."

She paused, her hopeful grin nearly audible. "Gwendolyn at TLC might remember you and Fido, but the police would have to know about your whatchacallit—sting operation—to ask. Right?"

Probably. Jack tried not to think about the law of amateur plumbing repairs: plug a visible leak in a pipe and a new, doubly damaging one is likely to spring in a less accessible place, like behind a solid brick wall.

If McGuire did find out about the loaners and Phil and followed up at the kennels, those vanishing files and vandalized log books would smell worse than Phil's morning breath.

Share that concern with Dina, and his little helper might spring new and scarier ideas to fix them, too. Switching the subject, Jack said, "Our temporary-change-of-address plan. Is Harriet okay with me moving in for a few days?"

She was napping when Jack followed Dina home and parked the Taurus, loaded with essential office files and equipment, in the Wexlers' garage. He'd declined Dina's offer to take him to his apartment and called a cab instead.

"Are you kidding?" Dina laughed. "Mom's thrilled to be harboring a fugitive. And his dog."

"I'm not a fugitive." Jack glanced down at a tenant unlocking her ground-floor apartment and lowered his voice. "Like I told you, the harder it is for McGuire to execute a search warrant on my car, the longer I can stall trying to explain what happened to my .38."

The delaying tactic included Gerry Abramson. Ignoring the insurance broker's increasingly hostile messages demanding a progress report was a lousy way to treat a client, but better than lying to him. Abramson didn't know that the Calendar Burglar had taken an early and permanent retirement.

In a perfect world, Jack could confide to Gerry why he

couldn't turn over Dina to the police without implicating them both in a homicide investigation. If the world were anywhere near perfect, a bullet to the brain wouldn't have taken Belle McPhee deHaven from it.

Dina said, "It's me who isn't convinced that your Plan B isn't charity."

"My soon-to-be former landlord calls it rent." Who wouldn't be happy with Jack for hereby opting out of his month-to-month tenancy. "Nothing's in stone yet, kid. We'll talk about it some more when I get there. Then if you or Harriet isn't comfortable with me moving in, I'll check into a motel."

"Phil stays, though. Okay?"

"Whatever." Jack snorted and pressed the end button. Being at least a rung below an ugly mutt with a skin rash on the preferred-roommate list did wonders for a guy's self-esteem.

As he entered his apartment, Sweetie Pie Snug 'Ems yipped and twirled, as though Jack hadn't already made a half-dozen trips to the parking lot and back. Ms. Pearl looked up from the videocassettes and DVDs surrounding her on the floor. Brows knitted in despair, she said, "Are you sure you don't want any of these?"

She'd asked the same question of the CDs, books, linens, a couple of lamps and the weather-band radio he'd carted over to her apartment.

"To tell you the truth, I don't know why I bought most of them."

Her gaze traveled around the room decorated in basic Motel 6, sans the ramshackle-barn-in-a-field-of-wildflowers artwork. "I feel like a home wrecker."

"No reason to. This is where I live. It never was home." Deciding that sounded a skosh shy of pitiful, he said, "Hey, I'm a guy. Four walls, a roof, indoor plumbing, TV, remote, a six-pack, a fifth and a recliner, and I'm happy. Everything else is just…stuff."

"Yes, but—" She sighed. "I suppose I'm too sentimental about things. And people." She patted a classic Hitchcock DVD. "I don't even know you that well, but I'll think of you when I watch this."

Jack knelt and scratched the Maltese behind an ear. "Did you see the small camelback trunk I hauled out of here?"

She nodded. "A lovely piece. Though a good coat of beeswax and a buffing would bring out the grain."

Rather than debate the merits of linseed oil versus wax, he said, "My grandfather made it. A poor man's wedding present for his bride. Grandma gave it to my mother when she married Dad. Neither of my sisters wanted it when they got married, so it was passed on to me."

Ms. Pearl smiled, evidently relieved he attached value to something, other than the minimum bachelor requirements.

"It's like this, ma'am. I'm pretty sure if, God forbid, this building caught fire, or a tornado was bearing down and you had time to save only one thing, it'd be Sweetie Pie."

"Well, I should say so." Kissy noises beckoned the Maltese. She hugged the dog to her bosom. "It scares me just thinking about it. The family Bible, photographs, china, the silver tea set—oh, my heart would absolutely break if I lost them."

"Except how many times have you seen newspaper photos, or footage of people whose homes have been destroyed, and they're clutching something they could replace at Wal-Mart for twenty bucks?"

Ms. Pearl frowned at the carpet a moment, then beamed at Jack. "Of course. Your grandfather's trunk. That's your Sweetie Pie, isn't it?"

It was the analogy he was going for, but in a manner of

speaking, for crissake. "It and what's inside are worth saving. All I could save, if I had to make a run for it." Jack's arm swept the room. "Everything else is just stuff."

By her expression, she understood and maybe agreed in some respects. Neither was the same as approval. "To someone with one heirloom to his name, yes. I suppose it is."

Chuckling, he went into the kitchen to fill a carton with canned goods and perishables. There wasn't much to begin with and less worth salvaging. Two iron skillets and a lidded wok were crammed in on top.

The Maltese shadowed Jack's final inspection for anything he might have overlooked. Moving hadn't been on this week's to-do list, but shit happens and you deal with it. With Phil in the picture, he'd have had to find another place with a fenced yard, anyway. The right one at the right price and he might break his cardinal rule about separation of work space from living space.

That or install a shower at the office, and teach Phil how to use the toilet.

The apartment key was unhooked from the ring and given to Ms. Pearl. "You're sure you don't mind handling an indoor garage sale?"

"It was my idea," she reminded. "Paying someone to haul your castoffs to the dump is a waste of money and plain old wasteful. I know for a fact Renee Hunt in Building B will want your dinette set. I'll take bids on the washer and dryer. Any number of tenants spend their Sundays at the laundromat."

The pair, used, had cost Jack a hundred dollars—not including spinal adjustments after dollying the heavy sons of bitches up a flight of stairs. He'd pay two hundred to avoid wrestling them down again.

He left Ms. Pearl believing whatever stuff she took was a fair exchange for womanning the sale, disposing of any leftovers and tidying his apartment. He'd deposit the check she'd mail to his office for the garage-sale proceeds, then write one to the landlord for her full month's rent.

"There's more than one way to skin a cat." The skillets clanked like cowbells as Jack slid the kitchen box alongside the camelback trunk. "Isn't that right, Gramps?"

The S-10 pickup with the lockable, steel-reinforced bedcover was demoted to secondary status when Jack bought the Taurus. The sedan was roomier, more comfortable and less conspicuous for stationary surveillance, but the truck had and still did serve a purpose. Among them, alternating vehicles made it more difficult to spot a tail, and in some venues, a pickup fit in, where a midsize sedan stood out like a vegetarian at a pig roast.

It was also registered to the agency as a commercial vehicle.

The distinction might not fly under Andy McGuire's radar. Then again, it just might. For a day or two, anyway.

Dina finished wiping down the spattered stove top.

Jack had insisted on cooking dinner, which was delicious, though its preparation had involved virtually every available pan and utensil, and the aftermath resembled a smallish food fight.

Earlier, he'd lugged in boxes of food, as well as cleaning and laundry supplies from his apartment. He'd also bought a giant sack of dog food, more groceries than the fridge and cabinets could hold and, to Harriet's delight, every cheeseball supermarket tabloid, plus the latest *People* magazine.

Office equipment and supplies were piled neatly in the corner of the dining room and table's far end. His clothes were hung on the overhead door tracks in the garage, and toiletries contained in a kit in the bathroom. At some point, he'd oiled the squeak out of Harriet's glider, even though it had been an early-warning system Dina had relied on for months.

Why, *no,* the perfect roommate didn't mind sleeping on the living-room floor with Phil. He wouldn't dream of uprooting Dina from the couch, since the second bedroom was a mishmash of Harriet's treasures, Randy's crap and Dina's few remaining worldly possessions.

Now Jack was laughing along with Harriet at a *Designing Women* rerun, just as he had the *Golden Girls* rerun preceding it. No doubt, *Kate & Allie* would soon have them both in stitches.

"What a great guy," Dina snarled under her breath. Mom had probably penciled his name in her will by now. The supposed rent, partial utilities and part-time assistant's wages he'd paid Dina almost filled the doughnut hole in Harriet's prescription coverage. And then some.

Jeepers, if it wasn't for the notes and that taped confession he'd hidden somewhere, life would be good—freakin' marvelous— until he got around to surrendering them and Dina to the police.

She flung the dishcloth at the sink, and stepped down off the wooden stool. "C'mon, Phil. You need to go out."

The mutt lying on the linoleum didn't seem to share that opinion. Squatting down, she lifted a mud-flap ear. "If it wasn't for me, you'd be at the pound scratching yourself bald. Now up and at 'em."

Phil scrambled up, as though her tone had triggered a major bladder spasm. Dina stalked past the TV and batted aside the drapes Jack had closed, along with the rest of the curtains. Had Harriet objected? Do donkeys fly?

She rolled the balky patio door shut behind her, and dragged an aluminum lawn chair to the farthest reaches of the pitted concrete slab. Heaven probably wasn't humid, rife with mosquitoes, gnats and hard-shelled brown bugs that clung to the screens like winged leeches. The patio was just the nearest thing to it, in a six-hundred-square-foot duplex whose population had doubled. And both new occupants were male.

Crickets tuned up in the mulberry tree. The moon hadn't yet crested the rooftops, and city lights washed out the stars. The air smelled like an Almighty steam iron pressing wrinkles from the yard. Phil's tags jingled as he whuffled along the perimeter of the warped board fence, having forgotten what his new world smelled like in less than an hour.

Cars passed on Spring Street, casting out brief musical interludes, snatches of conversation, laughter, beer cans and fast-food sacks. Ah, yes. Another enchanted evening in the 'hood.

A swath of light poured over the patio. Dina gritted her teeth, expecting her mother to inquire, "Is anything wrong?" then chide her for being unsociable.

The heavy glass door rumbled open and shut in its tracks. Jack said, "We need to talk."

Dina exhaled, amused to hear a man speak that immortal phrase. "I'll be in in a minute."

"Privately."

"Good luck with that. Fame is supposed to last fifteen minutes. Out here, privacy is barely fifteen seconds."

He moved to stand beside her chair. They'd both changed into shorts and flip-flops. The hairy thigh looming in Dina's peripheral vision was muscular, but Jack spent about as much time sunbathing as she did.

He said, "I'm not the least bit interested in jumping your bones."

"Really." She looked up, pretty much at the bent elbow crossed over the other arm at his chest. "Gosh, the better we get to know each other, the more we have in common."

"If circumstances were different, we'd be on our third date by now. But just in case that's what's bothered you since I got here, I don't have to blackmail women into sleeping with me."

Oddly, it took a moment for Dina to frame a response. His third-date supposition was ignorable. Yes, the possibility he'd use that audiotape as sexual extortion had occurred to her. So had driving him so wild with desire, he'd give her anything she wanted, including an orgasm, provided her critical components were still operational. Envisioning herself as Mata Hari was as hilarious as Jack morphing into the villain in a porno flick.

"Good to know," she said. "Not that I ruined my manicure worrying about it."

"I wouldn't blame you if you had, as fast as I moved in."

"I invited you."

"You invited Phil. I wasn't part of the original package." Jack shifted his weight. "Hard to believe what's happened in less than twenty-four hours. Or that you'd volunteer to help me disappear for a while."

It was also surprising the dog responded to the name given him almost as recently. Phil lumbered onto the patio and sprawled out as though his skeletal system had liquefied.

Dina gained her feet and looked Jack in the eye. "Your living here isn't a trade-off, either. I'm guilty. It's making me a little crazy not knowing when I'll say that to a judge, how long the sentence will be and that Mom—" She shook her head. "Can't go there at all."

Jack reached out to take her arm. She sidestepped away. "You haven't done anything wrong," she said. "Much less killed your ex-wife."

"Trespassing on private property, abetting flight to avoid prosecution, obstructing justice—"

"Hey, I'm on your side, okay? The point is, I'm not helping you out of a lot bigger jam than I got myself into, hoping you'll let me off the hook."

A corner of his mouth quirked into a half smile. "You're sure about that?"

A valid question, one he had an exclusive right to ask.

Dina hesitated, struck by the wonder of consistent honesty with someone else and with herself. Innumerable, well-meant white lies to preserve her one-sided marriage had become as unconscious as blinking. The habit made it easy, even natural to tell Harriet, "Yes, you're getting better every day," and presenting unpostmarked greeting cards with a "See, I told you Randy wouldn't forget your birthday." Or Mother's Day. Or Christmas.

But leveling with a private investigator in baggy-ass shorts and a ragged Budweiser T-shirt? For possibly the first time in her life, there were no illusions to uphold or manufacture.

"This afternoon, when you said you had to ditch your apartment and temporarily abandon the office, offering to let you stay here was pure, unadulterated Good Samaritanship." Dina's shoulder hitched. "It wasn't until after I'd sprung Phil from Merry Hills that I thought competing with him for your new best friend might help you forget where you hid that tape and your notes."

Jack laughed. "Looked for them, huh?"

"Not yet."

"Well, I'll save you the effort. They aren't here. And I duplicate everything—notes, photos, reports...."

"Taking your money," Dina went on, "thinking you might give me a break I don't deserve was worse than suddenly backing out on a place for you to stay."

Through a slit in the drapes, Harriet was angling a tabloid inches away from the drugstore magnifying glasses she seldom wore even in front of her daughter. Her mother's vanity was outward. Dina's was directed inward.

"I don't want your money," she said, "but it's a godsend. I like having you around, but damned if I know why, and it bugs the crap outa me. And yeah, I want to help you, but not to score brownie points with you, or God, or anybody else. I'm doing it for Belle. A woman I'd have envied—have *resented*—if I'd passed her on the street, because her shoes cost more than my rent."

Jack nodded, then stared down at the concrete, as though translating a rune etched in the chips and cracks. Now it was Dina's hand rising to comfort him, then lowering, before he deflected it, as she had. Reining in emotions was tough enough without compassion butting in.

"Okay." He cleared his throat and looked up at her. "Sounds like we're square."

"Yep."

Stretching a T-shirt sleeve to dab the sweat off his forehead, he said, "Mind a couple of questions, before we go in where it isn't cooler?"

She laughed. "I saw you set the thermostat back a couple of notches. You're on your own if Mom catches you."

"She did. It's back to friggin' eighty-two in there." A resigned sigh, then, "Last night at Belle's, did you see any lights on anywhere? Not lamps or fixtures, necessarily. A clock on the stove, or the microwave. The security system's control panel, a cordless phone dock. Anything electrical."

Dina thought back. "I can't say for sure, but I don't think so. The house was so dark, I didn't click on the penlight, for fear somebody would see it from outside."

He cocked his head. "But you must have. Unless it *was* reflected lightning I saw through the window wall."

A toe traced a crack in the concrete. She *umm*ed, then said. "Well, the penlight kind of turned itself on for a second after I dropped it."

"Uh-*huh*. Slick."

"Up yours, McPhee. I was scared—totally creeped out, if you want the truth. Why I didn't faint when those security lights came on, I don't know."

"Hey, I panicked a little around the edges myself, out on the terrace. I guess which of us set off the motion detectors is a toss-up."

"But…if you were on the terrace and I was inside, does that mean the other detectors I saw were fakes? Or broken, like the one over the mudroom door?"

"Neither. I'm almost sure, not all of them were equipped with battery backups. If they were, some of them lost juice faster than others."

Jack paused a moment. "This morning, Andy McGuire flashed crime-scene photos at me, taken with portable lights. Belle was in the Jacuzzi in the master bathroom. The jets were off. By my count, the bathroom had eighteen recessed fixtures. Half as many regular fixtures. A fancy chandelier over the tub. All of them *off*."

His lips flattened. "Altogether, how's that add up to you?"

Still reeling from the horror and pain those pictures must have caused him, Dina stammered, "The killer. He shut off the electricity." The answer fostered a "But why?"

Jack's voice was harsh, raspy. "To fuck with the time of death. Like a medical examiner's determination is ever as definite and precise as it is on TV shows."

Dina waved away a belated apology for his language. Murdering a woman in her bathtub was an obscenity in itself.

"When the jets were on," he continued, "the water temperature was between 98 and 104 degrees. Federal law won't allow thermostats to go higher than that. As a general rule, a dead body cools about a degree and a half per hour. That's one way an M.E.

determines time of death. How or if partial submersion and a gradually decreasing water temp affected that, I don't know. It's a safe guess, the killer thought it would."

"And that mattered because…"

"Again, it's speculation, but unless the shooter was just getting his jollies, there's only one logical reason."

Jack moved to the patio door. "Now let's go boot up the laptop, plug in your phone line and see if we can find some more."

Loath to admit that quintessential reason escaped her, Dina said, "You want to prove yourself wrong?"

"Sure, if I can." He chuckled. "If I don't, I'll know I'm right."

13

Jack closed his notebook and rose from the wrought-iron settee. "Thank you for your time, ma'am."

"My pleasure, Mr. McBee. Do ring me if you have any more questions."

Two can play the name game, lady, he thought. "I'd do that, Mrs. Porter."

A visual standoff ensued. Laura Proctor blinked first. Excellent. Now they understood each other.

She escorted him through the museum she called home. Jack had upgraded his Armani suit with a Kohl's dress shirt and tie, but sensed his hostess showed him to the door more from fear he'd pocket a Renaissance French what's-it, than etiquette.

Naturally, it was all he could do to not boost one of Catherine de Médicis's *authenticated* crystal doodads while Mrs. Proctor's back was turned. Wherever Belle was, she'd laugh herself loopy when Ms. Pearl sold the bauble for a quarter at his former apartment's garage sale.

Jack drove off realizing how lonely Belle must have been. The few neighbors he'd talked to were oblivious. Everyone pulled into the garage attached to a hermitic haven, paying scant, if any attention to the world outside the windows. That's what home was. A refuge.

For Laura Proctor, like Belle's other so-called friends, speaking ill of the dead was akin to a lemon slice drenched in honey: the sticky sweetness hadn't masked the puckery aftertaste. All seven women he'd interviewed that morning were reduced to tears carefully dabbed from their eye corners, while damning *dear, dear Belle* with the faintest of praise.

Each of them all but called her a low-class, ignorant gold digger. At the core of every humorous anecdote was an insult; each complimentary noun implied its antonym.

Carleton adored Belle, they meowed, as if he were hardly the first wealthy man besotted by a busty, flame-haired vixen. The allusions to Pygmalion transforming a gutter wench into a princess were unanimous. So were insinuations that once a wench, always a wench regardless of how skilled and patient the mentor, or how eager to please the student.

Last night, while Phil and Dina respectively whimpered and muttered in their sleep, Jack sifted remembered conversations with Belle for her female so-called friends' names. Why they'd rated mention, he couldn't recollect, but had a feeling Belle had ripped them up, down, sideways and repeatedly.

Lord, how she'd detested phonies, liars and snobs. He cuffed the pickup's steering wheel. "Except for Golden Boy."

The sobriquet attached to Carleton deHaven was coined five years prior when his bubble ascended on the get-rich-easy lecture circuit. Jack's and Dina's Internet surfing yielded increasingly awestruck references to deHaven's charisma, brilliance and groundbreaking financial philosophies.

From Jack's biased perspective, what he read seemed like a resurrection of Dale Carnegie's and others' positive-thinking strategies. For certain, deHaven's income derived from overpriced seminar and private consulting fees, and self-published how-to manuals, audiobooks and DVDs.

When Dina discovered that Golden Boy was also a hybrid tomato, a British bus line, a brand of fish sauce and a popular Frisco pizzeria, they'd laughed so hard, Harriet pelted them with sugarless candy.

Jack grinned and shook his head. The old girl was frail and in more pain than she let on, but had a pretty fair arm on her. And uncommon pragmatism, as he realized during the evening's umpteenth episode of carping at her daughter for neglecting her.

While she catered to Harriet's current whim, Jack had sat down on the ottoman. Quietly, he told her that Dina wouldn't grieve any less someday, no matter how much Harriet pushed her away, criticized her and hung haloes on Randy.

"I like you, McPhee," Harriet said with a benevolent smile. "Here's a piece of advice you might oughta think about before you start giving it." Her eyes narrowed. "Any fool with a shovel can dig himself a well. But nobody on God's green earth ever fell *out* of one."

Jack was imagining Belle's back-stabbing faux friends at the bottom of a very deep hole when a siren burped behind him. His eyes zipped to the S-10's side mirror, the revolving light bar reflected in it, then the speedometer. Reflex had eased up the accelerator. He was still nine miles over the speed limit.

Flicking on the turn signal, he pulled into a restaurant's front lot and rolled down the window. The patrolman who unfolded from the cruiser was a hoss: six-five, two-fifty and shaved as bald as a T-rex egg. The cop's jiggling holster strap might be carelessness, or overcautiousness. Good citizen Jack held the steering wheel at the prescribed ten- and two-o'clock positions.

"Morning, Offi—"

"May I see your driver's license, sir?"

"Wallet's in my inside pocket." Jack slowly opened his jacket wide with his left hand. Two fingers of his right tweezed out his billfold. The ID was slipped from its plastic sleeve.

Eyes twice older than the face they belonged to looked from Jack to the postage-stamp DMV photo. "You're Jack Limon McPhee?"

Affirmation brought a brusque "Step out of the vehicle, sir. Keep your hands where I can see 'em."

The ripple in Jack's belly said this wasn't a routine traffic stop. Arms aloft, he stepped onto the asphalt, asking the same question cops heard a dozen times a shift. "What's this about, Officer?"

It received the standard "Face the vehicle, hands on the bed, legs apart."

A smart chuck to the side of Jack's foot splayed them an extra, intimidating few inches. No, he didn't have a weapon. No contraband or anything on his person that might cause injury during a search. The wallet, sans ID, was shoved in his jacket pocket.

The pat-down drew stares from passing cars. A couple arriving for an early lunch gawked, as though trying to pick Jack out of last week's *America's Most Wanted* lineup.

"Okay. Bring one hand down behind your back."

Jack craned to squint over his shoulder. "I know the drill. I used to be a cop. I'm not resisting. I just want to know what I'm being arrested for."

A cuff snapped and ratcheted down on his wrist bone like dull-bladed pliers. "Probable cause, suspicion of homicide." The patrolman helped himself to Jack's other arm, wrenching it backward with practiced efficiency.

He winced at the cuff's metallic bite. The *Miranda* recitation sounded as atonal and distant as an echo. His Fourth Amendment rights, Jack understood. McGuire's probable cause for an arrest warrant was guessable and scared the hell out of him. Fear morphed into inane rage at the towing bill and impound fees he'd have to pay on the S-10.

For the second time in as many days, he was passengering a P.D. unit. As McGuire predicted, it was sideward in the backseat, cuffed and caged behind a thick sheet of Plexiglas. Sweat poured off him like oily brine. The odor mingled with the stench of dried puke, blood and urine.

An absurd remorse for a fine suit's ruination sent a laugh skittering up Jack's throat. The patrolman—S. Engels, by the nameplate above his pocket—glanced at the loon he was transporting.

Not even close to crazy, Jack telegraphed. The suit, the least of his current worries, was resolvable with lighter fluid and a match. When the world goes to shit, it's those abstract mental baby steps that keep you sane.

He and S. Engels parted company in the prisoner-intake area. Hoss had reports to write. Jack smiled for the mug shot. His prints were on file, but retaken because redundancy is the soul of a bureaucracy. The contents of his pockets were inventoried, bagged and sent upstairs. The cell phones' logged calls and their address books would be of particular interest to Lt. Andy McGuire.

An enthralling millennia was spent in a wire holding cell with a detoxing meth head, two jive-talking wanna-be gangstas and a rabbitlike older man who'd confess to anything for a get-out-of-jail-free card. Jack was then taken upstairs to a different, but identical interrogation room in the homicide unit.

The waiting game had walloped his sinuses and cleared his head. To the videocamera, he said, "C'mon, McGuire. Let's party. We both know I'm not gonna break down and cry for my momma."

The investigator let him stew a few minutes. McGuire strolled in with the air of an executioner with a brand-spanking-new rope. A cardboard file box was set on the floor between his chair and the wall, then he magnanimously unlocked the cuffs. "Better?"

"Peachy." Jack settled back in the chair, stifling an urge to rub his sore wrists. Behind his crossed arms, he flexed the circulation back in his fingers. "So, where'd the no-name tipster tell you to find my .38? In the Dumpster at the office? Conveniently located under a bush near the crime scene?"

"Smart-ass'll get you nowhere." The bagged and tagged weapon in question thunked on the table. "Ballistics matched the bullet recovered at autopsy."

Jack forced his mind and memory off the subject of that postmortem. "No prints other than mine, anywhere on the gun."

"Not a one." McGuire's expression fell short of victorious. "From the look of your office and apartment, I figured you were waiting your turn at a border crossing by now."

Jack couldn't stanch the pallor slithering downward from his hairline. "I told you Monday, the .38 was in the glove box in my Taurus. First thing after I left here, I checked." He shook his head. "Right then, I knew it was the murder weapon."

"Why didn't you call me and report it stolen?"

"Is that a rhetorical question?"

McGuire's grunt allowed that it was. Had Jack known the .38 was missing a week before Belle was killed, the muzzle would still point at him now. "Where did you find it?"

"Where you left it." A reproachful head shake. "A dresser drawer in your bedroom. Second from the top."

Under the pile of orphan socks Ms. Pearl wanted for miniblind dusters, Jack presumed. Had he not bailed from the apartment, the Dumpster or shrubbery scenario would have been substituted.

The search warrants led to the gun's discovery, rather than

the reverse. Except one fingerprint at the scene and a relationship to the victim don't constitute probable cause.

"Somebody's doing a sweet job of framing me for murder." He gave McGuire a tight smile. "What prompted the warrants?"

The deliberation extended several seconds. McGuire's answer might cue whether he believed the Easter Bunny left registered murder weapons in sock drawers for good little detectives. "A witness put your Ford at the deHaven house at about ten-thirty Sunday night. The individual was jogging, saw the residence was dark and memorized your plate."

Wouldn't ya know, Jack sneered to himself. I must have zoned out from boredom about the time Marathon Man laced up his cross-trainers for a nice run in the rain.

"Approximately ninety minutes later," McGuire said, "a uniform responded to check-the-well-being and trouble calls at that address. A vehicle of that description was observed in a driveway across the street."

"Of that description pertains to about what, about a thousand blue Tauruses in Park City? No approach. No tag, model year or VIN recorded by the responder. No suspicious-vehicle report to dispatch."

Jack leveled a "you gotta be kidding" glare. "Jesus. I'd truly love to hear how you reconcile me killing my ex-wife, then hanging around at the house for another hour and a half."

McGuire shot back, "Were you at that location at any time between the hours of noon and midnight on Sunday."

"I told you on Monday, I was working." Jack realized the error the instant it was made. "Working" is what he should have said during that interview.

For one, it was true. The rent-a-dog phone calls, the trip to the shelter, the meet with Cherise, surveillance at Belle's and interview with Dina were all hours billable to Gerry Abramson.

For that reason, Jack needn't have provided contact information for Cherise and Dina.

Being a typically sharp detective and inveterate note taker, McGuire said, "How's Cherise Taylor, the mall and your dog groomer fit with working?"

"Take my word for it" epitomized too little, too late.

"I'm not auditing your time sheets or tax deductions, McPhee." Failing that, McGuire stated, "Ms. Taylor mentioned a stalker is harassing you."

Grateful for the deflection, Jack said, "A mope that needs a new hobby." Possibly something besides serial lock picking, stealing guns, using them, then planting it.

Detailing Blankenship's vendetta would get Jack nowhere. McGuire might indulge him and canvass the apartment complex for witnesses who might have seen a fat fuck enter or exit Jack's building. If so, unless Blankenship told a witness he'd dropped by to dump the .38 in Jack's dresser, it'd prove precisely nothing.

"And what's with the dog?"

"Protection," Jack said, with a straight face. "While I was in the mall, the windows were down in the car enough, he wouldn't overheat."

"Your Ford, with a loaded .38 allegedly in the glove box."

"No." *Shit.* Jack hadn't lied on Monday, but the selective truth had tripped him up, anyway. When he met Cherise at the mall, she'd already taken Phil to Merry Hills.

McGuire knew Jack had been pulled over in the S-10. If there was a God, let the assumptions begin.

"Your other friend, Ms. Wexler. I spoke with a Mrs. Wexler at the number you provided. She refused to answer questions about you and said she'd tell Ms. Wexler to call back. Didn't happen."

Jack gave him Dina's cell-phone number.

"Generous of you, but I already got it off your cell."

"I didn't know Dina's cell number, until she called me on it Monday afternoon."

"Real close friends, are you?"

Ignoring him, Jack went on, "I guarantee, Mrs. Wexler forgot to pass on your message to Dina. I told you her mother isn't well. And you did confirm that 911 for an ambulance."

McGuire blew a raspberry and sat back. The knot in his Father's Day tie was adjusted, the ends aligned and ironed smooth. "On Monday, you denied being at the residence. We have two eyewitnesses, plus print evidence contradicting that. You bucked me on volunteering the .38. We execute search warrants and find it in your apartment. Now you say it was stolen. You said you screwed off all day Sunday. Forty-eight hours later, you tell me you were working."

"Yeah," Jack said. "I'm not helping myself a whole lot here."

"Cabbage, me lad, if you were this stupid back at the academy, you sure had me fooled."

Self-preservation is a primordial instinct. It stokes feats of superhuman strength and endurance, miraculous cures, heinous crimes and political scandal. If the unvarnished truth were Jack's salvation, the decision would be academic.

It wasn't. Explain the stakeout at the deHavens, and he had to cite the Calendar Burglar. Do that and McGuire would ask why Jack believed the thief would hit that house, that night. Relating the kennel setup implicated Ms. Pearl, Angie Meadows, and Cherise Taylor impersonating Belle deHaven.

Above all, giving up Dina Wexler in the process would enlarge the frame to include her. Christ, even if it magically erased Jack from the suspect list—which it wouldn't—he couldn't do that.

Dina was a thief, a smart aleck, wore kids' department clothes, stuffed tissues in her shoes so they wouldn't fall off and snored in her sleep. Instead of assuming the best about a woman, then reality skewing the image, Jack had known the worst about her almost from hello.

It was like Harriet's damn fall-out-of-a-well analogy. Except the bottom kept sinking from under Jack, and he couldn't climb out with a friggin' crane.

"I didn't kill Belle deHaven," he said. "Your blind side that she was dead—murdered—flattened me like a Mack truck. We loved each other. It just wasn't the kind you marry for, or can stay married for without losing the best parts of it."

McGuire's index finger and thumb imitated the world's smallest violin.

"Nice, ol' buddy. You don't want to hear me out? Fine. Charge me and add my name to the arraignment schedule."

His former classmate and friend had the grace to look contrite, but said, "Do I need to buy a machine sandwich and a soda? Or is there a chance I'll make it home for supper tonight."

By his girth, skipping meals wasn't a habit. Trading insults would amuse squad members monitoring the video feed in an adjacent room. As they preach in cop school, it wouldn't de-escalate the situation.

"I was working from approximately ten Sunday till approximately two Monday. By law, at Monday's interview and now, that's all I'm compelled to tell you. My mistake was trying to cover my ass without disclosing my client or nature of the case. Instead, I should have let it hang."

"Exigent circumstances," McGuire replied. "They allow statutes prohibiting a licensed investigator's breach of confidentiality to be waived without prejudice."

"Uh-uh. That's why loopholes bear an uncanny resemblance to nooses. Bottom line, what you have on me satisfied the judge who issued the search warrants, but the gaps are big enough for the Mack truck that keelhauled me to drive through."

Jack scooted to the edge of the chair and rested his forearms on the table. "It's what's missing that exonerates me, Andy. A Lone Ranger print on an exterior door frame—interesting. No lifts taken off any doorknobs or interior surfaces? Including the breaker box shut off before or shortly after Belle died? Makes no sense."

"So you gloved up."

"After I touched the door facing? Come on."

McGuire's eyebrow raised. "And you're admitting you knew the electricity was off. That wasn't in the press release."

"Didn't have to be. You showed me the prelim photos, remember? When was the last time you used portable halogens *inside* a house?"

"Six weeks ago."

Startled, Jack cursed himself for conclusion jumping, then recalled a squib in the newspaper. "A homeless guy that croaked in an abandoned shack doesn't count."

"You asked…"

"Yeah, and here's another one. Earlier, you said the patrolman was responding to trouble *calls* at the residence."

"Did I?"

"How many calls? From whom? What time?"

"None of your concern."

"Well, the waterproof jogger's report wasn't one of them. You'd have thrown that at me from the get-go." Along with any neighbor's complaint of a suspicious person or persons skulking around the deHavens' backyard.

The motion detectors might have initiated a silent alarm to the security company. When no one answered at the house, a trouble call might have been forwarded to dispatch.

Jack said, "That leaves Carleton deHaven requesting a check-the-well-being on his wife."

"If you say so."

"Well, if not, when Belle didn't arrive in Little Rock as scheduled, I'd say that's more than passing strange. Wouldn't you?"

"I might."

"Still is, considering she should have landed eight hours before that well-being check." Jack sucked his teeth. "Kinda makes me wonder if it took that long for Mr. Airtight Alibi to realize it *would* seem more than passing strange, when his wife turned up dead."

"DeHaven is in the clear. Mrs. deHaven missed her flight. When the next and last of the day was weather-delayed, he assumed she'd opted to drive down."

"Missed her flight?" Jack repeated. "Shit yeah. She didn't live to make it to the airport."

"Sounds like a lefthanded confession to me, bud."

"*Think,* for God's sake. I had no reason to kill my ex-wife. The prenup gave deHaven five hundred thousand of them."

"How do you know?"

"She *told* me. I told her she was nuts to sign it."

"She didn't listen to you."

"She rarely did." Jack's advice on marrying Carleton deHaven at all was also ignored.

"You can't possibly believe I left a print, gloved up, killed Belle with a registered .38, sat in my car for an hour and a half, then hid said murder weapon in a drawer, hired a neighbor to clear out my whole friggin' apartment and moved in—*moved* somewhere else."

"Sure, I can." McGuire splayed his hands on the table and stood up. "Your motive is the oldest one in the book."

"What motive? I don't—"

"Soon as we take a DNA swab and the wee, tiny bun in Mrs. deHaven's oven turns out to be yours, the prosecutor may up the charge to capital murder."

Cops lied. The more adept and experienced the investigator, the more he loved the irony in lying to extort the truth. To Jack's knowledge, Andy McGuire had dealt most every card off the top of the deck. And still was.

"Belle was *pregnant?*"

"Funny, her husband said that same exact thing. Except he isn't the father. He had a vasectomy years ago. The lab confirmed he's still shooting blanks."

McGuire picked up the handcuffs. "Since I'm 99.9 percent sure God isn't the daddy, either, whose little cabbage do you reckon it is?"

Jack sat there, stunned. His mind whirled a hundred revolutions per second. One thought clicked into place. "An attorney," he said. "I'm invoking my right to counsel."

14

"Shit, the—" Dina yanked her hand off the saucepan's metal handle. Homemade tomato soup slopped over. The burner's jets crackled, licking at the spill, welding it to the side of the pan.

She abruptly turned off the burner and spun around. Stretched on tiptoes, she batted at the sink faucet. A practiced jab at the spigot with a wooden spoon sent cold water streaming over her palm. The burn crossing from the base of her index finger to the heel of her hand wasn't serious. Just stupid and careless.

Harriet had owned the copper-bottom cookware set so long, Paul Revere might have forged it, then leaped on his horse to holler, "The British are coming!" It was certainly manufactured before heat-resistant handles were invented.

"And a long time after pot holders were, you idiot."

The cold water's supposed power to soothe the sting did the opposite. Deciding her skin wouldn't blister, or if it did, it served her right, Dina shut off the tap and towel patted her hand.

A half turkey sandwich, stewed prunes and the soup bowl arranged on a plate looked almost festive. Whether Harriet agreed or not, after wasting most of her breakfast, she'd eat every bite, if Dina had to play the choo-choo game with the spoon.

As she whisked the plate from the counter, it seemed to levitate, then descend to the floor in slow motion. The dish split on impact. Soup whooshed up like lava; the bowl flipped over on its rim. The sandwich disassembled itself, and prunes bounced and cavorted on the linoleum.

"Oh, no-o-o." Dina's wail was punctuated by the spoon tinking off the floor. She slumped against the refrigerator. Hot tears rose and spilled over.

This morning, the VW flooded when she'd tried to start it. Prior to that, Harriet's blood pressure was taken three times, before the reading stuck long enough to chart it. Instead of refilling the oxygen machine's reservoir, she'd drenched it and the carpet with distilled water. By the grace of God, five dogs and a cat were groomed without serious injury or casualties.

Phil edged around the cabinet and sniffed at a prune shotput into the dining room. He grimaced, then advanced on the splot of turkey peeking out from under the toe kick. At Harriet's whisper-yelled "Dina! Are you all right?" he snatched his prize and skedaddled for the hallway.

No, was the correct answer. "Better than the plate I dropped," would suffice, because no one literally falls apart from anxiety. It just feels that way.

Twenty-eight hours ago, Jack was in the shower when Dina and Harriet left for a doctor's appointment. He'd made a list of Belle deHaven's neighbors and friends to interview, saying he'd be lucky if many were home and willing to talk to a private investigator.

Since then, he hadn't called, hadn't answered his cell phone or office phone. TLC's boarding information had Jack's office phone, as did the other files she'd taken. The only A. D. Meadows in the phone book hung up the minute Dina mentioned Jack's name.

Posing as a local veterinarian's assistant, she'd called the animal shelter and obtained Jack's unlisted home number. A recording informed her it was out of service. Neither of Park City's hospitals had admitted anyone named McPhee. The emergency room clerk refused to confirm or deny he'd been treated.

"My stars and garters, will you look at this mess?" Harriet chided. "I've told you and told you what happens when you get in too big of a hurry, but will you listen?"

Eyes closed, her head tipped back, Dina breathed, "Just…don't, Mom. Okay?" Next on the agenda would be a demand to define "don't," then a lecture on the frustrations of mothering a selectively deaf child. "Please," she said. "Sit down at the table and I'll fix you another plate."

"I didn't want the first one. I told you, I'm not hungry."

Dina's teeth clenched. "Fine. No problem. Stand there until you fall down in a coma, then I'll call the goddamn paramedics again."

A gasp, shuffling steps, the muttered "The thanks I get" soliloquy were adaptations of a hoary melodrama. Dina hated fighting obstinance with meanness. She'd read the how-to books, the pamphlets, seen the videos. Be cheerful. Be positive. Be firm. Embrace the depths of self-understanding, enlightenment and personal growth the caregiving experience afforded.

She chortled at the thought, then laughter rolled out in waves. She imagined her mother staring at her, the lunatic who'd overtaken the asylum. Still chuckling, she brushed the hair from her face and peeled herself off the fridge. As she stepped over the broken, splattered dishes to fetch clean ones, Harriet said, "I'm as mad at McPhee as you are, you know."

Dina laid half of her own sandwich on a clean plate, then spooned out another serving of prunes. "Why would I be mad at him?"

"For moving in and taking over like he owns the place, then off he goes with nary a goodbye." She huffed. "Dog and all, same as that brother of yours."

Rare digs at Randy were actually convoluted apologies. Why fence-mending was direct most of the time and oblique at others was as bizarre as twisting mutual concern about Jack into anger.

"Jack and Phil were invited to stay with us." Dina set the plate and soup bowl between Harriet's elbows. "Randy dumped the dog he never once fed, watered or cleaned up after, on you."

"He loved that dog," Harriet countered. "Randy's heart nearly broke when it died. Nor's it his fault that his career has him traveling all the time."

Aliens from Planet Zirko, Dina thought, kneeling to swab the mucky floor. That's what anyone eavesdropping on this conversational doublespeak would assume we are. Unless other mothers and daughters, maybe even fathers and sons, communicated like a radio bringing in three stations at once and none of them in English.

Underlying the static and gibberish was fear. Not that something might have happened to Jack. The certainty something *had.* And Dina could do nothing save worry about a man she didn't know well enough or long enough to phone his friends, relatives, business acquaintances—let alone have the slightest idea where his apartment was located.

The only one who knew that was tentatively accepting spilled prunes as a food source. As if Phil ever barked, much less could draw Dina a map. Whatever the mutt's ancestry, Lassie hadn't lived in the same zip code.

"Sweetheart," Harriet said, quietly. "McPhee's all right. I'm as sure as I can be."

"Then why hasn't he called?" Dina pushed the trash can back under the sink and slammed the cabinet door. Her mother wasn't aware of Monday's crosswalk incident. Jack had told Harriet that Belle deHaven was his ex-wife, but not about being questioned by a homicide detective.

"Your daddy used to go on benders now and then."

Dina bristled. "He did not!"

Harriet sighed and trolled her spoon back and forth in the bowl. "Earl wasn't much of a drinker, but men bottle things up inside. When they can't hold any more, they pour them into a glass."

She looked up at Dina. "Remember him saying he never had headaches, except once in a blue moon?"

Oh, yeah. One of those "if I had a dollar" things that would endow a nice trust fund. Dina anticipated what was coming, before Harriet said, "It closed down years ago, but the Blue Moon down on Cleburne Avenue was where Earl took his troubles."

She smiled. "How many he left there, I couldn't say. Doubtful any, though bar dogs aren't fools, aside from being drunks. But whenever six o'clock on a Friday or four on Saturdays came and went without him, I knew 'twas a blue moon."

So had Dina, minus the specifics. It's just easier for a kid to block out funny smells and a snarled, slurry "Lemme alone, DeeJee" than admit her white knight, her enduring first love, had flaws in his armor. Later, when she was a teenager, those faults and others proved her old man was a hypocrite who had no right to tell her how to live her life.

"Daddy never called to tell you he wouldn't be home?"

The spoon clinked in the now empty bowl. "We had an understanding. I trusted Earl to be where I believed he was. He trusted me not to check up on him." She chuckled. "In all those years, Earl Wexler was the only customer the bartender didn't call to the phone. Not once."

The reassurance was lovingly given, but temporary. After Harriet lay down for a nap, Dina washed the dishes, waffling between hope Jack had crawled in a hole somewhere to recover from the worst, gut-rippingest, skull-splitting hangover of his life, and the fact nearly twenty-nine-and-a-half hours was too long to be drowning his grief.

She started when Phil butted her hip. "Prunes working their magic, huh?" He trotted into the dining room, turned and panted back at her. "Keep your legs crossed a sec, till—"

Soft thumping sounds wended from the entry. The storm door's pneumatic closer seldom engaged the latch. Sometimes, the air trapped between the storm door and solid wooden one made haunted-mansion noises.

Phil's head pivoted from Dina to the door. She flipped suds off her hands and jumped off the footstool. Those ghostly bumps in the night had never rattled out, "Shave and a Haircut, Two Bits."

Jack's fist was raised for another chorus when Dina yanked open the door. Rumpled, bag eyed, his five-o'clock shadow a sandy, nascent beard, he grinned as though she were the best thing he'd seen in recent memory. "Hi, kid."

"Damn you, McPhee." As he stepped inside, her sniff test detected fermentation, but not the alcohol variety. "Where in the hell have you been?"

"Missed me, didja?"

"No." She wrapped her arms around him and hugged him. His clothes stank, and he smelled riper than a farmer that still plowed behind a mule, and Dina couldn't have cared less.

Jack held her, his chin propped on her head, exhaustion as palpable as his heartbeat. "I'm sorry you were so worried."

"Not me. I knew you were okay. It's Mom who's been a nervous wreck."

"Uh-huh."

"And Phil."

"Uh-huh."

"I might have been a little concerned, but with work and everything…" Dina stepped back, feeling foolish, probably because she was making one of herself. "And well, you know, to be honest, it's not like we're close friends or anything."

He nodded, a sly glint in his bloodshot eyes. "It's a wonder you recognized me when you answered the door."

"Darn right, the way you look." She gave him the up-and-down. "I hope you have a great dry cleaner. That suit's a wreck."

"I'm a wreck. The suit's totaled." He glanced at the hallway. "I'll tell you all about it after I grab a shower. That is, if it won't wake your mother."

"The water won't. The singing? From what I heard yesterday morning, you should stick to humming."

He chuckled, then bent down and kissed her cheek. "You're a hard woman, Ms. Wexler."

Fingering the side of her face, she watched him stride out to the garage for a clean change of clothes. *No, I'm not hard, and neither are you. I don't know why, but I have a feeling that, until a few days ago, we were both a whole lot better at faking it.*

Soap, a tankful of hot water and a shave did not make Jack a new man. Just a cleaner, nicer-smelling version of the rapidly aging one McGuire had streeted after the twenty-four-hour custodial hold expired.

A cab to the impound lot conveniently located as far from the police station as the city limits allowed, then bailing out the S-10 ate another couple of hours.

He'd be a liar if he said the experience was worth the grin on Dina's face when she saw him. But it was close. Real close, as a matter of fact.

Everything permeated with Eau de Jail was crammed into a garbage bag. The pair of black lace-ups rode the bubble for a moment. Jack cautioned himself against getting carried away.

"It's only Wednesday," he said, rinsing shaving cream and stubble down the sink drain. "The way this week's going, you may need 'em for an arraignment before it's over."

Dina, bless her, had fixed them each a thick turkey sandwich and monster glasses of iced tea. Jack started to sit down at the table, then motioned at the patio door. "Our conference room must be ninety-five in the shade, but maybe we ought to take this picnic out there."

A round metal table between their lawn chairs held their drinks. The chair's webbing creaked and bowed like a hammock under Jack's weight, but was sturdier than it appeared. The triangular work of turkey Dina had sculpted immediately drew hungry flies and Phil. The first recognizable food Jack had seen since yesterday vanished without a crumb.

Smiling, she inquired, "Want another sandwich?"

Six, please, Jack thought, but declined. He doubted if Harriet napped away the afternoon. If his campout on the living-room floor was an indication, she was a light sleeper and a restive one, despite all the medication she took.

"My day in the twilight zone," he began, "by Jack McPhee." He summarized being taken into custody, the mounting evidence against him and his attorney's advice against providing a DNA sample unless McGuire obtained a search warrant for it.

"Steve Trujillo is a smart guy for a lawyer," Jack said, "but you aren't bluffing when you're holding aces. The preliminary autopsy report indicated that Belle was about four weeks' pregnant. It isn't mine—guaranteed. Steve was concerned the DNA wasn't just for a paternity test."

"Why else would the police want it?"

"Don't know. But as Steve reminded me, I don't recall touching that backdoor facing, either. There's no way crime-scene techs found anything inside the house with my genetic fingerprint. Outside? Extremely doubtful, but Steve was afraid of another connecting dot."

Jack reached for his glass. "He was also daring the prosecutor to ante up a homicide charge, or release me."

"Stand by for the second of what'll probably be a million whys." Dina waved her sandwich. "So why, already?"

"Formal charges render the search warrant moot. The cops could swab my appendix, if they wanted to."

"Hey, I'm eating. Swabbing anything, I really don't need to hear about."

"Then chew this, while you're chewing. When Belle and I had lunch last week, she pretty much told me she was trying to get pregnant. Yesterday, I hear from McGuire that deHaven had a vasectomy before his previous wife divorced him."

Dina swallowed, then hesitated as though the food might slide down the wrong pipe. "Well," she murmured, "maybe it wasn't her husband's baby she wanted."

"Or she'd had a hot 'n heavy one-nighter with her tennis instructor." Jack picked at a thread dangling from the hem of his shorts. "Yeah, I thought about that. Had plenty of time to think about it. Except there's two things I know about Belle. She never, ever screwed around on me. I honestly couldn't have blamed her if she had."

"You would have, though."

The automatic protest was too lame to vocalize. "Okay. I *shouldn't* have blamed her if she had. But the other thing I do know is the majority of our fights were about me refusing to grow up, settle down and start a family."

"She wanted kids, even then."

"Doesn't every woman?"

"Most, I guess." Dina's eyebrows arched. "Some don't, but get the stupid idea that babies fix lousy marriages. If they're lucky, they come to their senses after a pee test gives a false positive."

If it had. The kits weren't infallible, but their accuracy had increased dramatically since Belle streaked to the drugstore in a panic whenever her period was fifteen minutes late.

Dina said, "You don't think she knew about the vasectomy."

Jack shook his head. "Add it to the list of wild-hare notions, but this is my take. The stork doesn't cooperate. Belle assumes she's the problem. The OB-GYN says she isn't. Hubby's snip job can't stay secret, if he's fertility tested. He lies and says the ol' swim team has never scored a bronze, let alone gold, so he'll eat more oysters and rest longer between meets."

Dina burst out laughing. "Stop it. I mean it. This isn't funny."

Not a bit, Jack agreed. Sarcasm was a coping mechanism. Also a habit, but when the going's tough, the tough get snide. Especially if the subject of derision was a blue-ribbon jerk.

"The clock keeps ticking," he said. "Belle is now either disillusioned with the marriage, or okay with it, but carrying deHaven's biological child doesn't look promising. An anonymous donor-swimmer could solve everything. What's done in the lab, stays in the lab."

An affair, Jack admitted silently, would be cheaper and net the same result. Had Belle conceived while they were married, he wouldn't have questioned who the father was. And if they'd *had* a child, McGuire's second bombshell would have left Jack wondering for the rest of his life.

Dina stared into the ozone, nibbling her lower lip. Almost visible were scenes from Harriet's soap operas to commercials for Jerry Springer's paternity ambush shows.

"Secret vasectomy, secret artificial insemination, huh."

Ice cubes tinked as she drank deeply from her glass. "Poetic justice, I guess." A finger squeegeed the frosty condensation. "Passing off a child, though… *Evil* may be too strong a word, but *selfish* isn't strong enough."

If an appropriate one existed, it wasn't in Jack's vocabulary. "However it happened, pregnancy wasn't the murder motive. Belle wasn't far enough along for any champagne toasts."

"You're sure?"

"I'd have been the second one to know." True, if the order didn't include Belle. "Could be," he lied, "she'd packed a bottle of bubbly for the trip to Arkansas."

Unmentioned and unnecessary was that Belle didn't live to celebrate anything, or to discover her husband was surgically sterile.

Jack didn't expect the moist, cold hand Dina laid on his arm. Even less, the blunt "She did what she did, Jack. How she could have, what she was thinking, died with her. It's good you got it off your chest. Now let's work on saving your butt."

He looked at her. Nodded, then grinned, instead of exploding out of the chair, flinging it into the yard, cursing and demanding who the hell Dina thought she was, talking to him like that. About Belle like that.

"Okay," he said, as though she'd suggested a refill on the tea. "After Harriet's nap, if you can leave her alone awhile, I'll introduce you to the fine art of lying for a living."

15

"I thought we were going to your office."

"We are." Jack ducked and squinted out the Taurus's windshield to check the street sign's hundred block. "This is the scenic route."

He knew without looking that the answer didn't satisfy Dina. Supplying constant explanations was one of many reasons why McPhee Investigations was a one-man operation. Jack lost plenty of arguments with himself without a tiebreaker frowning at him from the passenger's seat.

"Make yourself useful," he said. "Watch for 4722."

"Three blocks up, in the middle. The even house numbers are on your side of the street."

"Gee, thanks. I hadn't noticed."

"Mary O. Blankenship, 4722 Nebraska Avenue," she said. "Brett Dean Blankenship's mother. She's lived there for at least two years."

Jack's head whipped sideways so fast, his neck popped. "And you know that, how?"

"Well…" Dina's drawl insinuated *Elementary, my dear Sherlock.* "The computer searches you did Monday night on Blankenship included his address. This morning, when Mom was so worried about you, I kind of looked him up in the kitchen phone book. He wasn't listed, but Mary O. had the same address."

She grinned. "I was just guessing about her being his mother."

"You didn't call him. Please, tell me you didn't call him."

"I started to, then I decided if he had beaten you up or something, he probably wouldn't admit it."

Jack blew out a sigh. "People are usually a little reluctant to discuss assault and battery on the phone."

"Especially with a stranger."

"Uh-huh." He slowed as he approached the 4700 block. "What made you think Mrs. Blankenship has lived here only two years?"

"At least two years," she corrected. "Because that's how old the kitchen phone book is. There's lots of notes, doctor referrals, billing codes—*stuff*—written in the front. Saving it's easier than copying everything into new ones."

Jack's archived directories harked back to the annual delivery cycle exclusive to Ma Bell. The handwritten information in them was obsolete; the doodles were priceless.

The yellow brick tract house at 4722 Nebraska was well-kempt, but trimmed in garish plum with an apple-green front door. Parked in the driveway were two subcompact Chevys: a cherry-red, late-model four-door, and Moby the Dickhead's older, grimy white one. Jack speculated it must be Mom's hand-me-down, and Brett Dean was not properly appreciative of her generosity.

"Wow," Dina said. "Somebody smacked him but good."

The caved driver's door, front fender and duct-taped plastic over the window indicated a T-bone collision with an approximately same-sized vehicle. Anything with a higher profile would have crushed the Cavalier like a soda can.

"Do you think he's…all right?" Dina asked.

"Yeah. Relatives of fatalities don't have the cars towed home and plunked in the driveway."

She snorted. "You're all heart, McPhee."

"Well, they *don't*." Jack went through the intersection, then pulled into the corner house's driveway for a U-turn. "I want the mope off my back, not in the morgue."

"He could have put us there," she allowed. "But his car sure wasn't damaged like that when he tried."

"That Grand Theft Auto getaway might have caused it. A block or few from the cop shop, the side streets are residential with two-way stops. By the damage, I'm guessing he blew one and got clipped."

Jack swung into the curb a house down from the Blankenships'. "Want to pay a sympathy call, or wait here?"

"We're going—" Dina glanced down at her bare legs, tennis shoes and shorts. "I'm really not dressed to meet anybody."

"Oh, for God's sake." Jack unlatched the seat belt and shouldered open the door. Before it shut, she'd scrambled out the passenger's side.

As they strode up the sidewalk, she muttered, "I just wish you'd told me about this, is all."

"Spur of the moment. Gotta be nimble, kid. Ready for anything."

What she muttered next was garbled. It didn't sound complimentary.

The woman who answered the door was above average height, roundish at the torso, but svelte compared to her son. Tired yet friendly eyes peered from glasses with stylish rectangular lenses. "Yes?" She looked past Jack at the driveway, then the curb for an identifying vehicle.

"Mrs. Blankenship?" Jack's smile assured her he was neither

a salesman nor a serial killer. "We heard about Brett Dean's accident and thought we'd stop by and see how he's doing." A raised hand, then, "Sorry, we should have called first. If we're intruding…"

"No, no, of course not." The dust cloth waving them inside disappeared behind her back. "My boss let me take the week off, but I can't seem to find time enough to clean."

The living room had a cozy, lived-in quality, instead of an impersonal, reserved-for-company feel. From furnishings to accessories, Mary Blankenship was into barnyard country collectibles in a big way. A lopsided corduroy recliner, ginormous TV and slew of video gaming equipment marked Brett Dean's territory.

"Y'all go ahead and make yourself comfortable. There's soda in the fridge, or I can make—"

"Thanks," Dina said, "but we really can't stay. We just wanted to make sure Brett was all right."

Jack draped an arm over her shoulder, signaling "Nice job" and a hopeful "Now zip it and let me do the talking."

"He's asleep at the moment." Mrs. Blankenship smiled toward a hallway. "Those pain pills he's on sure knock him out."

"From the look of his car," Jack said, "he's lucky he wasn't hurt a lot worse."

"Coming out of it with two fractured wrists and a broken ankle?" She rolled her eyes. "'Who cares?' he says. 'What am I s'posed to do all day? Can't work the computer, can't play video games. Can't hardly feed myself.'"

Her voice was higher than her son's, but the snivel in it was pitch-perfect.

"Men are so-o negative." Dina flinched, as though an insult had accidentally slipped out. "He'll adjust in a day or two. Good grief, it just happened yesterday."

"Not yesterday. Monday morning." Mrs. Blankenship hastened to add, "But you're right about being negative. Mostly, I think Brett Dean's mad at himself. He won't admit it, but the wreck *was* his fault. He ought to be thanking the Lord that the lady and her two kids in the other car didn't get a scratch."

"Amen to that." Jack's hip gently butted Dina in the ribs. "I guess we'd better run along and let you get back to your cleaning." He reached behind her for the doorknob. "Next time, though, we will call first."

"No need to. I'll tell Brett Dean you stopped by, as soon as he wakes up." She hesitated, then sighed. "This is awfully embarrassing, but your names must've gone in one ear and out the other."

"Melville," was the first one Jack thought of. "Herman Melville."

"And I'm Jane Austen."

"Well, it was very nice to meet you both. Come back anytime."

They were barely out of sight before Dina smacked Jack's arm. "Herman Melville. Are you nuts?"

"A Freudian slip. If you'd gotten a good look at Blankenship, you'd word-associate *whale,* too." He unlocked the car door and opened it. "After you, Miss Austen."

When he got in on the opposite side, Dina said, "I should have made up something instead of teasing you. Mrs. Blankenship was so nice to us, and what if Brett Dean is more of a reader than she is?"

"A description will tag me, and more than likely you." Jack pulled away from the curb. "Originally I wanted to find out if he had an alibi for Sunday afternoon. It's a leap backward from killing Belle to attempted vehicular homicide, but Moby's got more loose screws than a hardware store."

"You think he hates you enough to frame you for murder?"

"Maybe." Jack shrugged. "Underestimating a whacko isn't wise. As for being smart enough to pull it off? The more I considered it, the more doubtful it seemed. But like I told you, his background info on Belle made me hinky the day he showed it to me."

"Then why didn't you ask Mrs. Blankenship where he was?"

Several evasions were evaluated and rejected. "I intended to invent a mutual friend who said Brett Dean got shit-faced Sunday afternoon, then wrecked his car." He glanced sideward. "If he was home, or Mrs. B. knew where he was, she'd have Mama Beared me in a heartbeat."

"Exactly. So why—? Oh. Oops." Dina scooted lower in the seat. "Jeez, I thought I was brilliant getting her to say it happened Monday afternoon. Great assistant, I am."

A better one than you realize, Jack thought. The immediate, relaxed rapport with Mrs. Blankenship and natural ability to steer a conversation were impressive. Her body language jibed with every remark and comment, the unifying "men are negative" feint, in particular. A close second was deferring to him on their names and not batting a lash at Herman friggin' Melville.

"You're taking me back home, aren't you." Dina's fingers tapped a riff on her thighs. "Firing me on my first try must be a record."

"I'd demote you to pencil sharpener before I'd do that. And I never use pencils."

He wheeled into the parking lot of what once was Gavin & Giffen, Park City's premier department store. The five-story redbrick jewel of the downtown shopping area had lost her luster before malls were built on the town's south and west sides.

Urban renewal fever had demolished a dozen other landmarks before rock-bottom property values turned the survivors into gold mines in the rough. Gavin & Giffen's conversion to prime office space and loft-style condos made living and working downtown cool again.

"Last stop on the scenic route," Jack said. "Gotta pick up Yancy Nilsson, my IT guy."

Dina looked at the dashboard clock. "Wouldn't it have been quicker for him to meet us at the office?"

"Yancy doesn't have a car." Jack flashed her a grin. "And won't for about a year. He'll get his learner's permit around Christmas, though."

"Yeah, right." Dina's expression progressed from amusement to disbelief to unwilling acceptance. "You aren't joking, are you?"

"Nope." He pointed. "See for yourself."

The string bean exiting G&G's revolving lobby door inherited his mother's Asian bone structure and father's Nordic coloring. When Yancy grew into the best of both worlds, he'd be a babe magnet without even trying. At the moment, he'd give a hundred IQ points to look like every other kid in school.

The Taurus's backseat was heaped with the rest of Jack's wardrobe and his extra pillow. Dina scooted closer to Jack to make room for Yancy in the front. While they got acquainted, Jack rubbed hips and thighs with the world's shortest burglar and tried not to forget where his office was located.

The place wasn't as tidy as he'd left it, but McGuire and Company hadn't trashed it, either. Contrary to popular assumption, the tornado-aftermath simulation wasn't standard procedure for off-scene evidence collection in homicide investigations.

"Okay, troops." Jack took a twenty from his wallet. "First order of business is you two going to the diner. Buy the boss a jumbo black coffee and whatever you want."

They looked at each other, as if mentally flipping for carhop duty. "Age before beauty, Munchkin," Yancy said.

Dina inhaled through her nose. "Not funny, Willy Wonk. Neither is Elf, Dwarf, Leprechaun, Shrimp, Shorty or Ewok. Got it?"

"Both of you, scram," Jack ordered. "Then scram back."

The door hadn't shut behind them when he punched the speakerphone to play back his messages. He'd accessed by cell phone and erased earlier ones from Ms. Pearl, Cherise, McGuire, his attorney, prospective and peeved current clients and robot telemarketers. The digital scorekeeper said four newbies were in the batter's circle.

"Jack, it's Cherise. I'm really worried about you—"

Delete. "So am I."

The next two didn't require the temporary privacy he'd bought, either. The last message sat Jack down in the desk chair. "As of now," Gerry Abramson began, "3:12 p.m. Wednesday, your services are no longer required. Your performance was subpar before your arrest for homicide. I expect the presentation of a written report, invoice and balance of the retainer on or before 5:00 p.m. Friday."

An "or else" kicker was implied.

The basis for the firing was ninety percent justifiable. Keeping clients informed, even if oral progress reports were of the "same shit, different day" persuasion lent assurance you weren't sitting at home in your underpants watching a Cardinals doubleheader.

Instead Jack had adopted a dog, the Calendar Burglar, her mother, evicted himself from his apartment and played cat and mouse with Lt. Andy McGuire.

If not for those derelictions, the pink slip's nonjustifiable reason would irk him a little. Abramson must have an unreliable informant at the police department. Jack had been picked up and held for questioning, not charged with homicide. Absent that, the media couldn't legally name him as a suspect.

"Well, if you can't fix it, fuck it." He yanked his laptop from its carrying case. The meter was ticking. Twenty bucks in a perpetually starving teenager's hand converted to cheeseburgers, fries, onion rings, cheese sticks and the time needed to cook them. With Dina's supervision, Jack stood a fair chance of getting the coffee he'd ordered. If not, he'd brew his own.

From his pocket he took out a list of Harriet Wexler's prescriptions. A proper houseguest didn't snoop through medical paperwork when his hosts were occupied with nebulizer treatments. The corollary was that expecting a private investigator to keep his mitts to himself was akin to expecting Phil not to fart in the house.

Price comparisons at major Internet pharmacies didn't have Jack shouting hosannas. Too easy, he supposed, for one source to be the cheapest on everything *and* not ding customers for shipping and handling. By his rough calculations, Chinese-menu shopping—this from Column A, that from B—could shrink the remaining doughnut hole by three to four hundred out-of-pocket dollars.

The printer was spitting out Jack's pharmaceutical survey, when Willy Wonk and the Munchkin breezed in trailing a slipstream of deep-fryer grease. "Here's your coffee." Dina handed him a tall, lidded foam cup. "And here's your change." Three quarters, a nickel and four pennies pattered the desktop.

"Change?" Jack looked at Yancy, already chowing down on a deluxe tenderloin sandwich. "What a concept."

"She made me put back my candy bar."

While Yancy clogged his arteries, Jack showed Dina the

printouts. "This isn't comprehensive, but I bookmarked all the Web sites I browsed. Not bad, though, for a start."

"You did all this while we were at the diner?"

He waved a dismissal. "Just killing time, after I had the laptop up and running for Yancy."

Eyes downcast, Dina scanned each page as if it were a collection notice. "This would help so much." She folded the sheets lengthwise and dropped them in the trash can. "It means the world to me that you care enough to do that."

Of course he cared. Too damn much. "Then why'd you round-file it?"

"Because buying Mom's medications anywhere other than the approved, in-network pharmacy doesn't apply to the coverage gap."

Jack wasn't sure he understood. A surge of anger said he did. "Lemme get this straight. All of Harriet's prescriptions are filled at the same drugstore because you *have* to?"

"Rules are rules. A 'preferred pharmacy,' it's called."

"Even if you could buy some, or all of them, cheaper at a different store, online, wherever?"

She nodded.

"The same rule applies when *you're* making up that three-thousand dollar gap? You still can't buy them somewhere else? Somewhere less expensive for you?"

"I can," Dina said. "The money spent anywhere but the preferred pharmacy just won't count toward the doughnut hole. And until it's filled, none of Mom's prescriptions—old, new, dosage changes—are covered at all."

Jack spread his hands, his head shaking in disbelief. "I'm not arguing with you. I swear, I'm not. But that's the craziest racket I've ever heard of. It's not—"

"Fair," she finished. "Life isn't. That, McPhee, is rule number one." She looked at her watch. "Rule number two is, I have to go home and give Mom an injection pretty soon."

Yancy wadded the food sacks and directed a hook shot at the trash can. "You promised Dad I'd be back before dinner."

Oh, to be young again, Jack thought. With a cast-iron blast furnace for a stomach and a twenty-eight-inch waist.

"Then let's get after it."

While Dina fetched a fifty-foot phone line from the supply cabinet, Jack instructed Yancy to prepay two spoof-service sites, each for 120 minutes' usage. Yancy pointed out that twice the talk time from one provider would shave a few dollars off Jack's credit card bill.

True, but until now, Jack had worked the phones solo. Whether he and Dina could tap in two different phones off one account simultaneously, he didn't know.

"I can't risk the system allowing one of our spoofs to slide by unaltered." To an obviously perplexed Dina, he said, "What we're doing is controlling the display on outbound caller ID. Most people assume if, for instance, Dina Wexler and her home number come up, then Dina Wexler's calling them."

Jack jotted an 800-number, a PIN access number and the outbound identifier for Yancy to program in. "We'll do practice runs, but once it's set up, the outbound ID on your line will read '*Forbes* magazine' with a bogus phone number."

If a person could look both appalled and excited, Dina did.

"Like they say, kid. You can't believe everything you read. Law enforcement has spoofed bad guys for years. Now anybody with a credit card and phone can do it."

"Legally?"

"So far. Some politicians want it outlawed, because their opponents' campaigners spoofed voters. Identity thieves also used it to make it appear legit credit card holders were activating accounts from their home phones. Card issuers caught on and installed filters to recognize a proxy caller ID."

The bathroom would be Dina's private phone booth—hence the longer phone line. With her pretext as a magazine staff writer, she'd extract information from Carleton deHaven's public-relations manager and other sources regarding last weekend's seminar in Little Rock, Arkansas.

A timeline of deHaven's whereabouts on Sunday was crucial. If Belle's husband was glad-handing the minions all day, then his alibi *was* airtight. If God was on Jack's side, the same hotel desk clerk and concierge were on duty this afternoon.

"For your pretext," Jack said, "your name is Mary Jaymes. Common, but spelling out a minor discrepancy makes it sound a lot more legitimate."

On the off chance someone balked, Dina would dictate the spoofed number for a callback. The secret was to not hang up. She'd then signal an SOS to Jack. After the callback's supposed dialing sequence ended, he'd answer the still open line, "Forbes, Editorial Department," as though it had just connected. A second of dead air would infer the call was being transferred, then Dina would answer, "Mary Jaymes speaking."

In the past, Jack had modified his voice to pull off the flimflam. Not once had a callee noticed the dial-back number didn't ring.

His own pretext was Jim Mathews, a security specialist contracted by each respective airline—commuter and national— that serviced Park City and Little Rock. If the party who answered the call was female, Jim Mathews would have a charming Texas twang. If male, Mathews was a curt, "don't tell me what you can't do, buddy" kind of a guy.

The prickly Mathews was entertaining, but his "aw shucks" persona was a lot more fun.

While they worked the phones, Yancy Nilsson racked up an extra zero, probably two, on Jack's Visa card. Internet data mining had become pricier since a legislative crackdown in January 2007. Cell-phone and landline calling records, credit reports, real-name information on e-mail accounts—virtually any personal info—still orbited cyberspace. Obtaining it from brokers was just more expensive and time-consuming.

Jack's initial prospecting on Monday night had been cursory. A reluctance to tie up the Wexlers' single phone line and resorting to Model-T dial-up access was frustrating as hell.

Putting Yancy at the helm freed up Jack to make his phone calls and paid bonus dividends. For one, the boy typed about a million strokes a minute. Brokers' required prompts and general Web searching brinked on light-speed, and Yancy had a gift for what Jack termed, "Looking on a mountaintop to find a submarine."

More often than not, the teen eked out a whole fleet of them.

The reception area distanced Jack from the keyboard's ticky-ticky rhythm, the droning printer and fax machine's end-of-transmission beeps. Whether posing as good ol' boy Jim Mathews, or his coldly intimidating counterpart, the bathroom door was monitored for Dina's distress signal.

With Jack's back to the parking lot, McGuire's entrance caught him flat-footed. "My other line's ringing," he said, into the cell phone. Realizing his accent had evaporated, he added, "Thanks for yer hep, ma'am, and y'all have a nice day."

McGuire chuckled, quickly surveying the office. "Howdy, pardner. What kinda rodeo you having here?"

"Business as usual." Jack stood and sidled around the coffee table. McGuire deflected the cutoff at the pass. Jack said, "Hey, I appreciate you taking it easy on the search."

"We ain't the Gestapo, McPhee."

Okay, so much for killing him with kindness. Or halting his progress toward the desk. Yancy casually swept confidential paperwork into the top drawer, then lowered the laptop's screen. He nodded and smiled at McGuire as he emptied the printer's and fax's bales.

The detective smirked, not happy his sneak-a-peek had failed, but somewhat amused the kid had seen it coming. "What's your name, son?"

"Yancy." He sat back in the desk chair like a minimogul. "What's yours? Sir."

McGuire slanted a look at Jack. "Is he a protégé or a clone?" It was either a rhetorical question, or another observation took precedence. McGuire's finger tracked the phone line across the floor to the crack under the bathroom door. "Somebody making book in the can?"

Jack had had enough. "If there's an official reason for this visit, let's hear it."

His desktop computer's hard drive was returned in a plastic zip bag. "Real exciting crap on this one." McGuire regarded the laptop. "I'll bet what's on that wouldn't put me to sleep."

Jack didn't blink. Search warrants have a twenty-four-hour lifespan. The one executed on the office had expired. Requesting another at the same location with the same probable cause would raise a judge's curiosity, if not his hackles.

He rethought that supposition as McGuire removed a folded sheet of paper from his shirt pocket. "I went to your new address to search the Ford. The old lady who answered the door said it and you were not on the premises."

Jack mentally smacked his forehead. "I forgot about the vehicle search. That's the truth, believe it or don't." Removing the Taurus's ignition and trunk keys from the ring, he added, "If I wanted to give you the runaround, I'd have washed it, vacuumed it—the works." He laid the keys in McGuire's palm. "I haven't even cleaned the trash out of it for a week."

The detective tossed the search warrant on the desk and strode toward the door. Jack followed him outside, rather than let the Asian-Swedish pitcher with satellite-dish ears tune in to the conversation.

"The S-10 is a one-passenger truck, Andy. I had two of them. That's why I drove the Taurus this afternoon."

"Mm-hmm. Always som'thin', isn't there?"

"I also told you why it's been parked in the Wexlers' garage since Monday."

"Go back inside, McPhee."

"If you want copies of those glove-box, passenger's-door and trunk-lock photos, Yancy can download them off the camera and burn a disk."

"I said, go back inside."

Jack held up his hands. "Okay, okay. But you know in your gut who killed Belle, the same as I do."

"From all indications, I'm lookin' at him." McGuire slipped on a pair of sunglasses. "If I'm not, prove it."

16

"I don't like fish. It smells funny, and it tastes like fish." Harriet sniffed the flaky bite of flounder impaled on her fork. "But I like this fish."

"Thanks." Jack grinned. "I think." Personally, he could take it or leave it, but the steamed entrée and veggies conformed to her diet. Dina graciously deemed the steak he'd fixed the other night a rare treat, and wasn't referring to how it was cooked.

"You like tuna, too, Mom. And salmon."

"I eat 'em. That's not the same as liking 'em."

Dina huffed, "But you—"

"It's wonderful sitting down together for a meal," said Jack, the self-appointed United Nations. "Bachelors think feeding their faces in front of the TV ranks up there with microwave nachos, but they're fooling themselves."

Harriet slanted him a look. "Some folks fool easier than others."

He chuckled at the insult. "Obviously, you're feeling better than you were when we got back from the office."

A sinking spell was her diagnosis and it fit as well as any. Nothing dire, or definite, just a general malaise that rolled in and gradually receded, like an internal tide.

She'd insisted Andy McGuire's unannounced arrival hadn't

precipitated it. From her account, giving what-for to one of Park City's finest was the highlight of her day. Age and illness bestowed few perks. Impunity to tell a cop or anybody else to go chase his shadow was one of them.

"So," she said to Jack, "how are you holding up?"

"A little tired." The admission had the advantage of being true and corresponding to his excuse for disappearing for nearly thirty hours. "Pulling an all-night surveillance on not much sleep beforehand used to be a lot easier."

Dina pointed her fork at him. "Which is why you'll have the couch tonight. No arguments. Phil and I already voted."

"That old sofa's no featherbed," Harriet said, "but a far sight softer than a jail cot. I hear they're nothing but a slab of foam rubber with a dirty sheet on top."

Jack and Dina exchanged a silent "Oh, hell." Their eyes averted to Harriet, blithely nibbling an asparagus spear. Phil's nose crested the corner of the table near Dina's ribs, as if her sudden paralysis was an excellent opportunity to clean her plate for her.

"Some nights," Harriet said, "a sliver of a crack in a patio door lets in more than a couple of moths. But raise your bedroom window of an afternoon? Why, it's downright fascinating what'll drift in on the breeze."

Dina yelped, "You've been spying on us?" She appealed to Jack, as though expecting him to march off her mother to the gallows.

"How else am I supposed to find out anything? Both of you treat me like the dog." A finger jabbed the air. "I didn't say *a* dog, Dina Jeanne. I said *the* dog." Harriet pinched off some fish and lobbed it to Phil. She recited, "Finish your dinner. Drink your milk. Time to get up. Time for a nap, a poop, a pill."

"Hey, that's not fair!"

"Wasn't when I treated your daddy that way, either." Harriet's lips curled under, then smacked. "Like he wasn't a person anymore. Just a thing with not a brain in his head, long before his failed him.

"I didn't tell him about the bills. About borrowing from Peter to pay Paul for groceries. Troubles you and Randy were having…none of that, for fear it'd upset him."

She dragged deep on the oxygen cannula and exhaled a sigh. "Earl would've fretted somethin' fierce, too. What I didn't know is, upset's what keeps you feeling alive, instead of like the dog underfoot that can't think, or talk, or help fix a blessed thing."

A dozen emotions were reflected in Dina's expression. Resentment, sure. Guilt, admiration, despair, fear, love, regret, obstinance—those and others mirrored in her mother's face.

"You're right," Jack said. "Except on my part, maybe the secrecy was to protect me, not you. Whatever you may think of me, I don't want you to think any less."

Harriet harrumphed and stabbed a boiled baby carrot. "There you go, calling me stupid again."

"*Mo*-ther. He did no such thing."

"Did so." She glared at Jack. "If I believed you killed your ex-wife, do you think you'd have slept on my floor Monday night?"

"No, ma'am."

"Would your bony knees be under my table now?"

"No, ma'am."

"All right, then." She rounded on Dina. "As for you, missy, do you believe I'm so addlepated, I can't divine that McPhee caught you burgling that woman's house Sunday night? And her being murdered is why you two have been in cahoots ever since?"

The hand Dina rubbed over her mouth didn't quite hide a grin. "No, ma'am."

"Humph. You did till a second ago."

The Queen Mom, as Dina called her occasionally, had spoken. Harriet's official membership on the Save Jack's Ass Committee humbled him. He'd imploded the proverbial glass house she'd pretended was granite, along with the illusion that her daughter was a Rapunzel who spun gold from dogs' hair.

The collapse was inevitable without Jack instigating it. Delete him from the Calendar Burglar equation, and Dina's almost untenable disgust with herself and increasing carelessness would have proved her undoing.

Not for the first time of late, Jack thought about predestination. He used to joke about it being DFW, O'Hare, KCI—whatever airport you ran through or wasted hours in for a connecting flight to wherever you were going.

His definition never failed to get a laugh, particularly from a bored shmuck on the bar stool beside his in an airport lounge. It probably still would, though somehow, the punchline seemed flatter than it once did.

"McPhee." Harriet's tone insinuated it wasn't her first attempt to get his attention. His fork screeched across an empty plate he'd swear was half-full a moment ago. Seated on the floor beside him, Phil cocked a flop ear expectantly.

"I said, why do the police think you killed Mrs. deHaven?"

Starting with the .38, he related the evidentiary arrows pointed at him. Several were unwittingly self-inflicted. The majority were impossible to explain without implicating Dina and others, or violating client confidentiality.

Dina cleared the table, while he encapsulated the holes in McGuire's theory. "Homicide investigations hardly ever nail down every detail. A preponderance of evidence, beyond reasonable doubt—those come into play in the prosecutor's office long before a judge instructs a jury."

Jack drew finger doodles on his crumpled paper napkin. "The case against me isn't quite tight enough for a murder charge. Not yet. That's why they bounced me this morning."

Harriet flinched at a serving bowl whanging off the kitchen faucet. "Lord have mercy, girl. There won't be a dish left in the house if you don't quit slinging them around."

Dina's cheeks reddened, but she acted as though she hadn't heard. Silverware crashed on the bottom of the sink. A saucepan's lid clanged like a cymbal.

Harriet sniffed and tugged the cuffs of her sweater over her wrists. Back to business, it implied, and not her daughter's monkeyshines in the kitchen. "All right, McPhee. If you didn't kill that woman, who did?"

"Three candidates: Mr. X, a mope named Brett Dean Blankenship, or Belle's husband, Carleton deHaven."

More or less thinking aloud, he went on, "Mr. X is an UNSUB—an unknown subject. Someone with a personal motive, say a jilted lover, or an impersonal hired gun.

"Several problems with that. The biggest, it makes no sense for a lover to lay the murder on me. From my interviews with Belle's friends, it's a wonder they didn't hint she was cheating, even if she wasn't."

Harriet said, "Friends like that, you don't need enemies. Or maybe you do. Folks that wish you ill are honest about it."

Jack agreed. "As for a contract killer, he could have stolen my .38, provided that was part of the deal. Belle *was* shot execution style, but—" he shook his head "—I just don't buy it. Among other things, why shut off the electricity? Better yet, why leave it off?"

From the kitchen, Dina said, "I thought it was to confuse the time of death."

"The killer may have thought that," Jack said, "but immersion in jetted, hundred-some-degree water would have affected it, too. Possibly more."

"Why would a hit man care about the time of death?" Harriet said.

"He wouldn't. Whether the power was on or off goes to establishing an alibi."

Dina said, "Either way, Brett Dean Blankenship as the killer doesn't make sense, either. Why steal your gun, murder your ex-wife, then try to run you down with his car outside the police station?"

Harriet gasped. "Run you down?"

Noting Dina's neat subtraction of herself from the crosswalk incident, Jack said, "Aw, he missed me by a mile." He winked at her. "Excellent question, though. If he had the smarts to set me up, he'd have planted more evidence, tipped McGuire to Cherise Taylor's involvement with the kennel setups—plenty of loose ends available to wind around my neck."

"If," Dina said, "he knew about the kennels."

"He tailed me too often not to. Much as I'd like to believe I spotted him every time, there are thousands of small white cars in this town."

"Okay," she said, "except I still don't understand why you bothered talking to his mother."

"Process of elimination." Jack couldn't articulate the sensory cues a personal space exudes. Home isn't merely where the heart's supposed to be. It's where it beats loudest.

The house's jazzy exterior trim and Mary Blankenship's sporty red car were at odds with someone still enamored of hewed-plank paintings and rooster lampshades. The decor was as time-warped as her life. Brett Dean had commandeered the recliner—the dad chair—but remained the lazy, indulged kid she'd supported, cooked for and cleaned up after since the man of the house disappeared from the pictures atop the piano.

That contrast jibed with Mary's "boys will be boys" lilt when she said Brett Dean blamed the traffic accident on the other driver. As if he'd fibbed about an in-school detention, not causing what could have been a multifatality collision.

"Blankenship's an overfed brat," Jack said. "Also a freak, but how much initiative does it take to follow me in his car? Steer with one hand, slam Ding Dongs with the other. No sweat.

"But frame me for murder? Hell, Moby Dick—er, he'd have gotten more exercise than he's had in years. Plus, it required the stones to kill a woman in cold blood."

Jack thought Harriet's frown disapproved of his vocabulary.

"Well, if this Blankenship fella didn't do it," she said, "who did? Everybody *knows* her husband was in Arkansas when she was murdered."

"It does look that way."

"That man on the news said the police had confirmed he was."

Harriet sat up straighter, as though a lesson were about to be taught. "Time was when divorce was nigh as bad as murder. Then it made no nevermind to anybody if a couple bothered to take vows at all. Now it seems husbands and wives are killing one another right and left, like a divorce is worse than murder."

Dina laid her mother's pharmaceutical dessert course and water to wash it down with in front of Harriet. "I wanted a death certificate stapled to my divorce decree." She laughed. "Best of both worlds."

"What I'm trying to say is," Harriet snipped, "if you listen sharp, you can tell when the newsman is fudging. He'll say Mr. So-and-So was 'allegedly' here. Or 'reportedly' there. Hear either one of 'em, and ol' So-and-So's guilty as homemade sin."

She rolled a gel cap between her fingers. "But confirmed? Especially after a day or two's *allegedly* and *reportedly?* That's a sign to stop looking at poor So-and-So like he's a monster and start baking hams and a carrot cake to take to the house."

Green bean casserole was Jack's mother's comfort food. Canned onion rings, cream of mushroom soup and Italian-cut green beans on the counter harbinged a death outside the family as much as his dad's black suit hanging on the closet door.

Belle. They didn't know she was…gone. The funeral. They'd probably fly up for it. For Jack, and to pay respects to the daughter-in-law they'd loved and still sent birthday and Christmas cards to.

Images strobed in Jack's mind. In one frame, Bill and Norma McPhee exited a jetway, smiling and waving, then blanched, remembering why they'd come and embarrassed they'd forgotten for a moment. The next was of a casket resting on a skirted bier. Belle's leg crooked over the lip of the tub. A wall of gladioli, roses, lilies arranged by height and color spanning the width of a chapel. A cloudy green eye hooded and lifeless; the other a dark empty socket.

"DeHaven shot her." The guttural declaration startled Jack, as well as Harriet and Dina. His breathing was ragged, sour. "I'm—"

He stared down at the table, unashamed of the tears rising in his eyes and fighting to stanch them. He couldn't make up for anything he'd failed to give Belle in life. She didn't need his grief now. She needed his help.

A swallow of iced tea melted the jagged burr in his throat. "It had to be deHaven. Nobody else stood to gain from Belle's death." He looked up at Dina, then Harriet and down again, his composure still less than trustworthy.

"Gain motivates domestic homicides." A thumbnail planed

a defect in the table's shellac finish. "Money tops the hit parade—no pun intended. An anticipated windfall or to prevent a financial loss. Second is an emotional motive. Jealousy, revenge, to remove an obstacle, a threat and the ever popular 'If I can't have her, nobody can.'"

"Money," Harriet said, as if selecting a game-show category. "Rich people can afford lots of life insurance. Beneficiaries get twice as much if the departed didn't die natural."

Dina nodded at her mother. "*Double Indemnity*. It's one of her favorite movies."

"Mine, too. Except Belle didn't have any life insurance." Back on safe, factually solid ground, Jack added, "That would have been the first thing the police checked. Next was the prenup. A divorce would cost deHaven a half million."

"Dollars?" Dina slumped in her chair. Money in a lump-sum, six-figure denomination was beyond her comprehension.

"Spare change, it isn't, but nowhere near a straight-up division of marital assets. Which also assumes an amicable split, instead of, say, deHaven auditioning the next wife in advance. No apparent money motive and a Tupperware alibi is why his name fell off the suspect list and mine zoomed to the top."

An investigation always focuses on the obvious suspect, because in the majority of cases, the obvious doer is the guilty party. If cleared, the direction shifts to the next most obvious. As Belle's former husband, Jack would have been questioned had he moved to Nova Scotia after their divorce. An airtight alibi for his whereabouts would logically swing attention to deHaven again, albeit indirectly. An impatient or disappointed mistress; a business associate Belle suspected of malfeasance; a competitor choking on deHaven's dust.

"Ballistic proof that my .38 was the murder weapon suggests

more than it appears to," Jack said. "The shot that killed her shows proficiency with a handgun. I am. Practice keeps me that way. Anyone with access to a weapon damn well should be, in the event he ever has to use it."

Dina's eyes cut to Harriet. "Or should lose it." Her mother pursed her lips and picked at her sweater. "Go on, McPhee. Some of us are listening."

Another Wexlergram had been transmitted and received. Jack didn't know the code, and neither of them seemed inclined to translate.

"Handgun proficiency," he reminded. "McGuire told me deHaven isn't a registered gun owner. No weapons or ammo of any kind were found in the house. It isn't conclusive evidence he lacked the skill to fire the fatal shot. There just isn't any to the contrary."

Dina asked, "Do you have to be a registered gun owner to go to a target range?"

"You don't need a target range to practice," Jack said.

"Well, if I was planning a murder, I wouldn't want anybody to see me with a cap pistol." Harriet hesitated. "But wouldn't he need to practice with your gun? To get accustomed to it."

"An hour, maybe, if he was generally proficient already. The murder was premeditated. He may have jimmied my car the night of my last trip to the police range. If so, he had a week to practice with it."

"DeHaven knew you kept it in the glove box?" Dina asked.

Jack waggled a hand. "He's my ex-wife's husband. It's doubtful I monopolized their pillow talk, but drop a seed here and a seed there and pretty soon you have an orchard.

"Belle knew I have a concealed-carry permit. Also that I seldom walk around with a gun, like Dirty Harry. It's common sense—I'm unlikely to need a weapon at the office, which I'm not in, as much as my car.

"The clincher is, whoever stole my .38 popped the trunk first."

"It is?" Harriet frowned. "Oh. If he'd opened the glove box first, he'd have found the gun."

"Right."

"Which is a silly place to keep one, if you ask me."

Which made Harriet the second female to voice that unsolicited opinion. It went without saying that Dina agreed.

Jack sighed. "Once upon a time, not long ago, a hardworking, conscientious P.I. was surveiling a department store's loading dock. Inventory was shrinking. The manager wanted a line on who was walking it out the door and how.

"It's January, early evening, dark as midnight. Our hero was reviewing the symptoms of frostbite when a crowbar smashes the driver's-side window. There's a scuffle. Hero gets coldcocked and wakes up light a wallet, binoculars, camera equipment, etc."

Absently, Jack massaged a bump below the bridge of his nose. The schnoz he was born with was serviceable, but beatings add character. "The mugger didn't get the .38, though. Since I didn't expect trouble, it was locked in the trunk, where, as Belle often pointed out, it did me a helluva lotta good.

"Except blowing away a crack addict isn't my definition of self-defense and it might've happened from pure reflex. Yeah, he roughed me up, but hey. Nobody died."

Dina rose to let out Phil, sniffing at the patio drapes in a manner usually reserved for trees, tires and fire hydrants. A hand chafing the nape of her neck told Jack that the story's epilogue wasn't lost on her. Ignoring Belle's urging to carry the .38 for protection had saved a mugger's life, and ended hers.

"Her death wasn't your fault," Dina said, walking back to the table. "DeHaven would have taken that gun somehow, no matter where you kept it. Get over it."

"Dina Jeanne! That's an awful thing to say. The poor man—"

"Is a professional investigator," Jack finished. He jerked a thumb at the ream of data divided by subject in file folders. "With a shitload of homework to do."

And an able assistant who kicked him in the butt when he needed it most.

17

Jack buckled the seat belt. The abundant slack suggested its previous user was heftier than him, or the type who passively complied with rules and aggressively defied their purpose. Like a restaurant employee who obeys restroom signage about hand washing, then smugly dries them on a filthy apron.

He tipped his head back against the seat rest. He closed his eyes and blocked out the mechanical and human cacophony swirling around him, but shutting down two of the five senses intensified the remaining three. Smell in particular. The locker-room-meets-perfume-factory odors had him fumbling for a breath mint so he didn't have to taste them, too.

He hated to fly. Cruising altitude was bearable, up to the point where the childish lobe of his brain started whining, "Are we there yet? I'm hungry. I'm thirsty. I don' wanna sit still anymore and you can't make me."

Takeoffs and landings—that's what he hated. They resigned control to a stranger who resembled either someone itching for another go at the Luftwaffe, or the kid who chamoised Jack's car when he sprang for the deluxe hot-wax package.

Landings were a friggin' cheat. The tires touched down geographically by arrival time. Lumbering to the terminal and getting off the damn plane ate a quarter hour, depending on how many zip codes intervened and how much crap other passengers shoehorned into overhead bins the farthest distance from their assigned window seats.

Timing was everything, this trip. Jack had toyed with delaying until Sunday to better duplicate deHaven's theoretical flights between Park City, Missouri, and Little Rock, Arkansas— albeit in reverse order.

A Thursday schedule was different than a Sunday, especially prenoonish to midafternoon. Weekend business travelers tend to hop later evening flights, rather than leave home early, then twiddle their thumbs in destination hotel rooms.

Except a three-day wait was two too many. What would Jack do in the meantime? Progress on a premise liability investigation and a grandparent's child-custody petition sprang to mind. Then there was a public-defender hire for a client charged with armed robbery. The Supreme Court ruling that poor defendants deserved the same defense preparation as wealthier ones and at government expense hadn't silver-lined many P.I.s' pockets.

Government work paid like government work. Few clients on public defenders' rosters were guilty only of being in the wrong place at the wrong time. As usual, Jack's queries into the current case were asserting the prosecutor's contention.

By this Sunday, Jack might be decked out in jailhouse orange, socks and flip-flops. Hell, he could be tomorrow, assuming Captain America and the Car Wash Kid didn't screw up the air-safety statistics.

Yeah, well, statistics were really what had him strapped in a friggin' piccolo with wings and beverage service. Last night, Yancy Nilsson had called in the midst of Jack's and Dina's slog through a mountain of faxes, computer printouts and notes. "Simpson," Yancy said, instead of hello.

"Ashlee or Jessica?" The kid had the major hots for both, perhaps simultaneously in his dreams. When Yancy wasn't slaying online dragons, he surfed Internet fan sites and chat rooms for the latest cell-phone photos and gossip on his beloveds.

He said, "I guess you haven't gone over Sunday's passenger manifests yet."

"Just starting." Jack eyed the sheets in the respective folders. Stating the obvious with a kiss of accusation, he said, "You copied them when I wasn't looking."

"Robert K. Simpson," Yancy recited. "Flight 17, a DC-8, Little Rock to Park City."

Jack's finger followed down the page. "Got it."

"P. David Simpson, flight 219, a 737 from Chicago. Connecting flight, A-23, on a DC-8 from Park City to Little Rock."

The prickle of excitement at Jack's rib cage vaporized. "Nice try spotting the Simpson thing, but that Chicago flight departed there a few minutes behind flight 17 from Little Rock."

"The Chicago ticket could have been bought to throw everybody off. Dad says he's used the connecting-flight half of one lots of times. No questions asked, no problemo on a boarding pass for the second leg."

Dad Nilsson was also a six-foot-five-inch tax attorney who made grown IRS auditors weep. "'Simpson' isn't an uncommon name," he said, moving to a tray table beside Harriet's glider to confiscate a current telephone directory.

"There are 210,000 of them in the U.S.," Yancy stated. "Easy math—that's forty thou per state. Missouri's total population is roughly 5.8 million. Arkansas, 2.6. What are the odds a Simpson would fly out of Little Rock, and another Simpson into Little Rock, approximately five hours apart on the same Sunday in July?"

It sounded like a middle-school algebra story-question. Jack detested algebra, partly because he'd never given a rat's ass about Train X, Train Y or what time either of them left Baltimore.

"Okay," he said, because he did like Yancy and appreciated the kid's initiative. Tissue-thin phone book pages crackled through the *S* section. "But if deHaven needed two fake IDs to cover his tracks, why use the same last name?"

A pause, then, "You're the detective, Mr. McPhee. I just play one on the computer."

There were thirty-eight Simpsons in the greater Park City phone book. Two Bobs: Bob A. and Bob G. Two single-initial R. Simpsons, both probably female. Several Roberts, Robert Jr.s, Robs, a Robbie, a Robby and a Roberto. All with middle initials. Not a Robert K. in the bunch.

It didn't mean squat, Jack reminded himself now, as he had last night after Yancy hung up. Park City Memorial Airport drew passengers from a 150-mile radius. Robert K. Simpson's phone number could also be unlisted.

The turboprop piccolo with wings began descending, its throttle-back mimicking a stall. Or what he imagined a stall would feel like. He gripped the armrests as the glidey, gently pendulous seconds ticked by, braced to hear God's, or gravity's raucous laughter at the audacity of a multiton aircraft suspended on air.

A staticky, nasal voice on the PA droned, "Ladies and gentlemen, as we begin our approach to Little Rock National…"

The password entered in the newspaper archive database was taking forever to process. Dina arched her back, wriggled out the leg she'd been sitting on, then hiked a hip to tuck under the other one.

Like every chair in the universe, Jack's office model's seat was too deep to lean back against and too high for her feet to touch the floor. She'd learned by upper elementary school when the desks outgrew her that dangling both legs wasn't as comfortable as dangling one at a time. Even when no one was around to tease her, she felt shorter with her feet just hanging there at the end of her ankles.

"Nope," she said, going for cheerful. "Nobody here but me."

Earlier, the thrill of being Sherlock McPhee's trusty Dr. Watson had sped the morning's shearing of two longhaired cats' feces-matted hindquarters and a poodle's full-length crew cut. Strange how fast her excitement withered after she'd locked herself in Jack's office.

He'd advised against switching on the overheads or desk lamp to keep up a vacant appearance. Not that the office was dark. Light filtered through the tinted plate windows, and the laptop's screen glowed bright enough to read printed pages by.

Alone was relative, too. Vehicles passed by on the parking lot and on Danbury Street. Horns honked. Disembodied voices—mostly male—and occasional laughter were heard. Thuds, rattles and smoke-alarm howls echoed through the diner's common wall.

Dina's solitude was covert, not actual. No reason at all—in broad daylight, for pity's sake—to feel as if phantom centipedes were creepy-crawling up her arms.

At the screen's polite prompt, she typed in a new search parameter and clicked the mouse. "One moment, please…"

"Yeah, right." In cyberspace, a moment was relative, too.

With Yancy rehearsing for a tent-theater play and Jack snagging airline tickets barely in time to make the first flight, the computer snooping had fallen to her. A scribbled list of sites and their passwords hadn't netted much, besides eye strain. Evidently, TV P.I.s did this sort of scut work during commercials.

Dina sighed and swiveled to empty the color printer's tray. Yesterday, as deHaven's publicist told Mary Jaymes, ace magazine feature writer, photos of the weekend seminar had been posted on the Web site: deHaven at a lectern; deHaven shaking hands with the multitudes; book signings; happy hours; banquet table shots—deHaven, the only VIP not captured with a fork in his mouth.

He was a good-looking guy, she admitted. Tall, early fifties, graying at the temples. Tanned, fit and trim with an aura of lucking out in the gene pool rather than expending any effort on maintenance. In the photos, his smile muscles had received a serious workout, but his eyes were cold. Predatory, in Dina's opinion, which wasn't objective. In fairness, a man who made a living selling rainbows with pots of gold at their ends wouldn't get far looking like everybody's affable Uncle Lenny.

She moved aside Jack's key ring to lay the printouts flat on the desk's return. Between two square-headed silver keys, a little brass one winked at her in the light cast by the laptop screen. Her eyes flicked to the desk's center drawer's lock and back at the little brass key.

A moment later, she breathed, "Well, what do you know," as the drawer rolled open. "I'd have bet this was the key to the storage cabinet over there."

The pencil trough held several highlighter pens. "Wow, good thing I found *these*. They'll really come in handy when I have to, uh, highlight something."

Pulling the drawer open wider, she chatted, "No *wonder* Jack took his car keys off the ring, instead of giving me the one to the door. In case I needed a, er, staples. For the stapler. Or Wite-Out. *Not* because he was in a hurry to get to the airport."

Sticky notepads, loose business cards, paper clips, take-out menus—Mr. Neat's junk drawer proved he was human after all. She yelped, then sucked on a fingertip viciously stabbed by a pushpin.

At the back of the drawer, wedged in a corner under books of blank checks, was a rubber-banded envelope. The upper edge had been slit. The return address read, "George Stoughton, Public Defender's Office."

Inside was a small, spiral notebook and two cassette tapes. One of the latter was hand labeled Wexler, Dina J., Orig. The other, Wexler, Dina J., Dupl.

"Herman Melville," Jack said, having developed a peculiar fondness for the alias. "Postevent supervisor, F.D.I.C."

The initials stood for Financial Dividend Investment Counseling. A stroke of genius, Jack admitted, for Carlton deHaven to reinvent the vaunted FDIC's initials as a beard for his smoke and mirrors, MentalWealth seminars.

Why hadn't the Federal Deposit Insurance Corporation issued a cease-and-desist order? Along with indictments for fraud and other probable felonies? Hell if Jack knew.

Charles Dunwoodie, the hotel manager, shook Jack's hand, although clearly perplexed by the introduction. "Melville? Like the author?"

"Distant relative. All I write are reports and memos."

"Yes, well…"

"Let me guess," Jack said. "Our assistant event coordinator forgot to mention I'd stop by this week." He sucked his teeth. "That's two screwups so far this month."

Dunwoodie graciously replied, "It's possible your assistant informed my assistant and—well, just between you and I, my new girl isn't what you'd call upper-management material."

My girl? Fascinating how revealing a single word can be. "Considering you weren't expecting me, I do hope this isn't a bad time for you, Charles." He glanced at his watch. "I may be able to change to a later afternoon flight, if it's more convenient for you."

"Absolutely not, Mr. Melville." Dunwoodie practically clicked his heels together and bowed. "However, if you could pardon me for a moment or two, there is a matter of some urgency I must attend to before our meeting."

There was a chance Dunwoodie suspected Jack's cover story and was calling F.D.I.C. for the lowdown on Herman Melville. Could be he did have a bona fide priority to resolve. Instinct said the hotel manager was marking territory. He wanted to establish that he, too, was a busy executive unable to immediately cater to whomever waltzed in without an appointment.

Jack approached the desk clerk who'd surreptitiously watched the meet-and-greet. He took the guy for mid-twenties. Reasonably clean-cut, no visible tattoos, holes in both earlobes and bracketing an eyebrow. Ditch the hardware at home and you can make a couple bucks an hour more than a fry cook.

Jack's opening questions affirmed the clerk was on duty from 7:00 a.m. to 4:00 p.m. last Sunday. Noting the name badge, he said, "I'm the company complaint department, Michael. Believe me, I know conferences are nightmares for staffers trying their best to accommodate guests."

"Some are," Michael hedged.

"We've never had one yet where hotel employees wept when it was over." Jack grinned. "You wouldn't be the first to call Carleton deHaven a jerk, either." He tapped his leather portfolio. "Thirty-seven, at last count."

"Seriously?"

"Hey, you know how the world works, Mike. He who has the gold breaks the rules. I'm just the strictly confidential cleanup batter."

Still wary, but warming up, the clerk said, "I was off, Friday and Saturday. What I saw of Mr. deHaven, he seemed okay."

"Courteous? No over-the-top demands, nothing like that?"

A hesitation. "Not really."

Jack let silence stretch two beats, three….

"Well, room service caught it big-time on Sunday when he didn't have his pot of coffee, like two minutes after he called downstairs." A pause, then, "The servers flipped for who'd hustle it up to him. My girlfriend lost, but she made an extra five bucks cash on top of the gratuity. Mr. deHaven even apologized. Told her he had a wicked migraine and coffee always helped."

"Decent of him," Jack said. "I don't suppose you know when this happened?"

"Ten-thirty, eleven maybe." Mike shrugged. "That's why it took so long. The kitchen was hoppin' to get ready for the church crowd. You wouldn't believe how many townies pack into the restaurant for lunch on Sundays."

"You must have great food."

The clerk looked left, right, then lowered his voice. "Have you ever had great food in a hotel restaurant?"

Jack laughed. "Not on my expense account. I'm Super 8, IHOP and Mickey D's all the way."

Mike motioned to hold on while he checked out a guest. On the desk's belt-high staff side, a whisper-quiet printer proffered the guest's statement for Kenneth Liebowitz, 84552 StarCircle Drive, Atlanta, Georgia. During his overnight stay, he'd twice eaten in the restaurant, run up a fifty-seven-dollar bar tab and watched a pay-per-view channel in his room.

Had Jack been inclined, Liebowitz's American Express account number was his for the memorizing. Five minutes in the hotel's business center and he'd have a Social Security number, birth date, credit report, wife's and children's names and birth dates, employment history and previous addresses to go with it.

If the man's maternal grandmother had attended his wedding, or was deceased, either newspaper write-up would provide that worst conceivable security password: Liebowitz's mother's maiden name.

What Jack wouldn't give for the same amount of time alone with the keyboard taunting him a few feet beyond his reach. A fire alarm, bomb threat, faulty water main—any ol' act of God or vandalism would be splendid right about now.

"It wasn't Mr. deHaven that was a pain," Mike said, returning to Jack's end of the counter. "I don't remember the guy's name, but he was, like, a, you know, a director or something. Comb-over? Glasses? About your height, but a lot heavier."

Jack nodded, having not the slightest clue whom that description might fit.

"He was freakin' about somebody deHaven was supposed to pick up at the airport. Paced the lobby, yelled into his cell phone. Shoved around luggage carts and people that got between him and the door. I thought the dude was gonna stroke out, then boom, it was over. Maybe an hour later, Mr. deHaven and this other man pull up in a limo—"

Mike tensed. Overcome by a sudden need to consult the registration files in a desk cubby, he said, "I wish we had an F.D.I.C. seminar every weekend, Mr. Melville. Everyone I spoke to was as nice as he or she could be."

Jack knew without looking that Charles Dunwoodie had concluded his urgent matter and was standing directly behind him. "Impressive, Michael. Very impressive."

From the portfolio, he extracted an F.D.I.C. business card formatted and printed with the Web site's logo and contact information. "Our organization is always scouting for young up-and-comers—"

A hand clapped Jack's shoulder. The card was artfully plucked from his grasp. "So sorry to keep you waiting, Mr. Melville." To the desk clerk, Dunwoodie murmured, "If you'll excuse us, Michael."

Jack turned, biting back a grin. Like the song says, "You're nobody, till somebody loves you." Or in this case, wants you. Blatant head-hunting in front of the boss virtually assured Michael a raise, if not a promotion.

He also realized neither Mike nor Dunwoodie had mentioned Belle's demise. A subtle comment, such as, "How *is* Mr. deHaven?" could be taken as a condolence, or completely generic. Most telling was the desk clerk's reaction when Jack called the seminar's star a jerk. Meaning no reaction at all. Weird, if the clerk had heard about deHaven's tragic loss.

Little Rock PD uniforms or detectives who'd delivered the news and confirmed deHaven's alibi must have been preternaturally discreet. Or those witness statements McGuire was so proud of were limited to F.D.I.C. employees.

After Jack asked several questions he presumed a postevent supervisor might pose, he said, "Forgive me, Charles, but I'm not clear on a few amenity issues. Your valet parking, for example. Is it mandatory for hotel guests or can they park their own whee—er, vehicles, if they so choose."

"The service is optional." Dunwoodie sniffed. "Although the majority of those who stay with us prefer it."

"Is a room key card necessary to enter and exit the garage?"

"Until a few months ago, yes. Numerous complaints were received about the gate failing to operate, misplaced cards and the like. The system was dismantled and now a security officer patrols the entire facility on the hour."

"Security cameras? Lights?"

"Lighting, yes." Dunwoodie heaved a remorseful sigh. "I'd prefer not to go into detail, but incidents where the cameras captured, shall we say, indiscretions, encouraged their removal, as well."

In other words, videotaped evidence of married couples doing the Detroit Boogie with those other than their spouses were Exhibit A in divorce proceedings. Not many Park City hotels had parking garages, but Jack stowed away that tip for future reference.

"The do-it-yourself parking," he said. "Are areas assigned, or is it first come, first served?"

"The latter, Mr. Melville."

Feeling the hotel manager's increasing dubiousness, Jack switched tactics. "Before I forget, Mr. deHaven was concerned about the stain on the carpet in his room."

"Stain? What stain?"

"Red wine, I believe." Jack grimaced. "Nearly a full bottle, I'm afraid. Mr. deHaven instructed me to make sure no permanent damage was done. Or if so, to reimburse the hotel for any expense incurred."

"Oh, my heavens. A red-wine stain is worse than a…"

Bloodstain, Jack thought, as Dunwoodie hurried to the desk to check the room's availability for inspection.

DeHaven's weekend accommodations were a hike from the elevator alcove. While the manager slipped his passkey into room 220's electronic reader, Jack eyed the interior stairway directly across the corridor. Above the door was a combination Exit sign and dual emergency lights. No security cameras anywhere, unless the rubber tree at the end of the hall was wired for video.

A faint odor of nicotine contradicted the No Smoking placard on 220's door. By the lingering staleness, it was a relatively recent conversion.

DeHaven was a militant nonsmoker. Before Jack quit, Belle bummed a few when they'd meet for drinks. She couldn't resist the swimmy, head-lolling high they gave her. Short-lived, but perfectly legal. Carleton wasn't always in town during these revolts, but Jack knew Belle enjoyed them more when he was.

Otherwise, room 220 was a spacious, basic king-size bed, nightstands, bureau, armoire with requisite electronics and writing-desk setup. In front of the window was a club table and wing chairs where guests could sip the marginally palatable coffee brewed in the bathroom's Barbie Dream House coffeemaker.

Nice digs, but well beneath Golden Boy deHaven's standards—monetary and olfactory.

Dunwoodie bent double and scuttled around in search of the mythical wine stain. The cobalt-patterned carpet could absorb an arterial hemorrhage with no one the wiser. Jack dodged out of the manager's way, relieved there were no random splotches he'd be stuck paying to have cleaned.

"Were you surprised that Mr. deHaven didn't reserve a suite?" he asked.

Dunwoodie knelt to peer under the box-pleated bed skirt. "Um, well, yes, I suppose." He crab-walked to the foot of the bed. "Others in his entourage were on the concierge floor."

Jack couldn't pronounce *croissant* without a bourbon buzz. If then. In his vernacular, *entourage* was French for "ass kissers."

This trip, deHaven wanted distance from them. Privacy. The hotel's floor plan was posted on its Web site. A room in a dead-end corridor, one floor above the lobby, three below his lackeys and across from a stairway was tailor-made.

The nightstand's clock radio hoved into view. "Charles, listen, you've been a great help, but I do have a plane to catch."

Dunwoodie's joints cracked as he regained his feet. Dusting off his hands, he said, "A spill of the volume you mentioned might not be apparent for several days. Let me page a maintenance person—"

"Tell you what." Jack backed toward the door. "Send an invoice for any damages to my attention at the address on my card." He edged into the corridor. "We at F.D.I.C are eager to ensure a long and happy relationship with your hotel."

Dollar signs rose and shimmered in Dunwoodie's eyes. "Yes, of course, Herman. That's our objective."

"Herman" it was, finally. "This stairway. Does it access all levels of the parking garage? I figure I can zip down and out front to my rental car faster this way than backtracking to the elevators."

Dunwoodie's nose wrinkled at the thought of such an uncivilized exit. "Only the basement level, I'm afraid, Mr. Melville." He gestured down the corridor at an intersecting hallway. "The auxiliary elevators service the opposite end of the lobby and each garage level."

Jack chuckled and patted his midsection. "I'd rather ride, but this jelly roll says I need the exercise."

They shook on it, the manager still a skosh bewildered by the abrupt departure. Jack clattered down the concrete stairs, noting his watch's exact time. A land-speed record wasn't the intent. Hustle, not hurtle.

Dunwoodie had lied, of course. Compact security cameras with tiny red indicator buttons were mounted at each landing. Which meant Big Brother watched over the garage, as well. The hotel's liability in the event of a criminal assault, purse snatch or an on-premise injury guaranteed it. A clunkier, visible system had been replaced with a smaller generation of spy cams.

Evidence for criminal proceedings? You bet. For a civil case?

Aside from negligence suits against the hotel, no way, Jose. The simplest stopgap was dumping the footage every twenty-four hours. Long enough to preserve for a criminal- or personal-liability incident—brief enough to disappoint divorce lawyers and private investigators.

DeHaven's alleged egress and ingress via the stairs and out the basement garage remained alleged. While a subpoena could obtain a computerized record of room 220's key card's usage, the coffee service might have been a ruse for alibi purposes. Afterward, deHaven could jerry-rig the door to close but not lock. No key card needed to get back in. No record to make a liar out of him.

Jesus Christ on a chariot, McPhee. That ass wipe's a murderer, not a master friggin' criminal.

At the basement level, he shouldered open the heavy metal door. Twenty-three seconds from deHaven's room to the garage. Jack scanned the vehicles nosed into their respective blocks, then remembered Mike saying deHaven arrived at the hotel in a limo.

He hadn't driven to the airport. Duplicate ignition keys would circumvent the valet service, which deHaven undoubtedly used, but what if somebody saw him pull out of the garage? Or back in? And how would he later retrieve his car at Little Rock National without arousing suspicion?

He had to get to the airport somehow. A cab? The hotel shuttle? Possible. However deHaven managed it, he wasn't wearing custom-tailored threads when he left the hotel. But he must have dressed the part when he met Mr. Who's-It's incoming flight in a limo.

Provided he had murdered his wife…

Jack fast-walked, then broke into a jog toward the inclined ramp to street level. He had an hour and change to turn in his rented wheels, grab a boarding pass and strap himself into another damn piccolo with wings.

18

Dina's arm clapped the laptop and the sliding stack of loose papers to her chest. Their edges tickled her chin, the middle sheets gradually slithering downward. The hobo bag's strap dangling from the crook of her other arm and Jack's Captain Kangaroo-sized key ring in her hand weren't helping fit the agency's stupid door key into the agency's stupid key*hole*.

Behind her, a stern voice demanded, "Who are you?"

Papers slopped to the sidewalk and fanned out almost to the curb. Dina spun around. The sun reflecting off adjacent windshields backlit a tall, faceless man. Oh, dear God. Carleton deHaven. Every sheet of paper she'd printed had his name on it. "What are you doing here? What do you want?"

The man stepped closer, menacingly close, into the strip of shade fronting the buildings. White hair and features graven by at least twice Dina's years on Earth affirmed he wasn't deHaven. Still, that flinty glare pinned her back to the door.

"My name's Abramson. Gerald Abramson. I'm here to see Jack McPhee."

"The insurance agent?" An identity less terrifying than her earlier assumption. From a homicidal standpoint, anyway.

"Correct. And you?"

She wanted desperately to lie. And would, if any name other

than Jane Austen flitted through her brain. "Dina Wexler," she answered, as one might Lizzie "the Ax" Borden.

Rather than howl "Aha! The infamous Calendar Burglar!" Abramson's gaze averted to the key ring. "I wasn't aware McPhee had hired clerical help."

If *hired* equated with an agency paycheck, he hadn't. Which was none of Abramson's business.

"Hey, miss," yelled the more muscle-bound of two young men striding toward the diner's entrance. Both wore black jeans and boots, wraparound sunglasses and rottweiler scowls. "Is that guy hassling you?"

Yes, he was. Just not in the manner they implied. "Thanks," she said, "but everything's fine."

Continuing on, they darted skeptical glances as they swung open the diner's door. Not her mother's knights in shining armor, but it was nice to know some version still existed.

Undeterred by the anatomical rearrangement she'd spared him, Abramson snapped, "So where *is* McPhee?"

The gruff third-degree was beginning to piss her off. "Out of the office. Obviously."

"I can see where he isn't, Ms. Wexler."

"I don't know how to reach him at the moment, Mr. Abramson."

"Reach him is what I've tried to do all week. I've called and left message after message, before and since I fired him. He hasn't—"

"You fired him? When? Why?"

Suspicion narrowed his eyes. "You work here and you weren't aware of that?"

Dina knelt to scoop up the papers, baling them with her arm, like a conscientious clerical employee. She was careful not to let Abramson see their content, other than glimpses of several official-looking headers.

"Why wouldn't I fire him?" Abramson inquired, as much to the breeze as to Dina. "He hasn't provided a single written report. We haven't spoken since last Saturday. Even before the police arrested him for murder, his work has been completely incompetent."

"Really." This time, she was the aggressor, the invader of personal space. "First off, Jack wasn't arrested for anything. Questioned, yes. Charged with a crime of any kind? Absolutely not.

"Secondly, have you given one moment's thought to the fact the homicide victim was Mr. McPhee's former wife? That despite their marital difficulties, he'd have been devastated by her death, regardless of circumstances."

"Well, I—"

"You tell me." Dina pointed at the gold band he wore. "How *competent* would you be four days after your wife died?"

Abramson stiffened, his face flushing a deep scarlet. "My wife has Parkinson's disease. She's been dying a little every day for several years."

"Oh, God." She blew out a breath. "I'm sorry. For you and your wife. I truly am, but that doesn't change the grief Jack's dealing with. Someone he cared deeply about was killed—shot to death—in her own house."

Abramson studied her for a long moment, then nodded. "I didn't realize…. Should have, I suppose, as many years as I've known Jack."

"He does a pretty good job of acting tough." Dina smiled. "Okay, he doesn't, but he thinks he does."

"Yes, but tough isn't the issue, Ms. Wexler. One returned phone call, one e-mail—I don't think I'm unreasonable to have expected a response of some kind."

Dina couldn't argue. Particularly since protecting her was the reason for the communications blackout. Whatever intervention in her behalf Jack had planned for Monday morning, Belle's murder and Lt. McGuire's presumption of Jack's guilt changed everything.

Lying for investigative purposes was an occupational requirement. From what she'd seen and heard, Jack excelled at it. Where clients were concerned, his code of professional ethics was black-and-white.

"I appreciate your honesty, Ms. Wexler, and your loyalty." Abramson shifted his weight. "But business is business. Do remind Jack, as I said in my last telephone message, I want a final report and the balance of the retainer by five o'clock Friday afternoon."

"That's tomorrow." The purse strap wobbled off her slumping shoulder. If not for that pending homicide charge, she'd confess on the spot. She would anyway and leave out the empty-handed deHaven burglary, except how could she explain having the keys to Jack's office? Let alone why he hadn't surrendered her to the police.

State and city licensing boards weren't big on gray areas, either. Tell Abramson the truth and McPhee Investigations would soon be another empty storefront.

"Please," she said, "give him until Monday. That's one business day from Friday. An extra, lousy twenty-four hours."

"I can't. I've contracted with another investigator. He wants McPhee's notes and the report I've already paid for to avoid duplicating the casework. Assuming any was done."

With that, Abramson turned and stalked off toward a showroom-shiny Mercedes sedan.

"Reports aren't results," Dina called after him. "Bet ya a hundred bucks—make it a *thousand*—that Jack's replacement won't catch that burglar by Monday."

The insurance man shot her a look that should have scorched

the lettering off the plate window behind her. Anger evolved to circumspection. "You sound awfully sure of yourself, Ms. Wexler."

Once, just once, couldn't she shut her mouth before it got her in trouble? Then again, there were a couple of things of which she was absolutely certain.

"Why wouldn't I be? You fired the best P.I. in town." She jutted her jaw. "Instead of appreciating my loyalty to Jack, maybe you ought to have a little of it yourself."

Jack braked for a traffic light. Park City had grown since he left that morning. It must have. The drive from the airport to the Wexlers' seemed ninety miles long—most of it still ahead of him.

He scrubbed his face with a hand. His skin felt greasy and parched at the same time. Jesus. What was it about sitting on your duff in an airplane that wore you out? Praying you either survive or croak faster than you can say "Oh, shit" shouldn't drain your batteries to a click above lights-out. His lips hadn't even moved for fear his seatmate would get the wrong idea. Or the right one.

He ought to feel great. He was *this close* to having Carleton deHaven by the *cojones*. Yeah, a couple of sizable puzzle pieces were missing, but the picture was shaping up.

And yeah, he'd wanted deHaven by the *cojones* for years. The guy was a sleaze. A white-collar, rat-bastard con man. Belle was supposed to get wise and get out before the scam collapsed, as they inevitably do. Her calculated, cold-blooded execution, Jack never, ever anticipated.

"I should have." He joined the traffic herd moseying along an asphalt chute. "DeHaven's a flat-out, full-bore sociopath."

He welcomed the adrenaline gates nudging open a crack. Again, he thought of Belle's illicit Marlboro highs. His natural one simmering just slightly cleared his brain and the lethargy weighting his bones.

DeHaven thrilled at the hunt, the chase. Acquisition was the goal—personally and professionally. Attaining it was like an orgasm. Exultant, powerful, satiating but temporary. Those sensations could be achieved again, maybe exceeded now and then, yet eventually, with nothing else driving them, no emotional connection, the need to hunt, the hunger for the chase must be satisfied.

To plan and execute the perfect murder, outwitting the police and taking down Jack in the process was irresistible. DeHaven would rid himself of a wife he was no longer enamored of and avoid the cost and stigma of another divorce.

Instead of business associates and disciples beginning to question his personal judgment and by association, his financial acumen, he'd be a widower. The "poor man whose wife was murdered" rather than the romantic fool who marries in haste and repents in divorce courts.

Except a perfect murder is a myth, Jack thought. Homicide does go unpunished. Unsolved cases haunt investigators' days and nightmares. Worse and often harder to live with are the acquittals. Insufficient evidence or a jury's belief that "beyond a reasonable doubt" and the misnomer "beyond a *shadow* of a doubt" were synonymous proved it's the world that ain't perfect.

Crimes of passion were generally the ones that wind up in a cold case unit's file drawer. Premeditated murder?

"Mistakes," Jack said. "There are always mistakes. Tiny missteps. Big fuckups. Overthinking it. Overplaying the hand you dealt yourself from a stacked deck."

His chuckle sounded more like a death rattle. "Outfoxing the foxes is a helluva lot harder than it looks, Golden Boy."

Wheeling into a bank's ATM lane, he clamped off the thought that knowing and proving weren't synonyms, either.

The round-tripper to Little Rock had taken a toll on his cash reserves. Bribing rental car clerks in two states cost a friggin' fortune. Especially when it was the fifth and seventh gomers, respectively—God forbid it ever be the first—who coughed up the info Jack sought.

Yancy worked cheap, but yesterday's data mining and Dina's today were rolling up Jack's credit card balances like a space shuttle's odometer. The premium he'd paid for a couple of last-minute airfares, he didn't care to think about.

Or refunding Gerry Abramson's retainer by tomorrow. Every nickel of it. Not a single expense Jack had incurred was billable to National Federated. Mention the burglaries' kennel connection and Abramson didn't need a hired bird to follow the bread crumbs straight to Dina.

"Knowing and proving." Jack pulled another slice of his net worth from the ATM's metal lips. "Without me, Gerry's got *bupkis.*"

The ramifications were still playing Ping-Pong in his head when he parked beside the Beetle in the driveway. The S-10 had commandeered the garage, having more pawnable stuff stowed in it than in the Taurus's backseat.

"Home sweet home." Jack's breath caught. A four-letter word that packed that kind of a punch was usually profane, not profound. "Jeezus Louiseus." He slammed the car door. "Trot down to Arkansas for half a day and you come back the friggin' marshmallow man."

"You're home!" Dina's happy voice turned the corner of the garage a beat faster than she did. Her million-watt grin, that mop of hair flying every which way, the leap into Jack's arms, laughing and strangling him simultaneously, he hadn't let himself dream about.

"So is the kitchen on fire?" he teased. "Or are you just kinda glad to see me?"

No answer. No chance to. Not with his lips impulsively covering hers, then their tongues touching, savoring, exploring…until Jack had to stop, had to pull away, before his knees buckled and the impact with the driveway killed them both.

"Uhhh," she moaned, sliding down till her feet touched ground. "Whew, boy."

"Yeah," he sighed. "What you said."

Wobbling back a little, she looked up at him with a mixture of "Wow," trepidation, and "Well, maybe one more in case that was a fluke." He knew, because he was thinking it, too. And it scared the hell out of him.

"That wasn't supposed to happen," she said.

"Bound to, eventually." His casual shrug felt like a muscle spasm. "This, uh…"

Friendship didn't sound right. *Relationship* didn't, either, somehow. Maybe because Jack detested it. *Attraction?* So last week. *Conspiracy?* Not.

"This connection between us," he finally said. "It was there at the get-go. For me, anyway."

"Except it's backward," she said. "Usually, if you like somebody, like I think we like each other, you go out, get to know each other better, then if you hit a rough patch, you fix it, or you say, 'Gosh, that was fun while it lasted,' and forget it."

Jack scratched his head, not disagreeing with her, but uncertain if this was one of those times when a wise man should, or suffer the consequences.

"We," Dina went on, "started with the rough patch. The more we get to know each other, the rougher it is, and no matter how much we like each other, we can't fix it, and we can't just forget it, and 'Gosh, that was fun while it lasted' is—"

Jack shut her up the only way he knew how. He relished the softness of her lips, the taste of her, the feel of her lithe little body curving into his.

This time when they parted, he cradled her face in his hands. "I don't know how to fix all of it. There's no guarantee I can fix any of it. But forget it? Uh-uh. Whatever happens, happens, but I'm not walking away. Not now, not ever."

"Even if—"

He pressed a finger to her lips. "Even if."

19

Harriet looked at Dina, then to Jack and back again. "I don't want to know."

"Know what, Mom?" C'mon, Dina thought. Ask me why I have this loony grin on my face. Why inside, it feels like I'm balanced on one tiptoe on the rim of a volcano.

"Why it took you ten minutes to fetch McPhee in here." She muttered something ending in "broad daylight" and went back to watching TV and stroking Phil's head.

"Do you want to hear about Jack's trip?"

"Not especially." There was petulance in her voice and a tremor.

"Are you all right?"

"Not especially." Harriet bowed her back, as she sometimes did when angina tightened her chest and radiated downward. "Got me a gas pain that won't quit, thanks for asking." Her mouth pursed. "And that's all it is, so quit fussing and leave me be."

Her skin was neither flushed nor a porcelain grayish-blue. Respirations were shallower and quicker than Dina's, normal for Harriet. Scrutinizing every twitch and sniffle would irk a raging hypochondriac. If her mother weren't inclined to brave acute symptoms and complain about minor ones, Dina wouldn't hover so much.

Particularly now. Stress was exacting a toll on them all. Harriet's resiliency was already compromised.

In the dining area, Dina nodded Jack away from the chair nearer the wall he'd gravitated to for meals. It was the only one with a direct, diagonal bead on her mother. He was perfectly capable of monitoring Harriet himself, except he didn't have Wexler radar or years of experience recognizing the blips.

Dina also knew Harriet's silent Maydays when she saw them. A tissue dabbing sweat at her temples and mouth signaled a blood-sugar slide or chest pain. Her knuckle pressing up the oxygen cannula meant breathing difficulty. Fingers flexing, her feet tapping under the throw indicated tingling, numbness or cold associated with poor circulation—also symptomatic of respiratory distress.

The reported discomfort probably was just indigestion, Dina thought. Real or a sly insult to my cooking, as opposed to Chef Boy-ar-McPhee's. Why live in peace and harmony, when you enjoy being the stick poking a hornet's nest?

From the paper grocery sack Jack retrieved from the trunk, he took out two beverage cans clad in foam cozies. An eyebrow crimped as he held out one to Dina. "Beer?" he mouthed.

First he kisses her till her toes curl under, then he smuggles in beer disguised as sodas? And not the four-bucks-a-sixer brand she'd buy in November, refrigerate outside behind a bush and make last until March.

Dina felt her mother's sidelong squint at the tabs' merry pop-*whissh*. The container's coved top and gold band above the cozy was identical to a soda can. The escaping foam was thicker and frothier than a cola, but it slurped the same.

Only better. Way and wonderfully better.

Harriet was again entranced by *City Confidential,* though the volume was muted enough to eavesdrop. Dina slid the can across the table and bumped Jack's. "To whatever happens."

He winked, then drank to it. "That's the spirit."

A cold beer and a sit-down evidently took precedence over his changing clothes. The only concessions to comfort were draping his suit coat over another chair, a loosened tie and collar button.

The ceiling fixture's glare wasn't flattering to anyone, but scored every crease and the marionette lines in Jack's face. Sleep didn't cure that kind of tired, but counting back, Dina realized he hadn't had a full, dreamless night's rest in a week.

She smiled to herself. If the beer didn't knock him out, other prescription remedies were at her disposal. He might even thank her for it someday. If he ever figured out she'd drugged him.

"Did you eat on the plane?" she asked.

He snickered. "Been a while since you've flown anywhere, huh?"

Never, actually. If not for a few family vacations to the Great Smokies, the Rockies and Disneyland, she'd have never crossed the Missouri border.

"I can reheat the veggie casserole we had for dinner, and there's plenty of Jell-O salad."

To his credit, he didn't grimace at the menu. "Thanks, but I'm really not hungry. Should be, but maybe pretzels and snack mix are more filling than I thought." He glanced downward at a rustling noise. "Outski, you nosy mutt."

Nabbed with his snoot in the grocery sack, Phil schlumped back into the living room and flopped beside the ottoman. A dog's life wasn't merely seven times a human's; it was fraught with unending disappointments.

"So," Jack said. "Got anything interesting to show me?"

"Mm-hmm." A finger traced down her neck, then followed the scoop of her tank top. "And I found some interesting stuff on the Internet, too."

"Oh, yeah?" Eyes hooded, he blew out a growly sigh. "If I ever get you alone…"

"Promises, promises." There was plenty more double-talk where that'd come from, except Dina sensed the governess in a smock and elastic-waist jeans tuning in.

She wanted him, and was damn well going to have him. Give to him completely, body and soul…but not on a lumpy couch. Or a pallet on the floor. Not like horny teenagers half listening for Mom's footsteps in the hallway.

Jack wouldn't want her that way, either. The time for love-making would come and so would they. In private, if only for a few hours.

Moving aside the laptop, Dina slid over the sheaf of papers reordered after her charming repartee with Gerry Abramson. Yes, the man had a right to be angry. It was her prerogative to not remind Jack of the deadline. Messages stacked in his voice mail queue undoubtedly contained several from the insurance broker.

Beginning with the mundane, she showed Jack sheets of photos from the seminar posted on F.D.I.C.'s Web site. "Carleton deHaven was in most of them. I didn't waste ink on the ones without him."

Jack sorted through them, discarding a few at a glance. "No time-date stamps in the corners," he grumbled.

Professional, not amateur photography, Dina assumed. Or the shots were cropped to look that way. "I compared them with the seminar schedule. They're more or less in chronological order."

The beer sluicing down her throat brought an involuntary shudder. A half can and already a nascent buzz was commencing at her temples. Once a cheap date, always a cheap date.

"MentalWealth," she said. "These people really believe they can *think* themselves rich?"

"Every generation has a guru." Jack shrugged. "Positive thinking is better than wallowing in the negative. Like me being positive the ones raking in the cash aren't the pigeons flocking to these mumbo-jumbo conventions."

"Is that legal? Promising people they *will* get rich that way?"

"Never underestimate the power of greed, kid. If it doesn't pay off, the onus is on the pigeons for not believing *enough.*"

He bent over a photo sheet, then held it up, angling it toward, then away from the light. "Got a magnifying glass?"

Guy-speak for "Go get me a magnifying glass," knowing the two Harriet used to read with were on the tray table. He wasn't being rude. Men were genetically programmed to pose supply questions, rather than state demands. Primarily because women were genetically programmed to answer them.

After a few seconds' examination under Harriet's lighted, rectangular model, Jack turned the sheet around and passed Dina the magnifier. "Second row, third shot from the left. Tell me what you see."

A beaming fat man with a comb-over was shaking hands with F.D.I.C.'s dissipated has-been celebrity endorser. In the background, Carleton deHaven looked on, an elbow braced on a crossed forearm, a self-satisfied smirk on his face.

"Compare it to this one." Jack slid over shots of Sunday's informal brunch. In those, deHaven presided over a round table of nattering disciples. At each surrounding table, a Mental-Wealth associate held court with seven attendees not quite as enthused to break muffins with an aide-de-camp.

"Okay," she said. "DeHaven doesn't seem to be chatting up his group like the other men. He isn't eating much, either."

"Look closer at him, then at the later one in the hotel lobby."

Frowning, she bobbed the magnifier left to right. Obviously there was something important Jack wanted her to find on her own. As if she'd ever been a whiz at those What's Different? panels in the funny pages.

A final sweep begged a double take, then another. "The resolution's not great, so I can't be sure," she qualified. "Maybe it's just a shadow, but in the lobby photo, deHaven's hair is—"

"Creased," Jack said. "Hat hair."

"Could be."

"Well, it ain't a shadow. And he's wearing the same three-button sport shirt and jacket he wore at the brunch." Jack tapped images of others in both photos. "Everyone else at the brunch, then in the lobby, is in a business suit and tie."

He related deHaven's alleged late-morning migraine attack and the desk clerk's report about Comb-over's frantic pacing. "If deHaven didn't go AWOL midafternoon, why would Comb-over be in a tizzy about the endorser's incoming flight? No doubt, a flunky checked the parking garage and saw deHaven's car there. It's logical the minions kept dialing his room and his cell. Probably even knocked at 220's door a time or two, but they wouldn't dare get a passkey and barge in."

"Why not, if he was ill?"

"Also logical that at some point, possibly from day one at MentalWealth, deHaven convinced them to never invade his privacy. For all I know, he was screwing around on Belle every chance he got. In any event, if he hadn't established a do-not-disturb policy, going missing at this gig would be too risky."

Dina said, "He wasn't scheduled to speak again until the banquet that night. But if Comb-over did call deHaven's cell phone, why didn't he just answer it?"

"Because he was either in the Park City airport or on the plane, flying back to Little Rock. The background noise, either place, would give that away."

"He could say it was the TV," she countered.

"A migraine makes you extremely light and sound sensitive. A TV that loud would be excruciating. Plus, one PA announcement—at the Missouri airport or in flight—blasting in the speaker holes, and deHaven's screwed."

Dina had met her ex-husband's parents' and siblings' flights at the airport. Announcements and canned precautions were as constant as hospital pages.

"The hat hair is key," Jack said. "If the bastard wasn't sweating before or after he shot Belle, airplane cabins are stuffy as hell in February, let alone July. Besides that, just try and convince me that anybody with a migraine ripping his skull would sit in a hotel room with a friggin' ball cap on."

Excellent point. Gwendolyn Ellicot at TLC had migraines and prescription meds to combat them. The tablets were miracle drugs, but Gwendolyn had to lock herself in her office and lay her head on a dog pillow on the desk until the pain relented.

"You're thinking the ball cap was deHaven's disguise."

"Sort of." Jack leaned sideward to exchange his empty beer can with a full one from the sack. A waggled finger offered Dina a second round. She declined, rather than graduate from cheap date to a blithering, giggling idiot.

He cupped his hand over the tab to muffle the popping sound. "I figure he changed into faded-out jeans or shorts, and tennis shoes or sandals in the room. The dress shoes, slacks, sport shirt and jacket went into a small carry-on. Add a ball cap, the drugstore specs worn for both Simpsons' photo IDs and it's down the fire stairs."

"The sport shirt wasn't packed." Dina indicated the morning and evening photographs. "He wore that."

"No, he didn't. It's purple."

Not just purple. Bright, almost Barney violet.

"With the sports shirt buttoned," Jack said, "you can't tell whether there's a T-shirt under it at the brunch. Can't later in the lobby, either, but by then, it's under there for sure. DeHaven chose a memorable, can't-miss color he *wanted* to be seen in. But keep it on for the hustle downstairs and out the garage? Dead giveaway."

Dina looked down at the photos trying to imagine deHaven dressed as Jack described. In Web site publicity stills and previous seminar archives, deHaven was always business formal. Anyone accustomed to that uniform of sorts might not connect a man of similar stature and coloring in Sunday-go-to-Dairy-Queen clothes.

"But how do you know he wore glasses?"

"Done it myself a thousand times. Specs alter facial features more than you realize. For a few dollars more, you can buy lenses that react to sunlight and stay shadowy-gray indoors."

"Very impressive, McPhee."

"I have my moments." He grinned. "And the ticket agent at the Park City airport thinks P. David Simpson wore glasses."

"Cheater."

"Professionally, yeah. Personally?" Jack shook his head. "Just because you have me on a diet, I'll still read menus, but that's as far as it'll go."

"Define read," she said.

He chuckled. "Big boobs? Nice butt? Hey, I'm human. Usually I keep the drooling down my shirt to a minimum."

Ogling, but not touching, much less taking them home to hump their brains out in her bed was a new and refreshing concept for Dina. But if Jack didn't stop looking at her like that, Harriet was going to get a triple-X floor show any second.

Forcing her attention to the rest of the printouts, she said, "Speaking of P. David Simpson, and his brother, Robert K...."

"Brothers?"

"The elder went by 'Paul,' not 'David.'" Reproduced Ohio newspaper articles were placed on top of the photos. "On April 3, 1974, 148 tornadoes chewed an almost 2600-mile swath across a dozen states and into Windsor, Ontario. Over 300 people were killed. Nearly 5500 were injured."

Jack's expression hardened, his eyes flat and malevolent. "Then deHaven didn't buy a driver's-license-and-credit-card package off the street." He chafed his jaw. "Nah, too common criminal for a hotshot like him. He ripped off two disaster victims' identities."

"Oh, not just any two." Dina wriggled around and up on her knees to reach across the table. "I got in a hurry and misspelled his last name in a search box. The prompt said, 'Do you mean *Carl* Haven?' If it wasn't for the weird tangents Yancy went on yesterday, I'd have ignored it and started over."

"But there couldn't have been just one Carl Haven," Jack said. "Almost any name search brings up a million hits."

"It did. I knew Yancy would then enter 'Carl Haven + Robert K. Simpson' to narrow the field."

Her finger hopscotched from highlighted sentences and paragraphs in newspaper stories dated from April 4 to April 11. "Ellen Simpson, her daughter, Candice, and two foster kids, fifteen-year-old Carl Haven and twelve-year-old Melody Haven, made it to the storm cellar at their farm.

"Ellen's husband, Paul, her brother-in-law, Robert Simpson, and a neighbor, Vincent Pflanders, were killed trying to batten down the outbuildings."

Dina quoted Ellen Simpson, "'There wasn't nothing left of the barn. Over a hundred years old it was. Paul and Bobby's grandpa built it out of oak. Not a rafter, a feed trough—it's like a bomb blew it to bits, then scattered the splinters as far as the eye can see.'"

Jack drained his beer and slammed the cozy on the table. He scraped a fist over his mouth, muttering under his breath. "Even if I believed in coincidences, this can't be one."

Another page was presented. "Mrs. Simpson's obituary. She died of cancer in January 1991. I tried, but other than later tornado-related hits, I didn't find anything else on Carl or Melody Haven."

She hesitated, then admitted, "Well, I might have, if I'd stuck with it, but—"

"Glad you didn't. You nailed a wild goose. No sense in chasing it."

"Assuming Melody is his sister, I was hoping to track her down, so you could contact her."

Jack nodded. "If she's findable, I may, but Belle told me Carleton was an only child. Anything Melody could tell me about him would be ancient history."

He gestured at the rest of the pile. "Anything on how they became the Simpsons' foster kids?"

Damn. It hadn't occurred to Dina to look. Yancy would have zeroed in on their birth certificates.

"How about *Carleton deHaven*?" Jack asked. "We searched some the other night, but what's the earliest dated reference you found to him?"

Double damn.

"Jesus, cheer up, kid. I'm fishing out loud. That wasn't part of the homework assignment I gave you."

The leather portfolio he unzipped had fresh scuff marks on it. Road rash, Dina thought, from knocking it out of his hand when I jumped him in the driveway. Another few minutes, and she'd have had whisker rash.

"Hindsight," he said, putting several pages of her day's work into an inner file pocket. "I should have dug deeper into deHaven's affiliation with F.D.I.C."

A yawn overtook him—the head tilting, jaw breaking, king-of-the-jungle kind that left Jack's eyes watery and blinking. He apologized, adding, "Long day."

Coffee should be the next beverage course, but not unless he suggested it. He needed sleep, not caffeine, and there'd be Harriet to contend with. Though her mother appeared to have dozed off, there was a better than half chance she was faking it.

"I'll talk to McGuire, first thing tomorrow," Jack said. "Our circumstantial case against deHaven has to be more solid than the one against me."

Picking through the photos and printed material, he winnowed the stack to a select few. As he arranged and tucked them in the portfolio, he said, "Nice highlighting job, too."

Dina started. "What's that supposed to mean?"

"Exactly what I said. It'll make the show-'n-tell in McGuire's office a lot easier."

Her palms skated on the table as she pulled back and sat down in the chair. "Then today *was* a test. Sure, you needed me to follow up on some stuff. Giving me the keys to the candy store made it a twofer."

"Nope."

"Did you stop by and check the desk on your way from the airport? You must have another set of keys. It'd be stupid not to."

"To the office door, yeah." Jack's smile was weary, circumspect. "Okay, you poked around in my desk. BFD. I expected it, same as I expect Yancy to. Willy Wonk probably has dupes of every key on the ring." The smile widened. "The kid bores easily."

"Funny, I didn't see his name on an envelope with a notebook and cassette tapes in it. And I know it hasn't been there longer than a couple of days. The police would have found it when they searched your office."

"True." Jack splayed his elbows on the table. "Which is why it's safe there now. Locked in the drawer, right where I left it." His gaze leveled at her. "Isn't it?"

"No." A little head shake for emphasis. "It isn't."

Dina plucked up the rest of the papers he'd rejected and tapped them into a neat pile. Next, each photo sheet was meticulously aligned on top.

Giving her that full set of keys, instead of his spare door key *was* a test. Like tidying up now, while Jack's mouth worked, struggling not to ask what she'd done with the envelope. Waiting for her to tell him. Wondering if she'd destroyed it. If she had, whether he should be relieved or feel betrayed. And how much of either of those, or both, he could live with.

Slumping back, he rubbed his face with his hands, chuckling. "Man, I must be exhausted. You had me going there for a minute."

If he thought he could bluff her that easily—well, it was insulting, to say the least.

"The diner's smoke alarm went off, like it does about twenty times a day," he said. "So you locked the envelope inside my nice, fire-resistant supply cabinet."

Dina just stared at him, speechless. Between the desk and the cabinet, the envelope had jumped into her purse for a second, but why destroy it? The two people who mattered most already knew what she'd done.

A snide voice called from the living room, "Lord have mercy, Dina Jeanne, if you're not your daddy's daughter. Smart about a thing or two, but dumber than a toadstool on a stump 'bout most everything else."

20

"Simpson reserved a minivan at the Park City airport." Jack consulted his notes. "A two-day lease with a drop-off option—leave the keys under the floor mat, lock 'er up and go. Except a lot jockey saw the van in its designated space Sunday night. The mileage on the odometer was within 3.2 miles of what I clocked from Park City Memorial to the deHaven house."

McGuire had sat through almost an hour of circumstantial evidence against Carleton deHaven. Jack felt as though he were trying to sell his old friend a time-share condo. McGuire looked as if the sales pitch's steak house gift certificate and fifty bucks cash weren't as enticing as he'd thought.

The detective had made a few notes of his own. A good sign, considering a tape recorder captured Jack's every word—those of a prime homicide suspect. The outsourced lab the PD used hadn't yet ponied up the DNA test results.

The case against Jack didn't hinge on them, but impregnating his ex-wife and the implications were the strongest motives for a .38-caliber solution.

"Got addresses, Social Security numbers on these Simpson brothers?" McGuire asked.

"Working on it." Or would, when he went to the office. What's known as a credit bureau header would provide those and more. In this instance, pulling them violated the Fair Credit Reporting Act. Saving your ass from a murder rap hadn't made the list of acceptable guidelines.

"Fuzz, fuzzy, fuzzier," McGuire said. "The shuttle driver at the hotel in Little Rock can't describe any passengers he drove to the airport that morning."

"He might pick a composite from a six-panel field," Jack argued. "I could have mocked up deHaven's photo from a MentalWealth brochure—inked in glasses and a ball cap. Without five others for comparison, that'd burn the guy as a witness later."

"Assuming he'd recognize your theoretical Mr. Simpson." A pen weaved over and under McGuire's jazz-piano-man fingers. "I don't see the problem in deHaven phoning the limo service for a pickup at baggage claim. From what you've said, deHaven was supposed to meet Mr. Hollywood's plane on arrival. The flight was on time, deHaven was there on time—"

"How'd he get to the airport?" Jack flipped back pages in his notebook. "The limo was a one-way fare—Little Rock National to the hotel. DeHaven's vehicle didn't leave the parking garage."

"He took the shuttle. A cab. A bus. He hitchhiked."

"Weak."

"Says you."

"A Little Rock PD inquiry about any Simpson rentals that day might put some muscle in it. I got stonewalled yesterday. Suckered, more likely. Just because fifty-dollar bribes don't buy what they used to doesn't mean one Simpson or the other didn't rent a vehicle over the weekend."

"Whether one or both of them did, doesn't prove either of them was a deHaven alias."

No, Jack admitted. It didn't.

McGuire stood and stretched. The corner of the bull pen

where his desk was located was as cold as a refrigerator. Peculiar that his pale blue shirt had damp circles under the arms. Groaning as he lowered them, he remained on his feet, hooking his thumbs on his belt.

"I'll grant, post-9/11 airport security is a lot of hocus-pocus," he said. "Show a valid photo ID that matches the ticket and the credit card it's charged to, and you're good to go."

He looked up at Jack. "Except where's the gun come in? A .38 smuggled past metal detectors, X-rays and bag inspectors in two different airports? No way."

Helluva sticking point and it had bothered Jack, as well. DeHaven drove to the conference, so no problem taking the gun with him. Transporting it by air back to Park City, then stashing it to frame Jack was a giant hole in the puzzle.

"The odometer on the Park City rental could have covered a stop by F.D.I.C.'s office building," he said. "It *was* Sunday. The place should have been emptier than my bank account."

"Which is why installers replacing the carpet in F.D.I.C.'s offices received double time for working that day."

"And they didn't see anybody come in or go out."

McGuire shook his head.

Of course they hadn't. DeHaven was familiar with the layout and there were multiple entrances and exits. That the carpet layers couldn't be everywhere at once wasn't worth arguing.

McGuire *had* checked deHaven's alibi, though. Well beyond confirming the dates, times and movements deHaven provided, and the corroborating witness statements. His cop sense wasn't ready to accept that this wasn't a spousal homicide.

Atypical, yes. The premeditation was as intricate and delicate as a spider web. One tatted by a spider with a stopwatch and scant margin for error.

"You lied about me being the last person Belle talked to."

McGuire smirked. "All's fair."

"Then triangulate that landline call Belle supposedly made to hubby's cell. The one where she reportedly said she'd missed her flight and would take a later one. If I'm right, the signal bounced off the satellite tower nearest their house. DeHaven called himself on the landline phone and waited for his friggin' pocket to ring."

"Can't do it. No probable cause to look deeper than the call logs."

"The hell!" Now Jack was on his feet. "It goes to his alibi. Christ almighty. It's *key* to his alibi. The too-cutesy factor that was his biggest mistake."

McGuire heaved a sigh and sat down hard in his desk chair. "DeHaven and the chief are golf buddies. This isn't the only open homicide on the board. Got me three, four attempteds, with one vic up to his ankles in the River Jordan and sinkin' fast."

He waved at the oversize clock on a strip of wall between two windows. "In forty-one minutes, I'm testifying in court. *If* I'm sworn in before the judge adjourns for the weekend. Otherwise, Monday's gonna be déjà vu, except for the drive-by, or the fatality domestic I'll catch in the meantime."

"I know," Jack said. "It never ends."

"Nothing changes, except the names and faces."

"But you wouldn't be opposed to moving Belle's name from the open to the suspect-charged side of the board, would you." A statement, not a question. "Say, by eight, eight-thirty tonight?"

"Damned if you aren't a persistent—"

"A few hours of your time, a high-profile clearance, and the unit commander might think of somebody else's badge number when he assigns those incomings this weekend."

McGuire gave him the fish eye. "Not interested."

Hands aloft, Jack said, "No harm asking. It'd be more official with you listening in when I meet with deHaven, but 'flexible' is my middle name."

By now, deHaven should be opening a packet with copies of the most damning evidence and an unsigned letter. Jack had intercepted a courier and allowed him a look-see to prove the envelope's contents weren't explosive, illegal drugs, lethal microbes or cash. A hundred bucks for the delivery—another hundred for the messenger to permanently forget what Jack looked like.

Blackmailing the guilty worked in movies, but Jack was more than dubious about real life. Then again, deHaven wasn't as brilliant as he thought he was. He'd suspect Jack was the extortionist. But what if Comb-over or someone else at the seminar thought about Belle's death and hubby's disappearing act and did some checking?

F.D.I.C. data mined for new clientele. Cursory, if not full background checks culled greedy and broke prospects from greedy and financially solid ones. DeHaven had to wonder whether an IT tech had quietly been instructed to delve deeper into Golden Boy's past.

"Stay out of it, McPhee. And stay the fuck away from deHaven. Got that? *Way* away."

"I would, Andy. I swear I would if there weren't so many countries with no extradition treaties with the U.S. And several that do, but don't bust a hump finding rich bad guys. And if I didn't have a gut feeling that deHaven's scrambled ever since he found out Belle was pregnant. It ain't his. It ain't mine, either. Soon as that's confirmed, there goes his patsy."

McGuire surveyed the immediate vicinity. "Somebody is monitoring his financials."

"Excellent." And it was, since it also indicated McGuire's doubts about deHaven. "But how about Carl Haven's financials? Paul D. and Robert K. Simpson's? Every male killed in that '74 tornado outbreak? Daffy goddamn Duck's, for all we know."

Jack knuckled the desk and leaned forward. "He's gotta figure the spotlight's about to swing back. Even if he believes his alibi is flawless, the cops recanvassing business associates, friends, neighbors? Man, oh man. That kind of scrutiny makes conversations fizzle when you walk into the room. Especially for a guy whose living comes from selling pipe dreams to pigeons."

"Not interested," McGuire repeated, his gaze fixed on the BOLO alerts pushpinned to a cubicle's panel.

"Yeah, well. I tried. 'Preciate the listen." Jack started away, then turned. "But if you're out near the pavilion at Shiffen Park about, uh, say, seven-thirty, give me a call on my cell."

"Nice evening for a walk," Dina said. "Quieter than usual."

Jack grunted. Again. Since he'd come home from the office, then through dinner, it had been like cohabiting with a grouchy chimpanzee. A grouchy chimpanzee obsessed with his watch.

Dina slackened the leash so Phil could snuffle and snort and decide which blade of grass to pee on this time. The men in her life were such sparkling conversationalists, she could hardly squeeze in a word edgewise.

She ruffled the hair clinging to the back of her neck. "Sticky, though." The dark, clotted clouds seemed to suck up every breath of air and exhale none. The TV weatherman predicted the storm front inching up from the gulf across the Midwest wouldn't bring much rain to the Park City metro area.

"C'mon, Phil." She tugged the leash. "You're all show and no ammo, too."

The dog fell in beside her on the left. Jack marched like an automaton on the right. His hands were in his pockets, his expression pensive, his lips curled under.

"You know, this heat's giving me an idea," she said.

"Mmph."

"I think I'll take off my blouse and bra and go topless the rest of the way home."

"Mmph." Time check. An odd little spark in his eyes. "Better speed this up, kid. It's about time for me to pick up Yancy."

The highest consecutive number of words he'd uttered in several hours was about needing Willy Wonk to siphon information on the Simpson brothers reincarnate. Dina had suggested driving the VW to the office for some over-Yancy's-shoulder lessons on data searches. That way, if Harriet needed her, or the process dragged on a while, Dina had transportation home.

"Not tonight," Jack had said. "Your mom's had to tough it out alone too much lately as it is."

That unkind cut was intended to piss off Dina. It worked splendidly, until she remembered Yancy's tent-theater troupe had a dress rehearsal this evening, before their debut performance, Saturday night.

Confronting Jack would generate another lie. Instinct told her, whatever he had planned was risky, if not dangerous. His distracted antsiness hadn't escaped Harriet's notice, either. She'd mentioned it to Dina after dinner, while Jack stood on the patio looking for zoo animals in the clouds.

Now back at the duplex, Dina let in Phil, then unclipped the leash. To Jack, she said, "Would you mind seeing if his water bowl is full? The poor dog's liable to be dehydrated after irrigating the whole block."

"I've—" Jack struck whatever he was about to say and strode past Harriet into the kitchen.

Dina's lifted eyebrows signaled her mother, who was fiddling with a pill bottle at the table. Dina continued down the hall, into the bathroom and shut the door.

There on the vanity counter was her hobo bag, just as Harriet promised. Distrusting the strap to hold the purse's extra weight, Dina hugged it to her chest and pressed an ear to the doorjamb.

"Where's Dina?" she heard Jack ask.

"In the powder room. She'll be out in a minute."

An extended pause, then, "I'd better go, Harriet. Tell Dina I'll call her later."

Dina turned the knob and eased open the door a crack, listening for the storm door's rattle. Before the entry door pulled closed, she was running for the patio slider.

A knothole in the far corner of the fence was like an oval periscope. The Taurus's headlights blinked their remote unlock signal before Jack was in view. Dina squinted through the peephole and waved frantically at the patio door.

Jack opened the driver's side door and slid inside. Dina squeezed her purse, chanting, "Hurry. *Hurry.*"

The engine started; the car door closed. Dina glanced at the duplex. Phil stood with his nose smushed against the patio door's glass, as morose as the first out in a schoolyard dodgeball game. *Please, Mom,* screamed in Dina's head.

Jack reached over his shoulder for the seat belt. Dina readied herself mentally to revert to Plan B. He'd told her a professional investigator always had one, if not a Plan C, D and E. As a rank amateur, Dina wasn't confident in her second option, and didn't have a third.

The Taurus started backing from the driveway. Dina groaned, cursing the not yet darkness. The rear tires were in the street, the front end swinging right, when it stopped. Jack craned over the steering wheel. Scowled. Snarled a one-word curse a small child could lip-read.

Dina needn't see the porch light to know it was flipping on and off. Harriet, God love her, had come through.

Jack shifted into Drive and gunned the sedan forward. He leaped out, leaving the engine running, the door open. The instant he rounded the front bumper, Dina's hobo bag thudded on the other side of the fence.

She boosted herself up like a gymnast mounting a pommel horse. Foot braced on a plank, she cocked under the other leg and jumped.

A jab at a button on the Taurus's armrest unlocked the rear doors. Burrowing backward beneath the coats and blankets piled on the floorboard, Dina pulled the door shut as quietly as she could.

21

Jack's eyes flicked to the rearview mirror. He tilted it downward and a fraction left. On the backseat, his overcoat and the pillow and blankets under it were definitely jiggling.

Gravity, he supposed. His mobile closet was stacked almost level with the rear deck. In fact, the overcoat's charcoal-gray sleeve had flopped over on it, as if the invisible man had crawled inside for a snooze.

Tomorrow, he'd rearrange everything. Tidy up. Divide and conquer.

If he lived that long.

"If I don't," he said, "Ms. Pearl can throw the crap in with the rest of the garage sale stuff." He tried on a Bogart leer, then his raspy snarl. "Change the signsh to eshtate shale, shweet-art. You'll make a killin'."

He tensed. Eased up on the accelerator. Behind him, an SUV's headlights flashed a high-beam obscenity for slowing down. The overcoat was practically fibrillating.

DeHaven. Jee-zus, get a grip, dumbass. He's too tall to—

Instantly furious, he bellowed, "Dina, so help me God, you'd better not be hiding back there."

Silence. The coat stabilized.

Jack thought about her beeline to the bathroom after they

walked Phil. Her still being in the bathroom when he left. Coasting out of the driveway and pulling in again when Harriet flagged him with the porch light. Her saying she was sorry, she didn't want to be a bother, then pressed a dollar bill in his hand and asked him to buy a roll of sugarless mints on his way home.

"I'd send Dina," she said, "but it's getting dark and since you're going out anyway…"

By the dashboard clock, he should already be in position at the park. No time to turn around. None to wrestle a friggin' Munchkin dog groomer burglar out of the goddamn car and toss her in the nearest Dumpster. "I hope you suffocate back there. By hell, better hope you suffocate back there, before I get my hands on you."

The clothes humped and heaved. A small, red, sweaty face rose above the seat back. "Humphrey Bogart is spinning in his grave." Dina smeared a flap of damp hair off her brow. "How about kicking up the AC a little bit?"

"Do *not* even—"

"Oh, get over it. Two women outsmarted you. Big surprise. We don't have time for a tantrum." Dina scowled at the mirror. "Where are we meeting deHaven?"

Jack was still processing *outsmarted* and *tantrum* to less than calming results. "Who said anything about—?"

"You did. The Neanderthal act, the restlessness, checking your stupid watch every fifteen seconds. Plus lying to me about Yancy."

She grabbed the pillow and shoved it under her. To hell with his very expensive, dry-clean-only overcoat crumpled in a wad. "He told us at the office about tonight's final dress rehearsal and hinted like crazy about us coming to opening night."

Jack summoned what remained of his pride. "That's no excuse for you to sneak into my car. Did it ever occur to you that maybe I was trying to protect you?"

"Of course it did." Dina glared at him. "Right before it occurred to me that you're confronting a murderer—*alone*— with no way to protect yourself."

He almost lost control of the car when a huge, long-barreled revolver waggled in the mirror. It was practically an antique, but age wasn't relative to a .357 Magnum. Old or new, it'd blow a hole the size of a turkey platter in whatever happened to be in range.

"Holy *shit!* Is that thing loaded?"

"Well, yeah. I didn't bring it along to throw at him." Dina clucked her tongue. "I keep unloading it and burying the bullets in the yard, but Mom must have a case of them stashed somewhere."

Sweet Mother Mary, Jesus and Joseph. This was not real. There was not, could not possibly be, a four-foot-ten-inch woman in his backseat waving a cannon with a trigger and chatting about planting ammo like tulip bulbs.

Helluva hallucination, though. Stress. Nerves. Residual payback for a Scotch man knocking back four beers last night. Come to think of it, that third can had tasted funny. Evidently, oversleeping and waking up hungover and groggy wasn't punishment enough. Now he was imagining Dirty Harry Jr. in drag breathing down his neck.

If the figment of his imagination would shut up, he'd be fine in a second, but no. As he decelerated for a traffic light, it went on, "Like I said the other day, McPhee. If it wasn't for me, you wouldn't be in this mess, and— Oh, my God."

Just like that, the figment was gone. Poof. Abraca-friggin-dabra.

"Dina?"

A soft but insistent "Shh!" hissed behind and below his right ear.

The windows were up. Nobody could hear him. Or her, for that matter. Without turning his head, Jack commenced a visual survey for what spooked her into a nosedive. While clutching a loaded .357 whose barrel could at this very moment be aimed in a variety of potentially fatal directions.

Jack had followed that Audi sedan for at least a couple of blocks. The convertible behind them with four teenage girls in it wouldn't pose a threat, provided Dina could have seen them in the mirror.

The light changed; both lanes began moving forward as Jack's eyes roved to the black Lexus beside him. The driver's index finger beat time on the steering wheel with whatever was playing on the sound system. Either a cell phone was held to his opposite ear, or the man was singing along out of sync.

Nice ride, Jack thought as he switched off the dashboard lights. The LS model was much admired by executives, doctors, and luxury-car thieves. Fresh off the showroom floor, it fetched upward of seventy grand.

He lagged back to the apparent irritation of the teenyboppers behind him. The Lexus peeled off left at the next signal. After traffic swallowed it up, he said, "Olly and all that crap."

Fright-wig hair, a swath of ruddy skin, then a pair of eyebrows cautiously brooked the space between the Taurus's headrests. Jack reached to boost the air-conditioner to maximum cool.

"Don't tell me, let me guess," he said. "You hit the deck when you recognized your fence driving that Lexus." He gestured for silence. "No voodoo. Just effect, probable cause and common sense. I should have considered the angle sooner. It explains Gerry Abramson's impatience and why he's been on my butt since day one."

Dina's expression telegraphed dots connecting and an absence of some crucial ones. "Mr. Abramson came by the office yesterday, as I was locking up. Said he'd fired you, hired somebody else and wanted your report and a refund by five o'clock today."

"Oops." Jack smiled at the mirror. "The Lexus's driver is Wes Shapiro, National Federated's office manager. Gerry laughed when I mentioned Shapiro as a burglary suspect. He didn't want me diverting down that road. Obviously Gerry thought a fox was in his henhouse, but wanted proof."

Also clear in twenty-twenty retrospect was the Calendar Burglar's last transaction with the fence: a week ago Thursday. Jack wasn't aware of that theft until Gerry's call on Saturday, but he'd contracted with National Federated on Thursday afternoon.

Shapiro knew Jack couldn't identify the jewel thief in a matter of hours. Why not buy one final haul for half of the traditional ten percent cut?

By Sunday night when Jack had Dina try to contact her fence, Shapiro had folded the tent as far as she was concerned.

"He's worked for Gerry forever. Perfect setup, too, with access to other insurers' clients and policy information. Or Wes could figure out how to get it."

Memories of his appointment at National Federated clicked bright and clear. Shapiro saying he'd told Gerry for months to contact McPhee Investigations. The snipe about Gerry having the first dollar he'd ever made.

The first was a lie, the other, an anthem sung by every presumably underappreciated, underpaid employee. Which is why Jack hadn't paid much attention.

Well, actually he had, but in a different context. When Abramson dismissed Shapiro from his office, Jack felt sort of sorry for the guy, especially considering Gerry's reliance on Wes after Letha Abramson's diagnosis.

Therein must lay the tipping point. Letha's declining health shifted some of Gerry's workload onto Wes. For a while, Shapiro understood and sympathized. Eventually self-pity whined that he was running the business, but not profiting from it. The insult to compensatory injury was the toll that stress, sorrow and help-lessness had taken on Gerry's usual affability.

Shapiro had two choices: find a less moody, miserly em-ployer, or use insider knowledge to deepen his personal revenue stream.

"He may have started small," Jack said. "For sure, careful. Avoided mistakes that land other fences behind the razor-wire kind at the state hotel."

"That's why he used pay phones and prepaid cell phones."

Jack nodded. "Except if you found him, he's becoming too well known. By volume, if not by name." He glanced in the rearview mirror. "Burglary was your last resort, not a vocation. That friend of a friend of your brother's has to be a regular customer."

A crease tined between Dina's brows. She wouldn't reveal Randy Wexler's friend's name without persuasion. Jack was a pretty good persuader.

"Tooling around in a Lexus tells me Shapiro's gone Super-man, too. Unless a crook feels invincible, he doesn't drive a vehicle a tax bracket or two above his day-job income."

The dog-eared unexpected-inheritance story was almost a sure bet, but finite. It explained a few splurges or a boom-to-bust spend-athon. When splurges continue, people start to wonder. If the windfall was that big, or paid continuous dividends, why keep working at a dead-end job you bitch about constantly?

"So many perps," Jack said, as he approached the west entrance to Shiffen Park. "So little time."

The compass-point stone gates were patterned after the Arc de Triomphe in Paris. Bronze plaques embedded in each credited that source of inspiration, a 1902 dedication date, and identified the benefactor as A. N. Onymous.

A philanthropist with no ego and a sense of humor. As Jack always did, he saluted Mr. Onymous as he drove through the gates. Alas, they just don't build rich people and bas-relief granite arches like they used to.

The playground and picnic areas were deserted. The prospect of rain and encroaching darkness had discouraged all but a quartet of female joggers and an elderly gent walking a golden retriever.

"You're meeting deHaven here?" Dina's tone implied a major lapse in intelligence. "He can see you coming a mile away."

"And vice versa. Except it's a hundred feet at most with all the trees and shrubs."

The four sinuous entry roads led to the pavilion in the middle of the park. The original bandstand had burned to the ground in the 1920s. Its replacement and four others had suffered the same fate, until a concrete-company owner partnered with a metal fabricator to build a fireproof structure. The lucky seventh bandstand wasn't as large as the first, but its steel rafters and sheet-copper roof had defeated numerous arson attempts.

Jack parked the Taurus in the open and rolled down the windows. The engine dieseled, then shut down. Mugginess closed in, devouring the lingering coolness inside the car, but Jack needed to hear, as well as watch.

With century-old walnut trees circling in the distance, he was a sitting duck for a marksman with a high-powered rifle and scope. A shooter with a handgun would have to close much of the gap on foot.

"Okay, Annie Oakley. I'd be much obliged if you'd hand over that hog-leg—*gently*—and hunker down behind the seat."

"But that's—"

"Dina Jeanne, I do *not* have time to argue. Give me the damn gun and get your head lower than the window ledges."

The .357 whomped on the front seat. The barrel pointed at Jack, surely by accident. He turned it over, hefted it, shuddered, then laid it down again.

From under the seat, he brought out a .38 Police Special bought from a backroom dealer that afternoon. It wasn't registered to Jack or anyone else, hence doubly illegal to carry concealed. If deHaven came armed, they were even in Jack's eyes, though not the law's.

A queasy flutter in his belly pushed an acrid taste into his mouth. At least nothing was visible in the rearview, except a shadowy pillow and clothes.

"Can I ask you something?" Dina whispered.

"Uh-huh. Gotta answer like a ventriloquist, though."

"Are you scared?"

"Shitless."

Perhaps not the response she'd hoped for, but there you go. Jack was a background checker, a fraud investigator, an adulterer's worst enemy, a skip tracer and a missing-person finder. He'd never confused himself with Doc Holliday and neither had anyone else.

"How long do we have to wait?"

"The note I wrote said eight. It's nineteen minutes till."

The cell phone in his T-shirt pocket cheeped. Jack nearly kneecapped himself on the steering column. "Private" flashed on the caller-ID display. "Yo," was his noncommittal greeting.

"That you, McPhee?"

He gulped down a howl of relief. "I knew I could count on you, McGuire."

"Makes one of us."

Jack scanned the perimeter. "Where are you?"

"Fifty yards due southwest. Tucked up under a bush." Five seconds ticked by. McGuire chuckled. "Can't even see the whites of my eyes, can ya? Shades and natural camo, man. Can't beat 'em for night work."

"I owe you."

"Damn straight." McGuire dictated his cell phone number.

"I dial you back and we're good, right?"

"Affirmative. Clear."

Jack punched the number, let it ring once and canceled the call. The first deep breath in an hour or more was taken and released. He slipped the phone in his pocket and returned to eyeball-and-eardrum patrol.

"So you weren't coming here alone."

"Was until you hitchhiked," he said, opting for diplomacy. "McGuire was a gamble, not a sure thing."

"Promise you'll tell me when you see deHaven? I don't want to miss the arrest part."

Unless a weapon was involved, McGuire wouldn't charge out of the foliage the instant deHaven showed himself. It wasn't illegal to stroll through a public park with or without a satchel containing a quarter million in cash.

On the other hand, innocent people don't pay off blackmailers.

Explaining the finer points of the extortion to Dina through clenched teeth wouldn't be easy. In silhouette, a motionless jaw and lips flapping and contorting signified another unseen occupant, a hidden microphone and transmitter, or serious mental-health issues.

Like a verbal text message, Jack told her about the packet and blackmail note delivered to deHaven at his office. If he took the bait, Jack would hit Redial on his cell phone through his pocket, then stall his exit from the car until the display screen went dark again.

His snug pocket T-shirt allayed suspicion that he was wired for sound. Oh, he was, but cell phones had become as innocuous as ink pens. An open connection to McGuire's cellphone was a top-notch eavesdropping device, whether a tape recorder was nearby or not.

"Now that *is* slick," Dina whispered. "Did you think of it, or McGuire?"

"Old trick, kid. Done all the time."

On purpose and by accident. Bump the cell phone, jostle it in a pocket, or a purse and whoever you last dialed could be listening in on your current, live conversation.

No problem most of the time, other than burning up minutes on both phones. Very bad form if the spouse you called to tell about meeting a friend for dinner listens in on the hot date you're having with a lover.

Jack slapped a mosquito whining in his ear. Patted the .38 in his lap. Reminded himself to inhale. And exhale. His gaze swept the full darkness, jerking at shadows, at faint moon winks through tiny tears in the clouds, at nothing, expecting something to materialize.

Nocturnal birds sang and squabbled. A power line hummed a monotonous note. Rustling. Muffled snaps. Crunching. Squeaks. Poets who wrote of the night's unrelieved silence were out of their friggin' minds.

Eight twenty-three. Screw punctuality. DeHaven had laughed his ass off feeding the packet and the note into a shredder. Or he was out there, watching Jack sweat like a Clydesdale. Waiting for him to lose his concentration. Drop his guard. Stare too long at one spot.

By Dina's slow, even breathing, she'd dozed off. If the bugs weren't eating her alive, she was roasting in the airless nest behind the seat. Jack envied the oblivion with no relation to time. Missed her hushed voice. She made him think, made him laugh. Kept him honest.

He smiled at the paradox. Only it wasn't one. Actions don't always speak louder than words, much less character. Would he steal to buy medicine to keep his mother alive? To ease her pain?

Private again appeared on the screen.

"Yo."

"Duty calls." McGuire's voice intimated he was already on the run to his vehicle.

It was a few minutes shy of nine o'clock. Early for Friday night's gun-and-knife club to draw blood. Must be the heat.

Paranoia raised the hair on the nape of Jack's neck. A bogus 911 to dispatch would decoy McGuire. "What's the beef?"

"Stab 'n grab. Vic bled out before EMS arrived."

Jack wiped away the sweat beading his forehead. Somebody died. A legit 10-19 shouldn't feel like a reprieve. And wasn't. "Be careful out there. And thanks again."

"You hangin' in?"

For another fifteen, was Jack's immediate thought. Were deHaven aware of McGuire's presence, he'd make his move. In full darkness. Out of nowhere. "Negatory," Jack said into the cell, then clicked it off.

He keyed the ignition. He wasn't a hero or an idiot. DeHaven wouldn't leave any witnesses. But his vehicle in the vicinity would be damning to an extent.

He dialed back McGuire, who confirmed no parked cars were on the southbound road. Jack would meander through the other three, for general shits and grins.

"Blackmailing the bad guy," he muttered, "only works in the friggin' movies."

22

Jack shoved the holstered .38 under a suit bag in the trunk.

Tomorrow, he'd disassemble it and scatter the pieces in Dumpsters all over town. Eventually the cops would release its registered twin. Whether returned to Jack or scrap-heaped after a trial's conclusion remained to be seen.

He hoisted the .357 to add it to the makeshift armory.

"Oh, no, you don't." Dina gripped the barrel like a baseball bat. "This is my dad's, not yours."

"Well, it isn't going back in the house. A loaded gun lying around isn't protection. It's an accident waiting to happen."

So was a driveway tug-of-war with a cannon for the rope, but Jack wasn't about to turn loose. Neither was Dina.

"I'll unload it," she said, "after Mom goes to bed."

"And from what you told me, she'll reload it before breakfast."

Dina blew the hair out of her eyes, the better to glare up at him. "I don't expect you to understand, but to Mom, this stupid gun *is* my dad. As long as it's in the nightstand, just as it's always been, Earl Wexler is still here, still with her, protecting his family."

Her chin trembled and there were tears in her voice. "I don't care how crazy that sounds. I can't—*won't*—take that away from her. I'll be damned if I'll let you do it."

Safety and security were illusions. States of mind inconsistent with reality. Jack sincerely wished Harriet's symbol of them didn't have a trigger, but yeah. He understood. "Okay." He closed the trunk lid. "Annie gets her gun."

He turned the butt toward Dina. "If Little Annie promises to unload it and keep unloading it until Harriet runs out of ammo."

She laughed. "Think Phil will help me dig all those holes?"

"I'll take over the disposal end of it." Which included renting a metal detector to minesweep the yard. One thing about the Wexler women. They were never boring.

Harriet was shuffling around the corner from the kitchen when they walked in. Their faces must have told the tale. "No eye for an eye, huh. Pity."

"Mother." Dina set her purse and the gun on the table, then went to disentangle the oxygen hose before Harriet tripped on it. "Jack wanted deHaven to implicate himself. He didn't want to kill him."

Well, Jack thought, as he flopped on the couch, unless it was in self-defense. No, not even then. Dead murderers don't stand trial. They're spared the perp walk, the pretrial media feeding frenzy, the public humiliation. Couldn't happen to a more deserving guy.

"Will you quit fussing?" Harriet shooed Dina away. "Go let that silly dog out. He's wiping dog boogers all over my drapes."

Phil's head was craned behind the fabric, like Ichabod Mutt. Dina halted and looked at Jack. "Did you hear that?"

He assumed she didn't mean the back-to-school-sale commercial on TV. "Hear what?"

She pushed aside the drapes and tugged open the slider. "For a second there, I thought Phil growled."

"Nah. Probably something he ate is recycling itself."

If dogs were eligible for belching contests, Phil would have a wallful of blue ribbons. The other forced-air function at which he excelled hadn't yet qualified as an event.

The mutt backfooted from the door. He padded over between Harriet's chair and the dining area and sat down. Dina shut and relocked the patio door. "Maybe he's storm-phobic. It isn't thundering or lightning, but animals react to changes in barometric pressure."

Jack patted the couch cushion beside him. "I think the pressure he's—"

The front door burst open and crashed into the wall. Phil sprang forward. Teeth bared, he barked like a rabid Doberman.

Jack leaped to his feet, colliding with Dina. She screamed as a golf club arced down and cracked Phil's skull. The dog crumpled into a heap on the carpet.

"*Quiet!* Move away from McPhee." Carleton deHaven pointed a 9 mm Glock pistol at Dina. His hands were gloved; a finger curled around the trigger. "I said, *move.*"

Harriet's face was stark white. A quaking hand rose to her mouth. She stared at Phil, then up at deHaven, trying to comprehend what was happening.

"You." He nodded at Harriet. "Take off the Medi-Alert device. Careful…and drop it behind you. Very good. Now the cordless phone."

The handset banged off the portable oxygen tank.

"Now you, McPhee." DeHaven reached sideward. The five-iron probed at the narrow slot between the wall and the door. "Over toward the girl, where I can see you."

Nodding, Jack crossed his arms and sidled nearer Dina. She, too, was ghost-pale. Tears streamed from eyes at once terrified, heartsick at the blood trickling from Phil's ear, and icy with hatred for Carleton deHaven.

"Hold it. Close enough." DeHaven glanced away to leverage the door shut with the club.

Jack's thumb pressed Redial on the cell phone in his pocket.

Fingers tucked under his arms, his palm shielded the unit's lighted display. He prayed McGuire would realize it was a distress call. Prayed he'd answer, but not with a booming "McGuire."

"Nice tuxedo, deHaven. Which restaurant is missing its maître d'?"

"Very funny." The golf club clattered to the entry floor. "Tonight, the community opera is giving a special performance of *Pagliacci* in tribute to my unlamented, late wife."

Phil's inert body was nudged out of deHaven's path. "A private, invitation-only performance. To keep out the riffraff."

"Interesting choice of operas." Jack tamped his rage. He didn't have the luxury of indulging it. "The promiscuous Nedda represents Belle, no doubt. In your mind, anyway. Who plays you? Tonio, the fool? Or Nedda's husband, the clown that murders her in the end?"

DeHaven smirked. "Unfortunately, by the intermission, I was overwhelmed by grief. I left my guests to the buffet and Cristal and retired to the manager's office to rest, until the second act."

Tribute my ass, Jack thought. Glad Belle missed it. Buffalo wings, beer on tap and a shit-kickin' band were her style. There'd be a party in her honor, in this life or the next one, by God.

"How did you know where the Wexlers live?" he said. "Or that I was here?"

"And you call yourself a private detective? This *is* the twenty-first century. Pity you won't have time to adapt to modern technology."

Thinking between the inferences, Jack knew the Taurus had acquired an extra piece of equipment under a fender well or the bumper. A Global Positioning System tracker could be bought on eBay for a few hundred bucks, plus shipping.

"Sounds like you've finessed another almost perfect alibi. Except shooting us just adds three more homicides to the score."

Dina tried to stifle a sob. "Please, don't do this."

"Is that what Belle said when you aimed my .38 at her?"

"Shut up, McPhee."

"Four premeditated murders? Golden Boy, they're gonna put needles in *both* your arms."

"The police have no evidence against me. That ridiculous blackmail scheme of yours—"

"About the time that packet was delivered to you, I was with Lt. McGuire, laying out everything I sent you and more."

Harriet's fingers slowly closed around the remote—a decent weapon, if thrown hard enough. Her other hand was braced against the edge of the TV tray. Jack hadn't seen her move at all. Neither had deHaven.

A flying remote, the cluttered table toppling over—she'd distract deHaven. Startle him. Draw his fire. Sacrifice herself. Jack couldn't let that happen.

"You're bluffing," deHaven said. "If that were true, the police would have arrested me by now."

Then the tracking device wasn't on the car when Jack met with McGuire. The damn packet had set off deHaven. By no means, as Jack had planned.

He lowered his head, slowly shaking it, catching Harriet's eye. *Don't,* he telegraphed. *Not yet. Get ready.*

"What's this?" DeHaven backed up a step. His eyes and the Glock never wavered from Jack as he groped around on the dining room table for Earl Wexler's revolver. He pointed it at Dina. "This yours?"

She stiffened, but didn't respond.

"Well, I doubt it's McPhee's. But it better serves my purpose, regardless." He pocketed the 9 mm pistol. "It'll provoke fewer questions if Mrs. Wexler kills her daughter and her daughter's lover with it, then turns it on herself."

"Are you insane?" Dina shrieked, starting toward him. "Nobody—"

DeHaven thumbed the hammer. "Stop right there."

Jack grabbed her shirt and yanked her behind him. Two sharper jerks disguised his finger pointing at Harriet. *If* Dina saw it. Turning to face deHaven, Jack glanced sideward at Harriet. *Set.*

Phil's rear paw twitched. A halo of blood darkened the carpet above his head. The dead don't bleed. Nothing to pump it, when the heart stops. Hang on, buddy….

"It's your dear mother who's insane, Ms. Wexler," deHaven said. "The pharmacy bags in your car this afternoon and a telephone conversation with a chatty clerk were most informative."

Jack chuckled, waving a time-out, edging nearer, as if one motion impelled the other. "I don't know what you're smokin', but I want some."

"Elder rage, they call it," deHaven went on, spellbound by his own genius. "Tragic, when it occurs. Two of her medications can induce paranoid delusions. Another accelerates senile dementia. Anxiety. Pychoses."

The toe of his shoe prodded Phil's haunch. "Just look what your mother did to this poor, defenseless animal."

Phil snarled—twisted toward deHaven.

Harriet yelled, "Go!"

The tray table crashed to the floor. The .357 went off like a bomb. Jack slammed into deHaven, pile driving him into the dining room wall. The window shattered. Another shot squeezed off.

Jack pounded deHaven's wrist against the casing. "Drop the

gun—*drop it!*" A hand clamped his face, pushing, fingers claw-ing, gouging. He ducked, clenched his jaw. His head snapped up, ramming deHaven in the windpipe.

The heavy gun hit Jack like an anvil and fell to the floor. He cocked a fist and hammered deHaven square in the gut, doubling him over. A knee uppercut his chin.

Golden Boy smacked the wall again. Sliding down it, he sprawled at Jack's feet. Blood poured out deHaven's nose, the glove shredded by the window glass. His mouth hung open, con-vulsing like a fish out of water.

Panting, the acrid gunpowder haze as thick as fog, Jack scooped up the .357. The Glock was wrenched from deHaven's pocket. The floor suddenly heaved, tilted, rocking him backward.

He staggered into the living room. The patio door was shat-tered. The ottoman lay canted on its side. In front of the glider, Dina and Harriet were huddled over Phil. Blood smeared their hands, their clothes. Dog blood.

"Jack! Oh, my God."

At least that's what he thought Dina said. His skull felt as if it were wrapped in a mattress. It'd be nice if he could stretch out on one. Just for a minute. So damn tired—

McGuire and two patrolmen gangwayed in the front door, guns drawn and leveled. McGuire's lips moved. Why was every-body whispering?

"Party's over, man," Jack said. "Where the fuck you been?"

The uniforms glanced at Dina. She pointed, still whispering. They rushed past Jack into the dining room. Absently, he wondered how he could stand still while the duplex revolved around him.

Getting dark, too. Dina and her obsession with the light bill…penny-pincher.

McGuire holstered his weapon. The guns leaving Jack's hands made his knees rubbery. "Dog. Got get 'im...vet."

One leg buckled. McGuire grabbed for him. Pain screamed in Jack's head. The world went black.

23

Dina skewered a hole in a large cube of cheddar cheese. Into it, she inserted a tiny white pill, then a capsule. A spoonful of sugar wouldn't make the medicine go down. Not in this house, no matter whose name was on the prescription bottle.

Phil sniffed at the cheese. He looked up at her, his blue eye torpid, the lid adroop, fixed in a permanent, blind wink. The brown one told Dina he didn't fool that easily, but cheese was a vast improvement over yesterday's peanut butter Mickey Finns.

The crown of his head was shaved like a reverse mohawk with a crescent of blue-filament sutures in the middle. The exposed skin was a healthy pink, the gash mending nicely. Fur would regrow and hide the scar, but Dina would never forget that golf club whistling downward, the sound of the blade bashing his skull.

Phil gulped his pain-pill-antibiotic treat, licked his chops, then begged for a plain cheese chaser. She kissed his snoot. "Sorry, mooch. Not for another four hours. Now go take a nap, while I finish my rounds."

A saucepan of decaf tea poured into a plastic pitcher of ice was set on a tray. Seedless grapes, cantaloupe slices, plums and a bowl of rice cake chips more or less camouflaged four prescription bottles.

"Di-na," Harriet called from the living room. "When you get a minute, would you bring me a pair of socks? The blue ones, if they're clean. Same shade as my feet, seeing as how it's cold as kraut in here."

Breathe in, breathe out, Dina thought. Count your blessings.

Count *their* blessings. She hefted the tray and set off for the living room.

Harriet's rickety, throne-side trays had been righted. Restored or replaced necessities and clutter heaped each of them, placed just so, exactly as before, except somehow a clearing had been made large enough for a vase with a dozen red roses.

The ottoman, she complained bitterly, was lopsided and no longer rocked in tandem with the glider. Her scepter, the TV remote, was crisscrossed in adhesive tape and rubber bands. The Select and Info buttons had popped off. Up and Down had reversed polarity, but she wouldn't part with it for a truckful of roses. Not after she'd held it, like a grenade, to hurl at Carleton deHaven when he dispensed with Jack and came after them. Instead, as the patrolman escorted the prisoner past Harriet, she'd clocked deHaven upside the jaw with it.

Lt. Andy McGuire sat inches away from the ottoman, hunched over on a dining room chair, his elbows braced on his splayed knees. How he held a legal pad with one hand and wrote with the other was beyond Dina.

He'd apologized over and over for not responding faster to the cell-phoned distress call. Apparently, he just had again.

"If deHaven wasn't so in love with his scenario, we'd have had one of those so-called unfortunate outcomes." Jack rapped the arm winged in a cast with a metal bar holding it aloft. The fiberglass body cast extended diagonally across his chest and down to his waist. "My prize for keeping him talking is lurching around in a half-zombie suit for the next couple of months."

McGuire said, "The E.R. doc told me that uppercut to deHaven's belly is what blew out your shoulder. Generous of him to let his face meet your knee halfway."

"Generous of me not to finish him off."

Dina set down the tray on a rolling table at the foot of Jack's hospital bed. Even the narrowest one the medical supply house had available was a tight squeeze between the couch and Harriet's headquarters.

"With a pretty lady waiting on you hand and foot?" McGuire shook his head at the iced tea Dina offered. "I hope one of those pills is an attitude adjuster, Ms. Wexler. His sure could use improving."

"Since Friday night?" she teased. "Or is that a general observation?"

Harriet piped up, "Don't you go ganging up on McPhee." She plucked a tablet from Dina's hand and the tea to wash it down with. "If he hadn't pitched in to help, I'd have had to take my cane to that fancy-pantsed killer. I'd *still* like a crack at him for coshing Phil the way he did."

"You tell 'em, Rocky," Jack said.

The nickname had debuted with the flowers he'd sent before he was dismissed from the hospital. Harriet had spent Friday night there for observation, a floor below Jack, and assumed the bouquet had been delivered to the wrong room.

She'd laughed, then cried when she read the card's inscription: "Every Rockford needs a Rocky. Thanks for being mine. Love, McPhee."

Now he accepted his meds and the cold drink. His swollen eyes squinted at the fruit. The rice cakes were rejected entirely. "How's a guy supposed to get his strength back with this foo-foo crap?"

"You want something else," Dina said, "feel free to poke around in the fridge."

Jack appealed to McGuire. "As you can see, the pretty lady waiting on me hand and foot also has a vicious sense of humor."

"You should have heard what she said when you were deaf as a brick from that .357 going off." McGuire grinned. "What she was gonna do to you, if you up and died on her? Whooee. I still get goose bumps, just thinking about it."

"Oh, yeah?" Jack looked at her. "If I eat the fruit, will you give me a replay later? You know, for future reference."

When he'd stumbled from the dining room battered and bloody, Dina hadn't realized the close-range gunfire had deafened him or that much of the blood was deHaven's. When McGuire caught Jack as he fell and he screamed in pain, she thought he'd been shot in the head.

A torn rotator cuff, bruised ribs, a rebroken nose, facial lacerations, contusions and a concussion weren't minor injuries, but as Jack was fond of saying, nobody died.

"Here's a compromise," she said. "Eat the fruit and avoid armed, homicidal maniacs in the future."

"I'll think about it." Jack popped a grape in his mouth. To McGuire, he said, "Which reminds me, where'd deHaven's 9 mm come from? I thought you told me the house was clean for weapons and ammo when you searched it."

"It was. The Glock was registered to a Dallas resident. He reported it stolen from his vehicle about a year ago."

"A MentalWealth seminar groupie, by any chance?"

"We're checking. More likely, it migrated northeast into Missouri and deHaven bought it on the street." McGuire shook his head. "Not that he remembers anything about it, or calling Mrs. Wexler's pharmacy, or rigging your Ford with a GPS tracker."

"Doesn't remember," Harriet scoffed. "That's the best story he can come up with?"

Dina hooked a heel on the bed frame and boosted herself onto a corner of the mattress. Lt. McGuire hadn't invited either Wexler to audit his follow-up interview with Jack, but if Harriet had a bleacher seat, Dina might as well have the front row.

"He's sticking with it, ma'am. He'll plead not guilty by reason of temporary insanity to everything from home invasion to felony assault. Says the loss of his wife and unborn child caused him to snap and seek revenge on their killer."

"That would be me," Jack said. "Nice of him to keep my name in the publicity loop. All that free bad advertising for the agency."

"His child?" Dina said. "I thought deHaven had a vasectomy before he and Belle were married."

"He did. DeHaven now contends he and his wife discussed artificial insemination and it was fine with him, whenever she was ready. He was surprised to learn she was pregnant, because he doesn't remember her telling him she'd begun the procedure."

Harriet asked, before Dina could, "A woman can do that, without her husband knowing diddly-squat about it?"

McGuire exhaled a disgruntled sigh. "Few particulars have been made available to us yet, but it's my understanding that Mrs. deHaven may have visited a clinic in a different state."

In less carefully chosen words, deHaven's attorney was stalling, or frantically attempting to confirm that allegation.

"According to the news," Jack said, "deHaven doesn't recall busting in here with a five iron to whack Phil with, either. His lawyer's using selective amnesia as evidence deHaven wasn't legally sane Friday night. Like you must be nuts to grab a golf club, when you're already carrying a loaded Glock."

Dina said, "He must have sneaked around the house to look

in and seen Phil peeking out the drapes. And Phil either saw or sensed him. That's why he growled."

"No doubt. A .357 is a helluva lot louder, but a 9 mm in an enclosed space ain't quiet. One shot to take out the guard dog we didn't know we had, then a time lapse before the three or more shots to kill us would contradict his double-homicide–suicide scenario."

"Yes," Dina said, "but no matter how many shots were fired, I don't understand how he thought he could get away without anybody seeing him."

"He's a resourceful bastard," Jack said. "Black tux and a hot-wired stolen car he left running on the side street. A witness was more likely to get a good look at the vehicle than at him."

"We can't even prove he stole it," McGuire said. "The owner who reported it missing lives on the other side of town— nowhere near the community opera house."

McGuire's expression led Dina to ask, "You think there's a chance the jury will believe deHaven's insanity plea, don't you?"

"Ma'am, I gave up on guessing what any jury will do a long time ago."

"With you, me, McPhee and Dina testifying against him?" Harriet said. "Why, I'll go to my grave remembering every word that devil's spawn told us. And the pure evil in his eyes when he said 'em."

Dina would, too, but everyone present knew Carleton deHaven was a professional con artist. He'd convinced hundreds of people that they could think themselves rich. All he had to do was sway twelve of them that grief had driven him to exact biblical justice on Jack McPhee.

"Wait a sec," she said. "Am I missing something here? I mean, he *planned* to kill us, but he absolutely did murder his wife. Why hasn't he been charged with homicide, too?"

"We're working on it."

She combed her fingers through her hair, more confused than before, along with astonished and angry. "Jack already did the work. He told you Friday morning at your office. Now it's Sunday afternoon and deHaven's out on bail, free as a bird."

"Yeah, what'sup with that?" Jack said, a hint of a slur melting the edges off several consonants. A miserable night had ended his boycott against pain meds stronger than ibuprofen. His revised dosage schedule was every eight hours, instead of the prescribed six, but he wasn't grinding his molars and doing Lamaze breathing anymore.

"C'mon, McPhee. Even you admitted there are some big holes in your theory. You marked the trail, but I have to follow it and fill those gaps before the case moves to the prosecutor's office."

"If it ever does."

McGuire rapped his pen on the tablet. "I'll do my damned-est. I shouldn't have to promise you that."

Dina looked at Jack. "If? What if?"

"There's more than one of them, kid. Everything I gave McGuire is circumstantial at best."

"A *lot* of circumstantial," she said. "You told me, forty pieces of circumstantial evidence equals one piece of conclusive evidence."

"Sure, but…" An eye roll, a blink, then Jack leveraged his hand on the mattress to push himself up straighter. The pain meds' narcotic effect is why he'd tried to avoid them.

"Whew. Okay. We know the Simpson brothers, Carl Haven, Carleton deHaven connection isn't a fluke, but nothing proves it yet. McGuire says no security tapes or witnesses ID deHaven as Robert, or P. David Simpson in Park City around Belle's es-timated time of death."

"And like it or not," the detective went on, "deHaven doesn't fit the mold." He gestured, *Let me finish.* "Homicide is usually cut and dried. Anybody's gig. The premeditation here includes breaking and entering Jack's car to take his .38, then a second B and E to stash it in his apartment to complete the frame job."

"So what?"

"The more complicated and complex the scenario," Jack explained, "the tougher it'll be to prove a handsome white-collar financial evangelist had the skills and ability to pull it off. And the luck, for that matter."

Jack had told her the motive for killing Belle was expedience. From deHaven's viewpoint, murder was faster and less messy than another divorce. He'd be afforded sympathy for his loss, not criticism for another marital mistake. Yet the real lure was plotting and perpetrating the ultimate thrill-kill: a homicide that completely exonerated him as a suspect, and implicated Jack. Two birds, one bullet.

"Ma'am, I'll do my level best to build a solid case against deHaven," McGuire said. "But you have to understand, the prosecutor doesn't go to court with cases he's doubtful about winning. Especially murder."

"Because of double jeopardy, Dina Jeanne. A person can't be tried for the same crime twice."

"I know what double jeopardy is, Mom—"

"But there's no statute of limitations on murder. Andy can take his time and still hang Fancy-pants out to dry."

Andy? Dina bit back a grin. A Park City PD veteran and homicide unit detective had nothing on Rocky Wexler. Age was a rank in itself and she had a few decades on McGuire.

"Fifty bucks says Carl Haven's background will fit the common, ordinary perp mold. Seventy-five that Haven has a record, or was a felony suspect before he reinvented himself as Carleton deHaven."

"Huh?" McGuire's brow furrowed. "You want me to bet *against* building a case against him?"

Jack pondered a moment, then mumbled about brain fuzz. "Hell's bells. There's gotta be a way for me to hit you in the wallet on this."

"Call me when you find one." McGuire stood and slipped his pen in his shirt pocket. His expression sobered. "Or if you're inclined to straighten the kinks in your alibi."

Jack reached across his chest for an upside-down handshake. "I'll be drug free by the end of the week. Stop by for a brewski." He nodded at Dina. "I'll be sipping Scotch, if the pretty lady will fill that prescription for me."

"Don't go thirsty on my account. The property-crimes unit's closed case is a new homicide on the board for me."

Saying he'd let himself out, McGuire thanked Dina and Harriet for their hospitality and strode out the door.

"Well. Since I never got those socks I wanted," Harriet groused, "I guess I'll crawl under the covers till my feet warm up."

The thermostat had been dialed back a whole six degrees, so Jack wouldn't sweat through his cast. Not his or Dina's idea. Harriet's. Deferring to his comfort and griping about turning into a human Popsicle was her kind of a twofer.

"I'm sorry, Mom. You should have reminded me."

She harrumphed and shuffled toward the hallway. The protracted thumps of her cane measured her weariness. Afternoon naps were the purview of the young and the old; neither would admit to needing them.

Phil pulled himself up off the floor and followed her. He'd appointed himself Harriet's guardian whenever she left what had become the primary-care ward. Or perhaps to keep her company, since Jack had Dina to hover over him.

She leaned over to take away the fruit Jack had mostly ignored and returned it to the tray. "You're about to zonk out on me, too."

"Nope. The only time I get the remote is when the queen's in her chambers. I'm thinking there has to be a preseason football game playing somewhere."

Uh-huh, Dina thought. And you'll doze off between the hike and the quarterback sneak, too.

"But I can catch it in the second half," he said. The sheet tented as Jack bent up his knees. He patted the space beside him. "Since we have a little privacy for once, why don't you turn around and scootch up on my good side?"

Her mouth quirked at a corner. *Men.* Break 'em, bruise 'em, knock 'em senseless, and still they have only one thing on their minds.

"No, Dina. I'm not quite in shape for what you think I'm thinking." He scratched the three-day-old whiskers on his neck, destined to become a beard. Shaving left-handed was as untenable as Dina's doing the honors. "Not that I'm not thinking what you think I'm thinking. It'd kill me, but I'd damn sure die happy."

"Tempting," she said, "but I'd hate to miss out on you being at my mercy a while longer."

Rather than jiggle the bed, she hopped down, rounded the end, climbed over the arm of the couch and used the cushion to boost her butt up on the mattress again.

He'd joked about rolling over in his sleep some night and smashing her on the couch. Fortunately for them both, the spica cast provided about ten pounds of ballast.

Dina took his hand in both of hers. The skin was nicked and

scraped from the fight with deHaven. Two precise cuts marked where IVs had been shunted into his veins. Tears rimmed her eyes, unbidden, but recurrent, when she allowed thoughts about him hurting, instead of concentrating on healing.

She sniffed, raised her head, feigned a smart-aleck grin. "My hero."

The stubbled, battered face that had never been handsome arranged into a pensive expression. "How much of McGuire's and my conversation did you hear in the kitchen?"

"Zero. I really tried, but the food service and pill dispensing made too much noise."

"I didn't think so. Harriet caught my cue that it was a two-man discussion."

"Because…?"

"There've been some new developments in the fatality robbery McGuire responded to from the park Friday night. The cops have kept a lid on, pending notification of next-of-kin. The victim's sister and her husband were on a cruise to somewhere tropical. She was contacted about an hour before McGuire left his office to come here."

Dina shook her head. "The poor woman. Being thousands of miles away and finding out her brother had died of natural causes would be devastating enough."

Jack's fingers tightened on her hand. "I kept the volume low on purpose. With McGuire here, I was afraid how you'd react if you heard the vic was Wesley Martin Shapiro."

The name didn't register for a second. Dina hadn't known it, until she and Jack were en route to Shiffen Park. Before then, the man driving the Lexus was an intentional blur who meted out cash for medications and treatments her mother couldn't survive long without.

"But we just—" A shudder rippled down her spine. She and

Jack were probably the last people to see Wesley Shapiro alive. Except for his killer.

"It looked like an armed robbery gone south. McGuire had barely arrived at the scene when he picked up the cell-phone help call from me."

"Thank God he did. Or…" She waggled her head. "No *ors* allowed. *Ifs* and *buts*, either."

"Timing is everything, kid. If more elapsed after the meet at the park ended, McGuire would've let it go to voice mail."

Jack asked for and received a drink of iced tea, though the cubes had melted to chips. "It's procedure to search a homicide vic's residence. Shapiro's place was a moonlight shopper's warehouse. Electronics, guns, high-end power tools—"

"And jewelry." Dread welled in Dina's chest. He must have somehow convinced McGuire to delay the handcuffs and *Miranda* warning for a while.

Jack tugged her hand. "Don't go all pale and scared on me. Just listen."

"I already know what you're going to say."

"Doubt it. At least, the way you look, I hope not." He cleared his throat, hesitated. "Me and Harriet talked it over last night, while you were in the shower."

Last night? Dina frowned, wondering if she'd heard him wrong. McGuire hadn't told him about Shapiro until an hour or so ago.

"I'm not completely off the hook for Belle's murder. If deHaven is charged, his attorney may try to hang it on me. There's still a giant motive problem, but those kinks in my alibi McGuire referred to can't be straightened out without implicating you.

"The Shapiro homicide adds a new dimension. Property crimes think he was the Calendar Burglar and fenced merchandise on the side. The theory is, one of Shapiro's crew took exception to his slice of the pie and sliced up Shapiro instead."

Dina struggled to absorb what Jack was telling her. Even if the police believed Shapiro was the Calendar Burglar and a fence, what difference did it make? What she'd done was wrong, and not just legally. Harriet Wexler didn't deserve to be punished for being sick and broke, but that didn't excuse stealing to make ends meet.

"As it stands," Jack said, "one or both of us is involved in two unrelated homicides, multiple burglaries, harboring a fugitive— Lord knows what else. But a husband can't be compelled to testify against his wife, and a wife can't be compelled to do likewise against her husband."

A loopy grin suggested he was falling under the spell of Morpheus in pill form. "Neither of us will be completely in the clear, but no implicating, no perjury to avoid it. So what do you say?"

"Well," she replied, "I'd say one of us has lost his mind."

"Nope." His hand slithered out from between hers. The index finger raised. "For better or for worse. We've had mostly nothing but worse. Even worser will be better with you."

The middle finger unfurled. "For richer or for poorer. Poorer, we've nailed pretty much. Richer, we'll work on together. I have a feeling Abramson's gonna call to kiss and make up tomorrow. He can be the first to know—second, since I already told Harriet—that McPhee Investigations is expanding to McPhee Investigations and Poodle Parlor."

Jack's ring finger joined the others. "In sickness and in health. You've gotta stay healthy until they crack off my zombie suit. Then *we'll* both take care of Rocky. And Phil."

He reached to caress her cheek. "Look, everything I just said sounded fine, until I said it out loud. It doesn't help that I'm the least romantic guy on the planet. I also happen to love you so much, it scares me. What I'm not scared of is twenty-five to life with you and no chance of parole."

"I can't," Dina whispered. "I want to. But I can't."

"Okay, you don't love me yet. I understand that. Sorta expected it. After all, I've only been around a week, week and a half—"

"That isn't it. I *do* love you. Have for—" she smiled "—a week, week and a half."

His eyes held hers. "Life isn't fair. You told me that, the first night."

"And nothing's changed."

"The—" He groaned softly and leaned back. "Sorry. I'll never take sitting up for granted again."

"You need rest. We can talk later."

"No." He grasped her arm. "Listen to me. And I mean listen, not just hear. Where's the *fair* in your and Harriet's situation? Where is it in Shapiro cheating you fifty cents on every dollar, so you had to steal twice as much to pay for Harriet's prescriptions?"

"Jack, that's—"

"Where's the fairness in people denying ownership of most of that jewelry in Shapiro's house, because the appraisals were inflated and they want the insurance money not the sparklies?"

He paused, as if his words might need time to sink in. "In all of that, where's the fairness in you being the one and *only* fall guy?"

Dina looked away. "Somebody has to be. If I'd been a guy named Dean Wexler, you'd have handed me over to that patrolman at the deHavens' house."

"Absolutely. And by now, Dean's mama would be in a nursing home's Medicare ward and I'd be in a jail cell booked on first-degree homicide."

All things being equal, that was probably true. The police would have arrested Dina's alter ego, then Jack, when Belle's body was found. Among myriad other things, no one would have sneaked Phil from the kennel and erased Belle's name from the registration book.

Murderers were seldom granted bail, or it was set higher than Jack could have paid. From jail, he couldn't have collected the raft of circumstantial evidence against deHaven. At Jack's direction, his attorney might have found some of it, but the frame would be tighter, if not impossible to break.

He could have been convicted of killing his ex-wife. Carleton deHaven could have gotten away with murder. From what Lt. McGuire said, he might anyway, but if it went to trial, Jack's testimony as a private investigator and prosecution witness would be damning.

"I can see your gears turning, darlin'. Won't do any good. I've thought through every angle. You can move the pieces around on the chessboard however you want. Add some. Subtract some. There's no fair and square outcome. What *is*, is exactly how it was meant to play out."

"Like fate?" Dina chuckled. "Love at first tackle?"

Jack didn't reply. Not in words.

She sighed. "What about the money? Whether the people I stole from want their jewelry or not, I have to pay back what I took. Not just what Shapiro paid me. *All* of it. Every dime."

Jack smiled. "Some would say being Mrs. Jack McPhee for the rest of your life is punishment enough."

"It isn't. Not even close."

"There are different interpretations of restitution. Direct. Indirect. Community service. Steal a lawnmower and a Solomon-style judge might sentence you to cutting the grass for low-income seniors."

"What? Now I know you're—" Dina raked back her hair and clutched it in her fists. "Another Harriet Wexler. That money could fill the doughnut hole for somebody else. A lot of somebody elses."

"Funny, that's exactly what your mom said you'd say." Jack pulled her to his fiberglass-armored chest. "She also said you'd accept my proposal at the drop of a hat."

"I keep trying to tell you, we're nothing alike."

"Dina Jeanne. For crissake."

"Yes, I'll marry you. For better, for worse, for whatever happens, happens." Awkwardly, carefully she stretched to kiss him gently on the lips. "Except for McPhee Investigations and Poodle Parlor."

"Too breed specific? Okay. McPhee Investigations and Dog Grooming, then."

"No."

"McPhee Investigation and Clip Joint?"

"God, no."

"You're right. Negative connotation."

"Let me try." Dina feigned deliberation. "How about McPhee & McPhee Investigations?"

Jack eyed her warily.

"Somebody has to fill in at the office, while your shoulder heals. I'm already your assistant. Not much difference between that and an apprentice."

"The hell there isn't."

"You'll be here with Mom, so I'll keep on grooming for the kennels, too. But just until you're on your feet."

"I am on my feet. Just not at the moment."

"You said yourself, I'm a natural snoop. A year under your wing and I'll ace the test for my license."

"Aw, Jesus. Not the wing thing again." Jack's grimace and

pallor would have been alarming, had Dina not known the cause. "See, it's like I told Blankenship. The agency's always been a one-man operation."

Dina grinned and kissed him again. "That's the beauty of McPhee & McPhee, kid. It still is. And always will be."

NEW YORK TIMES
BESTSELLING AUTHOR

CARLA NEGGERS

A red velvet bag holding
ten sparkling gems.

A woman who must
confront their legacy
of deceit, scandal and murder.

Rebecca Blackburn caught a glimpse of the famed
Jupiter Stones as a small child. Unaware of their
significance, she forgot about them—until a
seemingly innocent photograph reignites one man's
simmering desire for vengeance.

Rebecca turns to Jared Sloan, the love she lost to
tragedy and scandal, his own life changed forever
by the secrets buried deep in their two families.
Their relentless quest for the truth will dredge up
bitter memories...and they will stop at nothing to
expose a cold-blooded killer.

BETRAYALS

MIRA®

Available February 24, 2009,
wherever books are sold!

www.MIRABooks.com   MCN2623

A terrifying new novel from

AMANDA STEVENS

Work is a welcome refuge for New Orleans homicide detective Evangeline Theroux. Feeling suffocated by her new baby, in whose eyes she sees only her dead husband, she throws herself into a high-profile murder case.

Reclusive writer Lena Saunders offers Evangeline a provocative theory of the crime: it is the work of a lunatic vigilante. Lena spins the sordid story of Ruth and Rebecca Lemay, whose mother brutally murdered her male children in an insane effort to root out an "evil" gene. The girls survived and grew to adulthood—but one is carrying on her mother's grisly work.

When the case takes a terrifyingly personal turn, Evangeline's whole life will depend on a crucial, impossible choice: the lesser of two evils.

the whispering room

Available wherever books are sold!

MIRA®

www.MIRABooks.com

MAS2628

Return to Virgin River with a breathtaking
new trilogy from award-winning author

ROBYN CARR

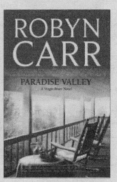

| February 2009 | March 2009 | April 2009 |

"The Virgin River books are so compelling—
I connected instantly with the characters
and just wanted more and more and more."
—#1 *New York Times* bestselling author
Debbie Macomber

MIRA®

www.MIRABooks.com

MRCTRI09

REQUEST YOUR FREE BOOKS!

2 FREE NOVELS FROM THE ROMANCE/SUSPENSE COLLECTION PLUS 2 FREE GIFTS!

YES! Please send me 2 FREE novels from the Romance/Suspense Collection and my 2 FREE gifts (gifts are worth about $10). After receiving them, if I don't wish to receive any more books, I can return the shipping statement marked "cancel." If I don't cancel, I will receive 4 brand-new novels every month and be billed just $5.49 per book in the U.S. or $5.99 per book in Canada, plus 25¢ shipping and handling per book plus applicable taxes, if any*. That's a savings of at least 20% off the cover price! I understand that accepting the 2 free books and gifts places me under no obligation to buy anything. I can always return a shipment and cancel at any time. Even if I never buy another book from the Reader Service, the two free books and gifts are mine to keep forever.

185 MDN EF5Y   385 MDN EF6C

Name _____ (PLEASE PRINT) _____

Address _____ Apt. # _____

City _____ State/Prov. _____ Zip/Postal Code _____

Signature (if under 18, a parent or guardian must sign)

Mail to **The Reader Service:**
IN U.S.A.: P.O. Box 1867, Buffalo, NY 14240-1867
IN CANADA: P.O. Box 609, Fort Erie, Ontario L2A 5X3

Not valid to current subscribers to the Romance Collection,
the Suspense Collection or the Romance/Suspense Collection.

Want to try two free books from another line?
Call 1-800-873-8635 or visit www.morefreebooks.com.

* Terms and prices subject to change without notice. N.Y. residents add applicable sales tax. Canadian residents will be charged applicable provincial taxes and GST. Offer not valid in Quebec. This offer is limited to one order per household. All orders subject to approval. Credit or debit balances in a customer's account(s) may be offset by any other outstanding balance owed by or to the customer. Please allow 4 to 6 weeks for delivery. Offer available while quantities last.

Your Privacy: Harlequin is committed to protecting your privacy. Our Privacy Policy is available online at www.eHarlequin.com or upon request from the Reader Service. From time to time we make our lists of customers available to reputable third parties who may have a product or service of interest to you. If you would prefer we not share your name and address, please check here. ☐

BOB08R

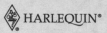

INTRIGUE

B.J. DANIELS

FIVE BROTHERS

ONE MARRIAGE-PACT
RACE TO THE HITCHING POST

The Corbetts

SHOTGUN BRIDE

Available April 2009

Catch all five adventures in
this new exciting miniseries
from B.J. Daniels!

www.eHarlequin.com

HI69392

SUZANN LEDBETTER

32450 HALFWAY TO HALF WAY   ___ $6.99 U.S. ___ $8.50 CAN.

(limited quantities available)

TOTAL AMOUNT	$	_____
POSTAGE & HANDLING	$	_____
($1.00 FOR 1 BOOK, 50¢ for each additional)		
APPLICABLE TAXES*	$	_____
TOTAL PAYABLE	$	_____

(check or money order—please do not send cash)

To order, complete this form and send it, along with a check or money order for the total above, payable to MIRA Books, to: **In the U.S.:** 3010 Walden Avenue, P.O. Box 9077, Buffalo, NY 14269-9077; **In Canada:** P.O. Box 636, Fort Erie, Ontario, L2A 5X3.

Name: _____

Address: _____ City: _____

State/Prov.: _____ Zip/Postal Code: _____

Account Number (if applicable): _____

075 CSAS

*New York residents remit applicable sales taxes.
*Canadian residents remit applicable GST and provincial taxes.

MIRA®

www.MIRABooks.com   MSL0309BL